# IRON WILLED WARRIOR

HANNAH SHIELD

IRON WILLED WARRIOR (Last Refuge Protectors Book 5)



Cover Photography: Wander Aguiar

Cover Design: Angela Haddon

Produced by Diana Road Books

# IRON WILLED WARRIOR

# CHAPTER ONE
# Brynn

"YOU'RE LATE, Agent Somerton. Where were you?"

I slid into the booth, gazing into the intense dark eyes of Special Agent in Charge Michael Stanford. My boss.

Wait, make that *ex*-boss. As of today.

Taking my time, I tugged the beanie off my head, smoothing my hair back into my signature high ponytail. "No offense, but I don't answer to you anymore. *Sir*."

Stanford regarded me with a deep frown creasing the corners of his mouth. I had worked with him for years now, and I knew that expression well. The man didn't like to be kept waiting. Yet I returned that glare with equal force.

"True," he said. "I suppose that means I should call you Brynn. And if we're going that far, you'd better call me Michael."

"*That's* not weird or anything."

We stared each other down. But laughter bubbled in my chest, and I couldn't keep it in. Then Stanford's sardonic smile appeared.

"How are you feeling?" he asked. "You ready?"

He was already starting with the questions? That meant he was uncertain. And that didn't sit well with me. Not at all.

It made nervousness do an uncomfortable dance in my stomach, and it was *way* too early into this mission for self-doubt.

I took off my puffy coat and settled into my seat while I glanced over the menu. "Can I at least order lunch before you grill me? What's good here?"

"Get the steak burger. It's fantastic."

I wrinkled my nose. "If I eat that, I'll have to stop for a nap."

"You could swing by and see Marie before you go."

That did sound nice, but I had a long drive ahead of me today.

I'd grown up in Denver, and I'd worked in the federal complex for the last five years. You'd think I would know all of SAC Stanford's favorite haunts by now, but the man could still surprise me. He'd suggested this cafe for our meeting today. It was off the beaten path and not popular with Feds or law enforcement. Which suited our purposes. We didn't want to be seen.

As far as Denver was concerned, I was out of here. I'd already moved all my things out of my place and given notice to my landlord. This meeting with Stanford was my last stop on my way out of town.

Stanford ordered the burger, extra caramelized onions, while I opted for a salmon salad. "Cold food on a cold day," he quipped, shaking his head. "I'll never understand it."

"Hoping it'll keep me sharp."

When the server returned to the kitchen, I leaned my elbows on the table. "I'm ready, sir. I mean, Michael." I shook my head. That really was weird. "I can't wait to get started, actually. Those assholes are going down, and they're not going to have any clue what's coming."

"I appreciate that enthusiasm. You can't afford to be cocky, though. We have a lot of unknowns. Too many things could go wrong."

We both sat back as the server brought over a basket of bread. I thanked her, but I couldn't help the frustration from creeping into my tone. As soon as she was gone, I let my scowl take over.

"Sir, we've been over this. I've proven myself. Dare I say, I've earned it. If you don't have faith in my ability to manage this assignment, then—"

He tilted his head. "Did I say that? I have faith in you, Brynn. Do not doubt that. Not for one second. But I also want to see you succeed."

A slow breath helped calm me. For a moment there, I'd heard my uncle's voice in my head instead of Stanford's. *What makes you think you can do this, Brynn? You're weak. Like all women are weak. Like your mother is weak.*

Stanford wasn't anything like my uncle. For one, he actually cared about me.

"I'm the best person for this job," I insisted.

"You are. I'd never let you do it if I didn't believe that."

Today, I would begin the biggest undercover assignment I'd ever undertaken. It was off the books, totally unofficial as far as any FBI records would show. It was the result of months of investigation and effort, with Stanford at the head.

A source had provided new intel recently, and we'd escalated our timetable. Things were suddenly moving fast. Maybe too fast, given Stanford's lingering worries. But I could do this. We were finally going to turn our investigation into action.

This case was personal for me. Not in a way that would cloud my judgment, but in a way that fueled my fire like nothing else.

"It's these other people I don't have faith in," Stanford said under his breath. "These...*Protectors*."

He'd laced that last word with as much derision and skepticism as possible.

The Last Refuge Protectors were a group of vigilantes operating out of Hart County, Colorado. All with military training, like myself. But unlike me, they were wary of the FBI. Our partnership with them was unconventional, to say the least.

On the FBI side, I'd been the natural choice for this undercover assignment, given my contacts and the circumstances at play. But it still hadn't been easy to convince SAC Stanford to put me in. I didn't do much undercover work. Certainly not something this deep or this dangerous. I'd served as a Marine in combat, but even then, I'd had my unit to rely on during missions. Not to mention air support.

But this mission wouldn't have existed at all if not for the Protectors. They also had resources of their own. Gear, weapons, technology, intel.

The truth was that we *needed* the Protectors to make this mission happen. Stanford knew that as well as I did.

"I'm not thrilled with it either," I said. "The decision's been made, and there's no going back. As you so often like to tell me."

"And you always hate hearing it."

"I do. At least we know River Kwon is legit. He's married to the lieutenant governor, for heaven's sake. My best friend. I wasn't sure about him at first, but he's a good guy, and that makes me believe the other Protectors are trustworthy as well."

"Kwon isn't your partner in this mission, though. You haven't even met this Cole Bailey character."

I groaned at the reminder. I had no idea what to make of Cole Bailey yet.

In an ideal world, we would've had more time to vet him. But under our time pressure, it wasn't possible. River had assured me Bailey was the best, and that he'd help us. No question. River had a way of getting on my last nerve, but he was an excellent operative. I trusted his word.

Starting tonight, I would have a week to get to know Bailey—and make sure he understood who was in charge—before we had to go into the lion's den together.

Stanford folded his hands on the tabletop, expression gruff. "What do we really know about Bailey, apart from his service record and current occupation? Very little."

"We've already discussed *all of this*." I kept my voice down, not wanting to draw the attention of our server or the couple of other patrons. But I was beyond frustrated. "Why are you rehashing it now?"

"Because you mean a hell of a lot to me, Brynn. That's not the kind of thing you and I talk about, and I figure that's the Marine in us both. We're hell-raisers when we need to be, but about other things, we're stoic."

"Yeah. That's fair."

"Truth is, you've become like a daughter to me and Marie. I hope you realize that."

I glanced down at the table, feeling my skin heat. "Thank you. I feel the same."

"And now I've gone and made it awkward."

I laughed. "Nah, I can handle talking feelings if you can. So long as we don't make a habit of it."

He winked. "Not likely."

The server brought over our lunches. I ate, though I wasn't feeling all that hungry. A lot of emotions were swirling around in my stomach. Gratitude. Nerves. Uncertainty.

Stanford reached into the messenger bag at his feet and brought out a manila envelope. Set it on the table and rested his hand on top of it. "The identity papers for your cover stories. We used Bailey's most recent photo from his bounty hunter license. His listed address is in Mexico City, but I couldn't risk going through any official channels there for more info. If we'd had more time…"

"We'll make it work." I took the envelope and peered quickly inside. It held several documents, as expected. There was also a burner phone, which would be the only means of contact between me and Stanford during this mission. My one remaining tie to the FBI.

"I've decided I want your updates daily," Stanford said.

I gave him a sharp look. "*Daily?* You're not serious."

I had already told him a complete communications blackout between us would be preferable. If anyone traced my mission back to the FBI, the entire thing could blow up in our faces. We'd compromised by agreeing to weekly updates. Now he wanted to renegotiate?

Daily was ridiculous. It was a risk.

But I also knew Stanford well enough to realize I shouldn't argue. "I'll do what I can to keep you informed."

"I said daily, Brynn. I mean it."

"All right, *Dad*. I'm thirty-three, not twelve."

His eyebrow lifted, but the corner of his mouth did too. "If anything happens, I'll do whatever I can to send in backup for you. And that includes any issues with the Last Refuge Protectors. If they try to shut you out, if they *burn* us, then I'll end each and every one of them. And Cole Bailey will be first on that list."

"Got it." I nodded, tucking the manila envelope into the large pocket of my coat.

"I just want you to remember," he said. "Even though we need the Protectors, that doesn't make you one of them. You can't let your guard down."

"I can promise you, sir, there's no chance of that."

---

I was an hour out of Denver, bobbing my head to my favorite playlist, when my phone rang. I answered it using my hands-free settings. "Charlotte! I was hoping to hear from you."

"I suck. I'm sorry. I really wanted to see you again before you left town, but the last few days have been nonstop."

I laughed. "I wasn't trying to make you feel bad. I get it. The lieutenant governor is in high demand these days."

"Unfortunately. But enough about me. How does it feel to no longer be a cog in the machine?"

"You mean, how does it feel to leave the good old FBI?"

I gazed out the windshield at the scenery flying past. A spring storm had dumped snow on the mountains and evergreens as far as I could see. But unlike Denver, where the snow had turned to muddy brown slush, it was a pristine white out here.

"It's…liberating," I finally said.

We were on an open cell line, nowhere near secure. So neither of us could discuss the nature of my undercover assignment. Even though Charlotte had been briefed on all the details.

She was one of the few people in the world, aside from Stanford, that I would gladly trust with my life. And I would lay down mine for her in return. We'd been best friends for well over a year now.

Charlotte was also my link to the Last Refuge Protectors.

Several months ago, the lieutenant governor had been attacked by Stillwater, a secretive criminal organization. With the help of River Kwon, Charlotte had uncovered crucial information about Stillwater, and they'd shared that intel with me and SAC Stanford. An FBI task force had taken over the investigation. But until recently, we'd had no idea who was really in charge of Stillwater.

My official story was that I'd resigned from the FBI out of

protest. I was disgusted with the Bureau's failed effort to take Stillwater down. And to some extent, that was true.

By going undercover, I would finally have the chance to stop the criminals who'd tried to murder my best friend and who'd harmed so many others.

"So you're on your way to Hart County?" Charlotte asked.

"I am. But not Hartley. I'm heading to Silver Ridge. I'm sure I'll see River at some point, but I decided to branch out. Do my own thing."

I hoped she got the hint. I couldn't head to Last Refuge, the Protectors' headquarters in Hartley, in case anyone from Stillwater had their eye on the location.

"If you have time, you could stop by my parents' place on the way," Charlotte said. "They'd love to see you."

I felt a twinge of discomfort, and then an ugly twist of envy. "I'd love to see them too. But maybe later. Not ready to change my plan just yet."

"Of course you've got your plan mapped out. You're the most together person I know."

"Perhaps I'm just really good at faking it."

Charlotte had an amazing family. Her parents were supportive, and her sisters never ceased to keep her entertained, even when they weren't getting along. In other words, she had exactly the kind of family I had always dreamed of.

It was so different from the way I'd grown up. Night and day.

When Charlotte and I had met, we'd both been extremely single. Then River had appeared. Her childhood friend and her ex's older brother. After a whirlwind of running for their lives and falling in love, they'd eloped. I was so happy for my friend. Truly.

I just wished her happiness didn't remind me of everything I'd lost. Or never really had to begin with.

"You *are* okay, right?" she asked. "You're up for this? You can change your mind if you have any concerns."

Wonderful. First Stanford had expressed doubts, and now Charlotte was fretting. It was like they *expected* something bad to happen.

"Don't jinx me when I've barely gotten started." I needed this undercover assignment. Not just to destroy Stillwater from the inside out, but to make me forget, even for a while, everything else that my life was lacking. "I know what I'm doing. I'm—"

I came around a curve, and suddenly the car in front of me slammed on its brakes. *Shit*. I was quick to respond, pressing hard on my own brake pedal.

I narrowly avoided the bumper ahead of me, stopping a few inches away.

*Phew*. Way too close.

"You still there, Brynn? Hello?"

"I'm here. There's some kind of slow down. Whole road seems to be stopped." I craned my neck, trying to see what was ahead. "I see emergency lights. Maybe an accident. I gotta go, Charlotte. I was probably going to lose cell reception soon anyway."

"Good luck, okay? Keep me posted if you can. I'll be rooting for you. Love you, B."

"Love you too."

I spent the next twenty minutes in stop-and-go traffic. As far as I could tell, there had been an accident involving a semi up ahead. And of course, this highway wove through mountains, and there was no easy route around. We had to follow a detour onto a smaller, two-lane highway.

I groaned, thinking of how long it was going to take me to get to Silver Ridge. But hey, I'd learned a long time ago not to let any obstacles stop me. So I turned up my playlist and sang along.

Eventually the traffic eased, and I was flying again, getting closer and closer to my destination.

Until there was a loud pop. My car veered hard to the left. Toward oncoming traffic. Gripping my steering wheel, I corrected, as honking horns assailed my ears. I made it to the right shoulder, up against a metal railing. Beyond it, a slope fell away into a rushing creek below.

I pushed open my door and jumped out. Frigid air rushed at me. It was twenty degrees colder, at least, than it had been in Denver. Inching along to stay away from the cars whizzing by on the road, I made it to the front bumper.

My front left tire had blown. The thing was shredded. I wasn't going anywhere on that, not unless I wanted to destroy the rim. And—yep. I'd lost cell reception. Just *great*.

My mind immediately flew to dark possibilities, but this wasn't evidence of a nefarious plot. It was just my old car and the bald tires I should've dealt with before leaving town.

*You're the most together person I know,* my best friend had said. When it came to my career, that was usually true. But the real Brynn Somerton was so much messier. Just getting by, day by day.

# CHAPTER TWO

## *Cole*

I *HATED* GOING UNDERCOVER. Yet I was on my way to Hart County, Colorado, right now for one of those spy routines. All because my friends had begged me to drop everything and step in.

It had been a long day already. Two excruciating flights and a hell of a headache getting through the rental car line. I wanted a damn cigarette, but I only allowed myself one a day, and I was determined to delay that gratification as long as possible.

And would you look at that? Flashing lights and a big orange barrier blocking the road. Of course.

With no other choice, I joined the line of cars branching off onto the alternate route. About fifteen miles later, I spotted a couple of vehicles pulled off onto the shoulder up ahead. I slowed, taking in the situation and assessing if they needed help.

A woman stood beside the first vehicle. She had a flat tire. *Very* flat. Sitting on the rim. A guy had parked his Land Cruiser behind her, and he stood with his hands on his hips. She was in a defensive posture. I didn't like what I read in their body language.

Something was up here.

It wasn't my business. It really wasn't. Didn't I have enough on my plate? But I was already pulling off to the shoulder.

I had a slight hang-up about people in distress. Especially women in distress. It was a visceral reaction, something I couldn't ignore. Even if it would've been smarter to.

But nobody had ever accused me of being a genius.

Pulling on my beanie, I got out of my car and approached, moving slowly out of caution and ignoring the twinge in my left leg. Too many hours crammed in a too-small airplane seat. As I neared, I picked up their voices over the noise of passing traffic.

"Don't be stuck up, sweetheart. I took the trouble of stopping. Just let me help. If you're worried about owing me, I'm sure we can work something out."

My spine straightened. Was this guy for real?

The jerk was in his twenties, built like a cornfed football player. Expensive sneakers and leather coat. The woman was pretty. No, make that gorgeous. Model gorgeous. Long black hair tied up in a ponytail at the crown of her head. Large eyes with thick eyelashes I could see from a distance. She didn't look frightened or flustered, but there was a wariness in her gaze. She crossed her arms, eyes bouncing over to me and back to the football player again.

I stopped about two yards away, undecided about how I should handle this. I preferred not to step in if I didn't have to. Because things inevitably got messy. I wound up getting involved, and pretty soon I was in deep, committed to risking life and limb even though I always got burned in the end.

Hell. I gripped the bridge of my nose. Why did I seem to find myself in these situations?

*You'll be going undercover against Stillwater,* my buddy Aiden

Shelborne had said. *We don't have anyone who can do this but you. Come on, Lynx. You can't say no.*

When did I *ever* know how to say no?

I was a bounty hunter operating exclusively south of the United States border. But I didn't track down fleeing sex offenders by wearing disguises or cooking up elaborate cover stories. Hell, no. My usual MO was to track the guy, march up to the dive bar or flea-ridden hotel he was skulking in, and make my presence known. The fugitive never had any doubt about who had arrived to ruin his Acapulco vacation.

*Me.* Cole Bailey, aka Lynx.

But Aiden was an Army brother and the founder of the Last Refuge Protectors, a group of men who—like myself—refused to stand by and watch innocent people get victimized by the scum of the world. And when I'd heard the mission was against Stillwater? There'd been no question.

I'd taken the first flight available, which connected through Houston, and then I'd flown on to Denver International. I'd chosen that airport because it was large, busy. Easier to go unnoticed in case anyone affiliated with Stillwater was watching.

The flight from Houston to Denver had been packed. I'd given up my aisle spot so a lady could sit with her ten-year-old daughter. Nobody else had been willing to volunteer. I had ended up in a middle seat in the back row. The loud talker at the window beside me had spilled his third Jack and Coke on my lap. Then he'd needed the bathroom and came back with white residue on his nostrils and a bad case of the sniffles.

When he'd asked to get up yet again, I'd glared without a word until he averted his eyes. He hadn't asked again.

And now this. The detour, the menacing jerk bothering a woman by the side of the road. As if the universe enjoyed making my life as complicated as possible. A cosmic joke against Cole Bailey, the guy who'd been punished for just about every good deed, and yet kept coming back for more.

*It's how you wound up married,* I reminded myself. *And then out on your ass with divorce papers in your hand.*

When was I going to learn?

The asshole football player took a few more steps toward the raven-haired woman. Reached out to grab her wrist. And that did it for me. The answer was *never*. I would never learn. I would keep on butting in and trying to help because my brain was wired that way.

Scowling, I started toward them.

I wasn't fast enough. The moment he touched her, the woman lashed out. She spun, and the football player in the fancy sneakers—who was twice her size at least—flipped through the air and landed on his back with a thud in the dirty snow.

Holy cow. Hadn't expected that.

I'd made it to them by then. Paused to look down at him. I probably had a look of shock on my face, but it was nothing to the stunned expression on his. It took him almost a full minute to get moving again.

"What the *fuck*." The football player jumped up, brushing at his clothes angrily. "You stuck up little—"

I grabbed him by the shoulder and pushed him back toward his SUV. "You'd be wise not to finish that sentence. Best be on your way. Unless you want her to come at you again."

As for the woman I'd been intending to rescue, she walked back over to her car. She spared a single glance at me, giving me a hard glare in case I had any ideas of making the same mistake this guy had made.

The football player's cheeks went even redder. Muttering, the guy stomped over to his vehicle. His wheels spun as he accelerated back onto the road, nearly hitting another car as he merged.

Good riddance.

I looked over at the woman. She was watching me with mild curiosity, along with that same wariness I'd seen earlier. And maybe a hint of smugness at the way she'd flipped him, which she richly deserved.

Wow. I was impressed.

I scratched my beard, which probably could've used a trim. "I pulled over because I thought you might need help with that guy. Clearly you didn't."

"Nope. But I appreciate the thought." She nodded once, with finality, like she really wanted that to be the end of it. She went to her trunk and pulled out a jack. Her spare was already resting beside her bumper. "Have a good day," she added. "Drive safe."

I was dismissed. Yet I lingered another moment, unable to shift my eyes away from her.

Those had been some kinda moves. She had training, and not just basic self defense. Not like I thought all women were helpless. Far from it. But this one was something else. Probably got hit on and bothered all the time by overeager admirers, and she showed them who was boss.

So why wasn't I back in my rental car and continuing on my way?

I gestured at the jack. "I hope I'm not speaking out of turn. But since I'm here, I'd feel like an asshole if I didn't offer a hand with that. Out of politeness. Nothing else."

Her smile was sharp. "I don't need a man to do hard things for me."

"Didn't say you did. I was just—"

"Thanks, but no thanks." She'd kept her tone even, but the message was clear. Step off.

"Fair enough," I said.

It was cold, and I was jonesing for nicotine and grumpy as hell from the long day I'd had already. I turned and walked toward my vehicle. Along the way, I gave in and took out my pack of cigarettes and my lighter.

The first lungful of smoke hit me with an instant wave of calm. There it was. Just what I'd needed.

I could stand here and have a smoke. After all, it was a free country.

Yes, the woman was beautiful. Attraction buzzed low in my belly, and my gaze kept straying in her direction. The elegant lines of her profile, the hidden strength of her body beneath the puffy coat and dark jeans. But that wasn't the reason I leaned against my car door instead of driving off.

What harm would it do if I stuck around until she'd finished changing her tire? I would know that nobody else would stop and bug her. Once she was on her way, I'd be on mine. Maybe in a slightly better mood before I got to Hart County.

So, I had some bad habits. If I hadn't made that clear yet.

I'd picked up smoking during my first deployment. After joining the Rangers, I'd been nearing a pack a day. Helped me smooth out the bumps so I didn't flinch at whatever came my way. My wife Shelley had hated it. Complained constantly that I stank whenever I was stateside.

Then I'd been wounded. Lost just about everything. The doctor had told me I should do my healing body a favor and quit poisoning it. But I hadn't managed to cut back until Shelley ditched me. I winnowed down my habit to one a day sheerly out of spite. My ex didn't want to be saddled with a one-legged husband? Fine. I would come back better than ever just to show her.

That had been five years ago. And I was still stuck on one a day.

My other bad habit? That one was obvious.

The pretty brunette kept glancing over at me. I managed to relocate my eyeballs on the forest across the road.

I couldn't manage to say no to someone in distress. The worst feeling in the world was knowing a person had needed me, and that I'd failed.

The habit rarely brought me satisfaction. Sadly, even when a mission succeeded, endings were never happy like in movies. That had been the case in my Army days. Same now that I was a bounty hunter.

I'd much rather be hunting down bad guys and knocking heads together than trying to fix something that was broken. I could repair a sink drain or change a flat, but I was *shit* at fixing anything of significance. My heroics were more the destructive kind.

The pretty brunette was fiddling with the jack. She cursed under her breath.

*Don't look,* I told myself. *Do. Not.*

Fuck me. I looked.

That same moment, there was a metallic-sounding snap. This time, she cursed nice and loud. Stood up. Bowed her head like she was praying for strength.

Then she turned and walked toward me, the long metal bar hanging from her hand.

I stayed very still as I leaned against my car door. Didn't smile, but a resting frown came naturally to me anyway. I just took another drag.

She cleared her throat. "So. Uh. It appears my equipment has seen better days. The hook snapped off."

"I noticed."

"And I made that whole speech about not needing anything from you. Which makes me feel kind of stupid right about now."

I exhaled in an almost-laugh, hooking a thumb toward my trunk. "You're welcome to borrow whatever you need."

"That would be great. Thank you."

I almost added that there was no shame in needing help. I'd needed plenty when I'd been in PT learning to walk again. But she seemed embarrassed already. I didn't want to add to that.

And secretly, I felt a jolt of deeper satisfaction than I'd gotten from the nicotine.

She waited by the hood while I went to my trunk for the jack and tools. I'd checked the equipment before leaving the rental lot.

I returned to her. "Are you in a rental car? Sometimes the agencies try to save a few bucks by buying junk."

"No, this is mine." She waved sheepishly at the beat-up Subaru. "But my ex used to borrow my car a lot. Who knows what he was doing. I mean, I know some of it, but..." She squeezed her eyes shut. "I'm not sure why I just told you that."

"Because you're having a bad day?"

Her shoulders sagged. "It's trending that way. That's why I'm going to swallow my pride and ask for your help. You seem like a good guy, and four hands will work faster than two. I'd really like to get back on the road. I have somewhere I need to be."

"Sure." I had half my cigarette left, but I stubbed it beneath my boot heel.

Faster we could get this done, faster we'd both be on our way.

"No gloating? No I-told-you-sos?"

"I'm just not being an asshole. Is that all it takes to be considered a good guy? I don't think my ex-wife would agree."

The brunette laughed, a soft sound that burrowed into my chest, and when it ended, she was smiling. A pretty, grateful smile like that was another hit straight to my bloodstream. I was so predictable. It was embarrassing.

We worked together on putting the jack into place and lifting the car. "Thank you again for this," she said. "I'm glad you didn't drive off."

"Happy to help."

Crouching beside her meant she was almost close enough to touch. She was younger than me, though I couldn't tell how much. The skin at the nape of her neck looked soft, sloping gently into the collar of her coat. Her pale coloring had a hint of pink at the cheeks. Was that from the cold? Or some reaction to me? I didn't flatter myself.

But yeah… She was something all right.

I almost asked for her name. In fact, I wanted to ask where she was from, where she was going. But I figured that was too friendly considering we were about to go our separate ways.

Still, I couldn't resist leaning in just as we finished. She smelled sweet, like flowers dipped in honey.

"There you go," I said. "Should be all set."

We both stood, taking off our dirty gloves.

"Thanks for loaning me your equipment."

I tapped my left thigh. "Well, I do know a thing or two about the benefits of good equipment."

In an instant, her pretty smile went hard. Then vanished altogether. Her eyes flashed down my body, then back up again, narrowing.

"Good equipment, huh?" She folded her arms over her chest. "Let me guess. You really know how to use it? Was that going to be your next line?"

I replayed what I'd just said. "I didn't mean it like that."

"Sure you didn't. That's why you were gesturing at your crotch. Very subtle."

"Hold on, I wasn't—" I'd meant my prosthesis. But I didn't owe her my life story. "You've got this wrong."

"I doubt it. I noticed how you were checking me out."

My jaw clenched. I'd definitely been checking her out. "Relax, you're not my type," I lied.

"You're not even close to mine. I don't go for assholes who pretend to be sweet."

"I wasn't pretending to be anything. Least of all sweet."

"That's good, because if you were, your act isn't anywhere near convincing."

"Then why are you still standing here? Your car is fixed. Nobody's forcing you to stay and gripe at me."

"You're right." She stalked to her car, got in, and drove away.

"Shit," I muttered. How had that gone downhill so fast?

I looked forlornly at the other half of my cigarette on the ground, regretting that I'd crushed it.

*No. Good. Deed.*

*Dammit.*

## CHAPTER THREE

DESPITE THE DETOUR, I made good time getting to Silver Ridge after the flat tire debacle. I followed the directions programmed into my GPS and found myself at a cute little house not far from Main Street.

My car pulled up to the curb, and I heaved a sigh. Thank goodness I was here.

Earlier this year I'd been to Hartley, the county seat, to visit the headquarters of the Protectors. Silver Ridge was about half an hour away from Hartley, and its architecture was just as charming. An eclectic mix of western, Victorian, and newer construction, combined with historic streetlights and signs that proclaimed *Welcome to the Hart of Colorado*. Cutesy puns were not usually my jam. But even I had to admit the ambiance of Hart County was inviting.

You'd never expect that a vigilante group like the Protectors had faced off with Stillwater not that far from here. An idyllic setting wasn't guaranteed to be peaceful underneath.

Grabbing my bag, I headed for the front door, not sure who this place belonged to. All I knew was that River had sent me this address. But it wasn't his, since River's apartment was over in Hartley. Also, this house was way too adorable for him. It was painted a cheerful blue with a white porch, and its driveway and sidewalks were meticulously shoveled free of snow. There was even a little gnome waving from the porch steps.

River opened the door as soon as I knocked. He took my bag and held out his other hand for a fist bump. "Hey, come in. How was the trip down?"

I couldn't hide my scowl. "A little drama. But no big deal." I took off my coat. For the drive, I'd worn a soft, long-sleeved Henley top and a pair of black jeans. So much more comfortable than my usual FBI dress slacks and blazer.

"Uh oh. If it put you in a mood, then it was clearly a big deal. What happened?"

"*You* usually put me in a mood," I pointed out. "And yet, I get over it."

"Exactly. I'm extraordinary. Therefore, whatever happened to get under your skin is worth hearing about."

"Your logic is frightening."

He grinned. "Thank you."

I hadn't been a fan of River Kwon when I'd first met him. The man had shown up to protect Charlotte, and I was protective of my best friend. Also, River was beyond cocky, and that tended to rub me the wrong way.

Okay, I could be a touch cocky at times myself. But I liked to know the score. When River had appeared on the scene, I hadn't known what to make of him. In the months since, he'd become a close friend. How could I dislike a man who made my friend so happy and treated her like a queen?

But that didn't mean I was willing to explain myself to him. Nope, I was better off forgetting the man who'd loaned me his jack by the side of the road.

I walked inside, spotted a kitchen, and made a beeline for it. There, I found a surprise waiting. A very pleasant one.

Keira Marsh stood behind the island, decked out in her

sheriff's deputy uniform, thumbs swiping on her phone. Then she looked up, set her phone aside, and smiled. "Brynn! It's so good to see you." She rounded the island, opening her arms for a hug.

"I didn't know you'd be here," I said.

"It would be weird if I wasn't. This is my house."

"Seriously? I had no idea you lived in Silver Ridge."

She puffed up with pride. "We closed after New Year's. My mom and sister have been *smothering* me with decorating help. They keep showing up with tchotchkes and furniture. I'm surprised the Hart County thrift stores have anything left on their shelves."

"Tell your mom and sister they're doing an excellent job of it." I glanced around. The house was full of overstuffed upholstery, cheerful patterns, and farmhouse touches. A few antiques here and there to create a sense of warmth and history.

"I know, right? I'd be annoyed at them butting in, but I gotta admit, they're good at it. My little sister Stephie especially. I don't have a design-conscious bone in my body. The timing worked out, though. When Owen and River mentioned you'd need a place to stay outside Hartley, I volunteered my guest room. So make yourself at home. Figured this was better than a hotel."

"So much better. You're an angel. Thank you."

I'd met Keira on my previous trips to Hartley. She worked for Sheriff Owen Douglas. From everything I'd seen, Keira was a good cop, just a few years out of college. Younger than me, but we'd gotten dinner and drinks and bonded over being women in the male-dominated law enforcement profession. I admired her dedication to her duties, even when she had to paint outside the lines to help the Protectors. That wasn't an easy balance.

As much as I respected her, I would've been hesitant tc

bring a junior deputy into a dangerous mission like this one. But Keira had dealt with Stillwater operatives before. And she hadn't lost her nerve. That alone made me admire her.

Of course, she wouldn't deal directly with Stillwater during the undercover op. That part would be all Cole Bailey and me. Speaking of…I wondered when my partner would get here.

Keira opened a cabinet, taking out a couple of mugs. "Want something to drink? I was just going to brew up some of my famous chai. Heavy on the honey and cinnamon."

"Yes, please. That sounds amazing."

"What sounds amazing?" River asked, strolling into the kitchen.

Keira smiled over her shoulder. "My famous chai. Want a mug?"

"You'd *better* make me a mug," he said, not missing a beat. "But I'm still curious about the drama that happened on the way down here."

"Drama?" Keira asked as she poured water into a pot.

"Not you too," I muttered. "When is Cole Bailey arriving? Is he staying here as well?"

River rested his hands against the butcher block top of the island. "I'm sure he'll get here soon, and no, we've got him bunking elsewhere. Tell us what happened, B."

He and Keira both paused, eyeing me.

I groaned. "Fine, I'll tell you. But it's not that exciting. It was just a flat tire. And this guy. Well, *two* guys. They stopped separately to help me change my tire, but clearly they were interested in…something else."

Keira's eyebrows knitted. "Not cool."

River quipped, "Are these guys maimed and lying by the side of the road? Do I need to call Trace for a discreet body cleanup?"

I laughed, tossing the end of my ponytail over my shoulder. "Not necessary. It was weird though. First, a young guy pulled over to help me and got offended when I said I could handle it myself. He didn't want to take no for an answer. Grabbed my arm."

River's eyes darkened. "The guy did *what?*"

"Don't worry about it. I handled him. But then the second guy showed up. And he seemed nice enough at first. I needed to borrow a jack, and he loaned me his."

He'd seemed to have a military vibe. Competent and calm, but interested in taking no shit. Like a seasoned staff sergeant. The kind of man I tended to respect.

Not bad to look at either. He hadn't been handsome in an obvious or classic way. More rugged. A dark beanie pulled over his hair, a full beard, scars on his forehead and cheek. He'd been leaning against his car, a cigarette pursed between his lips. Like a hero from an old Western movie if you'd traded the knit cap for a Stetson.

"But then he came on to me," I said. "And he wasn't clever about it either. It's fine for a guy to be interested. Whatever, I can brush that off. But there was no need to be crude."

"What did he say?" River demanded.

"I promise, there's no point repeating it. I'd rather forget it happened."

Keira made a disgusted face. "Why do men do that? Pretend to be nice to a vulnerable woman, only to try it on with her a minute later."

We both looked at River, and he held up his hands. "Don't expect me to explain my kind. We're not all like that."

"Clearly not." I just seemed to have a bad track record. Too many men in my life had made me believe they cared, that they were genuine, only to pull out the rug from beneath me.

Keira added spices and a few tea bags to her pot, then set

it on the stove. "The problem is, all the honorable men seem to be taken. Or not interested." She spoke that last part wistfully, like she had someone specific in mind. I'd have to remind myself to ask her about it later. We could trade tales of romantic woe. Or better yet, I could just listen. My history with men was just depressing.

River shrugged. "Sorry there's not enough of me to go around. Charlie is a very demanding woman."

I almost flipped him off, but Keira beat me to it.

A few minutes later, she poured us each a cup of chai. It was warm and sweet and spicy. Perfect thing to wipe away the last bit of tension I was holding.

"So, who wants to give me the inside scoop on my new partner?" I asked. "I assume Bailey is one of the good ones."

River leaned against the kitchen counter. "Lynx is solid. A skilled tracker, great shot, and a reliable operator through and through."

"I second all of that," Keira said. "Owen loves him too."

"He's a bounty hunter, right?"

River nodded. "Yep. Working in Mexico and Central America the last few years since leaving the Army Rangers. He tracks fugitive sex offenders and brings them back to the United States. Luckily, he was willing to drop everything to join this op. We didn't have a chance to fully brief him, but he's as eager to take down Stillwater as any of us. Should be here any—"

There was the sound of a car door closing outside.

"I assume that's him." River headed toward the door.

Before I could follow, Keira put her hand on my arm. "If you're worried about Cole being an honorable guy, you don't need to. He's been awesome every time I've spoken to him. Very professional."

"Glad to hear it."

I was grateful for the reassurance. SAC Stanford had been

stressing over nothing. The Protectors were good Marines, good special operators, or good soldiers, every one. They'd never bring in someone who didn't meet those same standards.

When Keira and I made it to the entryway, the door was open, and River was giving a back-slapping hug to another man. They both separated and turned, and my eyes made contact with the newcomer.

Both of us froze in place. Stared at one another.

It was official. This mission was screwed.

"Oh, hell no. *You're* Cole Bailey?"

# CHAPTER FOUR

## Brynn

COLE'S LIP CURLED. "YOU?"

River squinted at us both, glancing between us. "What's going on, exactly?"

"He's the guy. The one who helped me change my flat tire and then hit on me."

Cole scowled. "I didn't hit on you."

"You pointed at your crotch and said you have 'good equipment.'"

Keira's jaw dropped. River's head slowly swiveled toward the other man. "Dude. Seriously?"

"Whoa!" Cole held up his hands, taking a quick step forward. "That's not what happened."

"Now you're calling me a liar? Wonderful." I spun and went back into the house.

Footsteps pounded after me. "Hold on a minute." Cole followed me into the kitchen. Larger than life, and even more imposing because he was so out of place here among Keira's cute, welcoming decor. "Are you telling me this undercover op for the Protectors is with *you*?"

"It *was* with me. Not anymore. I'm not working with you."

Eventually, everyone showed their true colors. And this afternoon by the side of the road, Cole had shown me his. No way could I go into a dangerous undercover op with a guy like that.

"Hell, I never said I'd work with you," he barked. "I don't know a single damn thing about you except that you've got the wrong idea about me."

"First impressions speak volumes. I need an undercover partner I can trust with my life. Not someone who'll try to cop a feel."

River strode into the kitchen, Keira on his heels. "Okay, kids," River said. "There's been some kind of misunderstanding. Let's take a minute to breathe."

Cole and I glared at one another, chests heaving. Breathing was not the issue.

"Brynn, this is Cole Bailey, also known as Lynx. Cole, this is Special Agent Brynn Somerton. FBI."

If anything, Cole looked even more disgusted.

"Former FBI," I corrected. "Officially."

Cole turned his glare on his friend. "You didn't say anything about this op being with the FBI."

River shrugged. "I told you we were taking down Stillwater. You said you were in. We were saving the details for when you arrived."

"Hell of a detail to omit. I'm not working with a Fed. Find someone else."

I nodded. "Works for me. Find me another partner. Not him."

River threw his hands up in exasperation. "There *is* no one else. Not on the schedule we're working with."

"Maybe you two could discuss what happened earlier?" Keira said softly. "Five minutes. Couldn't possibly hurt. *Then* we can address the FBI thing."

I glanced over at Cole. He side-eyed me.

He went to the back door. Opened it. Looked at me like he expected me to go first.

"After you," I said.

Grumbling, he went into Keira's backyard, and I closed the door lightly on my way out.

Cole spun to face me. "For fuck's sake, I didn't point at my crotch."

"I saw what I saw."

"And yet you didn't see the whole picture." He bent and lifted the hem of his jeans on one leg, revealing the metal rod of a prosthetic leg. "*This* is the good equipment I was referring to."

My lips parted, but words failed me.

I had...not expected that.

But when I recalled the incident earlier, what he'd said... Okay, maybe I'd misinterpreted. The gesture hadn't been *directly* at his crotch. But still.

"How was I supposed to know that?" I sputtered.

"I don't know! It was a throwaway comment. I didn't mean a damn thing by it."

"But you could've explained right then."

"Why? I thought I'd never see you again. You'd hardly be the first woman to walk away with a shitty opinion of me."

"That's supposed to reassure me?"

He straightened to his full height and walked toward me, stopping when we were a few inches apart. "I'm just trying to clear this up so my friends don't think I'm a creep who propositions women who need help. It doesn't matter what *you* think of me."

I arched my spine, arms folded over my chest, ready with another comeback.

But then I thought back to how helpful he'd been with my flat tire. How he'd been perfectly nice before the "good equipment" confusion. He'd been checking me out, but no, that wasn't a crime.

*There is no one else,* River had said.

Ugh, what a mess.

Maybe we could salvage this. The enemy was Stillwater, not each other. If Keira and River and the other Protectors thought highly of Cole, I should give him a chance to prove himself.

Most importantly? I couldn't let this op fall apart before it had barely begun.

I put my hand over my eyes, then wiped it down my face. "All right. So we got off on the wrong foot."

He stared for a solid beat.

"That supposed to be a joke?" he finally asked.

"A joke?" Then I realized what I'd said. "It wasn't a reference to *your* foot. I mean—"

He snorted, glancing away and shaking his head. "I'm kidding. But you see how easy it is to say the wrong shit and get misinterpreted? Look, I personally witnessed some asswipe try to get aggressive with you this afternoon. I'm sure that kinda thing happens to you plenty. Impressive how you flipped him, by the way."

"Thanks."

"But I get why you jumped to the wrong conclusion when I said what I did. We both got our backs up. Got defensive."

"Yes, we did. I did." I could admit I was sensitive about men who pretended to be one thing, then proved to be the opposite. "I'm willing to start over if you are."

"Guess we could try," he said gruffly.

I held out my hand. "I'm Brynn Somerton."

"*Agent* Somerton."

"Former agent." My eyes looked heavenward. *Give me patience, please.* "We might as well go inside and talk through the details. Since we both came all this way."

"We did," he hedged.

"And this really isn't about us, anyway. It's about our common enemy."

"True."

I wiggled my hand. He still hadn't taken it.

He eyed my open palm another moment. Then he returned the gesture, and we shook. "I'm Cole Bailey. It's been…interesting to meet you, Brynn."

"Likewise."

His palm was large, fingers rough and thick, nearly swallowing mine. Our hands slid apart, and a shiver ran down my neck like a caressing fingertip.

Between the hat and the beard, I hadn't recognized him from his photos earlier, but now I saw it. The brightness of his blue eyes, ringed by crow's feet from squinting. A strong, square jaw line. Not bad to look at. Not at all.

The back door opened. "You two made up yet?" River asked.

That weird trance-like moment broke. We separated. "Yep. All good," I said. For now anyway.

I had no idea whether we could work together. But unless I wanted to face Stillwater alone, I had to give him a fair shot.

# CHAPTER FIVE

BRYNN WALKED TOWARD THE HOUSE. River stepped out of her way to let her pass. Then he turned toward me, blocking my path. "I trust the talk was productive," he said.

I was still standing there, my tongue not working well enough to speak.

A handshake with a potential teammate wasn't supposed to set my blood pumping. But from her? Shit. The sensation of her slender fingers wrapped around my palm had banished all the sense from my brain.

When I'd touched her, an image had flashed unbidden through my mind. Me gripping that ponytail on top of her head and tugging to angle her mouth perfectly toward mine.

*Nngh.*

Beyond inappropriate. I'd told her by the side of the road earlier that she wasn't my type, and that was complete bullshit.

*Shake it off,* I told myself. Her looks were irrelevant.

"Our talk was productive," I said, remembering River's question. "We established I'm not going around perving on random women. If that's what you mean. It was a misunderstanding."

He chuckled. "So we don't have to lock up our wives, nieces, and daughters around you?"

I coughed, gut twisting with discomfort over the lusty thoughts I'd been having about Brynn not moments before. It wasn't an issue. Regardless of any base-level attraction, I would never act on it.

I'd served with women. Worked with them. I was a professional. I didn't let myself get distracted by something as common as a pretty face.

And that wasn't even the problem here.

"Joke all you want, but I still don't see this working out. You should've told me what I was getting into." We were still standing in the open doorway. I glanced into the house, but Brynn had disappeared. "What the hell are the Protectors doing working with the FBI?"

"It's a long story, and I planned to explain it all when you got here."

"You didn't think I'd want to know a detail like that *beforehand?*"

"Oh, I knew you would," River said breezily. "Trace and I figured you'd get your panties in a bunch. That's why we decided to brief you when you arrived instead."

I muttered a string of curses. "'Cause you knew it would be harder for me to say no. Asshole."

He didn't even have the courtesy to look sorry about it. I should've expected this kind of deception from River and Trace. They were ex-CIA.

But my buddy Aiden? *Solo*?

I'd been tight with Aiden since our Army days. Neither of us were fun-loving, gregarious types, and we'd appreciated that about each other, even though our paths in the service had diverged. Aiden had gotten out as soon as possible, while I'd meant to stay in until retirement.

Obviously, that hadn't happened. But after I'd been wounded, his mom and sisters had sent me care packages.

Then the previous spring, about a year ago, Aiden had asked me to come to Hartley and lend the Protectors my tracking ability. I'd been happy to help an old friend. Hell, I'd shown up for his girlfriend Jessi's birthday to see them get engaged. This was how he repaid me?

"Did Aiden know about this clever plan of yours?" I asked.

"All of us agreed. I told you our timeline escalated. That was the truth. We had to get you here. If we could've come up with anyone else to represent the Protectors in this, we wouldn't have asked you."

"Jee, thanks." I shook my head, glaring at the half-melted snow in the yard.

As a bounty hunter, I had to liaise with law enforcement often enough. But I tried to keep my interactions with US government types to a minimum. All those agencies with their alphabet names? I wanted nothing to do with them.

This was why I worked outside the United States. Fewer regulations. Fewer lies. Sure, plenty of officials in other countries were corrupt, but at least I knew what to expect. They didn't pretend to be in my corner only to betray that faith in the worst way.

I glanced down at my left leg, though my prosthesis was hidden again by my jeans. The phantom limb pains didn't bother me much now after years of desensitizing and retraining my brain. But I still felt it at times. The awful, gut-wrenching sting of something that wasn't even there.

"Do the Feds have dirt on you and the Protectors?" I asked. "Is that why you're cooperating with them?"

"The FBI offered to scrub the files they have on us. Yeah.

But if Agent Somerton hadn't brought us the proposal, we would've told them to shove it. Brynn is my wife's best friend. Plus, I worked closely with her when Stillwater targeted Charlie last summer. Brynn is smart, and she's capable. A Marine before she was a Fed."

"Jarhead, huh?" Didn't necessarily change my mind, but it was something. Also explained the way she'd handled the football player guy when he'd grabbed her wrist. "I'm still not sure."

"Lynx, you know the kind of bullshit Stillwater is responsible for."

"Of course I do," I said gruffly. This fight was personal for River, Owen, Trace, and Aiden. But in the last several months, it had become personal for me too. River knew that. He also should've known I didn't want to discuss that particular topic.

*Luciana*. The woman I had failed to save.

"We've all dealt blows to Stillwater in the past," River continued. "You and Brynn can be the ones to finish it."

I exhaled. Fucking CIA spies with their manipulation. Of course I wanted the chance to end Stillwater, once and for all. Exactly the reason I was here. River had played me from minute one, and honestly, I couldn't even blame him.

"I'll listen to what Agent Somerton has to say." But I wasn't making any promises.

---

When we returned to the living room, Brynn and Keira were whispering quietly, heads bent together. They looked up as we entered.

"We're ready to get started," River said. "Brynn, I assume you want to do the honors. Lynx is eager to find out what's going on."

Keira touched Brynn on the shoulder. "In that case, I'll get going. I'm needed at the station." She smiled and nodded at me on her way out. At least I wasn't on Deputy Marsh's shit list too.

Brynn stood in front of the fireplace and clasped her hands behind her back. All business.

"Are we expecting anyone else?" I asked.

River dropped onto the couch, the cushion bouncing beneath him. "Nope. Just the three of us. More discreet this way, and I'm the most up-to-date on Stillwater anyway." He glanced at me. "I've been continuing my own investigation, as well as keeping in close contact with Brynn about the FBI's. Anything you need to know, Brynn or I should be able to tell you."

"I have plenty of questions. For starters, I want to know why this op is suddenly so urgent. You must've learned something big."

Missions like this lived and died based on intel. Everything depended on it. That told me that either the Protectors or the FBI had new intelligence on Stillwater, and it was significant.

But if the FBI was really in charge here, that was a dealbreaker for me. I was not sticking my neck out just for the Bureau to sharpen its axe should anything go wrong.

"We'll get to that," Brynn said. "But it'll make more sense if I explain how we got to this point."

"Then I'm listening." I took up a post behind the couch, bracing my hands on the back of it. I might've been tempted to sit down, but I'd already spent too many hours in a seated position. When I finally relaxed at the end of this frustrating day, I planned to kick back and not get up again until tomorrow.

Would I be heading back to Denver for the soonest flight to Mexico City? That remained to be seen.

I still had on my coat, so I unzipped it and took it off, tossing it on the back of the couch. Beneath, I'd worn my favorite gray T-shirt over well-worn jeans. Brynn's eyes traced my movements, lingering on the tattoos on my forearms, before quickly lifting.

It took a lot of willpower not to let my own eyes wander over her in a similar assessment. That wouldn't do me an ounce of good.

"So," she said. "Stillwater. I'm not sure how much you know."

"I know the business Stillwater is in." The organization was ultra-secretive. Operated from the shadows of the dark web. It offered services to smaller criminal gangs, like a twisted sort of consulting. Looking to expand your Oxy distribution channels without running afoul of the major cartels? Salivating to get into the human trafficking business? Not to mention hiring killers and paying off officials. Yeah, Stillwater could help you with all of that.

"I also heard about their attack on the lieutenant governor last year." I tipped my head at River, since I was referring to his now-wife. "River mentioned afterward that he and Charlotte discovered some actionable intel."

Brynn nodded. "Charlotte and River got access to an encrypted list of all of Stillwater's moles in the state and federal government. *Traitors.*"

Chills ran down my skin. Actionable intel indeed. "Then why haven't I heard of this before? Sounds like the kind of thing that should be made public."

"We decided not to go that route," Brynn said. "After River decrypted it, the Protectors agreed to share the list with my boss Michael Stanford at the Bureau."

I shot a glare at River. "You turned over intel of that value to the very government that allowed traitors into its ranks in the first place?"

"It allowed us to create a secret task force within the FBI," Brynn replied, though I hadn't been talking to her. "My boss, myself, and a handful of others were the only ones who knew. We flipped some of Stillwater's moles back to our side. In the months since, those individuals have been working for us as double agents. They've turned over essential information to help us understand Stillwater's operations and hierarchy."

I tightened my grip on the back of the couch."You mean, you let Stillwater's agents continue to work. To keep causing damage and screwing over innocent people. As if those lives don't matter."

Like Luciana and her daughter. More casualties of a system they'd had no chance against. Dammit. I pushed away from the couch, pacing across the room. Fury made my pulse race.

Yet Brynn responded with typical government callousness. "It was necessary to get us to the position we're in now."

"Sure, it's always necessary to step on someone if you want to make progress. Collateral damage. Cost of war. *Right?*"

These were the excuses those in power used to justify their actions. That kind of bullshit was extremely personal to me. It was the very reason I'd lost part of my leg and nearly lost my life. Some of the others in my unit hadn't been so lucky.

"I don't like the secrecy either," Brynn said softly. "But we had to do it."

River cut in. "When Brynn first proposed this partnership to the Protectors, we knew keeping the list secret was part of the deal. Every one of us signed off on it, including Trace."

"I *didn't,*" I growled. "You could've told me about this before. You chose not to." I tried to get my heart rate under control, but my body wasn't listening. Aiden and Trace had asked me to become an official Protector last year, and I'd declined. But that seemed beside the point right now.

"Look," River said, "we brought you in because Stillwater knows the rest of us. Me, Trace, Aiden, Owen. Stillwater's watching for us to make a move. We needed an outsider. Someone we can trust with this. And that is *you*. We've confirmed through the FBI's sources that you're not on their radar."

"And what about her?" I lifted my chin toward Brynn. "You said she's best friends with Charlotte. And she's an agent. How is it possible Stillwater won't see her coming a mile away?"

She huffed. "I'll be in disguise as part of my cover story. But Stillwater isn't watching me, anyway. To them, I'm a washed-up agent who just resigned. They'll underestimate me. Same thing you're doing."

My jaw was clenched tight. I stopped and leaned against a wall, my fingers itching for a cigarette. "So your secret FBI task force has been working with this intel. Why's this coming to a head now? What's the rest of it?"

Brynn licked her lips and went on. "One of our double agents shared new intelligence. Something that the typical Stillwater operative or lieutenant doesn't even know. We found out who's *really* in charge. The man at the very top of their hierarchy."

I blinked at her, letting that info sink into my head.

Stillwater conducted its business in the shadows, relying on a decentralized organization to shield those truly in power. If Brynn's task force had discovered its real leader, then it was no wonder that news had changed everything.

And...maybe it was slightly more understandable that the Protectors had chosen to go along with this. *The chance to go after the head of Stillwater*. That wasn't something I could just walk away from with no regrets. As River had definitely known.

"You're sure?" I asked.

"Positive. Not only that, we know where he'll be a week from now. A secluded resort in Arizona. This is our best shot at getting access to him, and we have to take it."

I rounded the couch and walked toward her. "I need to know who I would be working for. Who's in charge of this op? Is it the Protectors? Or do you still answer to the FBI?"

Brynn lifted her chin and crossed her arms as I neared. "Only the FBI task force knows my real objective. And I told you I resigned from the Bureau as of this morning. We're making our own calls."

"Who is *we*?"

"Me and the Protectors. And you, assuming you're a part of this."

"But do you report to the FBI? Yes or no."

"I've already answered that."

She was talking around something, refusing to be pinned down. I knew those tricks. I'd seen them every time I'd dealt with a Fed. "See, I don't like how vague you're being. I don't believe in happy partnerships where everyone's equal and gets along great. Ultimately, someone's going to have to come out on top. This is either an FBI op, or a Protectors one. So I'll repeat my question. Do you report to anyone inside the FBI? *Yes or no.*"

My blood was up. From the flush in her cheeks, so was hers. We were less than a foot apart. I caught the sweet scent of her, and it warmed my chest. Making me want to lean in even more.

Brynn tilted her head and gave me a hard stare. The look of a pissed-off soldier who'd been backed into a corner. Sorry, make that Marine. Jarheads hated being called soldiers.

Would she keep fighting me, or would she finally answer the damn question?

Then, she exhaled.

"No," she said. "I do not."

"So this is a Protectors op? We'll be working for and answering to them? *Only* them?"

"Yes. But as far as this op is concerned, I am the commanding officer."

"I'm not ready to agree to that." Was I just imagining it, or had we edged even closer? Still staring each other down.

"I've spent months learning everything I can about Stillwater," she said. "Between the two of us, I should take the lead. I have no doubt River and Trace would agree."

River coughed. I'd forgotten he was even in the room. I forced myself to take a step back to clear my head. Getting angry was not going to help.

"We can work out the details later," River said. "Just say you're in, Lynx. We need you for this."

Brynn glared at me a few seconds longer with those dark brown eyes.

"I want to be in. I'm considering it. But I can't go into a mission with someone, especially undercover, unless I know for sure she'll have my back." I thought I'd said that in a calm, rational tone. But Brynn scoffed and threw her hands up.

"I've been standing here trying to explain everything, trying to be the reasonable one, but you barely listened after you heard *FBI*. I won't let this mission be jeopardized by somebody with an axe to grind."

"I'm supposed to pretend the Bureau won't knife me first if this goes south? You were an agent until, what, five minutes ago? Why should I expect more loyalty from you?"

"You know what?" Brynn said. "I could do this without

you. I'll go undercover by myself. The Protectors can provide support and emergency backup."

I barked a laugh. "That would be incredibly foolish."

"Better than dealing with *you*."

"Guess what, honey, I'm not feeling too keen on you either."

Her nostrils flared. I inhaled at the same time. I could smell her fury layered over that sweeter scent, and I could definitely see it. Her pupils were dilated, tiny beads of sweat appearing at her temples.

"If you call me honey one more time," she murmured, "you're going to find yourself missing the other leg."

Brynn turned and walked out of the room, heading for some other part of the house. A door slammed.

River sighed and closed his eyes. "Even I'm not dumb enough to call a Marine *honey*."

Perhaps that hadn't been the best call. I had a problem filtering my words when my temper flared.

Fuck. Now *I* was the asshole.

# CHAPTER SIX

A FEW HOURS LATER, I strolled through the Silver Ridge historic business district. Locals and tourists streamed in and out of the shops and restaurants. Ready for a fun-filled, low-key night.

Too bad I was still very much keyed up.

Silver Ridge had just opened a small ski resort with a couple of lifts on a nearby mountain. Nowhere near as big as the famous destinations like Aspen and Breck, but this was still a happening place. I could see why the Protectors had chosen this town for Cole and me to launch our mission. Easy to blend in as just another vacationer, here for the spring skiing and the mountain scenery.

Of course, nothing about Cole Bailey had proved to be *easy* so far. I hadn't spoken to him since he'd called me "honey" that afternoon. And I didn't intend to. Not until he'd learned some basic civility. He'd been nice enough when I was a damsel with a flat tire, but the idea of me as his commanding officer? Nope, that had been too much for him to take.

Neon lights and classic rock spilled from the bar up

ahead. When I walked inside, I found a mixture of skiers and hipsters mingling around tables and playing darts.

I spotted Keira right away. She stood up from a stool at a high-top table, waving me over.

"Good, you found it," she said over the music, leaning in for a quick hug. She'd changed out of her deputy uniform and into a pair of dark jeans, a chunky turtleneck sweater, and hoop earrings. Her curly hair was piled into a poof on top of her head.

"It wasn't that hard to find. Silver Ridge isn't exactly New York."

"Or even Denver?"

Smiling, I took off my coat and draped it over my stool before I sat down. "I like the town so far. All the fresh, cold air cleared my head. I needed it."

"Uh oh. Does that mean the afternoon meeting with Cole didn't go well?"

"Ha. That's an understatement. Are you sure you like that guy? There's not another Cole Bailey running around with the same face but a completely different personality?"

"Not unless he's got an evil twin." Keira nodded toward the bar. "Which Cole do you think that is? The good one or the bad one?"

I shifted on my stool to look. And groaned.

*Really*? He couldn't find another bar in Silver Ridge?

Cole was taking off his coat and pulling up a seat at the bar. Must've walked in right after me. Was the guy following me around like some creeper? But then his head swiveled, taking in the surroundings, and our eyes met. He was surprised to see me too. I felt my frown deepen.

He turned away first.

*Guess what, honey. I'm not feeling too keen on you either.*

Keira whistled. "Now *there's* some animosity. Dang. I can

feel it from across the room. I thought you two had smoothed things over."

"We did. But it got bumpy again after you left."

"What happened?"

"Cole doesn't like that I was FBI. Or...anything else about me, apparently."

This mission wouldn't even exist without the work of the FBI task force. If the other Protectors were fine with my FBI pedigree, what did it matter to Cole? Our undercover mission would be off the Bureau's books. It *would* be a Protectors mission, like I'd said.

Well, more or less.

Okay, I'd fudged a bit there. I had told Cole I wouldn't report to anyone within the FBI. I'd failed to mention my daily reports to SAC Stanford. But keeping Stanford updated wasn't the same as *answering* to him. Even if Stanford might try to issue orders. I didn't have to accept them.

I wasn't an FBI agent right now. But I wasn't really a Protector, either. I'd promised Stanford that I wouldn't let down my guard during this mission, and I would keep my word.

This alliance was tenuous already. With Cole Bailey in the mix? It felt impossible.

"He's a hot head," I said. "Even worse, he's the kind of alpha who's happy to rescue a woman, but balks at taking orders from one."

"Huh. I didn't get that impression from Cole before. Seemed like he had no problem working with women."

"All I know is *I* can't work with him."

"I thought the Protectors didn't have anyone else to replace him as your partner." She propped her elbows on the table. It was noisy, and we were keeping our voices down, so I wasn't concerned about being overheard.

"They don't. I haven't got anyone in mind either, and

there's no time to bring in someone else anyway." Not to mention, we'd already created fake identity papers for Cole's cover. It wouldn't be easy to get new ones. "My only remaining option is to go it alone."

"*Alone*? Against—" Keira glanced around us, then whispered, "Stillwater?"

"If that's what it takes." But I didn't want to think about that right now. I needed tonight to regroup. I would touch base with SAC Stanford, let him know what was happening, and then I'd figure out what to do next. Tomorrow. "Do you want a drink?" I noticed Keira didn't have one yet.

"Dean's working bar tonight. He does table service. Here he comes."

A good-looking guy was making his way over to us. He wrapped Keira in a hug, and I noticed the way her face turned dreamy when she was tucked into him for that brief moment.

Then he held out his fist to bump against mine. "So you're Brynn. Welcome."

"My reputation precedes me?"

"In a way. I'm a friend of Owen's." Dean's hair curled over his ears and at his nape, overdue for a haircut. Stubble framed his easy-going smile. He winked, handing us a couple of menus.

"Dean is another unofficial Protector," Keira explained, her tone rich with admiration.

A line appeared between his brows. "Not exactly. I help out with certain things when I can."

"He served in the USMC, like you, Brynn."

I felt my expression light up. Always enjoyed meeting a fellow Marine. "Semper Fi. Where were you stationed?"

Dean's smile stayed, but it wasn't as carefree as before. "Swapping stories will have to wait. Gotta make my rounds before my customers get restless. What can I get the two of you?"

We ordered a couple of beers and some nachos. After Dean left, I glanced pointedly at Keira. She was biting her lip.

"He got out of here fast," I said. "Did I say the wrong thing?"

"No, it's not you. He's laid back about almost everything, but Dean rarely gets into the specifics of his military service. I wasn't thinking when I brought it up."

"*Ah*." I understood without needing to know more. Not everyone was able to talk about their deployments. Certainly not with someone they'd just met in a crowded bar, even a fellow Marine.

Keira was staring at the tabletop, so I put my hand over hers. "Not your fault either," I said. "He'll know you didn't mean anything by it."

"Yeah, that's true. Dean's great. He helped rescue Owen's girlfriend, Genevieve, from a killer last year. The same incident that first brought Cole to Hartley."

"Right." I'd heard all about it from River. That had been the Protectors' first brush with Stillwater.

"Dean was their driver during the rescue op. Owen wants to make him a full Protector, but that's just not going to happen. Dean doesn't touch weapons anymore."

A Marine who'd sworn off violence? I could fill in the blanks for myself. But whatever had really happened in his past, that was Dean's business. I wasn't going to push.

Keira sighed, glancing at the bar. "When I told him I was moving to Silver Ridge, Dean looked for a place here too. He's a snowboarder, and he was excited about the new resort here. He teaches lessons during the day and bartends at night. But he's kind of a nomad, you know? I have no idea how long he plans to stay in Hart County."

A different server brought over our beers. Not Dean. We thanked the girl, then sat forward again. I took a long swallow of my drink, enjoying the play of hops and yeast on my tongue.

"You and Dean sound close," I said.

"Not as close as I'd like to be. I've dropped plenty of hints, and he let me down gently." She rolled her eyes. "He thinks I'm too young."

"How old are you?" I knew she wasn't that long out of college, but I didn't know numbers.

"Twenty-six. Dean's thirty-four. Barely seems like a difference to me, but I guess he's seen a lot more of life than I have."

"*Ah,*" I said again. This was all becoming clearer. "If he's a nomad, then maybe he's doing you a favor, even though it doesn't feel like it. Plenty of older men wouldn't turn down the attention of a younger woman. They'd just enjoy her for a while and leave her in the dust."

Wow, that had sounded bitter.

I laughed to lessen the harshness of what I'd just said. "I'm sorry. You don't need my cynicism rubbing off on you."

Keira sipped her beer. "Were you speaking from experience?"

"Unfortunately." My fingers slid through the condensation on my glass. "I was with a guy who promised me the world. All I really wanted was his love, but even that was too much to expect." I forced a smile. "That's why I'm a cynic. But you're way ahead of me. You're crushing on a far superior guy. Even if Dean isn't the one for you, you've got excellent taste."

"That's looking on the bright side. Dean's an amazing guy."

"Then I'm glad he's your friend."

"Suppose it's better than nothing." She lifted her glass, clinking it against mine. "Dean is renting a place next door to the bar," she added. "Cole is staying with him."

My eyes hit on Cole again. He'd turned in his seat, watching me over his shoulder. We both looked away.

I cleared my throat.

"Why'd you move to Silver Ridge?" I asked. "You're a lot farther from the sheriff's department headquarters."

"My patrols take me all around the county. Plus, my parents and sister moved nearby. A lot of bad things have happened around Hartley in the last few years, you know? My family wanted a little distance."

"Stillwater," I said under my breath.

She nodded solemnly. "But there's not really an escape. Not until Stillwater is gone, and then there will be new bad guys to fight. That's why I asked to join the Protectors myself."

I grinned. "Really? Good for you. They need some feminine energy."

Her glossy lips pursed. "Owen said no. He lets me help out here and there, but he claimed he needs me to focus on being a deputy. I realize that I don't have that military credibility, and I don't have the same training. But I've accomplished a lot. I'm proud of who I am. I was top of my academy class. Yet once again, I'm told I'm too young and inexperienced. How will that change unless they give me a chance? It's bullshit."

She accentuated the last word by setting her glass on the table with a thump.

"Have you ever killed anyone?" I asked.

"Yes. Last year. Well…Owen and I were firing on the same guy, so I can't be sure, but I aimed to kill. And I don't regret it." Her voice gained in intensity. "I'm not delicate, any more than you are."

"But it's hard to hear no. I understand. I've been there."

"Really?"

"Are you kidding? So many times. I've had to prove myself

over and over again. As a Marine, as an agent. I heard it from my own family."

*You're weak,* my uncle sneered. *You're never going to cut it.*

I forced that voice out of my head.

"It took years to get where I am," I continued, "and it's still not easy. You just have to keep proving the doubters wrong."

She groaned. "That's what I've been trying to do. It's exhausting."

"It can be. But it's worth it. You should sign up for extra trainings. Take hand-to-hand combat lessons beyond the basics that the department offers. It'll make you a better cop, and Owen might change his mind about sending you on Protectors missions."

She chewed her lip, hesitating over her next words. "Or *you* could teach me. I've been undercover for a sting operation before. A larger department down south needed female officers to pose as underage girls. I loved catching those predatory bastards and sending them to jail. I could step in as your partner on the Stillwater mission."

I reached across the table and squeezed her hand. "Maybe a few years down the road, I'll take you up on that. Not yet."

Keira sighed. "I knew you were going to say that. Had to try anyway."

"And I admire you for it. It takes bravery to put yourself out there."

"I'd like to put my bravery to more productive uses."

"I'm sure you'll get your chance. Eventually."

On my periphery, I felt Cole's gaze on me again. That man was proving impossible to ignore.

But if he had something to say to me, he'd have to make the next move.

---

Keira and I talked for a while longer. A couple of guys stopped by to chat us up, but we politely brushed them off.

And would you look at that? Cole was eyeing me again.

Was he trying to turn me to stone with that glare? Or beam some kind of message into my brain?

I started to get up. "I'll get us another round."

"No, I need to hit the bathroom anyway. I'll be right back."

While she was gone, I took out my phone. I sent Charlotte a quick text, saying I'd made it to Silver Ridge.

CHARLOTTE:

Riv said there were some fireworks when you arrived?

ME:

You have no idea.

CHARLOTTE:

How bad is it?

ME:

I'll figure something out.

CHARLOTTE:

You're worrying me. And you're worrying River.

ME:

He just doesn't like when he's not in control of everything.

CHARLOTTE:

Pretty sure that's you.

Ha. We were all a bunch of control freaks. That wasn't going to change.

The stool across from me scraped against the floor. A heavy body sat down.

It wasn't Keira.

Cole set a beer in front of me, then set down his own. "I'm here to apologize."

I tucked my phone away. "So that's why you've been staring at me the last hour?"

"I was deciding what to say."

"Can't wait to hear the rest of it." I tugged the beer closer and took a sip. Same ale I'd been drinking before.

Wait.

I looked toward the bar and spotted Keira standing with Dean, both of them watching us. "Keira said something to you. She told you to come over here?" I hadn't noticed her talking to Cole. She must've done it while I was distracted with my phone.

*She'll make a good operative after all,* I thought. That woman was more devious than I'd given her credit for.

"She did. But I already planned to apologize. I shouldn't have called you 'honey.' That was unnecessary."

"Getting straight to it, aren't we?"

"I'm a candid guy."

"Then I'll be blunt as well. You wouldn't have called a man *honey,* I assume. You have a problem with me being a woman."

He grumbled, tapping his fingers on the table. "I have valid concerns about you being an FBI agent. *Former* agent," he corrected, before I could do it. "That's nothing to do with you being a woman."

"What a concession."

"But you can't deny that Stillwater enjoys victimizing women in particular," Cole said. "So can I look at you and not be aware of that fact? No. I can't."

My hand tightened on the glass as my spine stiffened. "Are you saying I have no place going undercover? That I'm not strong enough for this?"

"Hell, no. I'm not saying that. I've seen you in action, and so has River. Plus, your experience speaks for itself. I'm not questioning your abilities. Okay? Let's just get that out there."

I exhaled, the tight knot of muscle between my shoulders easing a bit. "Then what *are* you saying?"

"That you cannot go undercover alone. And yes, that is partly because you're a woman. Because I cannot stand the thought of the sick leader of Stillwater, whoever he is, ordering his thugs to hurt you." He'd said all this in a rough whisper, just barely audible over the background music. His blue eyes were intense on mine.

"Didn't think you cared," I said.

"The things Stillwater does? I don't want that to happen to anyone."

"But you're not talking about *anyone*. You're talking about me."

"True. I am." Cole was on the other side of the table, but he leaned over well into my space, close enough I got a whiff of spicy cologne with a hint of tobacco beneath. The combination went into my lungs and lower, hitting below my stomach with a swirl of flutters and spreading heat.

This time, it was me who blinked first. Averted my gaze.

"I accept your apology. I'd rather not do this alone." For one, because SAC Stanford would probably try to jump in as my partner himself before he let me go unassisted. His wife Marie would kill me. "But you don't trust me. I don't trust you. We're at an impasse."

"We can start over."

"For the second time in one day? Don't you think that's excessive?"

The muscle in his jaw pulsed. Another stare-off ensued.

Gah, why did his eyes have to be so blue?

Dean, the bartender, appeared beside the table. He had a couple of shot glasses in one hand, a bottle of top-shelf whiskey in the other. “On the house,” he said. “How about a toast?”

“To what?” I asked.

“Making new allies.”

Cole lifted an eyebrow at me in a silent question. *There’s more at stake,* I reminded myself. And maybe, just maybe, I’d been all wrong about him. I *wanted* to be wrong about him. So we could get back to the mission and fighting Stillwater instead of each other.

I nodded.

Dean splashed amber liquid into each glass. Cole lifted his up. I did the same, then tossed it back. The smooth burn trailed down into my stomach, leaving warmth behind.

Cole moved more slowly, bringing the glass to his lips while his eyes didn’t leave mine.

We both set our glasses down.

Dean grinned. “You going to stay here and chat? Work out your differences?”

“I don’t think we’re being given any other choice,” I pointed out. “I sense a conspiracy.”

“You’re right about that. River has been texting me nonstop for updates, and Keira has orders from Owen to lock you two in a room until morning if necessary. I hear you’re on a strict timetable? They want you to be best buds and prepping for the op by tomorrow.”

“We’ll figure it out,” Cole said.

I lifted an eyebrow. “We will?”

“Yep.” Cole tapped the table by his empty shot glass, and Dean poured another. “You should leave the bottle.”

Dean glanced at me.

I made a beckoning motion with my fingers. “Every Marine worth her salt can hold her liquor. Bring it.”

The bottle thumped onto the table. “Then I’ll put it on

River's tab." With a wink, Dean spun and headed back to the bar.

"Guess we have to find a way to get along," Cole said, pouring me another shot.

"And we have to do it fast." Whether we liked it or not.

It was going to be a long night.

# CHAPTER SEVEN

THE NEXT SHOT slid down even more smoothly than the first couple. I still wanted a cigarette, but whiskey was the next best thing. Took the edge off enough.

Of course, several hours of cooling my temper had helped with that, too.

Brynn was across from me, tracing a finger around the rim of her empty shot glass. Conversation and laughter continued, the rest of the bar oblivious to the two of us.

"Another?" I asked.

She nudged her glass across the table. Amber liquid splashed, filling the small cup to the brim.

Somehow, we had to get to know each other. But with this woman, I didn't even know where to start.

"Just gonna sit there and drink me under the table?" I asked.

"At least we're not arguing."

A smirk tugged at my lips. "This is true."

One of us would have to open up first. Seemed that it was gonna be me. We'd already had two disastrous attempts at making a first impression. So far, Brynn and I hadn't made it through one conversation without someone getting pissed. But maybe the third time was the charm.

After Brynn had stormed out of Keira's house earlier, River had taken me to Dean's place with strict instructions. *Fix this*. As if this whole debacle was my fault. Well, calling her *honey* had been all me. Not my finest moment.

But one thing had kept rattling around in my head all afternoon.

*They'd found the head of Stillwater.*

They knew his name. The man ultimately responsible for what had happened to Luciana and her daughter. I wanted him bad. Wanted him *dead*, if I could help it. This op would get me there.

And I'd meant what I said, too. It was a terrible idea for Brynn to go undercover against the head of Stillwater by herself. This was going to be a dangerous mission. Fatal if our covers were blown. But Stillwater wouldn't just make Brynn disappear. They'd make her suffer first. Could I really let her face that alone if nobody else was going to step up?

Pouring us each another shot, I thought, *Here goes nothing*.

I opened my mouth and started talking. "I was wounded in Afghanistan. Little over five years ago. My Ranger unit was clearing the way for a convoy." I kept the details vague because it was classified. Plus, it still messed with my head to talk about this, even years later. "We were ambushed."

She said nothing. But I had her attention. Brynn was completely focused on me.

"I was airlifted to Germany. Drugged up and in-and-out of consciousness for a while. When I came to, I found out I'd lost my left leg below the knee, and two of my teammates were KIA."

"I'm sorry."

I nodded. "Trust me, that's not the worst of it. My unit got blamed for missing the signs of the impending attack. My *dead friends* got blamed, even though it was all BS. People covering their asses and pointing fingers. That was vicious enough. But while I was in recovery, trying to get my shit back together, I heard rumors about what had really happened." I tossed back my shot, squeezing the glass, then forced myself to set it aside before I broke the thing. "We'd had a CIA officer working with us. He'd withheld information about insurgents in the area to protect a *fucking source*. Leaving us twisting in the breeze."

"Why didn't the CIA officer delay the convoy? Or redirect it? He could've come up with some excuse to avoid revealing his source."

"I've asked myself that a hundred times. Best I can tell, it just wasn't convenient. He figured we had a 50/50 chance of making it through and decided to roll the dice instead of troubling himself. Afterward the CIA spook was reassigned, but he kept his job."

She sucked in a breath. "That's unbelievable."

"You're tellin' me. After that, I was done. Couldn't get that medical discharge fast enough." So much for the career I'd spent fifteen years building. I'd felt betrayed. *Broken*.

Brynn poured us each another shot. "I see why you don't like Feds. You don't hold it against River or Trace for being ex-CIA?"

"No, because Trace got burned in his own way. And River was smart enough to leave." I grunted as the whiskey slid down my throat. "I'm not a fool. I realize it's valid to protect avenues of intelligence. But the callousness. The pure disregard for the lives of men and women who'd devoted their lives to their country. Not something I can easily forget."

"Can't blame you." Brynn leaned forward, elbows on the table. "Some things should be sacred. And when you learn they're not, that somebody you trusted betrayed you.... It's a hard lesson." She laughed darkly. "Want to know my official cover for resigning from the FBI? That I'm disgusted with its failure to stop Stillwater. But there's a lot of truth behind that story."

Brynn looked around cautiously before she went on. The occupants of the nearby tables had moved on and left empty glassware behind. There was a crowd over by the bar and the dart boards, but this area was deserted.

I rubbed my jaw, waiting for her to explain.

"I was close friends with one of the FBI special agents who turned out to work for Stillwater."

My brows shot up.

"He was involved in the attempt to kidnap the lieutenant governor. He lied to my face countless times. Hurt people I care about, plus who knows how many others. I—" Her voice cracked, and she swallowed. "Not saying it's the same as your experience. But I know what betrayal feels like."

I studied her, feeling like I was getting a real sense of Brynn Somerton for the first time since we'd met.

I tugged my pack of cigarettes from my back jeans pocket and set it on the table. It was getting late, and that meant it was almost tomorrow. Close enough. "I could use a smoke."

"Fine by me."

We got up, gathered our things, and I left the remainder of the whiskey bottle behind the bar.

Brynn's walk was steady and confident. No sign she'd just matched me taking five shots. Or was it six? Plus her beers.

Damn Marines. They could absolutely hold their liquor.

As for me, I was a touch more wobbly than usual. Maybe it was the long hours I'd spent on my prosthesis today. That didn't slow me down when shit got real, but the aches did build up. So I took my time, and Brynn seemed content to keep a leisurely pace by my side.

Once we were outside, she and I tugged on our coats. Our breaths made puffs of white in front of our faces. Brynn rubbed her hands together as I flicked my lighter open and lit up.

I closed my eyes, inhaling deeply.

"Enjoying that?" she asked.

"Hell yeah, I am. Only get one a day. I'd better enjoy it."

When I opened my eyes, Brynn plucked the cigarette from my lips. She brought it to her mouth and took a drag.

"Be my guest," I said.

She shrugged one shoulder. "Sorry. You made it look so tempting."

"I don't mind sharing."

"Also, I might be just a *tiny* bit drunk."

Laughter burst from my chest, surprising me. "Glad I'm not the only one."

I was already feeling loose and comfortable after the whiskey. Then seeing her lips where mine had just been…

*Don't get ideas,* I told myself. Good thing she didn't like me. Because this woman would be very hard to resist.

Brynn took the cig from her mouth and held it up. I parted my lips, and she placed it between them. She was careful to keep her fingers from brushing me.

"Let's take a walk," she said. "I'll tell you more about the op."

"Sounds good." The cigarette bobbed as I spoke.

This was the calm before the storm. So much had built up to this moment, and like an idiot, I'd nearly let my temper interfere. If I wanted the head of Stillwater, I had to find a way to connect with Brynn. *Partners.*

That was the only way for us to go into the upcoming mission and come out of it alive.

# CHAPTER EIGHT
## *Cole*

"WHY ONLY ONE A DAY?" Brynn asked.

We'd been walking for several minutes down a side street. The noise and neon of Main Street still drifted toward us, but over here, it was dark with only a few scattered streetlights. Yet the moon painted Brynn's black hair with a silvery glow. I could make out the shape of her beside me.

The end of my cigarette burned orange-red.

"My habit used to be a pack a day," I said. "In the hospital after I was wounded, docs told me I should quit. This is what I settled on." I didn't want to get into the rest of that story. My wife leaving. How the bitterness fueled me. It wasn't that kind of story time.

"You were going to tell me more about the op," I reminded her.

She nodded. "So, less than a month ago, the task force learned who's really in charge of Stillwater. The mastermind behind the entire enterprise. His name is Garon Westwick. A businessman and investor who's secretly building an empire as a criminal kingpin."

I let that name percolate in my brain. *Westwick*. The man responsible for so much chaos and suffering.

"Never heard of him."

"I hadn't either. Immediately, the task force started putting together a profile on him. Planning possible cover stories for approaching him."

"You mentioned new intel from a day or two ago."

"That's right. We'd already learned that Westwick has attended a wellness resort in Arizona the last few years. Just recently, he scheduled this year's trip. He'll be teaching an exclusive business seminar at the resort to a group of entrepreneurs. And we've got two tickets."

"Aren't those swanky kinds of events usually booked months in advance?"

"Sure, but Westwick decided to set this one up spur of the moment, apparently. The seminar booked up fast. It'll be a group of about twenty small business owners. Perfect chance for us to get close to him."

*And do what?* I wanted to know, but we'd get to that. Practical considerations had to come first. I took another drag, exhaling smoke through my nose. "You've got your cover in place? What about mine?"

"The moment the Protectors gave us your name, the task force got to work on it. I've got ID papers for you and me. Social media presence, passport, driver's licenses. We had to go through back channels, so the ID documents aren't quite good enough to fool an official scanner. "

Few fake IDs on the black market were that good. "Then I assume we won't be flying?"

"Nope. It's drivable."

"Right, Arizona. That's good." I rubbed my hands together, wishing I had gloves. "I grew up in Idaho, but I'm not used to the cold anymore."

There was a sign at the end of the street for a pub. Brynn tilted her head toward it. "Want to go in? Looks like they've got a fire going, and they're open late."

"I'm not a shivering flower. You don't have to rescue me." My lips slid into a smirk.

She pushed my shoulder toward the pub door. "Just go inside. I'm cold too. I don't have a cigarette to keep me warm."

This place was far quieter than the lively spot on Main Street where Dean worked. It looked like a converted house. A maze of small rooms, shadowed corners. Flames crackled in a fireplace. Candles flickered on tables, and couples huddled together at the bar. The vibe was pure romance.

I looked at her. She looked at me.

Brynn chose a back room that was otherwise empty. She sat at a tiny, circular table that was hardly big enough for just me, let alone the both of us. Which meant we were huddled together, knees knocking as we maneuvered for space. One of her legs wound up between mine.

We took off our coats, and a server came by. "Kitchen's closed, but the bar's open another hour. What can I get you?"

We both ordered sodas. We'd had enough whiskey. The moment the server was gone, I took out my phone and looked up Garon Westwick.

His photo came up at the top of the search results. A man around forty—my age—with sandy blond hair and a wholesome smile, arm around his wife on one side and a couple of teenage daughters on the other. Westwick was a middle-class kid who'd taken some early luck in the stock market and rolled it into a huge investment portfolio. He was a rising star in the business world.

"Known for bringing a kinder, gentler perspective to investing," I read from the guy's bio on Wikipedia. "This is the head of Stillwater? An organization that haunts the dark web and helps child traffickers make a buck?"

"I know, hard to believe." Brynn had scooted her chair closer so she could read along with me.

"Nah, I think the opposite. Figures he'd seem like Mr. Perfect. Hypocrisy doesn't surprise me." It disgusted me though. Made me all the more determined to see this guy brought down.

I barely noticed when the server dropped off our sodas. Neither of us touched them. If Brynn was like me, that whiskey wasn't sitting so well in her stomach anymore. Especially when I scrolled back up and looked at Westwick's picture again. His daughters. Their pretty blond hair and bright smiles, like they believed the world was a generous place, and they had nothing but happiness ahead of them.

Meanwhile, Westwick was helping ensure that other people's daughters vanished and never found their way home.

I had to lean back in my seat and stare at the ceiling a moment.

"He doesn't have a very high profile yet," Brynn said. "But from everything I can tell, his influence is growing. At the same time, Stillwater is growing too. They want to expand beyond this region. They're already recruiting moles inside the government more broadly. Foreign countries too."

That much, I already knew. "I'm aware they operate outside the states."

"I can show you the other evidence the task force has compiled. If you want to assess it yourself."

"Not necessary." I had no doubt River and the Protectors had paid close attention to the evidence before giving the go ahead on this op. What I wanted to know was the when and the where.

How long did I have to wait to get my hands on this guy? A week wasn't soon enough. Yet also, it was *too* soon. Ops like this took time to prepare.

I put my phone down on the table. "So we're posing as resort guests? Attending this seminar?"

"Exactly. We're entrepreneurs who want to rub elbows with Westwick and learn from his success."

I tasted bile in my mouth. "What's the plan?"

"River's going to provide me with a flash drive loaded with some kind of virus. Once we upload it to any one of Westwick's devices, River and his hacker friends will be able to use it to get inside Stillwater's digital operation."

I was no computer expert, but I could imagine how that would go. Stillwater was decentralized. Very few people understood the total picture of their operation. As its chief, Westwick would have that bigger picture. Unfettered access. He would want it at his fingertips, so his devices would hold the key.

"Once they're inside his digital world," Brynn went on, "River's hacker network will take over. Gather all the proof they need and dismantle Stillwater's organization from the inside. River says it's a playbook he's run before, though not quite on this scale. They'll be able to set up stings to arrest Stillwater's major players and lieutenants from the top down. And they'll drop a bomb of evidence on the media and law enforcement, all anonymous and with no ties to the FBI."

"And how long will all of that take?"

"That part isn't up to us. You know how it is."

Sure I did. How many times had I been the guy receiving orders without knowing the endgame, or when it would come? But I wasn't in the Army anymore.

"Wouldn't it be faster just to make Westwick disappear?" I asked lightly. "I don't like the thought of having him right there in our grasp, and then walking away." I wanted this guy to suffer for what he'd done. And I wanted to see it.

She gave me a hard glare. "And allow someone else to take his place? No way. That is not an option. When we're done, we leave Westwick alone and let the authorities handle him."

I grabbed my soda and pulled it closer. Sipped the icy,

sugary drink. "Tell me more about our cover. Who are we posing as?"

"I'm a social media influencer. You're my manager."

"Social media types have managers?"

"How old are you again?"

"Old enough not to give a shit about influencers and their managers."

Brynn snorted. "Well, you'd better figure it out. This is the cover we've got."

I wasn't impressed. "And how, exactly, are we going to upload River's virus onto Westwick's devices? I assume he'll have security."

"I'll get close. Sweet-talk him. Get him to let down his guard."

"You're a honeypot." Fuck. How had I not seen that coming? "And you actually considered going into this alone?" That was a rhetorical question, so I didn't need an answer. She *wasn't* going into it alone. That was for damn sure. So instead, I asked, "Exactly how close are you planning to get?"

"Whatever it takes."

"If you're cozying up to that asswipe and he harms you, you can't expect me to stand aside."

"I need a partner for this op. Not a bodyguard."

I sat back, folding my arms. "What about a boyfriend?"

She barked a laugh. "I'm sorry, *what*? You want to be my boyfriend, Bailey?"

My eyes lifted skyward. "I'm saying my cover should be that I'm your boyfriend. Then I'll have all the reason I need to stick close to you. When you're alone with Westwick, if anything goes sideways, I'll barge in playing the jealous boyfriend. Perfect diversion."

"I don't think so. You'll be there for support, not to take over if you think I'm the slightest bit in danger. It has to be my call."

"And there you go, talking like you're commanding this mission. I haven't agreed to any such thing."

"We're back to that again?" Pink spots appeared on her cheeks. Brynn was sensitive about being told she couldn't do something, and I understood that about her now. She didn't want me looking down on her as weaker, bossing her around. But I wasn't a fan of taking orders either these days.

"Trace is the leader of the Protectors," she said through gritted teeth. "He can decide which of us is commanding the op."

"No, this is between you and me. I only see one way of resolving it."

"And that is?"

"I'll arm wrestle you for it."

She stared at me, mouth dropping open. Then barked a laugh. "I thought you were serious."

"I am."

"Right." She grabbed her drink and pursed her lips around the straw. "Either you're funnier than I gave you credit for, Bailey, or you're drunk."

I'd sobered up, but if this went sideways and anyone asked, I planned to blame the whiskey. "We need some way to work this out. It needs to be fast."

"But since when does the commanding officer have to be the strongest? I'd prefer the smartest. The wiliest."

"I agree. You didn't flip that football player earlier by being stronger than him in terms of brute force. I'd say you were wilier."

"Therefore, I should be in charge."

"But you haven't gone head-to-head against *me* yet."

"You want me to take you outside and flip you?"

"I'd love to see you try."

Mischief glinted in her dark eyes. "I can't beat up on a one-legged guy."

"Oh, now you've gone and pissed me off." I planted my elbow on the table, hand open. "My two arms work just fine. Let's go, Marine. Prove you can best me. The Corps' honor is on the line."

That did the trick. There was no way she could say no.

With a scowl, Brynn mirrored my pose with her elbow on the table. Gripped my hand.

"Three, two, one," I said.

She went hard and fast from the get-go. Trying to overwhelm me with force in the first few seconds. A sprinter going straight for the finish line. I could see her strategy playing through her head like pieces moving on a chess board. She thought I would underestimate her strength. Or that I would take it easy on her, having some innate hesitation about physically overpowering a woman.

Neither was true.

I was ready for her attack. But instead of pushing back with my own muscle power in opposition to hers, I let go of her hand and grabbed her around the middle with both arms. Yanked her right off her chair and into my lap. She gasped in shock. I had her arms pinned, her body against my torso. With another quick movement, I got her legs wedged under one of my thighs.

"You asshole. Let go of me." Brynn struggled wildly, trying to break free.

"I will. As soon as you admit I won."

"You didn't win!"

The server poked her head into the room, eyes widening when she saw how we were tangled together. "Is everything all right?"

Brynn clenched her teeth into a semblance of a smile, but her eyes glared that she hated me. I'd loosened my grip slightly, and Brynn's elbow found the opening. I coughed when she jabbed me right in the stomach. Ouch.

"It's a little game we like to play," I said. "She's my girlfriend."

*"Like hell I am,"* Brynn hissed under her breath.

The server didn't seem convinced, but she also didn't look like she wanted to get in the middle of this. "We're closing soon," she warned.

"No problem," Brynn said.

"We'll be good," I added.

Brynn waited until the server had gone, then turned another murderous look on me. "You did not win. You cheated. Everyone knows the rules of arm wrestling. Your elbow can't leave the table. And you definitely can't do... Whatever the hell that was."

"See, you're still thinking like an FBI agent. Garon Westwick isn't going to play fair. If he feels threatened or if he wants something, he'll use every dirty trick he can think of. We can't follow some idealistic set of rules. Not if we want to win."

"I see your point," she said tightly. "Now let me go."

I did, and she scooted back onto her chair. She wouldn't meet my eyes. "I suppose you're in command now. Congrats."

"Do I detect a hint of sarcasm?"

"If you didn't, then your sarcasm detector needs adjustment. *Sir.*"

I chuckled. Nudged her arm with the back of my hand. "Relax. I don't want either of us to be in charge. If we're going to get through this, it will have to be as equals."

Surprise softened her features. "I thought you said earlier today that equal partnerships don't work. Somebody always has to come out on top."

My mind raced immediately to the gutter, thinking of the dirtier interpretations of those words. Nope. I wasn't going to follow that thread.

"I meant between the FBI and the Protectors. Groups with completely different methods and agendas. Between the two of us, I think we can figure things out diplomatically. Like we're doing right now."

"You just overpowered me and pinned me against your body so I couldn't move," she deadpanned. "Which part of that was diplomatic?"

I scratched my forehead. "That was only to prove a point. From now on, we talk things through. As teammates. Equals."

She sat back, crossing her arms. "All right. And if we can't agree, we defer to River or Trace."

"Works for me."

*Unless it's about the ultimate fate of Garon Westwick,* I added silently. Once he was in front of me, I had no intention of turning that piece of shit loose again, regardless of anything Brynn or the Protectors or any task force might have planned.

But we would just have to deal with that problem when we came to it.

# CHAPTER NINE

## *Brynn*

"HOW DO YOU NOT HAVE A HANGOVER?" Keira asked.

"Marines don't get hangovers." I poured her a cup of coffee and passed it across the island to her.

"That's what Dean says too," she grumbled, then tipped back the mug to take a hefty swallow. "I thought I would be making you a big breakfast to absorb all the alcohol you and Cole drank last night. I was surprised you could walk out of the bar at all."

"It's a talent of mine."

Keira rubbed her face and yawned. "Any chance you could make breakfast for me then? Because I'm still half asleep."

I laughed and started searching for an omelet pan. I'd already spotted some eggs and bacon in the fridge. "Have no fear. You'll be eating well in no time."

Despite getting to bed late, I'd woken up bright and early and well rested. I preferred sleeping in the nude, sheets right up against my skin, and I had to give credit to Keira's mom and sister. They'd picked out guest bed linens with an amazing thread count.

I'd pulled on a T-shirt and a pair of cotton shorts, no bra, and I'd left my hair down instead of pulling it up. Since it was just us girls this morning.

Obviously, Cole and I had gone our separate ways last night after agreeing to work together as equals. When I had gotten home last night, Keira had grilled me. I'd assured her that Cole and I were good. Aside from his ideas about playing my boyfriend. That, I didn't want to think about right now.

I had been very low key about that stunt he'd pulled. Demanding to arm wrestle, only to put me into a submission hold. I probably should've been more pissed off than I had been. But to be honest, when he'd had his arms and a leg snaked around me, I hadn't minded the sensation. He'd been close enough that he could've kissed me. Just leaned in and brushed his lips against mine.

I hadn't minded *that* thought either. Which was ridiculous.

But it didn't matter that I found the man slightly charming despite his constant grumping and his hot-headed temper. He'd agreed to be my partner for this mission, and that was what I needed. Nothing more.

Whenever I fully let down my guard around an attractive man, I lived to regret it. No way was I going down that road again.

Keira wandered off to start a load of laundry. While the bacon sizzled, I went to the guest room to grab my phone. I had a couple of messages from Charlotte, and I assured my best friend that we were back on track.

Then I remembered my *other* phone. The burner.

Crap, I hadn't written Stanford last night with an update And given his dad-like tendencies, he was probably annoyed. Sure enough, I had three texts waiting on the burner. He'd entered his number under the initial "S." I typed out a quick response.

S:

How goes it?

Update, B?

Hope I don't need to drive to Hart County. Marie won't be happy.

ME:

Sorry Dad, busy night. My arrival started out bumpy, but getting better.

S:

Bumpy how? Is it your partner?

ME:

Partner won't be an issue.

S:

He'd better not be.

I laughed quietly to myself. If I told Stanford everything that had happened yesterday with Cole, he would hit the roof.

ME:

I've got this. It would help if you'd trust me.

S:

It's the others you're working with who I don't trust.

ME:

Are you ready for retirement, old man? You're repeating yourself.

S:

And you're living dangerously. I don't recommend it.

ME:

Ha. More later. Bye.

S:

Hold on, task force just gathered some new intel on the target for his profile. It's concerning. Sending to you to read and consider.

ME:

Wilco.

S:

Stay vigilant.

ME:

Always do.

I set the phone aside, rolling my eyes. Why did I have to deal with so many grumpy men on a daily basis? Almost made me want to spend more time with River. *Almost*. At least he smiled and joked around while he was annoying the crap out of me.

Did I trust Cole after our night of bonding? Not completely. But I didn't *dis*trust him either. We had come to an understanding. For now, that was enough.

The scent of burning bacon reached my nose, and I cursed. I'd forgotten it.

I ran to the kitchen only to find Cole by the stove, leaning casually against the counter. He was dressed down this morning in gray sweats and a hoodie. The rectangular outline of his pack of cigarettes stood out in his front pocket.

"Forgot you were cooking?" he asked.

"Got distracted." I nudged him aside with my hip to put the well-done bacon on a plate. "What're you doing here?"

"Dean and I stopped by a bakery for cinnamon rolls."

"That's thoughtful."

"His idea, not mine. I think it was an excuse for him and Keira to check on our progress. Did you just wake up?"

"Actually, I've been up for hours. Bright and early. You?"

"I'm always up early. Hopped to Dean's kitchenette for a cup of coffee."

"Hopped?"

"I don't always feel like putting on my leg first thing. Prefer to shower without it. I have excellent balance. You have no idea." Cole slapped his stomach over his hoodie. "All in the core."

"I would've liked to see you in action."

"On this mission, we'll be seeing a lot of each other. So you probably will."

I glanced at him and found him smirking back.

"Last night did the trick, huh?" Dean asked.

We both turned. Dean was setting down a paper bag on the kitchen table. Keira stood beside him. "And you didn't even have to lock them in a room," Dean said to her.

I grabbed the bowl of scrambled eggs, which I'd left warming in the oven, and brought that and the bacon to the table. "Nope, Cole demanded we arm wrestle. And the rest is history."

Dean and Keira went quiet, trying to figure *that* one out, and all I could do was laugh.

"It made more sense in the moment," Cole said defensively.

"But who won?" Dean asked.

"I did."

I pointed a finger at Cole. "Because you *cheated*."

"You're just jealous you didn't think of it first."

"Have no doubt, I'll get my revenge." But we were grinning at each other, which took the bite out of my words.

"Actually, now I'm back to worried," Keira quipped. "You two are not acting normal. Either you're suddenly best buddies, or you're plotting to kill each other."

Cole pulled up a chair at the table. "Only time will tell."

---

After breakfast, Cole and I convinced Keira and Dean we didn't need a babysitter. We were getting along just fine. We had a huge amount of work to do to get ready for this op, and only a week to do it.

*Nope, no pressure. None at all.*

Leaving Cole in the living room, I went to my room to change into jeans and a sweatshirt. My short shorts felt a touch too casual for mission planning. When I came out, I had my hair sleeked back into its usual ponytail.

Cole was sitting on the couch. I sat right beside him. We were partners in this, and we had to count on each other. And that meant not being squeamish about being near the man. It had nothing to do with his suggestion from last night about playing my boyfriend. He hadn't mentioned that again, so I assumed the subject was officially dropped.

"I thought we'd work on our cover stories today." I put the manila envelope that Stanford had given me on the coffee table. Our fake identity papers spilled out when I tipped the envelope.

Cole picked up my new driver's license. "Brianna Waverley," he read. "She's a blond?"

"I'm wearing a wig in the photo, but I'll actually be blond by the time we head to Arizona. Between the hair and makeup, I'll be unrecognizable."

"Yeah, I agree. Picture barely looks like you."

"Plus, Westwick prefers blonds, so there's that."

Cole grumbled something inaudible under his breath, tossing the ID onto the coffee table. "What else do I need to know about her?"

"As I mentioned last night, I'm playing a social media influencer who's developing her own lifestyle brand. Brianna is eager to grow her business and learn from the little seminar Westwick is putting on." On my phone, I pulled up the fake Instagram profile. "Here she is, in all her hash-tagged glory."

Cole thumbed through Brianna's Instagram grid. It was full of posts and reels about wellness, interior design, plants, and skin products. Stuff I liked, honestly, so I didn't have to fake my enthusiasm in the videos. The account was sleek enough to look professional, but not distinct enough to draw too much attention.

"This is elaborate," Cole said. "How long were you working on this again? These posts go back months with tons of likes and comments."

"All fake, thanks to River and his hacker network. They made the account look like it's grown over months instead of weeks. This is enough to back up my cover story if Westwick decides he's curious."

"What about facial recognition? If he does a reverse photo look-up?"

"I asked River the same thing. He said he would take care of it. It's nothing to worry about."

"And where will the real Brynn Somerton be during the op in Arizona? Have you figured that out?"

Did he think I'd forget a detail like that? "I'll be camping in a remote location and considering my life choices after leaving the Bureau." Keira would park my car at a backpacking trailhead. That way, if anyone inquired, I would officially be nowhere near Arizona. Full deniability for the FBI. *And* for the Protectors.

Cole crossed his arms over his broad chest. "And do you have anyone back home who will be worrying about where you are?"

I switched my phone screen off and set it on the coffee table. "Are you asking if I have a significant other?"

"Or brother or nosy neighbor or whatever. Just getting a

sense of possible weaknesses in your cover. Anyone who might ask questions about you being MIA."

"Then the answer is no, I don't have a boyfriend. Or a husband or sister or anyone who's going to be checking up on me. As for you, we'll set up a similar kind of alibi. You can be out fishing or something. Colorado is great for disappearing into the wilderness."

Cole ran his fingers through the short chestnut strands of his hair. "Nah, I think another reason River chose me is that very few people are concerned about where I am."

"I know how that is." Aside from Charlotte and Stanford, who knew all about this plan, I didn't really have anybody.

There was an awkward pause, when both of us shifted on the couch, waiting for the other to ask a prying question.

"Anyway." I grabbed his fake driver's license from the pile. "You'll be Cameron Clay. My manager from San Diego."

Cole grumbled again. "I don't know a single thing about Southern California."

"Isn't that where Aiden is from? He's supposed to be your friend. Ask him. Also, there's this amazing thing called YouTube."

He glared.

"Like I said yesterday, you'll be there for support. The less you say to anyone, probably the better. I'll be doing all the talking."

"What about security? Does Westwick have bodyguards?"

"A man named Donovan Ryker heads Westwick's security detail, with a rotating roster of other guards depending on the situation. We expect Westwick will have no more than two at the resort, plus Ryker himself."

I pulled up a photo of Ryker. The man had a military-style haircut, thick neck, hardened features. Like many of Stillwater's henchmen, Ryker was a mercenary. Rumors tied him to multiple foreign wars and international incidents before he'd taken on a personal security role for Westwick. Ryker was the type to handle dirty work and make problems disappear.

The FBI had its eye on him, but evidence and witnesses against Ryker had a tendency to evaporate. Cole could read all about it in the report the task force had put together.

"You'll help me get around Ryker so I can cozy up to Westwick," I said. "According to the profile we've put together on him, he's partial to younger women. That's why I'll be playing younger too. Twenty-five and naively optimistic." Not like my cynical thirty-three-year-old self at all, but I'd taken acting classes in college. I'd also been practicing makeup techniques to smooth out the fine lines around my eyes. I could pull this off.

Cole glowered, his expression turning downright scary. "*Really* not a fan of this. You *sure* I can't grab Westwick and drive him out to the desert? So much easier."

I gave Cole a stern look. We'd already gone over this last night. But I assumed he was just venting. Hearing about this stuff made me furious too. "That reminds me. I got a message this morning about some new info. Something that's relevant to Westwick's profile."

"New info from who? The FBI task force? I thought they weren't involved anymore."

"It's just an update they sent me through secure channels. Relax." Never mind that I'd been texting with SAC Stanford that morning.

On my laptop, I accessed my secure drop box. There was a new document. I opened it, edging closer to Cole so we could read the screen together.

"Looks like the task force just discovered a former nanny of the Westwicks," I said. "One of the few people who's directly reported anything negative about him." Since the man kept his reputation squeaky-clean, this was significant.

The nanny, a young woman named Petra, had come to the

United States through an agency after being matched with Garon and his wife. She was hired to care for the Westwicks' daughters while the girls were in middle school. But quickly, the ideal job she had been promised turned into something far darker.

As we read, Cole muttered curses, and I clenched my teeth.

Westwick and his wife had docked Petra's pay for the slightest infraction. Eventually stopped paying her at all. Even forbade her from leaving the home. But far worse, Garon had been relentless about making advances. He'd made it clear that if Petra didn't submit to him, she would be punished. He also used his head of security, Donovan Ryker, to threaten and intimidate her, making her terrified for her life.

"She ran," Cole read aloud. "Reported the Westwicks to the police. Then Westwick used his connections to hush it all up. She got deported back to Finland."

When the whole ordeal had begun, she'd only been nineteen years old.

Westwick pretended to be an upstanding family man on the outside. But inside, he was exactly the type of scum who'd start an organization like Stillwater.

"I'm telling you, we can just abandon him with no phone and no water a hundred miles from civilization," Cole said. "The elements and vultures will take care of the rest."

"I'm tempted. Believe me. I already suspected Westwick had done this kind of thing. This is the most detailed account we've found because Petra was brave enough to try speaking out about it." And Westwick had pulled strings to silence her.

Cole pushed up to standing and walked over to the fireplace. Turned around and faced me, his large hands on his hips. "You plan to draw this asshole's attention. It's pretty clear what he'll try to do to you once you're alone."

I huffed. "You think I'm not aware of that? Please. That's the entire plan. To use his predatory tendencies against him. Don't even think about telling me we need a new approach, because it's not going to happen."

"And I'll be—what? Chilling by the pool while this is going on?"

"You'll be running interference. Giving me room to work. I'll have a way to contact you, some means to send a signal if things truly get dire. But they won't. I'm more than capable of handling this."

"But I'm not capable of sitting and twiddling my thumbs the way you're asking. You're using yourself as bait. And it's beyond obvious that you'll resist asking for help even if you need it. You'll take foolish risks just because you want to prove you can do it."

I stood and marched over to him. "Careful. I will not let you talk down to me like I'm some junior agent who's never run an op before."

"And I won't let you relegate me to a support role when I'm supposed to be your partner."

He took a step toward me, and I reacted, pressing my palm flat against his chest. Then Cole used my arm to spin me around, putting my back to the fireplace. He planted his hands on the mantle to either side of me. He'd caged me in, his bulky frame leaving only a centimeter of space between us.

"Is this your new technique every time we have an argument? Pinning me? I might have to resort to defensive measures. Like kneeing you in the balls."

"Save that for Westwick."

"I'm trying, but you keep testing me."

Cole leaned even closer. Lowered his voice. "Brynn.

There's a better way to get this done. You'd be safer if I can stay close." Cole's heat surrounded me, his determination rolling off of him in waves like a heady scent. Not to mention his *actual* scent, warm spices with hints of cigarette smoke, which had no right to be such a perfect combination.

"You want to play my boyfriend."

"It could make you even more enticing to Westwick if you're already taken. A man like him has everything. A wife, family, career. Yet he wants to lie and steal and cheat to get more. He craves power and secrecy. He'll love the idea of stealing you from me."

Huh. I wished I'd thought of that myself. "For a guy who claimed I'm not your type, you keep trying to get your hands on me, Bailey," I joked.

"I'll be playing a role. Nothing more than that."

"Yet we struggle to get along for ten minutes straight. Now we're supposed to be in a relationship? I just have my doubts we can pull this off."

He fixed me with an intense look. That fiery gaze started moving down my body.

Cole had subtly checked me out before, even though he'd denied it. But this time, there was a different glint in his eyes. A shameless, open hunger, layered with possessiveness. Like he'd destroy anyone and anything that stood between us.

Cole's eyes lifted to meet mine, and the breath whooshed out of my lungs.

He finally pushed back from the fireplace, taking several steps away from me. "Still skeptical?"

I swallowed. My mouth had gone dry, and my skin was damp with sweat. "That was…a good start."

"Suppose we'll need some practice to perfect it." His voice was rough.

I studied him, biting my lip. "Meet me at the bar where

Dean works. Eight tonight. In the meantime, I'll give you access to my secure files. So you can read up on everything else we've gathered on Westwick."

"Roger that."

We both stood there another moment. That same intensity still thick in the air.

"See you tonight," he finally said.

When Cole had left, I slumped onto the couch, my head falling back. I needed a cold shower.

But tonight, we'd be at it again. Practicing this fake relationship of ours. And at the resort, we'd be inseparable. We would have to convince everyone there, including Westwick, that we were in love. Okay, maybe not *in love*, but sleeping together.

Given the way Cole had just looked at me, I was on my way to believing it.

What had I gotten myself into?

# CHAPTER TEN

I GOT to the bar a couple minutes before eight. The place was packed, even more than the night before. Guns N' Roses blasted through the speakers. I pushed through the crowd, scanning for Brynn, but she wasn't here yet. So I pulled up to the bar instead, finding a sliver of space at the end.

I'd spent all afternoon reviewing the files on Garon Westwick and the preparations for the mission. Brynn's task force, along with River's hacker network, had been hard at work. I'd been relieved to see how thoroughly they'd outlined the situation. Blueprints of the resort, profiles of other guests who had already booked rooms. Had to hand it to the Feds. They'd done well with this one, and I gave a lot of the credit to Brynn.

If anything, I should've been feeling more relaxed tonight now that Brynn and I had reached some kind of understanding and we'd solidified our cover stories. But instead my fingers tapped impatiently against the bar top. I wasn't a fan of surprises, yet this mission kept delivering one after the other.

Earlier, when she had challenged me to prove I could be a convincing boyfriend… Let's just say, I didn't have to rely on my nonexistent acting skills. I was attracted to her. No denying it. Which was great for pulling off this fake relationship thing. But sure as hell inconvenient when it came to not blurring the lines.

After a few minutes, Dean made his way over to me. "Here again? I thought you got enough whiskey last night."

"That's why I'm sticking with beer." I ordered something on the lighter side. A session ale that wasn't heavy on the alcohol. "I'm meeting Brynn."

Dean poured my beer and brought it over. "I can't figure the two of you out. Are you at each other's throats? Or did you find your vibe?"

"Hell if I know," I muttered. "Technically, we're working tonight. Practicing."

"Practicing? Do I want to know what it is you'll be practicing?"

"Just don't be surprised by how we're acting tonight."

Dean laughed, clearly confused. But he would catch on fast. He knew we had to get our cover stories straight.

Truth was, I didn't know what to expect tonight either. What had happened earlier... Jeez, it had been a challenge not to get hard when I'd been right there in front of her, giving her the thorough eye-fuck that I had been denying myself since we'd met.

But that attraction wasn't the reason I had suggested tweaking our cover story. By playing her boyfriend, I would be able to stay close to her at all times. Brynn would have to be alone with Westwick at some point, but I could make sure that happened on her terms when she was ready. I didn't put anything past that asshole. Maybe he preferred to sit back and let his Stillwater lieutenants get their hands dirty. But if he'd held his nineteen-year-old nanny prisoner inside his house, then he was capable of plenty.

The whole idea was that Brynn would make herself irresistible. I had to be in the position to step in if her methods proved a little too effective.

But contrary to my claims, I had zero acting ability. I'd been all confidence and bravado with her earlier. Now, the real test would come. I much preferred a straightforward approach. Both with work *and* with women. Playing games was not my thing.

I checked my watch and noticed with annoyance that Brynn was ten minutes late. Where was she?

Then the crowd parted as several heads turned. Axl Rose wailed on the sound system. My jaw wanted to drop, but I kept it firmly in place.

Dean said, "Wait, is that *Brynn?*"

She had worn thigh-high, stiletto boots. A denim skirt about the size of a postage stamp. And a tight tank top that showed off her assets. Her hair was down, draping in long dark waves around her face and past her shoulders. More makeup than before, which somehow made her appear younger and more vixenish at the same time.

Dean set down the glass he was drying. "Didn't know all that was hiding behind the government façade. I mean, wow."

I glared at him. "Watch it."

He laughed, holding up his hands. "Didn't mean anything by it. Not like I'm going to make any moves on her. Are you?"

"My concern is purely professional."

"Sure it is."

Brynn's eyes found mine, though her expression didn't change. She walked up to the other side of the bar, resting her elbows casually on the top, an easy smile on her lips.

*Shit.*

"By the way," Dean said, "you have a little drool right here." He pointed at the corner of his mouth. Immediately I went to wipe my face, finding nothing, and the jerk cracked up.

"Fuck you. I'm supposed to be working."

"Good luck then, my friend."

Turning away from Dean, I leaned back against the bar to watch my undercover partner. I was far from the only man who'd noticed her. The guy right next to her turned to face her, leaning in to say something. She shrugged.

Should I go over there? Or sit here and keep drinking my beer? All I knew was that the tug of possessiveness in my belly was very real. The hell was up with me? I'd known the woman for less than two days.

It was this stuff about Garon Westwick. The knowledge that Brynn intended to use herself as bait. And the memory of what had happened to Luciana. That had to explain why I was suddenly so protective of a former FBI agent who didn't even like me.

I had to sort this out in my head. She was in character. That was the point of tonight. To practice our cover stories. I chugged the rest of my beer as I stood, set it on the bar, and put her in my sights.

She wanted to see if I could hold my own as her fake boyfriend? Brynn was about to see exactly how convincing I could be.

I started pushing my way through the crowd.

Another bartender, a woman, was taking Brynn's order. The guy next to her pulled out his wallet, clearly intending to pay. Brynn smiled sweetly, her straight white teeth flashing without a trace of her usual attitude. Way too innocent. I wasn't sure I liked that.

Then she put her hand on the guy's arm, and I *definitely* didn't like that.

There were still a few people between us, and they scowled at me when I tried to push past them, so all I could do was watch. The bartender poured mixers into a shaker, while Brynn spoke to the guy beside her. He wore an expensive ski jacket and had a pair of neon green sunglasses perched on his head.

"What's your name, beautiful?" Green Sunglasses slurred loudly. Couldn't have been older than twenty-five, and he swayed like he'd already had one tequila shot too many.

"Brianna."

"Sexy name for a sexy girl." The guy was flirting with the subtlety of a sledgehammer, his body language all cocky smugness. He had to be the most obnoxious guy in this place, and Brynn had zeroed in on him in five seconds.

The kid tugged a thick roll of bills from his wallet and tossed it onto the bar top. Even the bartender rolled her eyes as she set a martini glass down and took the money.

The kid leaned in and murmured something in Brynn's ear. Then his hand landed on her hip and slid toward her butt.

Oh, hell no.

Brynn's smile widened dangerously. I could tell she wanted to punch him for whatever he'd just said. But she didn't. Instead, she eyed me on her periphery. A challenge. *What are you going to do, Cole?*

She was playing her role, so I had better play mine.

"Excuse me," I said to the other people waiting. I ignored their complaints that I was cutting in line. I reached Brynn and slid my arm around her waist. "I've been looking for you."

"You know this old guy?" Green Sunglasses asked.

*Old guy*? Was this kid serious?

I pulled her closer, the lines of her body meeting mine and was gratified when the smug kid's hand got knocked aside. I wasn't a super possessive guy by nature. I rarely got jealous, and that was something that my ex-wife had complained about. Among the *many* things that hadn't pleased her about me. But right now, the act felt all too natural.

Brynn shrugged. "This is Cameron. He's my boyfriend."

"*Boyfriend*? But I just bought you a drink."

I spared a glance for the kid she'd been flirting with. He looked annoyed, and I didn't blame him. The man was an innocent bystander in this dress rehearsal of ours. Even if he did seem like a dipshit.

"I'll pay you back," I said. "She doesn't need anyone to buy her drinks but me."

The kid lifted his chin. "Fuck you, dude," he slurred. "If you were satisfying her, she wouldn't be dressing that way."

I took a quick, threatening step in his direction. The kid stumbled back, knocking into a woman. Her beer spilled all over him. There were shouts.

Brynn grabbed my arm and pulled me in the opposite direction through the crowd. Along the way, she ditched the martini on an empty table.

When we reached a shadowed corner, she spun around to face me, her hand still on my arm. She was laughing. "I'd say that went well for a first try."

"But did you have to pick the most asinine idiot in the room to cozy up to?"

"Couldn't help it. I seem to be a magnet for those."

"You're having way too much fun with this."

"It was pretty funny."

"Won't be funny when it's Garon Westwick you're flirting with."

"No, but that guy was no Garon Westwick."

I glowered over my shoulder in the direction of the bar. The kid's green sunglasses were still visible on top of his head. Looked like he was wiping himself off and arguing with someone else. Probably the woman he'd bumped into. The kid was irrelevant, but I still wanted to teach him a lesson for his behavior to Brynn. A visceral lesson he wouldn't soon forget.

This was why I hated undercover work. Playing a character, constantly switching gears. I preferred to keep things simple.

*Track down the threat. Neutralize it. The end.*

Brynn wrapped her arms around my neck. In those heeled boots, she was as tall as me. Eye to eye. Chest to chest.

"What are you doing?" I asked.

She brought her lips close enough to brush my ear. "I'm practicing, *Cameron*. The reason we came here tonight. The boyfriend story was your idea, if you recall."

Trickles of heat flowed through my veins. "Only because you insist on using yourself as a honey trap. I'm still not crazy about that plan."

"You did well with the jealous boyfriend act, though. I almost believe you're attracted to me."

*Because you make me want to push you up against the nearest wall and ravage your mouth,* I responded silently. *How's that for attraction?*

But more than that, I was worried for her. I didn't like emotions getting in the way of my work, and with this woman? All my wires were getting crossed. I was so far out of my element with this mission.

She rubbed her cheek against my stubbled one. My hands found her hips, and Brynn started swaying seductively to the Led Zeppelin song now playing on the speakers. Never thought you could slow dance to "Black Dog," but Brynn was making it work.

"You're being all stiff and awkward." She laughed softly and pulled back a bit so our eyes met again. Her lashes fluttered. "Where's that look you gave me earlier? The one at

Keira's house. Like you…you know, like you were crazy for me."

"You mean, for Brianna."

"Exactly. There's a lot we haven't worked out. Are Brianna and Cameron a new couple? Have we been together a while?" She lifted one hand to run her fingers through my short hair, and the tips of her nails scratched against my scalp. I closed my eyes, enjoying the sensation and letting myself relax.

"A few months," I said. "New enough that Cameron is unreasonably territorial."

She nodded. "But also long enough that Brianna knows how to soothe him."

"Seems like she does." Everything else in the bar faded, and my vision tunneled on the woman in front of me. "What about kissing?"

Her eyes widened. "What about it?"

"Is that off limits? Just trying to figure out how far this practice is supposed to go."

"I mean…no. Not off limits. We'll probably have to." Her voice had dipped.

"Probably. At some point. Tell me if you don't like anything I'm doing," I murmured. "Okay?"

"Yeah. Okay."

If she wanted to practice, I figured I might as well oblige.

I gathered her against me. Her breasts pushed into my chest. I dropped my head to press my lips to the pulse point at her neck. It thrummed wildly. Brynn tilted her head at the contact of my mouth on her skin, and her fingers tightened on the collar of my shirt. She made a soft sound, barely audible compared to the music playing overhead, but I felt it in her throat.

*Fake,* I reminded myself. *This is all fake.*

As we danced, Brynn's eyes kept lowering to my lips. Was

she in character? Had to be. But the heady cocktail of chemicals in my bloodstream, rushing straight to my cock, was the real damn thing.

Each song blended into the next. The bar lights a blur of neon in her eyes, even though I'd had only the one beer.

"You could kiss me now," she said after a while. Barely a whisper. "Might as well get it over with."

She made kissing me sound as exciting as getting her teeth cleaned at the dentist.

But if she wanted a kiss? Well, I could deliver.

I brought my lips to hers. She didn't pull away. Instead, she wiggled even closer to me. Grabbed onto my shirt. I'd meant to start this gently, not going too far too fast. But she was urging me on.

My tongue traced the shape of her lower lip, and when she opened to me, I licked inside. Brynn tasted sweet. Like she'd been eating candy before she'd arrived at the bar. No trace of alcohol, because she'd left the martini the kid had bought for her. That guy didn't matter.

Nobody mattered right now but the two of us. The way our bodies were in sync. She wanted natural, and I couldn't imagine anything more natural than this.

I couldn't remember the last time I just let go, gave in to exactly what I wanted. She was giving me all the signals, and at the moment, I just didn't care what was pretend and what wasn't.

All I could think was, *More, please.*

I changed the angle of the kiss, deepening it. Brynn was right there with me. Then she took over, and I loved that even more. Because *this* was the real Brynn, a woman who didn't shy away from being in command. And while I didn't take orders easily, not from anyone, I was happy to let her drive. If only so she could show me exactly how to make her feel good.

Our tongues tangled and danced, giving and taking, and it made me wonder what being in bed with her would be like. I had the feeling Brynn was no pushover when it came to sex. Like every interaction we'd had, she would make me work to be in charge, and damn, did I want that opportunity.

Then she pulled away from me with a gasp, her eyes glazed. Her lips were parted. Pink and wet from the friction against mine.

My cock was like steel. I still had my arms around her, so I separated our bodies by a few inches. "You okay?"

She breathed a laugh. Her hands went to my shoulders, as if she needed me to steady her. "I'd say we aced the assignment." She blinked a few times. "Nice job."

*Nice job?*

Her words calmed the situation in my pants, enough that I wouldn't embarrass myself. Right. Of course this was a job. I'd enjoyed it though, and that wasn't a crime. In fact, I thought we were on a roll.

"Enough practice for tonight?" I asked. "Or..."

"Oh, no, that was plenty." Brynn let go of me, breaking all contact between us like she'd flipped a switch. She looked at the ground, straightening her top. "*Definitely* enough practice."

Mentally, I wanted to slap myself. *Nice job indeed, Lynx. Nice fucking job.* Clearly, I was the only one who'd felt that chemistry.

But I sucked as an actor, so it was a good thing I enjoyed kissing her, wasn't it? No way I could play the obsessive boyfriend otherwise.

This was fake, and I would just have to keep repeating that, because my body kept trying to forget it.

## CHAPTER ELEVEN

# Brynn

THAT KISS.

*That kiss.*

I had not been prepared for it. When Cole's lips had melted over mine, his tongue in my mouth and his strong arms around me, I had forgotten all about the undercover assignment. Whether I was Brianna or Brynn. I had just wanted more of it.

I hugged my arms around my middle. "Would you walk me back to Keira's? I'm freezing my assets off. Ready to change into my sweats."

Cole was all for more "practicing," but that was way too tempting. Nope, I had to put a stop to this so I could get my reactions to the man under control. Step one was to get out of this bar and out of this ridiculous outfit so that Cole would stop looking at me like he might eat me alive.

Yet he kept doing it, those blue eyes running over me like he owned me. "Where's your coat?"

"More layers would've ruined the effect of Brianna's outfit."

Cole chuckled. He took off the heavy flannel jacket he was wearing, leaving just his long-sleeved undershirt. "Here." He draped the flannel around my shoulders. Cozy warmth enveloped me. Which strangely made me shiver as I thought again of that kiss. "Best I can do for now," he said.

"Oh, it's fine. Perfect, actually." I stuck my arms into the jacket and buttoned it. The edges fell almost to the tops of my thigh-high boots.

Cole straightened the collar. It had rolled up on one side. His fingers brushed my neck, and just that brief moment of skin-to-skin contact made my whole body blush.

"Are you being Cameron right now? Or just Cole?"

His face twisted up. "Hell if I know."

"Either way, all of me thanks you."

Seriously. I had to get a grip.

We'd been talking about leaving, and yet we both kept standing there. Cole seemed to be deep in thought, but for the life of me I couldn't read his expression. "What?" I asked.

"Nothing. Let's go."

He put his hand on the small of my back, ushering me through the crowd. Like it was the natural thing to do. But my head was spinning.

That afternoon, I had gone over to Main Street to do some shopping for my cover. It wasn't easy to find short shorts and mini skirts at this time of year, but there was a cute thrift shop that had all kinds of variety. I'd lucked out with the boots. They were the kind I would wear for a special occasion. Maybe a third date. They made me feel sexy and confident. But for Brianna Waverley, flashy clothes were an everyday necessity.

And yes, I'd been freezing on my walk here from Keira's place. But that was hardly going to be my biggest challenge in this mission. I'd walked into this bar wanting to draw attention. To give Cole some inspiration for getting into character as my possessive older boyfriend.

Perhaps it had worked a bit too well.

The kid at the bar had been an obvious mark. Showboating for his friends, leering at every female in the vicinity. I'd made a beeline for him the moment I saw him. But still, I hadn't *asked* him to buy me a drink. Hadn't done anything overly flirtatious either, aside from a brief touch on his forearm when I complemented his neon ski jacket. The kid had taken it upon himself to throw his money around, insisting he pay for my martini.

When Cole had arrived, the kid had made things turn ugly fast all by himself.

Had I enjoyed seeing Cole get all gruff and protective? More than I should have. It had been a long time since I'd been kissed. In fact, the last man I'd kissed had crushed my heart and ground it into dust.

That had to explain this confused, achy longing I was feeling. But it didn't help that I had Cole's warm jacket and his steady hand on my back. The moment we were outside, I sucked in the dry, icy air. It cleared the swirl of messy thoughts in my brain.

Unfortunately the relief only lasted until I saw who was waiting on the sidewalk.

The kid who'd bought me the martini stood by the curb with his four friends. He scowled when he saw me and Cole. "That's them."

Crap. I was too tired for this.

Just as I clocked the guy's presence, Cole muttered "Green Sunglasses on your three."

"Yeah, I saw him."

"Hey," the kid yelled. "That was bullshit what you pulled in there." I had no idea if he meant me or Cole.

But Cole stepped out in front of me. "No idea what you're referring to, son."

"You and your girl made me look like an idiot."

"Wasn't hard," I said. The kid's scowl deepened, like a

toddler about to have a tantrum. "I didn't ask you to buy me a drink. I didn't hit on you."

"Then why are you going around dressed like that? Huh?"

Cole shook his head. "I suggest you and your buddies go back inside and forget about this. Unless you want your night to get a lot worse."

The kid sneered, gesturing at his friends. "There's five of us and one of you, old man."

*Really*? I didn't count?

That would not do. Not at *all*.

I walked forward, standing shoulder to shoulder with Cole. "Dibs on the two on the right," I murmured. Which included green sunglasses boy.

Cole sighed. "Fine, I'll take the left two. And whichever of us finishes first takes the one in the middle."

"Works for me."

We spread out. Meanwhile, the kid kept yapping. "I don't hit girls, even slutty ones, so you'd better get out of the way, babe. Unless you wanna come with us right now and we'll show you a lot more fun than this dude ever will."

I laughed. "Last chance, sweetie."

The man on the far left moved first. Lunged at Cole with his fist raised. Cole blocked the punch and returned it with two quick jabs to the man's torso.

Green Sunglasses turned, about to go after Cole from the other side. I got in his way. Didn't want to mess up the kid's dental work unless I truly had to, but then, he made it an easy decision for me. Green Sunglasses grabbed me by the arm, trying to shove me out of the way. So I twisted my body as my fist smashed a hook into his chin. He careened backward, sprawling half on the sidewalk and half in the muddy street. His green sunglasses clattered onto the asphalt.

The other guy I'd called dibs on came in next. Fists flying. No holding back on account of me being female, and I appreciated it. I stepped out of his path and kicked him at the knee. He toppled next to his friend.

I glanced over to see Cole twisting another guy's arm at a painful-looking angle. The guy cried for mercy.

And the middle one? That guy was already running down the street. Seemed like he had thought better of engaging, unlike his buddies. But I doubted there were any broken bones. Just bruised egos.

Cole stood, brushing off his hands on his jeans, and walked over to me. "Probably best not to stick around. I don't want to have to explain this to Sheriff Owen. I can skip the lecture."

I snorted. The sheriff did have a tendency to be uptight, especially when it came to writing up incidents that caused him a headache. Cole and I were supposed to be keeping a low profile in Silver Ridge.

I was more than happy to move on before the boys got any ideas about a round two.

---

On the walk back to Keira's, my blood was singing. The exercise had heated me up enough that I didn't need Cole's jacket anymore. But I didn't take it off.

"Nothing like the endorphins from a good fight," I said, shaking out my hand. I'd need to ice my knuckles later, but it was worth it.

"Agreed. I mean, I can think of one thing that's even better for a dopamine rush, but a good fight is close second." Cole had his eyes on the dark street ahead of us instead of on me. But his smirk said it all.

"Well, it's been a little while for me when it comes to either of those activities. Fighting or, you know, that other F word." Much longer, in fact, for the second.

We both laughed, and I felt blood rush into my face. A sudden burst of shyness after the wild night we'd had. Good thing it was dark and he couldn't see me blushing.

"I thought we fought well together," Cole said, voice dropping lower.

"Me too."

As for doing that other F with him... *Brynn, get that out of your head.*

We needed a new topic of conversation, so I went with the first thing that came to mind. "How do you like your prosthesis?"

His smile faded, the relaxed mood between us turning to tension again. "If you're really trying to ask if it's a limitation—"

"I'm not." I hadn't meant to screw up the good vibes so quickly. Last thing I'd wanted to do. "I know other people with prostheses. But it's different for each person, so I was curious about your experience. If that's too private, I understand."

Cole rolled his shoulders. "I don't mind talking about it. It was tough at first. In the beginning, you just get a temporary fit, because the stump tissue is still shrinking."

"Sounds painful."

He grunted. "It sucked. At first, I couldn't stand the prosthesis more than half an hour at a time, which just pissed me off. I wanted to get back to where I'd been before. Back on my feet, literally. Within several months, though, I had the hang of it. This particular one, I've had a couple years. I can wear it for days now, depending on how much I'm on my feet. It's not an issue."

"I don't doubt it. Never meant to suggest it was. You didn't consider returning to active duty?" An amputation didn't necessarily end a military career, even for someone like Cole, being a Ranger. It would've been incredibly difficult to jump through the Army's hoops to qualify, but if anyone could do it, I would've bet on Cole. The man had a bull-headed, stubborn streak, that was for sure.

"After the way it all went down? Hell no. But." Cole scratched his chin, pausing on that word. "Did I think about it? Sure. The Army was my career. Pretty much everything I knew. To lose it all in one fell swoop. That was tough."

I couldn't imagine. He had told me some of this before, but I got the sense there was far more to it. There had to be, going through something like that. The trauma of the injury. Not just the healing and adjusting to a changed physical existence, but all the mental shock it would entail too. When I thought about it, his strength blew me away.

"I hope you had people supporting you through it. Family and friends."

His expression remained carefully neutral. "Not so much. No family to speak of anymore. After I came home, my wife decided she'd had enough of me. So she took off pretty soon as well."

I stopped walking, turning to him. "Are you kidding me? That's unbelievable."

He shrugged. "I had my Army buddies and their significant others who stepped up. Aiden's family especially was great. I'm not complaining. My buddies who didn't even make it home..." He cleared his throat, shaking his head.

Instinctively, I reached out to squeeze his upper arm. I'd lost people too in the service. But I didn't want to compare my experiences to his. Each loss was a uniquely brutal punch to the gut, a pain all its own that never fully went away.

His bicep tensed. Then released.

"I have nothing to complain about," he said. "And yet I'm still a grumpy asshole. Go figure."

I smiled. "I'm getting used to it. You're not so bad."

"Careful. You almost sound like you like me."

"I know, it's worrisome."

We resumed our walk, but closer than before. Arms brushing. Every once in a while, Cole's hand would rest on my back again, as if keeping me steady. I was doing just fine in my heels, but I didn't mind it.

"What's on the agenda for tomorrow?" he asked. "We haven't talked about what gear and weapons we're bringing with us. I'd like to know more about Westwick's head of security. Ryker."

"Tomorrow's good for that. I think River's planning to come by. You'll also need some new clothes for Cameron Clay."

He groaned. "Shopping. Can't wait."

We kept chatting about the long list of preparations still ahead of us. Only a few days to get it all done. But really, it felt like we were just filling the silence. Because there was something new between us now, and I suspected Cole didn't know what to do with it, any more than I did.

We reached Keira's house and went up to her porch. I turned around, not reaching yet for the door. "Thanks for walking me back."

"No worries." He was standing in my space. Nearly as close as he had earlier in the bar, when we'd been in character. Yet I felt an urge to pull him closer.

This was a problem. A disaster waiting to happen.

I crossed my arms over his flannel jacket. "Look. I need to say this. Please don't take offense."

"I'm listening." But his eyes were wandering down the length of my body.

I shifted on my heels. "About what happened earlier. It got a bit…heated."

"The fight? I thought it was pretty low key, all things considered."

"I mean before the fight. In the bar."

"The kiss?" he asked innocently.

"Yes, Cole. The kiss. You know that's what I'm talking about."

His feet shuffled forward, his weight moving from hip to hip. He reached out his hand and braced it against the front door behind me. "You thought the kiss was heated?"

"That's what I just said."

"And here I was thinking you hadn't noticed."

My chest was tight, and I felt lightheaded. "Don't get me wrong. It's great we're getting along better."

"Mmhmm." He nodded. "Much better."

"But this will be tricky. The fake relationship part of our cover."

"I imagine so." His eyelids went heavy as he glanced at my mouth.

I leaned against the door, my limbs turning liquid. "We need to keep things professional. There can't be any more misunderstandings."

"Misunderstandings about what?"

I felt the soft breath of his words against my mouth. And I had no clue what I had been about to say. None whatsoever. "I'm…uh…"

His nose nudged mine. I sighed. His lips were right there, and it would barely take a move to continue what we'd started earlier. *Practice*. It was supposed to be practice in front of an audience. But here, it was just us.

"We could try it again," he said. "For the sake of clarity."

The door flew open, and I stumbled backward. Cole grabbed my shoulders before I fell.

"Oh! I'm sorry. I thought I heard voices." Keira stood in the doorway, eyes wide. "Did you want to come in?"

"No," I said, heart beating a mile a minute. "We were just finishing our chat."

Cole touched his fingers to his lips, while Keira glanced between the two of us.

"Here. Cole, this is yours." As quickly as I could, I started unbuttoning his jacket.

"That's all right. You keep it." He stopped me, wrapping my fingers inside his larger hand. "I'll get it later."

"You sure?"

"Yeah." He stuck his hands in his pockets. "I'll see you tomorrow, B."

I felt a secret thrill that he'd used my nickname. It was what my good friends, like Charlotte and River, called me. Did Cole know that? Or had he come up with it on his own?

"Goodnight, Cole."

"Night." He nodded, eyes lingering, before he turned away and jogged to the sidewalk.

"What was that all about?" Keira asked.

I let out a heavy exhale. "This is bad."

"Why? What happened now?"

We went inside the house, Keira closing the door behind me. I flopped onto the couch. The soft fabric of Cole's jacket rubbed gently against my skin. "I think I like the guy."

"No kidding." Keira sat in the chair across from me. Her lips pressed together as she tried and failed not to laugh. "Dean texted that the two of you were about to set the bar on fire with that make-out session. All of Silver Ridge has figured out that you like him."

"You and Dean are such gossips."

"What? The Protectors told us to keep an eye on you. I take my job seriously."

"We were practicing our cover story. Cole suggested he play my boyfriend, and I agreed. Because it makes sense. He'll be able to stay closer to me throughout the op, and it will probably make the head of Stillwater even more interested if I'm unavailable."

"But your practice with Cole got a little too real? According to Dean, he was about to ask you two if you needed a room."

With a huff of frustration, I collapsed sideways on the couch. "I am an FBI special agent. I shouldn't be reacting to a kiss like a girl on prom night."

Then I realized what I had just said. I'd used the present tense when describing myself as an agent. Which just proved how much Cole distracted me.

We were about to go into a life-or-death situation together, and I couldn't afford to screw up.

"Why is it so bad if you enjoy kissing him?" Keira asked. "Or even if you like the man? I'm sure you can both keep that separate from your undercover mission. And later, if you decide you want to pursue something more with him, then—"

"No," I said emphatically. "Please don't finish that sentence. Because that's not going to happen."

The last thing I needed was to get some confused crush on my undercover partner. I hardly knew Cole. We'd just barely started to trust one another.

But this wasn't even about him. Not really. It was *me*. Whenever I really liked a man, my heart tended to gallop ahead, leaving my rational brain in the dust. I'd made that mistake before. I couldn't do it again.

"I *will not* fall for Cole Bailey. Not now, and not ever. You can quote me on that." I sat up, unbuttoning his jacket as I went, then tossed it onto the back of the couch. I'd return it tomorrow. Right after I gave Stanford his daily update. Something Cole would be furious about if he knew.

"Sorry," I said to Keira. "Thank you for talking this through with me. I'm…embarrassed, honestly."

"Don't be. This is a stressful mission, and we're all

counting on it to go well. It's a ton of pressure on you and Cole."

"As it should be. We can handle it." I breathed a few times. Solidifying my resolve. "We're going to see this through to the end."

"Now you're talking. Stillwater is going down. I can't wait to see it."

"Neither can I."

But as I got ready for bed, I kept replaying the evening in my head. The fierce blue of Cole's eyes on me. His lips. The deft strokes of his tongue. How I would've let him kiss me again if Keira hadn't interrupted us.

*I* probably would've kissed *him*.

But starting tomorrow, I'd be all business. All of my focus would go to this mission. Defeating Garon Westwick and Stillwater.

And after it was over...

There would be nothing but friendship afterward. Not for me and Cole.

I couldn't let myself fall for the wrong guy again. Not *ever*. The damaged remnants of my heart just couldn't take it.

# CHAPTER TWELVE

FIVE DAYS LATER, we were on our way to Arizona. The undercover mission had officially begun.

After driving all day, we walked into the Sunset Rocks Resort. Desert plants grew all around, creating a lush atmosphere despite the arid climate. Palm trees, saguaro cactuses. Blooming bushes with pink flowers. Calming music played overhead. It was like a fancy spa. *Way* too fancy for me. At least it was warm.

I straightened my linen button-down, feeling way out of place here. But at least I was a confident guy. I was good at storming into places that I didn't belong.

In contrast, Brynn strode into the lobby like she was born to do it. She wore a sundress that swirled and flowed around her curves. Tall wedge sandals that made her legs look a mile long.

The clerk at the desk looked up, smiling. "Checking in?" His gaze bounced from Brynn, to me, then back again.

"Sure are." Brynn swept her dyed honey-blond hair over her shoulder. "I saw the pool on the way in. Can't *wait* to get out there." Her Brianna voice was far bubblier than her real one. In fact, everything about her was slightly off the Brynn I knew. Brighter and sunnier, which made me feel even more like a grump by comparison. Luckily, that fit my cover.

The scent of her new perfume filled my nose. Coconut and pineapple layered with tropical flowers. The blond hair and the new wardrobe were disorienting, given how little they fit the real woman beneath. But my reaction to her was the same.

She rested her elbows on the counter, and the clerk's eyes darted briefly downward to her cleavage. The movement was so quick it would be easy to miss. But I caught it. I edged in right behind her and scowled at the guy to make sure he knew I'd seen.

"Cameron Clay and Brianna Waverley," I said gruffly.

His Adam's apple moved as he swallowed. His name tag read *Lance*. "Yes sir, of course. I just need your ID and a credit card."

I took the fake from my wallet. I'd tried out the credit card a time or two, but this would be the first real test of the documents the FBI task force had created. Sweat dampened my armpits, though I wouldn't let my nerves show.

Brynn studied her nails beside me. Meanwhile, Lance studied my ID.

I put my hands on the counter and leaned forward, doing my best to be intimidating. And my best was usually pretty strong. "I want a bottle of your most expensive champagne delivered to the room. And no housekeeping service during our stay unless we ask for it. We won't want to be disturbed."

"Yes, Mr. Clay. I can put in that request." Finally, Lance smiled, handing back my fake ID. "Great news. We've upgraded you to a Jacuzzi suite. No additional charge."

Brynn squealed and nestled into my side. "Doesn't that sound romantic, baby?"

I grunted an affirmative, still frowning, though my inner

relief was palpable. No issues with my ID. The FBI hadn't screwed that up, at least.

Nearly everything else, including the gear hiding inside a secret compartment of our vehicle, was from the Protectors. Them, I had more faith in. But either way, we were here. Past the first test and in the door.

Brynn slid away from me, flitting around the lobby as if admiring the luxurious decor. But she was scoping out the place, just like I was.

"You're here for the small business seminar?" Lance asked.

I nodded. "But we plan on making the most of the trip."

"Oh, I'm sure." He grinned. "Ms. Waverley seems very... energetic."

I glared at him until he went back to tapping on the computer.

Lance the hotel clerk gave us our keys and a map of the resort, and then we were on our way to the room. I carried our bags myself, having declined the bell hop service.

Brynn slid an arm around my waist. "Nice touch with the champagne," she murmured.

"I didn't like how closely he was looking at my ID."

She laughed, as if I had said something charming, and gazed at me adoringly as some other resort guests passed us. "You're worrying too much."

*I'm not worrying,* I wanted to protest. If anything, I didn't feel like I was focused enough. All this touching and cuddling after five days of zero contact between us? Could she blame me for being distracted?

As for *The Kiss,* which in my head started with capital letters, that subject was off limits. It hadn't been repeated in the days since, and neither of us had brought it up. But it was still there like a blinking neon sign in my head.

We reached the room, and I swiped the keycard. Brynn

went past me, cooing at the furnishings. The place was all white. The bedding, the walls, the upholstery on the chairs and couch. *Everything*. I couldn't imagine the laundry bills for this place. The bleach alone. Jeez.

I joined her at the windows, which took up the far wall opposite the bed. We had a view of the resort's manicured grounds, and beyond that, rolling hills of red rock.

I turned around, unable to avoid the most dominant feature of the room. The king-size bed, which we would be sharing for the next several days of this mission. Beyond, the sliding door to the bathroom was open, revealing an expanse of white marble. And there was the Jacuzzi tub. Even bigger than I'd been expecting. Plenty of space for *anything*.

Nope, I wasn't going near that tub. It was going to be nonstop ice-cold showers for me from here on out.

This woman was killing me.

Room service arrived with the champagne and two glasses. Brynn kept snapping pictures with her phone in its shiny, pale purple case. Something else River had provided: cell phones for this mission, uncrackable and untraceable to our real identities.

But as soon as I had the door closed and locked, Brynn pulled the curtains, and her demeanor changed instantly. Without a word, we checked the room for audio or video surveillance. We found nothing.

I grabbed my bag to unpack our guns. Securing our weapons, those we'd brought inside, was next on my priorities. Taking out my multitool, I used the screwdriver to open up an air vent. I taped a plastic envelope holding my handgun and ammo to the duct, making sure it was well concealed. I secured a second gun to the underside of the drawer on the nightstand. The tactical knife, I taped under the sink in the bathroom. If housekeeping did decide to visit, they wouldn't find anything unless they were specifically looking.

I had a few more important items, but I didn't unpack those yet. I'd find another place for them.

Meanwhile, Brynn kicked off her shoes, typing on her phone with purpose as she sat on the couch.

"Checking in with the Protectors?" I asked.

Brynn nodded, not looking up. "I'm letting them know we've arrived. No updates on their end." After a couple of minutes, she set the phone aside and stood.

"And the flash drive…" I began. She knew what I meant. The virus program that River had provided to upload to Westwick's devices. It was disguised to look like a tube of lipstick.

"In my purse. We're set." She was tense. I could feel it across the room. And she had claimed *I* was the worried one?

But was Brynn tense about the op? Or was it about me and this room we'd be sharing? More specifically, the bed. Which she had avoided looking at, just as she avoided looking at me now that we were alone.

Since The Kiss, we had kept things strictly platonic. It had been nothing but work and preparation. Preparation and work. No more practicing our cover story. No more *misunderstandings,* as Brynn had called it.

But I'd gotten the message. She wasn't interested. Brynn had made it very clear that, no matter how much chemistry I might've felt when we kissed at the bar, it was all one-sided.

Yet I hadn't been able to shake it off, either.

After we'd kissed that night, I had jerked off frantically in bed as I'd replayed the whole thing in my mind. The little moans she'd made as our tongues glided together. The way she'd melted into me. I'd jerked off again in the shower the next morning. In the days since, I had needed a *lot* of extra long showers. Dean would probably wonder when he saw the water bill.

Now Brynn and I had to share a bed. And a Jacuzzi tub

big enough to fit both of us, naked and soapy and slippery. A picture I should *not* be imagining. I was acting like the horn dog Brynn had accused me of being the first day we met.

Which made me feel even more shitty when there were certain details about my agenda on this mission that I was keeping from her.

I had a strategy, though. I would not initiate any kind of touch, even when we were in character. I would leave that to Brynn. Or rather, Brianna. She was the sweet, vivacious, affectionate one. Meanwhile, Cameron was a possessive grump who got joy from very little. That much, I could handle.

If she was nervous I'd do something inappropriate, I wanted to assure her she had nothing to be concerned about.

"What's up?" I asked. "What are you thinking about?"

"The plan. Contingencies."

"Isn't that what we talked about the entire fourteen hour drive here?" And the five days before that. Certainly hadn't discussed anything personal.

"Yes, but I hate this part of a mission. When we're in the open, on the move, but we haven't encountered the enemy yet. I can't sit still."

That I could understand. Garon Westwick and his head of security would arrive tomorrow. I expected they'd send a man ahead to prep and secure their rooms. That was something I intended to find out today. Until we had eyes on the enemy and had a sense of what we were really dealing with, we'd both be antsy.

Planning was all well and good, but a mission didn't truly take shape until you were in the thick of it.

"We could relax, since that's what Cameron and Brianna came here to do," I said.

Brynn finally glanced at me, eyes flashing. "Relax?"

"Take a bubble bath in the fancy tub." I quickly added, "Just *you,* I mean. Alone. I wasn't suggesting...anything else."

*Smooth, Lynx. Very smooth.*

Her cheeks pinked. "We should take care of that errand. Setting things up for River, like he asked."

"I'll take care of it. I could use a walk around the resort to get a feel for it." I didn't want to leave her alone, but Brynn could handle herself. We could both use some breathing room.

"Then I'll go hang out by the pool. Meet some of the other guests and make some posts for Brianna's socials. I need to change." She took a few things from her bag, went into the bathroom, and came out wearing a silky cover-up. I assumed she had a swimsuit beneath. She grabbed her phone and a room key. "See you in a bit."

"Later."

The door snicked closed.

"Fuck," I muttered. Fifteen minutes into the op, and I already wondered how I was going to make it through days more of this.

---

The rest of my unpacking was next, including the tools I always carried to make adjustments to my prosthesis. With those chores finished, I changed into pool wear. Shorts, a tee, and slip-on shoes. As much as it bugged me to go around unarmed, it couldn't be helped. Damn undercover work. Even a grumpy asshole like Cameron Clay wouldn't carry a gun to the resort pool.

I did have the rest of those important items to unpack, though. Had to find the right kind of hiding place.

Before leaving, I set up a few secondary security measures so we'd know if anyone came into the room. A tiny folded piece of paper, along with one of Brynn's long hairs, positioned carefully in the doorframe. Old school, but effective.

With a small daypack over my shoulder, I walked down the hall, allowing my usual gruff expression to take over my face. Time for some recon.

When I'd been planning my cover over the last few days, I had tried to keep it simple. My usual mantra for most things. There was no way I could pull off playing someone totally different from me. I wasn't Brynn with her acting skills. So Cameron Clay had to be rough around the edges. A loner. He was Brianna Waverley's manager, but he wasn't some fancy agent working at a big talent agency. Cameron was more of an opportunist. The type of guy who had met a pretty, talented girl and latched onto her. Men like that were a dime a dozen in this world, and I had to expect that Garon Westwick would understand it.

He didn't have to like me or believe I was a decent manager. Just had to see that I was possessive of the woman I considered my property. And Westwick would *definitely* understand that.

As far as clothes for my persona, I had gone with warm-weather resort wear. Shorts, cargos, lightweight shirts. Not all that different from what I typically wore in Mexico or Columbia or Belize when I was working. Plus a couple pairs of nicer pants and a sport coat in case I had to dress up. As I strolled around the resort, I was glad to see that I fit right in. While this place was upscale, most of the guests were dressed down. Heading off to the pool, spa appointments, or yoga classes.

I walked the winding paths that led from building to building. The spa was in a separate area, as were the gym and tennis courts. Hiking trails branched away from the property and into the rocky hills. I made a note of possible hiding places, both for myself or for weapons.

Or for stashing a body.

But I lucked out when I walked around the rear of the main building, on the side with the delivery entrance and the employee doors. I spotted a thick metal door marked *Roof Access*. A chain looped around the handle with a padlock securing it. But the padlock wasn't actually locked.

I tugged the door open, finding a stairwell. At the top, another door led onto the flat roof of the main building. It was covered in tarpaper with air conditioning units lining one side. There were some wooden crates turned upside down and positioned in a circle, with a large glass ashtray on one of them. Cigarette butts piled high. A few empty beer bottles and a dry fifth of Jack Daniels.

Unlike the rest of the resort, this was purely a functional space for maintenance and storage, but it looked like the employees had converted it into a break area. Judging by the chain and padlock, they weren't supposed to be up here. Nor was I.

This would do *very* nicely.

I lowered my daypack to the ground, unzipping it. A smaller bag was inside. My personal goody bag. Among other things, it held zip-ties, a gag, and a syringe filled with enough sleepy-time meds to knock out a full-grown man in seconds.

I found a nice hiding spot inside a stack of discarded pieces of metal, ductwork, and other debris. Odds and ends that the maintenance crew had left here instead of hauling offsite. My bag of goodies vanished behind a rectangle of metal. Easy for me to recover later.

Then I took out my smokes and lit one up, taking a seat on a wooden crate. A sense of calm flooded me. Brynn was an epic distraction for many reasons, but I couldn't forget my ultimate goal here.

After she planted that virus on Westwick's devices, and River had gotten whatever access to Stillwater's network that he needed, that wasn't the end of my mission. No matter what Brynn or her former FBI friends had to say about it. I intended to make sure she stayed safe. That was a given.

But afterward, I would personally see that Garon Westwick suffered for every evil thing he'd done. And ensure he never got the chance to repeat it.

# CHAPTER THIRTEEN

AFTER LEAVING THE ROOF, I was careful to shut the access door. Then I took the nearest entrance back inside the main building.

I had one last objective before finding Brynn. I wondered if she was relaxing by the pool right now. If she'd made friends with the other guests already. No doubt, she'd attracted attention.

In our preparations for the mission, River had given us a layout of the resort. One room in particular he'd circled. That was where I headed now. It was in the employee area of the main building. I walked casually down a hallway, ducking into the open doorway of a closet when a couple of cooks rushed past in their kitchen uniforms. Once they were gone, I continued down the hall.

The door I wanted was closed. Locked when I jiggled the handle. I glanced up and down, listening for anyone else coming. River had assured me there were very few cameras around the property except on the primary entrances and exits. But this area was still busy.

When I heard nothing, I took a lock-picking set from my pack. About a minute later, I had the door open. There was some electronic equipment in here. Lots of wires and lights. Not my specialty, but River had been clear about what to do.

Kneeling, I dug into my daypack. Mostly it held the usual stuff. A water bottle and sunblock, plus my cigarettes, though I'd used up my one smoke for today. Part of me wished I'd waited for Brynn to share it with me. But she hadn't done that since the night before we kissed.

At the very bottom of the pack, my hand closed around a small plastic device. I shook my head. River and his gadgets.

I plugged the device into the hotel's modem. Then took out my phone to send a quick message to River. He wrote back, telling me to stand by. Minutes passed. I heard voices out in the hall. Sweat began to bead at the back of my neck. If somebody caught me in here, it wouldn't be easy to explain.

*Come on, Riv. Hurry the hell up.*

Finally, he messaged again, saying we were all clear. He now had access to all the hotel's internet-connected systems. I unplugged the device and stuck it into my pack. Carefully opening the door, I stepped out, re-locking the room as I left.

In the next hallway, a man in navy cargos and a black polo stepped out of a guest room. I barely spared him a glance, though my mind was working fast. His clothing pinned him instantly as security. But I also recognized the guy. The shoulder-length hair, the mole on his chin.

This was one of Garon Westwick's bodyguards, a guy named Troy Manning. Brynn and I had studied the lineup of Westwick's regular security team so that we would be ready. Manning was a former cop who had left the force in disgrace after a corruption scandal.

So he was the advance man that Ryker, Westwick's head of security, had sent. And his room was in the same hall as mine and Brynn's, which suggested Westwick's would be close as well. That could be both good or bad.

"Excuse me. *Sir*."

I froze in the middle of the hall. Looked back over my shoulder.

Manning was striding toward me. "You're staying here?"

I couldn't tell what that look meant. The scrutiny in his expression. But I quickly considered my options. That little spy device in my daypack wouldn't mean anything to most people, but to a security expert?

I turned a little more, adjusting my pack on my shoulder. "What's it to you?"

Brynn and River had both assured me that Stillwater didn't know me. Had no idea that I had struck that Stillwater storage facility with the Protectors last year. But if they'd been wrong? If Westwick's security team had been briefed about the Protectors, and I was among them?

This entire mission could be screwed before it had barely begun.

My breathing slowed as I tried to read the other man. Keeping my hand concealed at my side, I tightened my fingers into a fist.

But then Manning smiled sheepishly, holding up his hands. "No offense. Just curious if you're military." He pointed at my prosthesis, which was clearly visible beneath the hem of my shorts. "My brother lost his left leg above the knee in Iraq."

I turned fully toward him, fingers easing out of their clenched position. "Oh yeah? Appreciate his service. But no, mine was a motorcycle accident."

I felt him looking me over. Assessing. I'd been out of the Army for five years, and my hair and beard had grown out, but some of those military habits were hard to break. A way of standing, of carrying myself that could give me away. I cocked my hip.

He nodded like I'd passed. "Tough break, man. Do you still ride?"

I chuckled, trying to keep to my Cameron Clay persona. "My girl wishes I didn't. Good thing she doesn't make the rules. I do."

Manning laughed, and we kept chatting. He wanted to tell me all about his motorcycle. *And* his girl, who was waiting for him back home in Vegas.

Did Manning know he worked for the head of Stillwater? As a bodyguard, he would see plenty. Ryker, Manning's boss, had threatened the nanny who Westwick had been keeping prisoner. Maybe Manning had been involved in that. He'd been a corrupt cop before his bodyguard days.

He was a threat, no question. But was he also a potential weakness I could exploit?

"I travel a lot for work though," Manning was saying, "so what my girl doesn't know doesn't concern her. If you know what I mean."

"Right on." I grinned, wondering if I would end up killing this guy too. "That's what you're doing here in Arizona? Working?"

The door across the hall opened, and another face appeared. One even more recognizable, making my pulse leap and my muscles involuntarily clench tight.

Donovan Ryker stood there, frowning at the two of us.

Manning jumped, since he'd just been caught goofing off. "Ryke! Hey. Didn't see you there."

"Who is this?" Ryker asked, staring at me, his voice oily and threatening. A man who didn't mess around. My initial shock had faded, and now I was wary, my mind spinning out what this could mean.

Ryker wasn't supposed to have arrived until tomorrow.

But Cameron Clay wasn't the type to cede an inch, even around a tough guy, so I just stared back. "I don't know, who the hell are you?"

Manning laughed and clapped me on the shoulder. "This

guy is funny, Ryke. He's staying down the hall. We were just chatting."

Ryker's hard gaze turned to his employee. "Then I suggest you get back to what you should be doing."

Manning practically clicked his heels together and took off down the hall. What was he up to? Prepping security for Westwick's arrival?

Unless the head of Stillwater had already arrived. A whole day early. Dammit, I wanted eyes on Brynn.

Ryker stepped out, closing the door most of the way behind him. He looked me up and down, pausing on my prosthetic leg, but unlike Manning he didn't comment on it. Instead his scrutiny increased. There was a long pause.

"What was your name again?" he asked.

"I didn't say. What's yours?"

Ryker didn't answer.

I didn't intend to antagonize the man. But there was no buddying up to him, either. He would've found that more suspicious.

I lifted my chin. "Whatever, man. My girl's waiting for me by the pool."

"Enjoy yourself," Ryker said, though his tone suggested I do something else to myself entirely.

If Ryker had recognized me as someone affiliated with the Protectors, then I would find that out very soon.

I had to get to Brynn.

---

When I reached the pool, Brynn was sitting in a cabana, holding court like the most popular girl in school. Relief flooded me at the sight of her, just knowing she was safe.

I'd had no reason to suspect otherwise, but dammit, I had a weakness for this woman.

I slowed my pace as my mouth went dry. Her cover-up was open, revealing a pale pink bikini underneath. She had her sunglasses perched on her head, legs tucked sideways in her chair as she laughed at whatever the woman beside her was saying. Several other guests looked on. They all held drinks like they'd been relaxing here for a while.

She gave me a playful look when she spotted me. Waved me over. "Cameron, there you are! I was just telling everyone about you. They're here for the seminar too. This is—"

"Need to talk to you, B," I interrupted. "Now."

She pouted. "But baby, I want to introduce you to my new friends."

"*Now*, B," I repeated.

The two couples around her shifted uncomfortably, clearly unsure of how to handle my rudeness. They were older, maybe fifties or sixties. I vaguely remembered their names from the guest profiles we'd reviewed. They seemed harmless enough.

But this was an opportunity for me to establish my character as an asshole *and* get her alone to warn her. I was a fan of efficiency.

Brynn sighed, unfolding her legs and standing up slowly. The fabric of her cover-up swished around her, and the triangles of her bikini top tightened on her breasts. "Sorry, everyone. Cameron isn't known for his patience." She laughed it off, managing to come across as sad, embarrassed, and hopeful all at the same time. "We'll be back soon."

"We'll save your seat, dear," a woman said, shooting me a glare to make her disapproval known.

Yeah, Cameron Clay was a jerk. There was no denying it.

Brynn grabbed my arm, and we walked to a quiet corner of the pool area. "That might've been slightly more dickish than necessary," she said. "You're supposed to come across as possessive, not pathological."

"I needed your attention." My eyes flicked down to the cleft between her breasts. A few tiny beads of sweat dotted her golden skin. And below that, the smooth expanse of her belly…

"What's going on?" she asked, forcing me back to the moment.

*Focus, Lynx.*

"Donovan Ryker is here already. Which means Westwick might be here."

Her fingernails dug into my arm. "*What?*"

I put my arm around her and drew her closer so I could speak into her ear. "I saw Ryker in the hall just now. Plus another bodyguard from Westwick's security team, Manning. According to your intel, Ryker was supposed to arrive with Westwick."

"They always travel together." Brynn bit her lip. "That means Westwick changed his schedule. I wonder if something's up."

"That's my thought as well. So much for us settling in." It was a good thing we had gotten here today. Yesterday would've been better, though. We'd barely had any time to get our bearings.

"But he's still having the seminar on Saturday morning, I assume?" she asked.

"I have no idea. I came straight here after seeing Ryker. He seemed suspicious of me. No clue how much to read into that."

"From what I've heard, Ryker is just paranoid that way. It's why Westwick trusts him so much. But the change in timing…" She shivered, leaning into me. "I don't like it. We need to inform the Protectors and the—" She closed her mouth on whatever she'd been about to say.

"And who else?" I asked. "The task force? We agreed they

wouldn't be involved any further." The last thing I wanted was the FBI butting into this mission.

"Relax, Cameron," she said with a tight smile. She played with the collar of my T-shirt. "People are watching."

I resisted the urge to look. She was right. We were in public. This wasn't the time or place. "We should go back to the room."

"Later," she whispered. "We've drawn enough interest already. But I'm glad you're here." I didn't know if she was being Brianna or herself. Either way, her words calmed me.

"Me too."

She gave me a soft kiss on the cheek that made my spine straighten.

I wanted to shield her. Drag her away from here and deal with Garon Westwick and his thugs myself. But I couldn't do it without her. I knew that.

This woman had me tied up in knots, and there was no way out but ahead.

# CHAPTER FOURTEEN

## *Brynn*

COLE WAS ON EDGE, and I didn't like it.

I feathered the longer strands of hair on top of his head. "Do you need a cigarette? I can get you one."

His eyes closed briefly. "Already had one today."

"I know. I can smell it." I leaned closer and breathed him in. Partly because we still had an audience over in the cabana. But partly just...because.

"I'm good, B."

He wasn't used to being undercover. But he had plenty of experience with plans going to shit. So it didn't surprise me that he was already shaking off the bump in our schedule. If Westwick was early, we would adjust. We could handle anything that came our way. I believed that.

Except maybe this insistent chemistry between us. It was confusing and overwhelming, and I couldn't seem to avoid it. No matter how much I'd been trying to.

I still had my fingers in his hair. Cole took my hand by the wrist and tugged it gently down. Okay, message received. He didn't want me touching him unless absolutely necessary. Maybe I'd been laying it on a bit thick today.

I had a thing for this guy. A stupid, inconvenient crush. It could become a problem if I let it, so I *wouldn't* let it. I'd made a rule for myself. When we were alone, I had to steer clear. For my own sanity, not to mention the sake of the mission.

Yet my eyes wandered over him. He'd rolled up his sleeves, revealing those sexy tattoos on his forearms. An eagle in flight on the right side, and on his left, the words *Always Endeavor*.

"Introduce me to your friends, Brianna." Cole smirked. "I'll decide if they're worthy of you."

In other words, back to our cover story. "Sure, baby. Whatever you want."

The skin around his eyes tightened, almost a flinch, and I had no idea what it meant.

I spun on the ball of my strappy sandal and made my way back to the cabana. I managed not to react when I felt his warm hand slide into mine.

At moments like this, our cover stories gave me the perfect excuse to give in to temptation. Even if Cole didn't seem to enjoy the contact. He'd been acting uncomfortable since we'd arrived at the resort. He was attracted to me. That much was obvious. I'd seen the way he admired my body just now in my bikini. That hunger in his gaze. But he didn't *want* to be attracted to me. And that, I could sympathize with. This would be easier if I weren't attracted to him either.

We stepped into the cabana. It was raised from the rest of the pool area, the sides draped with white fabric that billowed in the slight breeze. Every eye turned toward us.

"Hi again, everyone." I hugged his arm, tugging him closer. "Cameron just got word about a sponsor pulling out of a collaboration with me, and he gets very defensive on my behalf." I smiled at him, fluttering my lashes. "Baby, I told them all about how you're my manager."

He grunted some kind of response, which was good enough. I planned to talk enough for the both of us.

The tactical part of my brain wanted to know if Westwick had really arrived early, and why. Why had the man scheduled this seminar at the last minute, only to change his plans? Hopefully River could work his magic and find out more. Same with Stanford and the task force, though I'd have to be more careful there.

I was anxious for the next piece of intel for our mission. But right now, I had to act natural. So did Cole. We had to sell this.

I went around introducing Cole, or rather Cameron, to the four people I'd met so far, all of them already profiled as attendees of the small business seminar. The most outspoken was Molly, a woman in her fifties from Dallas with the teased hair to match. She was here with her husband, co-owner of her chain of bakeries that she hoped to expand with Westwick's entrepreneurial advice.

It frustrated me that these kind people were paying money to hear someone like Garon Westwick speak. I didn't like lying to them either. Putting on this show as Brianna and being something I wasn't. But if everything went well, these resort guests would have no idea we'd lied. They could go home in blissful ignorance. No clue that they'd come so close to an evil organization like Stillwater.

And Cole wouldn't need to know I'd been updating SAC Stanford this whole time, either. I'd brought the burner phone Stanford had given me. It was inside a sock in the hotel room, hidden from my partner and password protected. Another lie to dig at my conscience. But it was a practical one.

If we got desperate enough to need FBI backup, Cole would thank me.

We settled back onto the couch, me tucked against Cole's

side and practically in his lap. I draped my arm around his shoulders, feeling him tense up as he had been all day. Well, he was just going to have to get used to it.

"Cameron, isn't it a bit unusual for you to be dating Brianna if she's your client?" Molly asked. "Or am I mistaken about that? Especially since you're so much more mature than her?" She put an emphasis on the word *mature*. According to our covers, he was supposed to have about fifteen years on me.

Molly had mentioned that she had a daughter in college, and I'd gotten the sense that she was a mama bear type. From the way she had her eyes narrowed at Cole, our cover story was working. They'd accepted me as the young, naive twenty-something with a domineering jerk for a boyfriend.

"Isn't it rude for you to ask bullshit questions like that?"

Molly huffed, looking to her husband to defend her, but her other half was sucking down the rest of his rum runner.

"Don't mind Cam," I said. "He can be nice when he wants. I guess he bewitched me." I dragged my fingertip down the back of his neck.

Cole's eyes locked with mine, full of intensity. That look of his that could drive me wild. It tugged at something deep within me like a magnet.

Damn the man. He was so uncomfortable with me one moment, then hit me with that lust-filled gaze the next. Knocking me off balance.

Neither of us noticed at first when the others' heads turned, and new voices spoke on the patio. Excitement filled my veins, along with something uglier. More bloodthirsty.

Garon Westwick, the leader of Stillwater, stood just a few yards away. His ash-blond hair was slicked back from his face, his chinos neatly pressed. So unassuming. Like a suburban dad more than a high-powered investor. Certainly nothing like what you'd expect a dark-web criminal mastermind to be.

But that was how men like him always operated. Right there in plain sight, pretending to be righteous, hiding their evil behind closed doors as if their power would always protect them.

I'd thought so many times about how this moment would go. Should I hang back, play the shy card? Wait for him to notice me? But as I sat there, I knew that was the wrong way to go.

Cole put his hand on my knee, his palm hot against my bare skin. Like he already knew what I planned to do and wanted to stop me. But I was going to follow my instincts.

I jumped up and walked straight over to him. "Mr. Westwick, right? Sorry, I just couldn't wait to meet you. I'm Brianna Waverley. I'm signed up for your seminar."

Westwick had been chatting quietly with Donovan Ryker, his head of security, who towered over the other man. As soon as I approached, they went silent. I'd been careful to leave my cover-up hanging open, my bikini on full display. Westwick did a quick sweep of my body, and his clean-shaven face broke into a grin.

"Miss Waverley. Yes, I'm Garon. I'm happy to meet someone who's excited to hear me speak. I hope I live up to it." He laughed self-deprecatingly. Both his hands closed around mine, and I worked hard to keep my smile in place, though I was cringing with disgust on the inside.

I had looked killers in the face before. As a special agent, I had interrogated them. Heard them recount, with no remorse and a charming smile, the monstrous things they had done. I saw that same glassiness in Westwick's dilated pupils right now. Dead eyes that hid the depths of cruelty beneath. This was the guy who'd ordered kidnappers and killers to go after my best friend.

Oh, I was going to enjoy taking him down.

"It's a pleasure," I said.

"I promise, the pleasure is all mine."

Cole came up behind me. I felt his hand rest protectively on my waist, his body angling next to mine, as if he wanted to be sure he was in place to step in front of me at a moment's notice.

"Mr. Westwick, this is my manager and boyfriend. Cameron Clay."

"Cameron, is it?"

"That's right," Cole said.

The head of Stillwater shook Cole's hand. The men's knuckles turned white as they gripped each other's fingers. Behind his boss, Ryker shifted closer.

Molly and her husband hurried over to meet Westwick and ask questions about the upcoming event on Saturday. Cole's arm snaked around my waist and his hand splayed on my bare stomach. He subtly pulled me back from the group.

"You could've given me some warning you were going to do that," he murmured into my ear. "You ran straight for him."

"I had to make sure he noticed me."

"Oh trust me, he did."

After a few minutes, Westwick clapped his hands together. "I'd love to have you all join me for dinner tonight. My treat." He'd included everyone in our group, but his eyes connected with mine as he spoke, like it was an invitation directly to me.

---

"That was way too easy."

Cole paced across the room in his long black pants and

cream linen shirt. I swiped mascara onto my lashes in the bathroom mirror.

"I planned everything about my appearance and cover story to appeal to him. Is it that surprising that Westwick took the bait?"

"But I was standing right there. You would think he'd be a touch more subtle about it. The guy already has designs on my girlfriend after meeting you for all of five minutes."

I chuckled. Cole sounded like he was taking personal offense. Like this wasn't exactly what we'd wanted. "I did my best to give him the right signals. You should be glad I know what I'm doing." Westwick wasn't the type to get pulled in by a femme fatale. I had to make him believe I was a sweet ingenue who looked up to him for his business success. All the better for him to take advantage of me.

*Yuck*. I tasted bile in my mouth.

But soon, if this all went well, the state and federal authorities would have enough evidence against the man to put him away for good and shut down Stillwater forever.

Cole grumbled something inaudible as he paced.

I finished with my makeup and fluffed my hair. I really wasn't used to the blond, and the texture was off too from the bleach. "Westwick moved up his timetable for a reason, and I doubt it was for more vacation time. We have no idea how the rest of his schedule might change. He might even leave the resort earlier than we expected. We have to take this chance at him while we've got it."

Cole stopped in the doorway to the bathroom, visible behind me in the mirror. "I agree. But is it possible, even remotely, that any of your double agents inside Stillwater tipped off Ryker and his security team? Could we have walked into a trap?"

His concern was valid. Cole was asking the same questions I'd been asking myself. It would be foolish if we didn't consider it. But I'd already dismissed it.

"No. Our sources inside Stillwater never spoke to me directly. They would have no idea about my cover identity or that you were involved. Besides that, the FBI has a very tight leash on all our double agents."

But I would have to confirm it with Stanford though. Make sure our double agents were still cooperating and accounted for. I just hated doing that behind Cole's back.

"You know...I could touch base with the task force," I suggested, testing the waters.

But he leveled a glare in the mirror. "No way. Let's wait to hear back from River. See what he can find out through his channels. The FBI is far more likely to charge in here and make a mess of this, while screwing us over in the process."

"Except I trust them."

"And I *don't*. We already agreed this is a Protectors op only."

I exhaled, summoning patience. Yes, we'd agreed. And we had contacted River about Westwick's early appearance at the resort. River had promised to look into it. Since Cole was so uptight about anyone associated with the FBI, I would discreetly text Stanford my update later.

What else could we do right now, aside from continue trying to get access to Westwick?

I turned around and smoothed my hands over Cole's shirt. His spine went rigid. "Relax. Your nice clothes are getting wrinkled from all your fussing."

"I don't fuss."

My palms ran over his broad chest. Why did the man have to be so sexy, even when he was being impossible? His tongue traced his lower lip, and I backed away.

"There. All set." I grabbed my purse, which held Brianna's phone and room key. Of course, the flash drive River had given me was hidden inside the lining, along with a multi-purpose adapter that would connect to Westwick's phone and other devices. If I had a chance tonight to upload River's virus, I had to be ready.

"Wait," Cole said.

I turned around.

He brought his hands to the shoulders of my dress. It was made of semi-sheer fabric, just flirty enough to tease the outlines of my undergarments beneath. He tucked my bra straps in. Then he carefully lifted his hands away, avoiding any other contact.

"Now we can go."

"Thanks." I opened the door, ignoring the thickness in my throat.

# CHAPTER FIFTEEN
## Brynn

IN THE RESTAURANT, Westwick had reserved a long table in a private dining room. Molly and her husband were here, plus the handful of other seminar guests who'd arrived today. Westwick sat at the head of the table, and the rest of us gathered around. His bodyguards were nowhere in sight, but I had to expect they were skulking around somewhere close.

"You should have your arm around me," I whispered to Cole. With a huff, he obliged. The weight of his arm settled on my shoulders, and his fingers gripped my upper arm.

"See? That wasn't so bad."

The corner of his mouth quirked up. The first smile I'd seen from him all evening. Thankfully, Molly was talking loudly enough on my other side to drown out my comments to Cole.

Through drinks and appetizers, I asked Westwick questions about his background and investments. Of course, I already knew all the answers from River's research and my preparations. The other seminar guests kept things going from there, and Westwick seemed pleased to be surrounded by admirers. He went on and on about research and development. Emerging technologies. The importance of taking on risky opportunities.

Only Cole was quiet, giving off grumpy vibes beside me and barely joining in the conversation. Which was on point for Cameron Clay. But I pretended to be fascinated. The whole time, Westwick gave me plenty of attention, his eyes always returning to mine.

After we'd finished dinner and the plates were cleared, someone proposed going to the lounge for more drinks and dancing. I leaned over to Molly and gave her my most dazzling smile. "Are you coming too?"

"I could be convinced."

"You have to." I looked over at Westwick. "What about our host? You're not going to miss dancing, are you?"

Cole coughed. Yeah, I knew what he was thinking. I was giving myself a toothache with all this sugary sweetness. It was so not me.

But thankfully, the head of Stillwater was eating it up. "I wouldn't want to disappoint," Westwick said. "And please, Brianna, call me Garon."

Cole's hand tightened possessively on my shoulder.

The lounge had the vibe of an old-school jazz club, with brown leather chairs and low lighting. Our group had winnowed to a half dozen. We started with a round of brandy, which gave me plenty of opportunities to ask Westwick about the liquor and where it came from. A man like him loved nothing more than to prove how sophisticated and intelligent he was. Cole and I both took tiny sips so we'd stay sober.

I couldn't have asked for a better setup. Alcohol to loosen Westwick up, and dancing to get close. A chance to talk alone even in a crowded room.

Ryker and the other bodyguard, Manning, had appeared, sitting like lumps in boxy suits at another table, but that was fine. Cole was in the seat next to me, his thigh up against mine.

I just had to be patient. Wait for Westwick to ask to dance with me. I'd baited the hook earlier. Now I had to reel him in.

But then, shockingly, Cole beat him to it.

He held out his hand. "Feel like dancing?"

I paused a moment before realizing what he had in mind. Stoking Westwick's competitiveness. "Love to." I took Cole's hand. Westwick's eyes followed me as I left. I didn't see it so much as feel it.

We walked over to the small dance floor where a few couples were swaying to the jazz singer crooning from a small stage. Cole's hands rested on my hips. Steady and firm. I laced my fingers together behind his neck.

"Good idea," I said. "Reminding Westwick I'm taken."

"Figured I could be useful. Even if I still hate this idea."

"It'll be worth it in the end."

Cole hummed. Whether he was skeptical or agreeing, I couldn't tell. His fingers tapped lightly against my lower back along with the beat.

This was the first time we'd been pressed up against each other like this, chest to chest and belly to belly, since the night we'd kissed. It felt nice. More than nice.

I let the music sink into me. The warmth of Cole's embrace.

I noticed more couples joining us. Westwick was dancing with Molly just a few feet away, yet they seemed farther than that. Like Cole and I were inside our own bubble. It was tempting to forget where we were. Like Cole kept pulling me to some other place where Stillwater didn't exist and I could simply enjoy the moment without fear of what came next. How did he do that? And why did I keep responding this way?

I brushed my fingers down the back of Cole's neck, and he made a sound too low for anyone to hear but me.

The song ended way too soon, and a shadow fell over me. "Mind if I cut in?" Westwick asked. "More fun if we all change up partners, don't you think?"

Alertness filled me, chasing away the brief calm I'd felt. Cole and I shared a lightning-fast, silent communication.

"I don't think so, no," Cole said dismissively.

"Please Cameron?" I turned my widest eyes on him. "You said you were tired of dancing anyway. You wanted to get a drink, right?"

His hands briefly tightened on my waist before he let go "One dance." With a scowl at Westwick, Cole stalked toward the bar. But Westwick just smiled as he watched Cole leave.

"I don't think Cameron is a fan of mine."

"I'm sorry. He just...doesn't like me talking to other men sometimes." I smiled shyly.

"I'm not causing a problem for you, am I?"

"No, it's okay. Cam will get over it. He usually does."

Westwick's touch on my waist was a stark contrast to Cole's. Cold and clammy through my dress instead of warm. I rested my hands on the man's shoulders. Swayed with the music. All the time wishing I had a knife I could stick in his back.

But the long strap of my purse rested against my torso, a reminder of what was inside. That virus was all the revenge we needed.

"Cameron is your manager, correct?" he asked. "How long has he represented you?"

"For about a year." I repeated a few details of how Brianna and Cameron had met, how she'd fallen for him. "He's been good to me."

"I'm sure. But did Cameron actually want to attend this

seminar with you? Or was it your idea?" He angled his head toward me like we were sharing a secret.

"I guess it was mine."

"He doesn't seem all that happy to be here."

"He helped me take my business to the next level. Make more contacts in the industry. But…" I pretended to hesitate.

"Yes?"

"Never mind. I should be grateful for everything he's done for me."

We rotated in a slow circle to the music, and Cole came into view. He was leaning back against the bar, arms crossed as he watched us. Westwick moved his grip from my waist to my lower hips. *Keep going, asshole,* I thought. *I dare you.*

On the other side of the room, Ryker and Manning hunched together at a table, watching us too.

"You know, Brianna, you can't allow another person to hold you back from what you want."

"That's why I wanted to attend your seminar. I follow a lot of entrepreneurs online, study their advice, but yours resonated with me."

"Really." His focus on me sharpened. "You know, this afternoon I took a look at your Instagram account. You've built a nice little following. Your lifestyle brand could go far. But you have to consider your future. Is Cameron the best manager to achieve your goals?"

I tried to look guilty. "I'm not sure."

"We could meet up to discuss options, but it would have to be without your current manager. Cameron is likely to discourage you from changing anything. Especially if it would diminish his control over your career."

*There we go,* I thought. *Was the man truly this easy?*

I thought of Cole's worry—that we were walking into a trap. That Westwick and Ryker already knew our real identities.

"You think he's trying to control me?" I asked.

"Something as beautiful as you?" Westwick purred into my ear. "What man wouldn't want to own that?"

It took all my willpower not to push him away. Or better yet, pull him closer and squeeze him by the jugular. *Remember the mission,* I told myself. *It'll be worth it when we destroy him.* But my defiant heart just couldn't let that pass. Without thinking, I asked, "Are you saying *you* want to own me? Shouldn't a person get to be in control of her own career? Her own life?" A hint of genuine anger had sneaked into my tone.

Thankfully, he laughed. "I like you, Brianna. You're feistier than I imagined you were."

I smiled and shrugged. As if I'd been teasing him.

His long fingers massaged circles into my hip, just over my behind. "I think we'd get along very well together. *Very* well. If you can get time away from your overbearing manager this weekend, then we can talk business. See what we can do for each other."

"I'll…" Fighting back my disgust, I finished my sentence. "Think about it, Mr. Westwick."

"I'm sure you will. And you'd better call me Garon." His phone made a noise. Westwick took it from his inner blazer pocket to look at it. He frowned. I tried to get a glimpse of the screen, but he kept it covered. "I'm sorry, Brianna. Forgive me for being rude, but I'd better take this."

"Oh? Is it important?"

"The kind of thing that can't wait." With a wink that he probably thought was charming, he walked toward the exit. He waved at his bodyguards, signaling that he didn't need them.

Cole was still watching me, but I went casually toward the restrooms.

As soon as I was in the hallway, out of sight of Westwick's

security, I jogged past the bathrooms and went through the door at the opposite end, which led back to the lobby. I wanted to know who had called Westwick. What was so important that he had to deal with it right now?

Did it have something to do with his decision to move up his arrival?

I heard Westwick's voice just around the corner. "When exactly will you get here tomorrow?" Then a pause while he listened to the answer. "No problem. Of course. But—"

The rest of what he was saying faded out as he moved. Westwick was walking away. I heard his footsteps receding. Edging forward, I peered around the corner. But the man was gone.

"Can I help you, Ms. Waverley?"

I spun around and found the clerk who had checked us into the reception earlier. Lance, the one who'd been ogling my cleavage. I smiled. "I was just looking for my boyfriend Cameron. He wandered off."

I hoped Lance didn't realize that Cole and the others were in the lounge. Or that I'd been spying on Garon Westwick.

He eyed me, but I couldn't tell if it was skepticism or interest. "Have you tried your room? I haven't seen him pass by."

I brightened. "Of course. Silly me. Have a good night."

I took off before he could ask any more questions.

The hallway was deserted as I walked toward the guest rooms. A few voices murmured behind closed doors. I listened for Westwick, unsure which room was his.

I thought I could hear his baritone.

I came to a stop, pressing my ear against that room. But there was nothing. Dang it. I'd been hoping to hear more of Westwick's conversation. He was expecting someone tomorrow, someone *important*, which could explain his early arrival. Did it have something to do with Stillwater?

I had to get back to the lounge and find Cole. Let him know what I'd learned.

But when I turned, I nearly ran into a wall of muscle. "Just what are you doing there, Ms. Waverley?" Donovan Ryker asked. "Because it looked like you were listening at Mr. Westwick's door."

Shit. How had I failed to hear the man approach? *Because he's a trained mercenary*, I answered myself.

Time to bluff. And above all, stay calm. "He left the lounge to take a phone call. I was just hoping to catch him. Continue our conversation. But it's fine, I can wait." I tried to walk around the man, but he grabbed my upper arm.

"Ow, let go of me!"

"What's your interest in Mr. Westwick?"

"None of your business."

"It's very much my business who gets close to my boss." Ryker pushed me up against the wall hard enough my head smacked the drywall. I could've fought back with equal force and then some. But Brianna Waverley didn't have training in hand-to-hand combat. If I used any of my skills, it would blow my cover.

Ryker opened his mouth to say something else. Then he suddenly wrenched away from me. Cole slammed the man into the opposite wall of the hallway, his teeth gritted in a snarl.

"Get your fucking hands off her."

Lance, the hotel clerk, appeared at the end of the hallway. "What's going on here?"

Ryker took a menacing step toward Cole, who didn't back down. "This piece of shit attacked my girlfriend."

I reached for Cole's arm. "It's a misunderstanding."

"It was," Ryker said, a warning in his voice. "And I trust it won't happen again." With a last glare in my direction, he stalked toward the lobby.

"Do I need to call the authorities?" The clerk's tone conveyed that was the last thing he wanted to do, and he visibly relaxed when I shook my head. Doors started to open up and down the hall, heads peeking out to see what was happening.

"No. We're going to our room." I pulled Cole down the hall. I had to get us both out of there before we did something stupid. Like following Ryker and continuing that fight, because one thing was certain—it wasn't over.

# CHAPTER SIXTEEN

WHEN WE MADE it back to the room, Brynn went inside first. I gave her a nudge to go ahead of me, and she frowned over her shoulder. But I wasn't letting that woman out of my sight again.

I slammed the door closed. Locked it, then flipped the security bar. Once all that was finished, I turned around and leaned against it.

"What the hell were you thinking?" I asked.

She went over to the bed and sat on the edge of it, kicking off her sandals and setting her purse aside. "I was doing my job."

"Without telling me what you were planning?"

It had been awful enough watching her dance with Westwick. Seeing the man touch her, while knowing the things he was responsible for. This whole time I'd known Brynn would play the honeypot. And there she was, laying the trap. Being as sweet and naive as possible to draw him in. I could imagine the possibilities that had been running through the man's mind, and it had made me sick.

"Westwick got a phone call," she said. "He mentioned it was important. I had to try to learn more."

"Did you?"

"Not as much as I would've liked."

I ran my fingers through my hair. I'd seen Westwick leave to take the call. I'd seen Brynn's curiosity too, but she'd gone for the bathrooms. I had wondered if she was foolish enough to try following the man when his bodyguards were just yards away. But I'd decided to give her space.

Then Ryker had left the bar. Brynn hadn't come back. And that had been enough for me.

"You should've let me know," I said. "You could've signaled me."

"I couldn't risk it. Ryker and Manning were right there watching us."

That was a fair point, but I was still pissed. "I'm supposed to be your backup. How can I back you up when I don't even know where you are? Anything could've happened in those few minutes."

"You got here in time, didn't you? I'd say it went fine. I was trying to take advantage of an opportunity. I'm trained for this. The only thing at risk was my cover. If I'd had to kick Ryker's ass, it would've meant a lot more questions."

Her voice was all confidence, yet her hands were shaking. I suspected it was anger rather than fear. The fight in the hallway had affected her far more than she wanted to admit. But it had affected me too. *Terrified* me when I hadn't been able to find her.

I walked over to her. Sat beside her on the bed. "There was a lot more at risk than just your cover."

She exhaled a shuddering breath.

"Brynn, listen—"

She interrupted me. "Clearly we've made an enemy of Ryker, but I can fix this. I'll smooth things over with Westwick. The important thing is, I don't think Ryker suspects I'm an undercover operative. He thinks I'm a nosy kid who's going to overhear the wrong thing."

"Our cover isn't my primary concern right now."

But she went on. "If anything, Westwick will take it as a good sign that I came to his hotel room. He'll think he's got me wrapped around his finger already." She stood up, hugging her elbows, eyes darting over the room. "I could act shy around him tomorrow. Intimidated, even. He'll like that. We can spin this so that it's—"

My jaw creaked as I gnashed my teeth together. I closed the distance between us. The absolute fury I'd felt in that hallway, the sheer violence I had wanted to inflict on Ryker for hurting her, it all reared up inside me again.

I spun her around to face the full-length mirror on the wall. "Look at this, Brynn." I lifted the strap of her dress so her shoulder was clear in the reflection. Red marks showed where Ryker's fingers had been digging in. "If Ryker was so brazen in a public hotel hallway, what would he do if he caught you with that flash drive? What if I can't reach you then?"

I'd barely been able to stand watching Westwick with her. After knowing her for a couple of hours, the man was already trying to seduce her. I could only imagine what that trash had planned for her.

But later, when I'd walked down that hallway, found Ryker with his hand squeezing her shoulder and the look of terror on her face, my guts had dropped to somewhere near the southern hemisphere.

When I'd pulled Ryker off her, I hadn't been thinking about the mission. Only Brynn.

How she had felt in my arms when we had been dancing. How I'd wanted to keep her safe. Not just as her undercover partner, but as a man who wanted to shield a woman he was starting to care about.

"We're supposed to be teammates in this, remember?" I asked. "Equals. Yet you're taking the brunt of the risk."

"I can handle it."

"I know you can. That doesn't make it sit well with me."

"I'm sorry this mission isn't satisfying your need to be the hero."

"It's more than just that! I want you, and I don't want *any* other men touching you."

Hell. I'd shouted that loud enough for anyone in the hallway to hear. My control was near its breaking point. My face burned, and I saw my own reflection in the mirror. Wild eyes and flushed skin like I was barely keeping my shit together. Because I *wasn't*.

Brynn's body rose and fell against my chest. Breathing hard. I eased my grip on her, letting my hands fall. But I still stood there right behind her, our bodies touching. Her expression in the mirror was a mix of confusion and frustration.

"You're saying that because of our cover stories," she said softly. "Getting close, acting like we're in a relationship. It's intense."

"I shouldn't crave you like this. We barely know each other. But I can't pretend I don't feel it." The words came out like they'd been raked across gravel. I forced myself to take a step back. My eyes found hers in the mirror.

All I could do was keep going. Finish my confession, because it was entirely possible she'd tell me what an inappropriate asshole I was being.

"Maybe you're right and it's this fake relationship thing, and it's got all the wires crossed in my brain after less than a single day. All I know is that you're someone to me, someone who *matters*, and I protect what's *mine*."

Brynn turned. Took an unsteady step toward me.

And crushed her mouth to my lips.

My hands shot out to catch her, while my mouth moved against hers, ready to take whatever she would give me. I'd been aching for this, and being able to touch her, taste her—it was such a relief. An instant release of all the tension that had been winding tighter inside me for days.

I walked us backward to the bed. Landed heavily on the edge of the mattress, pulling her down beside me. She had two handfuls of my shirt, and I eased her fists open. Laced our fingers instead as our mouths sought out the different ways we could fit together.

Her breaths came too quick. Almost frantic. I smoothed my fingers through her hair and pressed a kiss to the corner of her mouth, then her chin, moving down the column of her throat. Arousal pumped in my veins. Kissing her had only affirmed what I already knew. I craved this woman, and it was hopeless to deny it. But it wasn't just about sex, either. Scratching some itch. I respected her. I *liked* her.

This might end badly. Probably would end badly, in fact. A dangerous undercover op was a terrible time to start something between us. What if this was just the roles we were playing, messing with our heads?

But was it better to keep ignoring the pull I felt toward her? I'd tried doing that. Hadn't worked. I was a straightforward guy at heart, and when I wanted a woman, I let her know.

Yet no matter how much urgency I felt, I couldn't be rough with her either. I usually wasn't great at being gentle, but that was what she deserved.

"This is such a bad idea." Her breath puffed near my collarbone.

"Maybe. Probably." My lips brushed a featherlight kiss just above the bruises on her shoulder. "But there's no pressure, B. You can think about what you want. If that's me, I'll be here."

"You just threw an awful lot at me. Serious words like *mine*."

"At least I didn't talk shit about the Bureau. Or call you honey."

Her mouth quirked. "Thinking would be good. I need to take a few minutes. With you right there, it's a lot of temptation." She got up, took some clothes from a drawer, and went to the bathroom, shutting the door behind her.

I blew out a breath, hoping I hadn't screwed everything up.

Perhaps it would've been smarter to keep my mouth shut. Keep what I wanted to myself. I knew the woman had trust issues, though I didn't know all the details of why.

But tonight, *she* had kissed *me*. Not because we had an audience. Not because it was our cover story. It had just been us. I'd told her how much I wanted her, but she'd been the one to pull me closer.

In my book, that meant something.

---

While Brynn was in the bathroom, I quickly stripped out of my pants and shirt, hanging both in the closet. For sleeping clothes, I'd brought sweatpants. So I pulled those on over my boxers.

Brynn came out, pausing when she saw me. Her fingertips ghosted over her shoulder. I wondered what I could do to take the sting away.

"Do you need ice? Is that bothering you?"

"It's nothing. Just a little sore." Her eyes darted over my bare chest.

I could've let my gaze linger on her too, because she looked good as always. A loose tank top, cotton shorts. Face scrubbed of makeup. But I sensed uncertainty from her, so I went to the bathroom myself and took care of getting ready for bed.

I splashed water over my face and neck, washing off the day's sweat and frustration. I was glad to put Westwick, Ryker and Stillwater out of my mind for the night.

But Brynn? She was in my head. Under my skin. Everywhere.

My cock perked up. But we would just have to wait and see.

After brushing my teeth, I opened the bathroom door. Brynn was sitting in a chair and staring off into space, deep in thought.

"If you'd rather not share the bed—" I began.

"I'm okay with it."

I chewed my lip. "All right. I'll stay on my side."

"Maybe I don't want you to."

My nerve endings lit up like sparklers. "You just let me know." I sat on the edge of the mattress and rucked up the left leg of my sweats. This was the first time she would see me without my prosthesis. But no point in hesitating.

I pushed a button on the side of the socket to release the pin and slid off the device, followed by the sock and the liner. I felt her looking. I could've tugged my pant leg down to cover up, but fuck that. Better she get an eyeful and decide now if she had an issue.

I was a confident guy. I'd been with women since my divorce, and they'd found me plenty attractive. But my wife had left me within two months of seeing my injury. That kind of thing wasn't easy for a man to forget.

"I'm not winning any beauty contests anymore," I joked. "That ship has sailed."

Brynn huffed. "Are you kidding? You might be the sexiest man I've ever seen."

I smirked, glowing with pride at her words. "Might?"

"I would need to get closer to find out."

"I've got no objections to that."

But Brynn stayed in her chair for several long seconds, long enough I thought she had decided to let the moment pass.

Then she got up.

Taking slow strides, she crossed the space. Stood between my spread knees and put her hands on my shoulders, assessing me. "Somehow," she murmured, "you keep getting sexier every day that I know you."

"Glad it's not the opposite."

When her brown eyes lifted after her perusal, they were dark and dilated. She knelt on the bed to either side of me, straddling my lap.

Huh. Whatever was happening right now, I was on board.

Brynn pushed my shoulders until I lay backward on the bed, taking her with me. We fell easily into kissing again. This was a new position, horizontal this time, but we found our rhythm. Tongues gliding, teeth nipping.

I rolled, taking the top position now as she fell back onto the mattress. Then I caught sight again of those marks on her shoulder. A splash of cold water over the mood.

Her hands slid up my sides. Reluctantly, I took hold of her wrists and put her arms above her head. God, she was beautiful. She was in bed with me. Willing. Moments ago, I'd been desperate to touch her, taste her, explore every part of her. Yet this didn't feel right.

"It's been a long day. And you got knocked around tonight." I dropped one more soft kiss to her lips. "We're going to save the rest of this for later."

She sighed. "Why do you have to do that?"

"Do what?"

"Be so…thoughtful. I want to believe you're for real, but it's hard to."

I almost smiled, but there was a sadness in the cut of her mouth. I didn't like it.

"When we met," I reminded her, "you thought I was an asshole. And you couldn't get away from me fast enough."

"I know. Instead, you keep making me like you."

"It's a devious plan of mine." I eased onto my side next to her, letting go of her wrists. Her eyes followed my movements. "Who was he?" I asked.

A crease appeared between her eyebrows. "What do you mean?"

"The guy who did a number on you. Who broke your heart."

Her mouth worked like she wanted to deny it. "How did you know?"

"A hunch." I remembered she had mentioned an ex at one point. But it wasn't so hard to follow this particular trail.

"I don't want to talk about it."

"That's fine. Just give me a name. I'm a bounty hunter. A name is all I need. Might take some time, but eventually this guy will just, *poof*. Disappear."

The sadness turned into a smile, though it didn't quite reach her eyes. "He's not worth the trouble."

"Few of them are. I'd still do it. If it makes you happier."

Brynn rolled onto her side to face me, snuggling into the pillow. "Who are you, Cole Bailey?" she whispered. "I can't figure you out."

"I'm a dick sometimes, in case you forgot. I lose my temper."

"You get upset when people are hurting. Hardly a fault."

"Yeah, and that makes me do stupid things. I say shit that gets me in trouble. I try to get my way."

"I know. And it gets on my nerves every dang time." She reached out to brush the hair from my forehead. "The problem is that it makes me like you even more."

I took her hand and kissed the tips of her fingers. If we were doomed to want each other, at least we'd go down in flames together.

# CHAPTER SEVENTEEN

## Brynn

I WOKE up to an empty bed.

I kicked off the covers and felt the other side of the mattress where Cole had been sleeping. It wasn't warm, which meant he'd been gone for a while. Worry swirled in my gut. Memories of what had happened last night with Westwick, then Ryker.

And Cole. Kissing him. Everything he'd said.

I jumped up, and that's when I saw the note and a to-go coffee cup on the nightstand. The coffee cup had *Brianna* written on it. I picked it up and took a sip while I glanced over the note.

*Went for a morning walk. Back soon. Cameron.*

Cole had brought me a chai latte. Spice and sweetness burst across my tongue. It reminded me of the chai Keira had made us at her house almost a week ago. I'd ordered a latte just like this at the coffee shop in Silver Ridge, too. I hadn't even realized Cole had noticed.

It was thoughtful. So like him.

*Ugh,* I was in trouble. I touched my lower lip, thinking of how hot and commanding his kisses had been last night.

But while he was gone, I had something to take care of. I'd failed to update Stanford yesterday. Taking another sip of my drink, I went to the drawer where I'd placed my socks, undies, and pajamas. The burner phone was stuck inside a wool hiking sock. Not the most devious hiding spot ever, but good enough. Cole wasn't the type to go through my things.

I sat on the bed, unlocked my phone, then opened the messaging app. But as my thumbs hovered over the keyboard on the screen, I hesitated. I could report plenty of things that would raise Stanford's concerns. Like Westwick's early arrival, that phone call Westwick had received. Ryker's suspicion of me and the confrontation with Cole. I'd meant to check in about the status of our double agents as well. But if the task force had news, Stanford would already have written me.

I glanced down at my shoulder. The marks had darkened slightly. Not much of a bruise, thankfully, but it was there. A reminder that the incident could've gone so much worse than it had.

So much had changed between Cole and me last night. And yet here I was, going behind his back to contact my former boss even though I had sworn I was done with the FBI.

I tipped my head back against the wall, letting out a groan of frustration.

This was why I should've kept my distance from Cole. Kept things strictly professional. Because as soon as I'd gotten close to him, started to really like him on an intimate, I'm-dying-to-kiss-you level, everything had gotten jumbled up in my head.

*Before you know it, you'll be in love with him. Remember how that turned out before? How pathetic would that be?*

But Cole was so different from what I'd expected. Every day, he showed me a little more of himself. I liked what I saw.

Yet I didn't know how to deal with his sheer...*intensity*. His need to care for me and protect me. My natural instinct was to resist, to declare I didn't need it, but he seemed so genuine.

Somehow, he had figured out that I'd had my heart broken. He had seen that in me. Maybe seen too much.

I realized where I was sitting. On the side of the bed that Cole had slept in last night. Even though his body warmth had fled, it still smelled faintly like him. He'd taken care of me last night when so many men would've been selfish. He had actually held my hand until I'd fallen asleep. When was the last time I had slept so deeply and comfortably?

Did we want each other because of the fake relationship? Or did this mean something more? I had no idea.

But maybe Cole was everything he claimed to be. A good man who wouldn't make promises he had no intention of keeping. The constriction in my chest told me how much I wanted that to be true.

I just didn't know how to trust it.

I started typing out an update for Stanford. But I didn't even know what I would write until the words popped up on the screen.

ME:

> C and I arrived at the resort yesterday as planned. W is here and we're proceeding. Can't risk further daily updates at this time. I'll be in touch when I can. Love to you and Marie. —B

With that, I switched off the screen and returned the burner to its hiding place.

I would do what I'd promised Cole. Treat this as a Protectors op, relying only on River and the Last Refuge crew for support. Stanford was going to be pissed, but he wasn't my boss at the moment. Wasn't my father either. He just had to deal with it. What was he going to do? Fire me?

I didn't even know if I wanted to return to the FBI after this.

After washing my face and brushing my teeth, I went back into the room just as Cole was coming through the door. He had a sheen of sweat over his tanned skin. A smile when he saw me. He wore a tee and mesh running shorts, which revealed even more of his legs than his swimming trunks had yesterday. More than I'd seen last night when he'd had on those sweats. It was a good look on him.

I had meant what I'd said last night. The man was incredibly sexy. And to me, the evidence on his body of his military service only added to it.

"Thanks for the latte." I went onto my toes to kiss him. A peck that quickly turned to something sweeter and deeper. He tasted like salt and black coffee, not a bad combination. Every time I got near Cole, it was difficult to pull away. But seeing the happy grin he gave me afterward was worth it.

"I thought about getting you something more to eat, but I noticed you don't usually have much breakfast."

"You noticed, huh?"

He put an arm around my waist. He smelled of sweat, but also fresh air and sun. "I like paying attention to you," he said. "I have no problem admitting it."

"Are you also ready to admit you were checking me out within two seconds of us meeting?"

"Oh yeah. Totally checked you out by the side of the road. Guilty as charged."

"I knew it."

He looked me up and down, like I was dressed to the nines instead of in my rumpled PJs. "I'm checking you out right now."

I laughed. "I've been checking you out too. Shamelessly."

*This is good, isn't it?* my heart said. *See how easy this feels?* Before I could start actively swooning, I broke away from him and grabbed my latte. "So what were you up to this morning, aside from coffee?"

"Did a lap around the resort while you got your beauty sleep." He winked.

"Is it going to be nonstop flirting from now on when we're alone? I've created a monster."

"I like flirting with you. It's not something I do often. Goes against my grumpy reputation, which is well deserved."

"Then why am I different?" I'd been kidding, but his face turned serious. He came toward me and cupped the back of my neck, drawing me closer.

"I dunno, B. You make me want to try for things."

"You make me want that too," I said softly. Even though I felt like I was letting him see too much of me again. With Cole, I couldn't help it.

"How are you feeling this morning?" he asked.

"Like I want to make progress on the mission." I took a reluctant step back. "We need to know how much of a problem last night's confrontation with Ryker caused." In fact, I was surprised I'd slept so well given that uncertainty.

"It just so happens I've been working on that. I think we're okay."

"Yeah?"

"I have intel to share. Among other things." His hand slid down along my back to my waist, giving me a gentle pat on my hip. "Get dressed. I've got something to show you."

---

We walked hand-in-hand down the hallway. I was glad when we didn't run into Ryker or Westwick. I wanted more time to assess things before I saw the head of Stillwater again. With

Westwick, it was all about strategy. A chess game. I had to consider the next move that would bring me closer to him, and how to do that without crossing Ryker.

Besides that, I was feeling a bit too warm toward Cole, and I was afraid Westwick would pick up on it. I was supposed to be having doubts about my boyfriend.

Yet the more this morning wore on, the fewer doubts I had about the man beside me. Even if I had no clue what we were doing.

We pushed through an exit door into the Arizona sunshine. The springtime weather was gorgeous. Blue skies, red rock hills, and dusky greens and browns in the desert beyond. Near the pool, we spotted Molly and her husband and stopped to chat with them because Brianna would have. Cole, playing Cameron, did an excellent job of acting annoyed.

Then we were moving again, skirting the walking path that wound through the resort. "What is it you wanted to show me?"

"We're almost there."

I realized we had made almost a full circle, coming back toward the main resort building but on the rear side with employee access. I figured Cole had a reason for taking the scenic way around.

Checking that we were alone, I asked, "What did you find out about Ryker?"

"This morning, I just happened to bump into Manning, Westwick's bodyguard. Figured I might find him out and about, and I was right. Unlike Ryker, Manning seems to like me."

"Since you bonded over motorcycles?" Cole had told me all about that conversation.

"Yep. I offered to buy him a coffee, and we got to talking. Manning had heard about the dust-up with Ryker. Apparently, Westwick was pissed about it. Told Ryker to back off. Manning even apologized to me. He didn't come out and say it, but he clearly thinks Ryker is a paranoid dick."

"That could be useful."

"Exactly what I was thinking. Dissension in the ranks."

"You don't think he was stringing you along?"

"It's possible. But I doubt it. Manning doesn't have that kind of an edge to him. Ryker is suspicious of us, we can't fix that, but Westwick doesn't suspect us. Our cover is safe for now."

We turned down a small maintenance path between the buildings. This was not the pretty, public side of the resort. There were a couple of dumpsters that already smelled unpleasant, despite the mild morning temperatures. Otherwise, the area was deserted.

Cole stopped at a door reading *Roof Access* with a length of chain wrapped around the handle. But the lock wasn't secured. He opened it, gesturing for me to go ahead.

After climbing a steep set of stairs, we came out onto a flat roof.

"I found this spot yesterday," Cole explained. "The restaurant employees sometimes come up for smoke breaks. One saw me having a cig myself, and he scurried off. But obviously didn't report me, since the chain is still unlocked. The employees don't want to lose their spot up here."

I walked around, glancing over the short wall that bordered the roof. The parking lot was below. "Nice," I said. "A fallback position?"

"That's what I was thinking. In case things go south and we can't make it to the car. We've got the high ground up here."

My original plan had been to rely on deception to get close to Westwick and then sneak away, leaving him none the wiser that his devices had been compromised. But after what had happened with Ryker last night? This was a very good idea.

"Nice work." I turned to face him. "Have you had your cigarette for the day?"

His gaze turned heated, and he sauntered closer. "I wanted to save it for later. Thought I might have a better occasion to enjoy a smoke."

"Is that so?"

"Not making any assumptions."

I smiled. "Of course not." Later sounded good. Something to look forward to. Our main focus had to be on the mission. Neither of us could forget that. But in between, a little relaxation and pleasure wouldn't hurt. All part of our cover story.

Cole dropped his mouth to mine, sucking gently on my lower lip, before stepping back again. "I learned a few more things. Another bodyguard arrived early this morning. Randall O'Hanlon."

O'Hanlon had been on our list of Ryker's security personnel. Another ex-cop. We'd seen his photo among those provided by the task force. I remembered bright red hair, a long nose, a hard scowl.

Cole opened his mouth to say something else. But then we heard loud voices below. Including a familiar one. *Westwick*. He was down in the parking lot.

Cole's eyes flew to mine. He signaled in the direction of the voices. We both crossed the distance in a crouch and hid behind the short wall bordering the roof.

"—a pleasure to see you again," Westwick was saying below. "Are you sure you don't want to join me for breakfast? It must've been a long drive."

I peeked over the side. Westwick was there, his ash-blond hair slicked back as it had been yesterday. This time he wore a pair of tailored pants and a sport coat, like he'd just stepped out of a country club. The man with him was around the same age as Westwick, but even more movie-star handsome. His broad shoulders filled out a red golf polo, and his leather loafers looked expensive. I felt a jolt of recognition, though I couldn't say for sure where I had seen this man before. Not in person. On TV, maybe?

Slowly, I took my phone from my pocket and lifted it to snap a few photos.

The man clapped Westwick on the shoulder in a friendly but commanding way, like the two were vying for the alpha position while remaining collegial on the surface. "I'd rather see the facility before anything else."

"Of course. Let's do it."

The two men walked toward an SUV with tinted windows. Ryker was already there, holding open the back door, and Westwick and his friend got in. Ryker slid into the driver's seat, and I spotted Manning in the passenger side.

The SUV reversed. Cole and I ducked down, staying there until we heard the noise of the engine receding. "Last night, when Westwick was on the phone, he said something about an arrival this morning. Did you recognize his friend?"

Cole shook his head. "Never seen the guy before. Have you?"

"I don't know. I thought so, but I'm not sure from when or where. I got some photos. I'll send them to River. See if he can identify the man."

Cole got up, then stretched out his hand to help me stand. We brushed off our clothes. "Makes me wonder if this is the reason Westwick moved up his schedule," he said.

"I was thinking the same thing. This meeting was important." Maybe the seminar at this resort had been an excuse all along. A convenient cover so the trip wouldn't draw as much attention.

"Too bad I didn't put a GPS tracker on Westwick's car," Cole said. "I'd love to know where they're headed."

"Same here, but they'll be back. We'll just have to be ready."

If I could get River's virus planted, then we wouldn't need to track him through the desert. We could crack open all his secrets and find out just what the head of Stillwater was hiding.

# CHAPTER EIGHTEEN

BRYNN and I took the quicker route on our way back. But we stopped short in front of our guest room door.

A massive bouquet of flowers sat there, all bright and tropical, blooms spilling over the sides.

"What have we here?" I bent to pluck the note from the arrangement and unfolded it to show Brynn. I had a bet who it might be from.

*Dear Brianna and Cameron,*

*My sincere apologies for the incident with my head of security last night. He tends to get overzealous on my behalf, but that's no excuse. I hope to see you at dinner tonight. And naturally, at the seminar tomorrow morning.*

*Garon*

Even though this was a good sign, it still irked me. If anybody was going to buy this woman flowers, it should be me. And this asshole had beaten me to it.

"See? Everything's fine," Brynn said. Not in her real voice, but Brianna's. "Garon knows it was a misunderstanding. You need to let it go, Cam."

Her eyes conveyed far more. Ryker, Westwick, and Manning had left the premises, but O'Hanlon could be watching from a nearby room. We hadn't seen him in person yet, so I hadn't gotten a read on him.

I put on my most intimidating frown. "We'll be fine if nobody else touches you." It didn't matter if I was being Cameron right now or myself. The sentiment was the same.

I yanked off the "Privacy Please" sign and swiped the keycard. As we entered, Brynn and I did a subtle check to make sure our low-tech security measures were in place. Nothing had been disturbed.

We also brought in the bouquet, setting it roughly on a table by the entrance, then proceeded to pull it apart in search of surveillance devices. But it was clean.

Brynn stretched her arms over her head, and I admired the exposed strip of stomach when her tank top rose up. "So at least Westwick believes our cover story," she said, "just like you heard from Manning. Garon wants to make nice. Unless he and Ryker are playing some longer game."

"Either way, I have to think Ryker assigned O'Hanlon to report back on what we do today." I edged closer, resting my hands on her hips. Didn't seem to be able to stop touching her. Good thing she didn't mind. Brynn's hands ran up and down my arms.

"Then we have to stay in character," she said. "Convince him we are who we say we are."

"We could spend the day in the room in as little clothing as possible. Not required, of course, but just throwing out options."

She smirked up at me. "As enticing as that idea is, I was thinking something more public."

"They might kick us out of the resort if we do *that* in public."

Brynn laughed out loud. Pleasure lit me up. I liked making her laugh and made a mental note to do it a lot more often.

"Does Cole Bailey have a naughty side? I'm shocked."

My cock pulsed at the thought of showing her just how naughty I could get. "I'm happy to demonstrate. But I'll leave the decision up to you." I pressed a kiss to her hair, lingering to inhale her scent. Shampoo and subtle hints of her perfume from last night, layered with the sweet notes that were just her. "I'm at your disposal."

I wanted to make sure she felt safe with me. I was up for anything. But when it came to getting physical, Brynn could set the pace.

"Good to know." Sliding out of my grip, she grabbed her laptop and set it up.

Brynn sent the photo she'd taken of Westwick's guest to River. Hopefully River and his hacker network could identify the man quickly. I wasn't too worried about that. River had a way of getting things done. He was a useful person to know.

I rested my bulk against the edge of the dresser. "I have an idea for today. Something that'll get us outside in public while keeping our cover intact. And it might actually be fun."

"Yeah? Tell me more."

"Finish up what you're doing. We can swing by the front desk to get what we need." I scanned her outfit. One of her Brianna sundresses. "And put on something you can hike in."

I wasn't used to enjoying myself during ops. Except when I was hauling in a fugitive, maybe. That part was always satisfying in a dark, vengeful way. But I rarely mixed business with pleasure. In fact, I would've said it was too risky. Distractions led to mistakes.

So was it wrong that excitement simmered beneath my skin as I thought of spending the day with Brynn, being able to touch her and knowing that she felt the same interest that I did?

I had to admit I didn't give a fuck. *Sorry, not sorry.*

For the moment, our mission and our desire for each other overlapped. I was going to roll with it.

---

Brynn switched into an outfit she claimed was hiking appropriate. To me, it looked like a sexy skirt made of stretchy material and a tight tank top, plus a pair of brand new pink hiking boots.

"You look like Hiking Barbie," I said. "Cute."

She winked. "Brianna has a signature look. What can I say?" Her honey-blond hair was pulled into a high ponytail, a nod to her own style. That small reminder of the real Brynn stoked my fire like nothing else.

I opened the door to our room, waiting for her to go ahead into the hall. After she'd passed me, I palmed her butt cheek beneath the short skirt and squeezed. *Nngh*. She had a tiny pair of boy shorts beneath. Hopefully this wasn't too forward, but I was in character as Cameron, and he was a handsy, possessive guy. Could she blame me?

Brynn smirked at me. She knew exactly what I was up to.

We headed for the front desk. Along the way, we ran into Molly and her husband, the bakers. As always, Molly greeted Brynn warmly, but her expression soured when she saw me.

"Cameron," she said, dripping with disdain.

I lifted my chin. "Yo."

Molly crossed her arms. "I heard about the incident with Garon's security last night. So unfortunate. Are you all right, Brianna?"

Brynn put a hand on Molly's arm. "It was nothing. Garon sent some flowers over to apologize. Just a mix-up."

"Well that was thoughtful. Some men know how to behave." Molly's eyes narrowed at me. Then she gasped, gesturing at Brynn's shoulder. "Are those…finger marks?"

Brynn's hand flew up to cover the bruises. "It happened last night, but it was an accident."

*Hardly*, I thought, my hackles raising yet again as I thought of Ryker hurting her. I was going to punish the guy. Make no mistake.

But Molly glared at me, as if she suspected *I* was the real culprit.

We said goodbye, resuming our course to the front desk. "I'm getting a reputation around here," I murmured. "Soon half the resort will want my blood for abusing the popular girl everyone loves." This felt different from them thinking I was a jerk. Even though they were judging Cameron, not me, I still didn't like it.

"It's all about perception. Planting the seeds in Westwick's mind that I'm not happy with you. It'll help if other guests are reinforcing that idea."

Right, so Westwick could swoop in and steal her from me. Shaking my head, we continued down the hallway. Having Brynn put herself at the mercy of Westwick, even briefly, was simply not a viable option to me. I would have to make her see that. But I knew it would take some convincing.

At reception, I asked for info on the local hiking trails. Brynn glanced over the pamphlets excitedly, while I made noise about getting drinks and lunch for us to take along. All amenities that the resort offered. I wanted to make sure that as many people as possible knew where we were heading.

Once we were equipped, we set out, me wearing the backpack full of supplies and my fingers entwined with hers. This hike would take us up to the summit of the rocky red hills bordering the resort.

The air smelled of sunshine and dust, free of the mix of perfumes and cleaning fluid at the resort. I inhaled deeply.

Since the Army, I had felt most comfortable outside under the open sky. In an area full of hostiles, that could mean more danger. Yet it was liberating too, a reminder that nature wasn't far away. In my experience, it was usually humanity that was the problem.

After being wounded, I'd hated being stuck in a hospital room. Staring at ceilings instead of blue sky. Feeling walls close in instead of the endless expanse and possibilities of the wilderness. I'd fought hard to get back to the same level of activity I'd taken for granted.

Since then, every time I was out in a place like this and moving on my two feet, *free,* I was grateful to be here.

And with Brynn hiking up the narrow trail in front of me, the view was even sweeter. Her toned legs, the curves of her hips and butt as the trail climbed. Her beauty was obvious to anyone who met her. Especially right now, with those clothes that hugged her curves. But Brynn was so much more than that.

I remembered my very first impression of her. Seeing her flip the guy who'd grabbed her arm by the side of the road. Even when that fierceness was directed my way, I admired it.

And I *really* admired the sheen of her skin as we stopped for a water break. A drop of sweat rolled down her neck and into the hollow between her collarbones. Would it be too much if I licked it off? Yeah, probably. But the thought of it, wondering what it would taste like, had my cock perking up.

Brynn wiped the sweat from her brow, her throat working as she swallowed water from the bottle.

"We're being followed," she said, the lip of the water bottle in front of her mouth and her voice low.

I moved into her space, giving in to the urge to kiss her temple. Salt spread over my lips. "We have been for a while, yeah."

We'd passed a few hikers when we had first started, but since then, we'd seemed to have the path to ourselves. But despite appearances, we weren't alone.

"He's stopped every time that we have," I said. "Trying to stay behind us so he doesn't catch up. Good thing, because I was afraid that O'Hanlon had dropped the ball."

"You're sure it's him? Westwick's other bodyguard?"

"Definitely. His red hair is like a stoplight. Just like the photo in his profile." I knelt to open my daypack. Beneath the snacks and drinks I had tucked inside, courtesy of the front desk staff, I had folded up a hand towel from our bathroom. I flicked one edge aside.

A gun lay beneath.

Brynn snickered. "I figured you had a strategy worked out for this excursion. But doesn't it seem a bit early to be picking off Westwick's men?"

I covered the gun, zipping the pack and slinging it onto my shoulder again. "I'm being a good boy. The bodyguard is safe, so long as he stays smart and keeps his distance." But I didn't expect anything more than surveillance. Sure, it was possible that Ryker had ordered O'Hanlon to get rid of me. But Westwick was busy with his guest, a man who'd given every indication of being important. Westwick wouldn't want the mess and distraction of resort guests going missing, especially attendees of his seminar who'd tussled with his head of security last night. Westwick was too smart for that.

No, this was an opportunity. Not just to solidify our cover story, but to assess the security team's abilities. So far, I wasn't impressed.

"What do you want to do?" Brynn asked. "Keep going and

see if he follows?" She sidled over and wrapped her arms around my neck. "Or should we put on a little show?"

As if I had to give that any thought. "I suppose, if you're that eager to get your lips on me again..."

"More like, you're happy for any excuse to get your lips on *mine*." The tip of her nose nudged my cheek, a tease more than anything else. "Do you think he can see us right now?"

I hummed, turning slightly to assess the surroundings with my peripheral vision. "Probably not. I assume he brought binoculars, maybe even a camera with a long lens, but we need higher ground."

"Guess we should keep hiking then."

"In a sec." Now that Brynn and I had given in to our attraction, I didn't need any excuse to kiss her. My lips brushed softly over hers, just to make sure she wanted this, but she grasped the collar of my shirt and kissed me back. The rest of me responded, longing to get her as close as possible. But too soon, she pulled back.

"Come on," she said. "Let's find a better spot so he's sure to see us. O'Hanlon will need something exciting to report back to Ryker and Westwick."

"There you go again, wanting to get dirty in public. I'm going to think you're an exhibitionist, B."

She reached around to smack my butt cheek. "I'm still waiting for that naughty side you promised."

Grinning, we continued hiking uphill. It was nearing midday, so the sun was getting intense, despite the cooler temperatures of spring. The other hikers from the resort had already made their way back for showers and the cool oasis of the pool, so aside from our shadow, we had the trail to ourselves.

About a mile later, we reached an overlook point. A flat area jutted out over the valley, a perfect spot for a break. The cliff above provided shade from the unrelenting sun, and there were a couple of smooth rocks that we could spread out on.

Brynn took the pack from me and unzipped it. "Lunch?" she asked.

"Yeah. I'm starved."

She handed me a sandwich and took one for herself. While I took a bite, I went to the edge of the overhang, stretching my arms up like I was catching my breath and admiring the view of the valley leading down to the resort grounds.

I caught a brief flash of movement. Red hair beneath a dark cap, then sun reflecting off of glass. Our watcher was about half a klick downhill, off the trail and partially hidden by some scrubby bushes and rugged looking trees.

Perfect.

I finished my sandwich in a few bites, then washed it down with water. Brynn was turned away from me, bent over to dig through my pack, which she'd set on the long, flat rock. I came up behind her, sliding my hands up her sides as she rose to standing, and I pulled her against me.

"Our friend can see us," I said in her ear. "O'Hanlon is watching." And I had to admit, even though I was no exhibitionist, the thought had my skin tingling. Especially when Brynn turned her head, eyes flashing with interest.

"I'm game if you are."

Keeping her back to my chest, I spun us and sat on the rock, pulling her down with me onto my lap. I splayed one hand flat on her stomach and brought the other to drape loosely at her neck. Her behind nestled against my crotch, and the warm weight of her was impossible for my body to ignore.

Burying my face against her hair, I said, "This okay?"

"Yes," she breathed.

She craned her neck so she could see me. I nipped at her

lip with my teeth before slanting my mouth over hers. My tongue pushed inside. More salt, the taste of clean sweat. Her scent and the fresh dry air mingled in my nostrils.

In this spot, with us facing the valley, our watcher would have a perfect view of everything we were doing.

I trailed kisses along her neck, pausing to speak while being careful that O'Hanlon couldn't read my lips. "If you want me to stop at any time, tell me you're still hungry," I said. "I'll act annoyed, but we'll head back to the resort. Okay?"

She nodded. "I'm good."

"You *are* good." Then I raised my voice. "You feel how hard you're making me, B? That's all you."

She whimpered, dropping her head back against my shoulder. "*Cameron.*" She'd used the name of my cover, but the way Brynn's hips shifted, rubbing herself against my thickening cock, was just for me.

Hell. I had to close my eyes. That felt incredible.

"But there could be other hikers." Her words echoed against the rocks. "Someone's going to see."

I held in my smile. Brynn was really getting into this. My acting skills were nothing much, but maybe I could step it up. "Let them. I saw the way you were dancing with Garon last night. You need a reminder of who you belong to."

The look Brynn gave me was hot enough to feel the burn on my skin. Like the sun was shining directly on me, though we were in the shade.

"Keep going?" I murmured.

She nodded. A smile in her eyes, no hesitation.

I lifted her up and maneuvered her so she faced me. Her knees were bent, thighs straddling my hips. I switched my grip to hook my left arm at her waist, as if I was forcing her to stay there. But with my other hand, I gently massaged her stomach through her shirt. I kept my kisses soft. Coaxing.

Letting her set the pace, even as I pretended to have complete control. Her tongue dipped past my lips, tasting me.

Yet as we continued to make out, the haze of desire started blotting out the rest of the world. Which meant danger. I had to remain aware of our surroundings. This woman meant a lot to me already. Probably too much, given how briefly we had known one another. I'd gotten glimpses of that secret vulnerability beneath her outer layer of strength. Which just made me want to protect her all the more. Not because she was a woman facing off against an enemy like Stillwater. And not just because she was my partner.

I had to protect her because, with every kiss and caress, she felt more and more like a part of me.

Damn, I was in so deep already.

I sat back slightly, enough to let my senses regain awareness. "Something wrong?" she whispered.

"Just looking at what's mine."

I'd said that for the benefit of whoever was listening, but that didn't make it any less true in the moment.

I brought my hands to her thighs and massaged the muscle under her bare skin. Leaning forward, I spoke into her ear. "Just keeping an eye on the trail. I was getting distracted."

She chuckled. "You and me both."

My thumbs made small circles on her inner thighs, inching inward. One swiped the edge of her tiny boy shorts beneath the hem of her skirt. Brynn inhaled, her pupils dilating. Her breath caught, and she squeezed my bicep hard. Nodded.

My thumb moved again, this time drawing directly over the crotch of her shorts. Her whimper was a soft, desperate thing.

"You like that?" I ghosted my lips over hers. I had thought my cock was hard before, but that was nothing to the way my shaft throbbed against my fly. "No one can see what I'm doing. You wanted to put on a show. Whether it's real is up to you."

Brynn widened her legs a bit more. Arched her back. "Touch me." Her words were rich with arousal. Her eyelids heavy, mouth pink and bee-stung from all the kissing.

Using that same thumb, I wiggled it beneath the edge of her shorts. Then slid into the juncture between her legs until I met slick wetness. Brynn whimpered. A long stroke, up and down over her most intimate parts, had her shivering. Her lashes fluttered.

"Don't stop. *Please*."

"I don't intend to."

With just that thumb, I explored her. Discovered the tempo she liked, the pressure. Brynn's hips rocked against me. My cock was trapped inside my own shorts, receiving just enough friction to get me hot and wanting. Sweat dripped down my back.

The last thing I wanted to do was tear my attention away, especially with her moaning like that, but I kept an eye on the trail as well. Nobody could accuse me of being unable to multitask. Thank you, Ranger training. This was an exercise in concentration. In pushing aside my own wants to focus entirely on my task.

My thumb moved in ever faster circles. Concentrating on her clit as her moans quickened and her body tensed like a bow string.

"I'm—I'm going to—" Brynn fell forward against me, her kisses frantic and needy. "C-*Cameron*." I was pretty sure she'd almost said my real name, but she'd corrected herself just in time.

I kept flicking my thumb until she started to shudder. My

middle finger sank inside her. She gasped and pressed her face to my neck.

"That's it, B," I murmured. "I've got you."

When she finally stopped shaking, Brynn sat back in my lap, blinking like she'd forgotten where we were. Nobody had bothered us. Actually, if any hikers had approached, they probably would've steered clear given the sounds Brynn had been making.

There hadn't been much mystery about what Brianna and Cameron were up to.

I kissed her, lips closed, as I slid my hand free and fixed her shorts and skirt. "Think that was enough of a show?" I asked.

Her cheeks flushed. But she lifted her chin defiantly. "I challenge any other couple at the resort to do better."

I kissed her again to hide my smile.

# CHAPTER NINETEEN

## *Brynn*

THE HIKE BACK to the resort was much faster than the trip out. It was downhill, but that wasn't the real reason.

I wanted to get Cole back to our room. *Now*.

I couldn't believe I'd done that. Letting Cole touch me, pleasure me, like I was made for it. He'd brought me to orgasm right there in the middle of the trail, fully aware that a bodyguard for the head of Stillwater was watching us. Anyone might've walked by. Of course, Cole had an eye on the area, but usually I was the one maintaining situational awareness.

But instead of being careful, I'd completely surrendered. Special Agent Somerton didn't do things like that.

And it had been *hot*. Hotter than anything I'd ever experienced. What was it about this man?

As we rushed down the trail, we didn't run into O'Hanlon or anyone else. Good thing, because I was in no mood to pretend to be Brianna. It had been hard enough to keep up the fiction when we'd been on the trail.

I didn't want Cameron. I wanted *Cole*. Wanted to give him just as much wild pleasure as he had given me.

We burst into the hotel room, already kissing, hands

roving. Cole managed to slam the door shut and flip the lock. Then he pressed me to the closed surface, his mouth dominating mine. Tongue sliding and stroking.

His erection had flagged on the way back, and now I felt him hardening against me again. I fit my hands between our bodies. Flicked open the button of his fly and moved the zipper down to reach inside.

My fist closed around his thickness, and Cole tipped his head back as he groaned low in his chest.

"Need you," I said hoarsely. "Right now."

"Bedroom."

"No. Can't wait that long."

His nostrils flared. Glancing around the room, he grabbed my wrist and dragged me to the couch nearby. Cole bounced on the cushion as he sat, then pulled me down onto his lap, just like we'd been positioned earlier on the flat rock overlooking the valley. But now, the soft upholstery of the couch provided a much more welcoming surface. My hips moved involuntarily, grinding me against him.

I'd never felt this kind of urgency. This uncontrollable frenzy to have a man inside of me.

Somehow, I pushed my shorts and panties down my thighs, lifting my legs to get them off. Cole pushed down his own shorts and boxers and his cock popped free, smacking his T-shirt over his stomach. He held his shaft at the base and squeezed.

"You sure you want this?" he asked.

Since my ex had left me, I had second-guessed every moment of intimacy with other men. Distrust had become my default. But being with Cole this way felt…simple. With him, I could just let go. Because I knew he'd be right there with me.

"I want it more than anything."

He notched himself at my entrance, and I sank down. His

blue eyes held me as his cock filled me inch by inch. Cole arched upwards, and I moaned at the sensation of him pushing deep. Taking my breath, touching places inside me I hadn't allowed any man in too long.

This was exactly what I wanted. What I *needed*.

I still had my skirt on. He pushed up the fabric and gripped my hips as we rocked in a faster rhythm. My chest was tight, the skin of my stomach flushed with heat. The way he watched me, the lust but also the awe I saw in his gaze, made tingles of pleasure race along my limbs.

"*Brynn,*" he said, just before he cupped the back of my neck and kissed me. His tongue licked into my mouth, owning me with hot, filthy strokes as his cock thrust into my pussy. The scents of sweat, salt, and sex mingled in the room.

I gripped his strong, broad shoulders and bounced in his lap. Pushing away everything but the pressure of him inside me, the perfect way my clit rubbed against him. And that hungry look he gave me. I couldn't get enough of that.

"So good," he purred. "Ride me like you mean it. Take what you need, because I can't last much longer, and I wanna feel you lose control first. Wanna see that pretty face twisted up with pleasure."

So Cole was a talker during sex. I loved that.

I was close. Every part of me tensing as electric pleasure built between my legs. Then his large hands squeezed my ass, his hips bucking hard, and I careened straight off the edge. My fingers grasped at his short hair and I rubbed my face against his, feeling the soft abrasion of his whiskers on my cheek. I rode him as wave after wave zapped through me and left me breathless.

I was still coming when Cole let out a choked cry, and I felt his spasms inside me.

When the intensity faded, our faces were still pressed

together. He hummed and trailed wet kisses across my cheek. "Told you my plan for today would be fun."

"You had this part planned too?"

"Not specifically. But was I hoping? Hell yeah, I was."

His arms wrapped around me like he didn't intend to let me go anywhere. I smiled with my eyes closed. I wasn't ready for this moment to end yet either.

He chuckled. "Been wanting to get you naked since the minute I saw you. Know what? I'm the exact kind of horny bastard you accused me of being." To accentuate the point, he pinched my butt cheek.

My eyes popped open, jaw dropping in pretend shock. "Scandalous."

We both smiled and then laughed. With the movement of my body, I felt him still inside me. *Oh*. He was softening, but yes, I felt him.

His eyelids got heavy. He exhaled and kissed me gently. "Hope you enjoyed that as much as I did," he said.

"Every bit." In fact, I wasn't opposed to more. It was just past lunchtime. We weren't due anywhere until dinner, and we'd certainly made an impact already today.

With luck, I'd have Garon's attention again this evening, as well as his competitiveness to steal me from Cameron.

But with Cole's lips on mine and our bodies still connected in the most intimate way, all I really wanted—even more than defeating the head of Stillwater—was to hold on to this warm, comfortable feeling. Maybe I should've been concerned about that.

---

Sadly, I couldn't linger there forever, so I got up and pushed my skirt back down. Cole was quick to tug up his shorts.

A jolt of shyness made me hesitate, which was ridiculous.

He had just been inside me, and I certainly hadn't shown any inhibitions on the hiking trail. "I'm going to get cleaned up." I started toward the bathroom, then added, "We could try out the Jacuzzi tub after. If you want."

"That is an excellent idea." His mouth quirked wickedly, revealing his incisor on one side. "Wouldn't want our room upgrade to go to waste. But I should see if River has written back yet."

I cursed myself for not thinking of it. "You're right. I'll be out in a minute."

I went into the bathroom. Too quickly, the perfect comfort I'd been feeling on the couch evaporated, replaced by the knowledge that I should be focusing on our mission. As Cole had just reminded me.

I didn't want this to be a mistake.

*Please don't let it be a mistake.*

After rinsing off, I wrapped myself in a towel and emerged from the bathroom. It was either that or put my sweaty, dirty clothes back on.

I stepped into the room, finding Cole on the laptop. "Nothing from River yet. I guess for the moment, no news is good news." He shut the lid of the device and leaned back in his seat, letting his eyes trace over me from head to toe.

"Shower's free," I said.

"Is that a hint that I smell bad?"

I tilted my head, giving him a sardonic look. Actually, his scent was already turning me on again. "After the hike and what we got up to after? I'd say we both need it."

"I'll shower. But I want you to come here first." His tone had dipped back to a lower octave. That voice was hypnotic.

I couldn't explain the effect this man had on me. Especially when he turned all grumpy and gruff.

"I'm supposed to follow your orders?" I asked, but I was already walking over to him.

As soon as I was close enough, he pulled me down to sit on the knee of his right leg. With his teeth digging into his lower lip, he hooked one finger into the top of my towel. "Can I?"

I lowered my hands, a silent agreement. *Do what you want to me*. Cole tugged again at the towel, and it opened, pooling around my hips. He groaned as my breasts and stomach came into view.

"Hot damn, you are gorgeous, B."

My nipples beaded in the air-conditioned chill. Cole brought a finger to one of them and circled the nub. My breaths came faster. His same finger drew a line between my breasts, down my stomach, and all the way between my legs. I gasped as he found those spots that drove me wild. Just a couple of times together so far, and he was getting to know my body well.

"Want to make you come again." He dropped a kiss to my collarbone. His tongue darted out to lick a bead of water. "But I want to do it in that big tub."

I playfully pushed away his hand. "Then get cleaned up. You're too dirty for the bath."

"I'll show you dirty." He pinned me with his arms and rubbed his salty cheek between my breasts. Laughing, I pushed at him and tried to get up.

"Jerk!"

Cole let me go, grinning. And my heart gave a powerful thump. I wouldn't have described this rugged man as beautiful before, but right now, that fit him perfectly.

I picked up the towel that had fallen to the floor. But Cole swiped it from me. "It's a crime to cover a view that spectacular."

My skin heated with a blush. I grabbed the towel back, draping it over my front. All Cole did was smirk at me, stand up, and start stripping his clothes on the way to the bathroom. I felt my eyes bugging as he shoved his boxers down, stepping out of them as he went. The tight muscles of his glutes flexed.

My towel fell to the floor, and I left it there.

When I followed Cole into the bathroom, he was sitting on the edge of the tub and removing his prosthesis. "Want me to switch on the water in the shower?" I asked.

"Nah. I've got it. Not my first time showering on one foot, honey."

"Right." I was an idiot. But Cole laughed, a sound I was coming to crave way too much.

"You just let me get away with calling you honey," he pointed out.

I totally had. But him saying it today sounded far different than before. Today, I'd kind of liked it. "Would you rather I get pissed?"

"No, I'd rather you let me kiss you." He set his prosthesis and the inner sock on the tile, then spread his legs so I could stand between them. Cole's hands rested on my hips, bringing me close enough to kiss each of my nipples, tongue flicking over them. Desire ignited my bloodstream. Pulsed between my legs.

Somehow, with Cole and me both stark naked amid all this white marble tile and bright light, this scene felt just as scandalous as what we'd done on the hiking trail. He was supposed to be my partner. Sleeping with him, in the middle of a mission no less, went against every iota of my training.

*Such a bad idea,* I thought for the hundredth time since last night. But this felt too wonderful to stop.

"Start the bath," he said. "I'll join you in a minute."

He got up, balancing on his right foot, and hopped to the shower. My mouth went dry as every muscle and sinew in his body went taut. His raw strength, built through hard work and years of experience, was undeniable. The scars on his skin spoke to his bravery. Everything he'd been through.

And then watching the shower spray roll down every angle and line of that breathtaking body?

I'd said before that he *might* be one of the sexiest men I'd seen. It was no longer a contest.

I managed to tear my gaze from him long enough to get hot water pouring into the tub. While it filled, I got in and rested my chin on the edge, still watching Cole through the glass walls of the shower. He was soaping up his arms, stomach, cock. Every couple minutes our eyes met, both of us smiling. But as he finished up, and the hot water lapped around my hips in the tub, it felt like the connection between us pulled taut. Rich with anticipation.

He switched off the water and pushed open the shower door. "This part might be less sexy," he joked.

"Not possible."

"Yet I suspect slipping on the wet floor and falling on my face is not a good way to impress you."

"You've already impressed me. Twice today, in fact," I added with a teasing wink.

"There's more where that came from. I promise." Cole sat down on the shower mat just outside the door. He'd already set a fresh, rolled-up towel within reach, and he used that to dry off a bit. Then, with a devious look, he spread the towel out to cover the short distance between the shower and the tub.

And proceeded to crawl toward me like some Apex predator toward his next meal.

He had said this wouldn't be sexy?

When he reached the side of the tub, he got in. I moved back to make room. Hot water sloshed around us both.

Cole relaxed with his back to one end of the tub. I turned around so that I sat between his legs, resting against his chest. His right leg was bent, the left stretched out. With us both in the tub, the water had nearly reached the top, so I switched off the faucets.

"Want to turn on the water jets?" he asked.

"I'd rather just sit with you." Settling back against Cole in the hot water, I was instantly surrounded by comfort. I breathed out and relaxed. "How does this feel so right?" I murmured.

He brought a hand to rest on my stomach. "I keep asking myself the same thing."

Neither of us spoke for a while, just soaking in the ambience.

"Would you tell me about your family?" I said.

His thumb drew a semi-circle on my stomach. I felt him swallow, and I thought he might not answer me. I remembered from our previous conversations that his family hadn't helped him after he was wounded. So clearly there were some kind of story there.

I was curious about this man. Cole intrigued me in a way no one else had in a long time. After my ex left, I hadn't let myself get close enough to someone romantically to get to this step. Not just sharing mind-blowing orgasms, but truths about ourselves. Whether *he* wanted to share his past with me was another issue.

"I never knew my biological parents," he said. "My mom was young when she had me, probably a runaway. That's the theory, anyway. She abandoned me at a hospital when I was two."

"Oh, Cole. That's rough." I was sure he didn't want or need useless platitudes. But it was still hard to hear.

"I ended up in foster care. Was placed with a few different families, and the last one stuck. They fostered a lot of kids, and Mom and Dad were older by the time I came to them. But they were great. If anything, they should've been more selfish, because they gave absolutely everything to us and kept nothing in the tank for themselves. Never stopped putting other people first." His chest moved against me as he breathed. "They both passed away while I was in the service."

"They sound like amazing people. You must miss them."

"They were. And...yeah," he said softly. "I do."

I rested my head against his shoulder. Reached for the hand that wasn't already touching me to lace our fingers. "Do you have foster siblings?"

"None that I'm close to. So that's why my family hasn't been in the picture for a while. What about you? What's your family like?"

"I didn't know my father either. My mom and I lived with her brother. My uncle. He was...not a kind man, unfortunately." Unlike Cole's foster parents, my uncle had been a jerk, and my mom hadn't been willing or able to stand up to him.

"Is this uncle still around?"

I knew that tone. It was the same one Cole used whenever he was getting protective. And potentially murderous towards anyone who'd hurt me. "Yes, but I haven't seen him in a long time. He wasn't physically abusive. Uncle Jim loved to tell me how weak I was, how I'd never amount to anything. What a fool I was for studying hard, or applying for scholarships, or thinking about enlisting."

"I'm sorry, B. Clearly he was wrong."

My eyes stung, and that made me feel ridiculous. I was glad Cole couldn't see.

"In a way, he did me a favor. Gave me something to fight against. It was the best feeling in the world when I made it through boot camp. Like a big middle finger to him and anyone else who'd doubted me." I blinked at the bathroom ceiling, but I was smiling. I hated that I still heard my uncle's voice in my head sometimes. But I had proved him wrong. About my career accomplishments, at least.

"I sent Uncle Jim an invitation to my graduation ceremony at Quantico after I finished FBI training. He didn't come, and I didn't expect him to. But I would've loved to see the look on his face. Knowing I was an FBI special agent." I closed my eyes. All kinds of emotions were bubbling up before I could stop them. "Thank goodness he didn't find out about my engagement and how *that* ended. Uncle Jim would've been the first to say I told you so."

"You were engaged?"

Dang it, why had I said that?

Probably because I'd been too comfortable. It was way too easy to let down my guard when I was with Cole.

He had already guessed that someone had broken my heart. Maybe I should just rip the Band-Aid off. Tell him the rest of my deep dark secrets, since the man had been so open with me.

I splashed warm water onto us. "It ended a couple years ago." Before I'd met my best friend Charlotte. "You've probably heard this one before. Girl meets the perfect guy. Falls in love. Not just with him, but with his family too. The big, happy family she always wanted. They decide to get married." Shame and anger swirled in my stomach. "Then, guy gets cold feet and backs out. Confesses he never loved her that much anyway."

My ex was a professional mountaineer. He'd been the guide for a climbing trip I took, and I'd fallen for him up on the summit of a fourteener. I had believed every pretty word that came out of his mouth. As if my life had turned into a fairy tale.

Cole muttered a curse. He turned me so I was cradled against his chest. Stroked my arm and kissed my hair. "That's a reflection on him, not you."

"But I was the fool who believed in him. In us. I should've known he was too good to be true." Full of promises and short on followthrough.

Then last year, I had learned that a fellow FBI agent, another man I had trusted implicitly, was working for Stillwater. And my faith in my own judgment had crumbled even more.

Which was just a reminder that I shouldn't get carried away. Whatever this was between me and Cole, however perfect he seemed to be, I had to be careful. Couldn't risk my heart. Not ever again.

Cole's fingers touched my chin, angling my head so my eyes met his. And it felt like he could read everything that was going through my mind.

"There is no shame in believing someone's promises. Even if they break them. That doesn't make you weak. You know that, right?"

"Of course I do." My throat felt too thick. I shrugged. Maybe Cole was thinking of his ex-wife. Maybe I wasn't the only one in this tub who knew what broken-hearted felt like.

"But I can think of more fun activities than talking about our past," I said.

"You did start it."

I shifted so I was kneeling between his spread thighs. Water sloshed around us against the sides of the tub. "And now, I'm starting *this*."

I pressed my naked body into his, and I kissed him.

## CHAPTER TWENTY

I KNEW what Brynn was doing. She didn't want to talk about her heartbreak, so she was distracting me with sex.

Was I a bad person if it worked?

But I was the last guy to force someone to share feelings if she didn't want to. If I could comfort Brynn and show her just how amazing she was, how lucky *any* man would be to have her, then I was ready and willing to report for duty.

I finally had her naked against me, all slippery and wet. While I had thoroughly enjoyed that quickie on the couch earlier, there was a lot more I wanted to try with Brynn. First off, continuing to admire her fine form.

I also hadn't missed the way she'd admired me when I'd been in the shower. And when I'd crawled over to join her in the tub. Yes, I'd been concerned about practicality. I'd slipped on wet tile out of carelessness before, and I didn't need the annoyance of a bruised tailbone or worse.

But I'd enjoyed putting on a little show for her, too. Seeing her reactions to me. Brynn hadn't made any secret of how much I turned her on. Which made a guy feel pretty damn good.

Time to return the favor.

She was in my lap, a position I was a fan of. I loved having her thighs spread around me, my hands able to squeeze the curves of her butt cheeks. Her nipples rubbed against my chest. I let Brynn be in charge of the kiss for a while.

But then I sat forward, laying her back against the far side of the tub and kneeling over her. Taking the dominant position. I sucked and nibbled at her lips, then moved my mouth to her neck and chest. I lavished kisses on the skin just above where the water lapped at her breasts.

The water covered too much of her, and that wasn't going to work. Not for what I had in mind.

I stretched up to grab a couple of folded towels from the shelf above us. This was one of the benefits of the upgraded room, apparently. An ample supply of towels. I positioned them on the ledge behind Brynn, where the frame of the tub connected to the wall.

Grabbing her by the hips, I lifted her up and set her there on the narrow stretch of tile. Now she was out of the water and in just the perfect place for my mouth.

"Not too cold?" I asked.

"Not cold," she said breathily. "If anything, I was overheating. Something about sharing a tub of hot water with an even hotter man."

"Then let's see if I can get you more comfortable." Pushing her thighs wider and holding one in each hand, I bent forward.

The flat of my tongue lapped over her core. She gasped and leaned further back against the rolled towels. Giving me full access.

I used my tongue to tease her. To trace her outlines and then slowly dip inside her opening. Brynn grasped at my hair. Her hips moved and her knees shook as she made the sexiest whimpers.

My cock strained toward her from where I knelt in the water. But right now, this was all about Brynn.

When she started begging, I flicked my tongue at a faster pace. Her moans echoed against the tile. Then I pushed two fingers inside of her and sucked on her clit. Her head fell back against the wall and she let out a breathy cry.

"C—oh. Don't stop. Please, don't stop."

She had been about to yell my name. Good thing she had stopped herself, because we had no idea if anyone could hear us. She could've called me Cameron like she had on the trail, but I was glad she didn't. This was real, and it wasn't for anyone but us.

I loved the wild sounds she was making, the way she lost more and more composure as I massaged her sweet center with my tongue. When she finally stopped shuddering, her thighs trying to close, I sat back on my heels.

Brynn slid down into the water. She had a soft, dazed smile on her face, and her hair was a mess.

The water was only lukewarm by now, but neither of us paid any attention. Especially when she reached out and stroked my erection from base to tip.

I closed my lips on a groan. This wasn't going to take long. The aching need for release had already tightened at the base of my spine.

We kissed deeply as she brought me closer and closer to climax. Then she bent at the waist to fit her hot mouth around my tip, and I was done for. I grabbed for the sides of the tub to keep myself steady, still kneeling, and just gave in to the incredible feeling of her mouth as the water lapped at my thighs. It all built up and crescendoed like a firework going off, light bursting behind my eyes, heat and release and perfect satisfaction.

Brynn sat up, licking her lips. "I think I like the tub."

"I *really* like it." I stretched out in the cooling water. Brynn lay on top of me and rested her head on my chest. It was going to be a few minutes before I could move again.

I couldn't remember the last time I'd been so content after sex. Maybe not ever.

*I need a tub like this at the house,* I thought, picturing how it might fit in the bathroom at my place on the beach. Would I ever get to take Brynn there? I could imagine her in a bikini and a see-through cover-up, sipping a margarita on my deck. Smiling at me.

I could feel it like an arrow to the chest.

Maybe that was too much to hope for. Who knew where this was heading? But I liked the thought of it. Liked the thought of falling into whatever this was between us. Enjoying it for as long as it would last.

---

Eventually the water was ice cold. I handed Brynn a towel after getting out myself. Once we were all dry, and I had my prosthesis back in place and my clothes on, we went to check the laptop.

Brynn made it there first. "We've got a message from River. He sent some info to the secure server." I stood behind her shoulder, one hand on the back of her chair, as she navigated to the new documents.

"Westwick's friend is named Eric Masterson." She glanced up at me. "He's running for a US Senate seat here in Arizona. He's been making the rounds on cable news. That's why I recognized him."

"Figures. But why did he show up for a morning meeting with Westwick?"

Together, we read the profile River had provided on Masterson. He was an Ivy League-educated businessman turned politician. He'd spent a lot of time campaigning about the importance of new technology, research and development that would give our country the edge in the future. Which matched up with things Westwick had said.

So it was no surprise that Masterson's campaign had received large donations from the companies owned by Garon Westwick.

Brynn opened a news article. Masterson's photo was below the headline, his arms crossed as he grinned at the camera. His wife and family were a little younger than Westwick's, but equally beautiful. A picture of perfect domestic bliss. But if he was affiliated with Westwick, how much of that façade was real?

Brynn kept scrolling through the documents River had sent, and she inhaled sharply. "Remember how they talked about touring a facility? Look at this."

River had connected Westwick to a new solar energy plant in the Arizona desert. The plant was massive, the size of multiple football fields. I leaned over the desk for a better look, while Brynn zoomed in on the satellite images. "This is a hundred miles or so from the resort," she said. "Out in the middle of nowhere. This could be the facility Masterson wanted to see."

"Hmm. Question is, what's so exciting about a solar plant?" I was no expert, but desert and sun pretty much went together. "Why did Masterson make a special trip out here to coincide with Westwick's seminar?"

"And then go without a photo op," Brynn quipped. "We know politicians love those."

According to what River had learned, the project had been in the works for about a year. Government approvals had come through shockingly fast and with little friction. Yet despite the man's social media presence and *nice guy* persona, Westwick hadn't publicized this investment. Instead, he'd tried to minimize his involvement. One of Westwick's companies had funneled millions of dollars through shell corporations to build it. River had connected the dots, obviously, but none of the public documents related to the solar plant mentioned the man at the top.

"If this has something to do with Stillwater," Brynn said, "Westwick would want the media as far away as possible. Especially if Stillwater's contacts inside the government pushed the project through using manipulation and bribes."

My hand rested on Brynn's shoulder, massaging the tension there. "So Westwick isn't just here to teach a seminar. He's using the seminar to create the appearance of a legitimate trip without the need to publicize exactly what they're doing."

Both Masterson and Westwick had high profiles, relatively speaking. They couldn't move around completely unnoticed. But the surface reason for the trip could conceal something more nefarious. Stillwater was all about hiding in plain sight.

Brynn nodded. "And that just makes me wonder. Is this solar plant really all that's out there?"

"You want to find out what they're up to in the desert?" I asked.

"Of course I do. Which means I have to get River's virus onto Westwick's devices asap. Tonight. Before Westwick changes his schedule yet again. I have to get him alone."

*Over my dead body,* I thought. "Or we could gather intel at the source. We drive out to the site of this solar plant after dark, and we find out if it's connected to Stillwater or not."

"You think we can get close enough?"

I gestured for her to let me take the seat. Brynn got up, and I slid into the place she'd left. River had included maps of the area around the solar plant, as well as more satellite images. Great resolution, too. These had come from government satellites, not just Google Earth.

I zoomed in.

"Looks like the main highway will take us within a couple of miles. The turnoff to the facility is here." I pointed at a narrower road that spurred from the highway. "There's a fence surrounding the perimeter. A gatehouse at the entrance." I tapped the screen. "And the front office building is here."

Brynn nodded along with my assessment. "Might have guards on patrol at night, but it'll be a skeleton crew," she mused. "They'll rely on their remoteness instead of a large security force."

"If this is really a Stillwater facility, they won't want too much personnel."

She laughed without humor. "Exactly. They'll happily send dozens of operatives to kidnap or kill a target, like the lieutenant governor. Wreak as much havoc and chaos as possible. But more guards around a place like this would mean more mouths to talk. Westwick likes his privacy."

"A weakness we can use."

The photos showed large trucks visiting the facility, probably with deliveries of materials. Plus construction vehicles in areas that looked unfinished. Were they still expanding?

"What about this?" She leaned over me and tapped on another building towards the middle of the property. "Another staff building? Electrical components of some kind?"

"I don't know what goes into maintaining these solar farms. Or what kind of machinery and electrical infrastructure they require." I was a bounty hunter, not an engineer.

"That's what Google is for. Right?"

Snorting, I pulled up the browser and searched. We spent some time reading up on solar energy plants. Most were either owned by utilities or by private investors who sold the energy wholesale to local power companies. "They'll have inverters and transformers to convert the power to a form that's usable by the utility," Brynn read. "Connections to the main power grid." But neither of us could identify everything we saw on the satellite images for Westwick's facility.

We sent a secure text to River, asking his opinion on the images. After all, he was the Protectors' resident nerd. And I meant that in the best way possible.

A few minutes later, River sent back the satellite photo with some parts labeled. He'd identified the centralized inverters that served each rectangular block of solar panels, as well as the other electrical equipment.

Then I added labels for the buildings that appeared to be for staff. "Building A" for the front office near the entrance. "Building B" for the one in the middle.

But there were other structures that didn't seem to fit the solar plant layout or the official public plans the government had approved. River couldn't identify them either.

"We need to get closer," I said. "Find out what's really going on there."

She nodded. "I say we hike in, time out their security guard patrols, and get a better look. We could approach from this side." Brynn pointed at the west perimeter of the facility, where the desert flora was thicker and the terrain more rugged. Small hills and canyons would provide cover.

"Perfect. You're pretty good at this, honey."

"Watch it." Grinning, Brynn wrapped her arms around my neck and playfully bit my ear. "You're not such a bad partner yourself. When you behave."

I turned my head to kiss her, anticipation making my pulse race.

I had a feeling that this excursion with Brynn would be *almost* as fun as partnering with her in bed.

# CHAPTER TWENTY-ONE

## *Brynn*

I WANTED to know what Westwick and Masterson had been doing out in the desert today. But first, we had to make it through another dinner.

Somehow, I had to once again smile at the head of Stillwater. Flirt with him. As if I was really Brianna, and nothing important had changed since the last time I'd seen the man.

Even though *everything* between me and Cole had changed.

Cole zipped up the back of my dress, his touch gentle, lingering at the nape of my neck. He'd already changed into his clothes for dinner. "B, from here on out, we stick together. No running off alone. No more risking yourself. Agreed?"

"For tonight, yes. We have a different agenda. Get through dinner, act friendly toward Westwick, and make sure he's not suspicious before we head out to the desert."

"I don't just mean tonight."

I sighed. I had known Cole was going to bring this up again. But my opinion hadn't changed. "Just because we're sleeping together doesn't mean you're suddenly in command. We need all options on the table."

Even our contingencies had relied on me getting Westwick alone in some capacity. Maybe something would change after we investigated the man's solar plant tonight, but if it didn't? We were back to the original plan.

I could tell Cole wanted to keep arguing, so I pointed out the time. "We need to go."

"This conversation isn't finished."

"But for now, it is." I marched to the door and opened it. With a wry look, Cole followed me, putting our security measures in place as we left.

Gentle music played as we walked into the restaurant. The hostess showed Cole and me to a table. Unlike last night, there were no plans for the seminar attendees to eat together. Everyone was relaxing tonight before the start of the event first thing tomorrow morning.

Cole was quick to take the seat facing the dining room, leaving me with the one facing the wall. I smiled when the hostess handed me a menu, but my expression turned cutting when I focused on Cole. "I know what you're doing," I muttered. "That spot should be mine."

"So you can wave and make eyes at Garon when he arrives?"

"*Exactly,*" I said through gritted teeth.

"I can wave at him for you." Cole smirked.

Like I didn't know what he was doing. But that was fine. Did he think I *wanted* to use myself as bait? Of course not. Allowing that man to touch me was the last thing on my wish list.

Last night, Cole had said he didn't want *any* other men touching me. The truth was, I didn't want that either. There wasn't a single man in the world I'd rather have in my bed than Cole. I was already attached, foolish as that was.

Cole lifted his water glass. "Westwick just arrived. And Masterson is with him."

I glanced up. There was a framed photo behind Cole's head, and in the reflective glass, I spied the two men. Westwick and Masterson were taking seats at a table in the middle of the restaurant. A large chandelier made of driftwood hung over their heads.

Interesting. Dining at that table was as good as a neon sign with an arrow. *Eric Masterson is here*. And yet, it fit with our theory. As a Senate candidate, it might be hard for Masterson to keep his movements secret. The resort visit was a cover. Maybe he was attending the seminar. Or maybe he was just visiting his friend. Either way, nobody outside their circle would know about their side trip into the desert.

Except Cole and me.

Twisting in my seat, I put on my most brilliant smile and waved. I caught Westwick's eye. He smiled back, tipping his head in my direction and reaching out to gently touch the shoulder of his companion.

Eric Masterson turned, one eyebrow lifting as he looked me over.

I wiggled my fingers in a friendly hello to them both before turning back around. "Are they still looking?" I asked Cole under my breath.

"Yep," Cole grumbled, slumping forward. "I'm sure they're talking about us. Or rather, *you*. I'm guessing O'Hanlon has reported what we were up to on the hiking trail."

My face heated, but not because I was embarrassed that the men knew we'd fooled around. It was the memory of how shameless I had been when Cole touched me. Plus the incredibly hot interlude with Cole on the couch… And in the oversized tub.

I crossed my legs. "That was the idea."

Tomorrow we would be spending all day in the seminar with Westwick. And maybe Masterson too, if he stuck around. With how quickly everything had been shifting, I was hesitant about making any assumptions.

As I'd said to Cole earlier, every option had to be on the table. We simply had no idea what tomorrow would bring.

If we were lucky, tonight's recon mission would open up some other avenue to use against Westwick. Some other means to infiltrate the inner workings of Stillwater.

But if it didn't? If we had no alternatives? I had to go back to my original tactic.

We couldn't let personal feelings get in the way of this mission. Could *not* allow this to fail.

Cole stiffened, a frown hardening on his face just before a voice spoke behind me.

"Ms. Waverley?"

I looked back. It was the hostess. She held a flute of champagne. "On the house, courtesy of Mr. Westwick."

I accepted the glass, lifting it in the man's direction. He grinned smugly.

"Didn't even send me one," Cole complained.

But less than a minute later, the hostess returned, carrying a lowball of scotch. She set it on the table, saying again that Westwick had sent it over. Yet another gesture to smooth over any hard feelings about the incident with Ryker last night.

We ordered, and while we waited for our food, I kept an eye on the dining room using the reflective glass behind Cole. Westwick's bodyguards weren't here tonight. "Did you notice who's missing?" I asked.

Cole nodded, taking another sip of his water. He'd ignored the scotch. "All three of the bodyguards. I dunno what to make of that."

Neither did I.

The important thing was that we'd cemented our cover story. Cole was doing an excellent job of playing my possessive, jealous boyfriend. I did my best to seem restless, even if what I *really* wanted was to lace my fingers with his and gaze into his eyes like I could never get enough. His leg brushed mine beneath the table, and our knees pressed together.

*What are we doing?* I wondered. Not for the first time that day. And probably not for the last.

---

Darkness surrounded us almost as soon as we left the resort. As a city girl, I'd always been amazed how quickly civilization faded once you were out in the wilderness.

We couldn't see a single thing beyond the glow of the headlights on the two-lane highway. Like we were headed straight into nowhere.

When we pulled off the highway, the desert made itself known as soon as we switched off the engine and lights. Hoots and howls, insects and larger things wrestling in the brush. Yet I felt infinitely safer out here than I had back at the resort. I would take vicious, hungry animals over Westwick and his crew any day.

Well, maybe my heart wasn't safe with Cole. But I was taking all sorts of risks with this mission, wasn't I?

Cole opened the trunk and used another key to unlock the special compartment at the back. "Let's gear up."

For tonight, mobility and stealth were paramount. We both changed into all-black head to toe. A black knit cap covered my bleached hair. I had wanted to work with the Protectors in the first place because they were well funded and equipped. And for this mission, they hadn't disappointed. We had plenty to choose from.

I strapped on my gear, checking that my weapon was ready and loaded. Grease paint blotted the paleness of my face. While I waited for Cole to finish, I took a swig from my water bottle.

"All set?" I asked him.

He popped the magazine of his handgun. Once he was satisfied, he inspected the items in his various pockets. I did one last inventory of my own.

"Yep, you?" he said.

"Let's roll."

Neither of us spoke much on the hike toward the facility. We had night-vision goggles, but I didn't put them on right away, just letting my eyes adjust to the sliver of moonlight in the sky and the brilliant blanket of stars overhead.

The air was cold and crisp. The trees and far-off mountains in silhouette.

Every so often we stopped and checked the map. Despite the late hour, after midnight, I was invigorated. Just being out here, kitted in tactical gear like an operative instead of masquerading as an influencer almost ten years younger than me.

This, right now, felt like the real me. Having Cole beside me only accentuated that feeling, like he had been my trusted partner for years instead of a matter of days. Like we *fit*, hand in glove or lock in key.

A mile out from the solar plant, the terrain got more variable, and we had to pick our way through hills and narrow canyons. Animals skittered away. Others watched us with glowing eyes from their hiding places.

"There are scorpions and rattlesnakes out here," I said, my upper lip curling. "Better be careful."

"Bringing back memories of the sandbox," Cole muttered.

"No kidding."

Once we found a high vantage point and checked for creepy-crawlies, we lay side by side. Cole's body was solid and warm against mine. I lifted a monocular for a closer view.

The solar farm lay below us. A seemingly endless sea of panels beyond a high, chain-linked fence. Bright lights marked the main gate to the facility. Just inside, there was a parking lot with a smattering of cars.

"There's one guard at the gatehouse," I said.

Cole held up his own monocular. "I've got eyes on a vehicle. A jeep patrolling the dirt road that borders the perimeter fence. Driver is alone."

I checked my watch, marking the time. The patrol drove along the west side of the facility. I switched my view to the other areas of the plant, but not much was visible from here. We would need to get closer.

At least the fence didn't look electrified. No signs of cameras on the fence line either. Once we had the patrols timed out, we'd be able to go over.

"What do you think they're really doing in there?" Cole asked.

I lowered my monocular. "From the info River sent, it seems like the solar panels are real. They're generating a lot of energy. Sending it on to the local utility."

"Sure, but all of it? I've been thinking. They could be using some of the energy for something else." Cole shifted, his hip bumping mine. "We know Stillwater has storage locations scattered around the Southwest. The Protectors and I struck one in Hart County. Loads of cash, documents. Plus those gold medallions Stillwater likes to hand out to its members like calling cards."

I huffed a laugh. "Stillwater gave up on those medallions last year after they realized what a liability the coins were. Wouldn't be surprised if they dumped the rest of them into the ocean somewhere."

He hummed. "Maybe. But I don't think this place is for

storage, anyway. The storage facility I saw before was nothing like this. It was hidden in the mountains. Manned by a single guard. Guaranteed, Garon Westwick would never have stepped foot near it. But today, he brought a potential senator here. So this is something far more significant."

"True. Even if they tried to keep the visit quiet, having either of their names tied in any way to this location means potential exposure. This is a risk. Something bigger than we've seen from Westwick before. But the reward must be worth it. Whatever he's got going here, it's valuable enough to justify the potential downsides."

Nobody outside Stillwater's ruling circle, not even the FBI's double agents, knew exactly what Garon Westwick was planning for the future of Stillwater.

Were we looking at it right now?

"If this is something bigger than we've seen from Still-water before," Cole said, "then it's fucking frightening."

"Do you know much about their activities outside the United States? That's something else that our double agents don't know, since they're all people working for state and federal authorities domestically."

"Some," he grunted. His lips pushed into a thin line.

I lifted my eyebrows at his vague, clipped answer. Like we were back to the first couple of days of trying to navigate this partnership, instead of...whatever we were now.

Cole turned his head toward me. I couldn't see him well in the dimness, but what I did see was conflicted. "There's something I haven't told you," he said.

My mind went to places I didn't want to go. Revelations I hadn't seen coming because I had been so eager to trust. "What's that?" I prompted.

*You're keeping things too,* I reminded myself.

I saw his Adam's apple move as he swallowed. "After I hit that Stillwater storage facility with the Protectors last year, I started looking for signs of them on my turf. It wasn't easy at first. You know how Stillwater works. Pulling strings from the shadows."

"Right." The anxiety burning through my stomach made me want to hurry him along. But Cole didn't seem to be in a rush.

He faced forward again to resume watching the dirt road that bordered the fence. Then he continued. "Given Stillwater's ties to human trafficking groups, I paid attention whenever word about traffickers crossed my radar. Somebody passed on my name to a mother, Luciana Rojas, who was searching for her teenage daughter Daniela. The girl had gone missing several months before. Luciana was desperate. Willing to do anything, seek help from anywhere, to find her kid."

Cole's voice was a monotone, a quiet drone in the desert bleakness. He paused briefly, and I thought of the similar stories I'd heard myself. "Awful," I murmured.

"Luciana suspected that Daniela had been taken by traffickers when the girl went to apply for a job. A common ruse to lure people in, and then they're spirited away, never to be seen again. I tracked Luciana's daughter to a warehouse on the coast, a way station for young trafficking victims on their way to being smuggled into the United States."

My gorge rose with fury. And with a sense of powerlessness, because the FBI fought against these kinds of evils all the time and none of it ever stopped.

"I was too late," Cole said. "Her daughter was gone. But you know what I did find? One of those gold Stillwater medallions. Proof that the traffickers used Stillwater's services. Guess they hadn't gotten the memo that the coins were out of fashion," he added bitterly.

I edged closer, wanting to feel Cole's warmth and hoping

he could feel mine. Still no sign of the security patrol on the dirt road.

A rustling noise came from nearby, startling us. In a split second, Cole had his weapon out, pointed into the dark. Two glowing eyes looked back. Then loped away.

It was another minute before my pulse started to slow, and Cole returned to his narrative. "I passed on the tip to a friend in the Mexican police. They raided the warehouse, seized computers and documents, but it was the same old song-and-dance that you and I have seen too many times before. Where it gets hushed up by corrupt officials. Wrapped in red bureaucratic tape. I tried rattling a few cages. Even contacted the Protectors, but River couldn't pull up any new leads for me. Eventually I concluded it was hopeless. The trail had gone cold. But Luciana wouldn't give up."

"What happened to her?" I asked, even though the resignation and frustration in his tone told me there was no happy ending.

"Luciana's body washed up on a beach."

I cursed. My eyes stung. "I'm so sorry."

"Her sister found my number among her things and that's how I heard."

"It sounds like Luciana meant a lot to you." I was ashamed at the jealousy that pricked my insides, imagining how close this woman had gotten to Cole. That shouldn't have mattered.

"She did mean a lot, but not the way you're thinking. It's because she was a good person who needed my help, needed protection, and I failed her. I'm convinced that either the traffickers or Stillwater killed her. Either way, every single person in the chain, from the scum who snatched Luciana's daughter all the way on up to Garon Westwick, are responsible. They all deserve to burn."

Everything about his body language, his voice, his eyes told me he meant that literally. Cole wanted blood.

"When you suggested we drive Westwick into the desert, you weren't kidding."

"No," he said with that flat, unwavering look in his eyes. "I wasn't. I've never intended to let Westwick walk away from this and trust that the FBI would eventually put him behind bars. That's the reason I initially accepted this mission. Not out of some vague sense of duty or the fact that the guys in the Protectors are my friends."

I exhaled, shaking my head. "And that's why you didn't quit when you found out I was an FBI agent." He had almost walked away. Now I knew why he'd changed his mind. Yet I wasn't sure how I felt about these revelations. Back in Silver Ridge, Cole had insisted up and down that he was worried about me going into this alone. Had that just been a convenient excuse? "Everything you said about us being equals..."

"I meant it. Even if I didn't necessarily agree about the endgame here, I knew I would need *you* to make it happen. As much as you need me." Cole shifted onto his side, gloved fingers reaching out to turn my chin so I would look at him. "I had a lot of reasons for sticking with this. What happened to Luciana was a big part of it, yeah. But from the moment I met you, I wanted to protect you, even if you didn't really need protecting. And now B, you mean so much more to me."

*You mean a lot to me too,* I wanted to say. But the words wouldn't come.

I hadn't told him about my communications with Stanford, either. I couldn't be too mad that Cole had come into this with his own agenda from the start.

But what now? Where did this partnership go from here?

"I understand why you didn't tell me about Luciana

before. You didn't trust me. I didn't trust you. It's different now, but—"

"It *is* different," he said emphatically. "That's why I'm telling you all this. I want you to—"

The faint rumble of an engine interrupted whatever he was about to say. We watched the same jeep slowly make its way along the fence line before turning out of sight again.

I checked my watch. "Twenty minutes between patrols." There hadn't been any other signs of human activity. The guard in the gatehouse hadn't budged.

"You were saying something before," I prompted. Cole hadn't finished his sentence.

But he shook his head. "Never mind. We should go and see what we can find out."

## CHAPTER TWENTY-TWO

WE CROSSED the open desert and stopped when we reached the fence. It was designed to keep out animals more than people, so it didn't take much for me to boost Brynn over the side and then climb over myself. We made our way past row after row of reflective panels. Brynn snapped photos as we went.

If anything, this place was too still and quiet. Eerily so. It made my thoughts even louder in my head.

I'd finally told Brynn about Luciana's murder and my personal stake in this mission. The moment had called for honesty. It would've been a lie of omission if I'd held it back, and I didn't want to do that with Brynn anymore.

I'd warned Luciana that she could be in trouble for continuing to speak out and demand answers. I should've known that her love for her daughter would never allow her to quit. I should've *protected* her. An innocent woman who committed no crime except loving her family. Instead, she'd had no one to help her, and I would never forget the shame of that.

Brynn had training and experience that Luciana never did. Beautiful and tough as steel underneath. Yet I also knew that if anything happened to Brynn, if I failed once again to stop Stillwater from harming a woman who'd needed my help, I would never be able to forgive myself.

"Listen," Brynn said, tilting her head.

I heard it too. A mechanical whooshing sound.

We kept going as the sound got louder. It was coming from a rectangular block of concrete. One of the mysterious structures we'd seen on the satellite imagery. Brynn and I paused as we reached it. The concrete walls only reached as high as my chest, metal grating on the top, with hatches on the sides that I assumed were for maintenance. Brynn twisted the handle of a hatch and opened it.

The humming noise got louder, and I realized what this had to be. A ventilation shaft with a fan spinning inside the concrete housing, circulating air.

I pointed down at our feet, and Brynn nodded.

There was something below us. Underground.

Brynn signaled for us to continue along our previous path, heading toward Building B at the middle of the property. I dipped my chin in acknowledgment.

But as we neared the circle of light around Building B, we found we weren't alone.

A guard stood in front of the building's entrance in full tactical gear, an M4 carbine strapped across his front. He had a casual but alert stance. The man looked exactly like the Stillwater operatives I had faced before. Mercenaries.

And wouldn't you know it? The door to the building opened, and Donovan Ryker strode out.

Brynn grabbed my arm and squeezed. I nodded. Now we knew for sure that Westwick and Masterson had visited here. This had to be a Stillwater facility. But why hadn't Ryker returned with his boss to the resort?

We stayed still, watching from our crouched position in the shadows. Ryker didn't pause, going over to a golf cart and getting in. He zoomed off toward the facility's exit. Whatever his purpose here, it appeared he was finished.

The door to Building B slammed shut, and the lock engaged with an audible thunk. The guard remained in place.

Brynn and I communicated silently. A brief but simple decision. Stay or go?

*Stay.* We both agreed. Now that we were here, we had to know more.

Building B had a single lens above a high-tech panel that controlled the lock. Maybe a fingerprint scanner. I hadn't spotted any other surveillance elsewhere in the solar farm. Cameras, like a larger security force, would be a double-edged sword. More surveillance and manpower would prevent trespassers from coming near. People like Brynn and me. But the more cameras and personnel hanging around, the more chances Westwick's secrets could leak.

If I were Westwick, I would allow only my most trusted people here. Which meant these guards were Stillwater loyalists. Probably handpicked by Donovan Ryker himself.

Getting past that guard would *not* be easy. And then getting inside Building B could be straight-up impossible. Unless we could somehow use the guard's biometrics for access. This could get messy.

Brynn nudged me. Another golf cart was zooming up the central path from the direction of Building A, the property's entrance. But it wasn't Ryker returning. It was another Stillwater mercenary.

Brynn and I both tensed, going for our weapons as the newcomer veered off the path and parked the golf cart within spitting distance of our hiding place. He jumped out and headed for the door, lifting his hand at the standing guard.

They fist bumped. Their laughter carried. I eased my hand away from my gun, keeping my breaths normal.

*Shift change.*

More evidence that cameras weren't watching, since I doubted these guys would be so laid back if Ryker or Westwick could check up on them. But nobody expected any trouble tonight. They were probably relieved that the boss had left the premises.

The guards were chatting, so I pressed my lips to Brynn's ear. "We can divert the guard going off shift. Question him."

"Affirmative. But we can't let him raise alarms after. We're ghosts tonight."

I held her gaze. We both knew what that would mean. And hell, I was proud of her. She wasn't thinking like an FBI agent anymore, worrying about jurisdiction and rules.

These were Stillwater mercenaries. Enemy combatants. That called for us to be just as merciless.

Quickly, we agreed on a plan. And then, we were on the move.

---

With the map of the facility laid out in my head, I cut across the dark rows of solar panels.

There was a bend in the central path through the property. A brief span that would be out of sight of both Building B's guard and Building A farther on. That's where I waited, drawing my weapon and getting ready.

Minutes later, I heard the whirr of the golf cart's motor.

I stepped into the path, aiming my gun. Shock rippled across the driver's features. He braked hard, swerving to the side. Grabbed for his radio with one hand, gun with the other.

But before he could get hold of either, Brynn popped up from the back of the golf cart. As the smaller between the two of us, she'd hidden inside the cargo compartment at the back of the cart.

She pressed the muzzle of her gun to the man's head, murmuring quietly. He snarled and went again for his weapon. Brynn smacked him in the nose. He shouted, but she muffled the sound by covering his mouth. I dashed forward, coming around the driver's side of the cart. Plucked his radio and his weapon. Blood gushed from the guard's nostrils.

Brynn shifted to the man's side, keeping her weapon on him.

"You're dead," he said thickly. I caught a faint accent, though I couldn't place it. "No chance are you getting out of here alive."

"If I were you, I'd be more concerned about myself," Brynn replied. "Hands off the steering wheel. Unless you'd prefer to end it all right here."

Of course, he wasn't going to live either way.

Spitting blood at my feet, the guard raised his arms. Brynn wrenched them behind his back and bound them with ties from our gear, while I tied his ankles. She stuffed a dirty rag into his mouth. No clue where she'd gotten it, but maybe it had been in the golf cart's storage compartment. Probably didn't taste so good.

I jumped into the driver's seat and steered us off the path, veering down a narrow gap between the solar panels. I parked the cart behind a ventilation shaft, out of sight and earshot of the buildings, but that brought us nearer to the fence line.

Brynn checked her watch. "We've got three minutes until the next patrol drives by."

"Keep an eye on the time for me? We'll let it pass. Then I'd love first crack at this guy."

"Wilco. Be my guest." She smirked.

We dragged the Stillwater guard out of the cart and onto the dirt beneath a solar panel. Laid him flat on his back. The guy tried to wriggle away. Brynn sat on his legs, and I held my gun beneath his chin.

He stopped moving. Stared with empty eyes. Breathed wetly through his damaged nose. I doubted that was pleasant.

Every Stillwater mercenary I'd faced had been well-trained. Unlikely to break under interrogation or torture. Especially not quickly, and we didn't have all night. But sometimes people gave away things that they didn't intend.

I kept the gun on him for a while. Three long minutes. Brynn counted them down.

The jeep's engine started as a faint growl. Grew louder as its lights came into view. Brynn and I didn't take our eyes off our prisoner. If he was going to escape or get the attention of his fellow guard, it would be now.

The jeep got closer. We weren't right at the fence line, but if there was a loud noise or a flash of sudden movement, the driver would probably notice. Assuming he wasn't an idiot.

With a violent burst of energy, our prisoner tried to buck Brynn off, shouting around his gag. I grabbed his damaged nose and squeezed.

The jeep drove past.

Once it was gone, I sat beside our prisoner's head, my knees bent and the gun aimed casually near my feet. Then I tugged the rag from his mouth.

"Fuck you," he spit out. "You're getting nothing from me."

"We know this is a Stillwater facility and that Garon Westwick visited earlier today with a friend of his. Eric Masterson."

No reaction.

"I want to know what you're guarding here. What did Westwick and Masterson come here to see?"

"If you know about Stillwater, you know they'll hunt you down."

"What's underground here?"

Dull eyes looked back at me. He wasn't giving me much, that was for sure. But his lack of confusion or surprise confirmed that we were right. Whatever Stillwater had going on here, the main action was beneath us.

"You think a man like Westwick gives a shit about you?" I asked. "You're disposable. But how about this." I moved the muzzle of the gun to his forehead. "Talk to me, and I'll let you go before the next patrol comes by. Nobody will know you said a word. You can take your paycheck and hope for the best. Even better, you can get as far away from Stillwater as possible before you wind up dead like the others my friends and I have killed. Stillwater seems to go through a lot of you guys."

More of a reaction that time. His pupils dilated, and the muscles near his throat convulsed, like he was just holding back from giving me something. Just to see if I was actually going to let him go.

His lips started to move. I waited.

"The deepest water is the quietest," he whispered. The Stillwater motto.

Then he lunged, upper body arching toward me. My gun cut a gash in his forehead. I barely shifted to the side in time to keep him from headbutting me. I pushed back against him with my weight as he did everything in his power to wriggle free.

Then just as suddenly, the man grunted, heaved several breaths, and went limp. The black handle of a knife stuck out from his rib cage.

Brynn had stabbed him. Precision aim, designed to kill.

"He knew you weren't going to shoot him." Her voice was rough. "Knew we wouldn't risk the noise."

"True." I looked at her for a moment. She was breathing hard. Hand still clenched around the knife handle. I reached over to loosen her grip. Her expression had closed off.

"You good?" I asked.

Every kill, no matter how justifiable, took something from you. It was a reality I'd come to terms with long ago. I also expected that Brynn had killed before. But there was something extremely personal about killing a man with a knife. It was more intimate than a gun. Visceral.

My heart rebelled at seeing the slickness of blood on Brynn's gloved hands. I had meant to dispose of this guy, and it pissed me off that Brynn had to do it instead. That mark was supposed to be on *my* hardened soul, like so many others. Not on hers.

And that was the problem with getting involved with your partner. I wasn't treating her like an equal right now, was I? I was thinking of her as my protectee. Someone I was meant to shield, who wasn't supposed to risk herself to shield *me*.

She pushed up onto her hands and knees. "I'm fine. Help me get this mess cleaned up so we can get out of here."

# CHAPTER TWENTY-THREE
## Brynn

NUMBNESS DULLED everything inside me on the drive back to the resort. I'd always appreciated that when going into battle. When the buzz of anxiety and second-guessing in my head went quiet, and nothing but the mission mattered. Neutralize the target, reach the objective, *survive*.

The part I didn't like as much was when the ice thawed. As it inevitably did.

I rubbed my hands absently against my black pants, and Cole reached across the cabin. Captured my left hand with his larger one. His strength grounded me, and I appreciated that, but it felt like he was questioning me too. *Are you all right?*

Right now, I didn't want to be questioned. Especially not by him. Because with Cole, I was tempted to fold myself into his arms and let him take the burden of what I was feeling.

If I did that, then I wouldn't deserve to stand beside him as his partner.

I had done what I had to, and there was nothing else to say about it.

With the guard dead, we'd had a body to dispose of. Ideally, we would've dispatched the guy *without* leaving a blood trail. But not everything went according to best-laid plans. We'd stripped the Stillwater guard's vest, jacket, and pants, then stuffed the body in the maintenance hatch of the ventilation shaft and kicked dirt around to cover the blood.

Cole and I had argued over who would drive the golf cart to the exit. If we left the dead man's car in the parking lot, the others would realize within hours that their colleague had never left at the end of his shift. Cole had insisted he would fit the guard's clothes better, which I supposed was a fair point.

He'd masqueraded as the dead guy, while I'd climbed the fence and retraced our path through the desert, thinking the whole time that I'd murder Cole if he let himself get caught.

But he hadn't. He'd used the dead guard's key fob to locate his vehicle in the employee lot. Then drove right out of the Stillwater facility. Thank goodness the guard at the gatehouse hadn't looked too closely. The darkness had helped.

The dead guard's car was out in the desert now. With luck, we had at least a day or two before Stillwater realized their man hadn't made it home. Especially if the guard wasn't due back on shift tomorrow.

No, make that today. Because it was almost four AM. I sighed, dropping my head back against the passenger seat. What a night.

We knew for sure Westwick was up to something in the desert. Something hidden beneath those fields of solar panels. And we had confirmed that Stillwater faithful were guarding the facility. The kinds of men who Westwick and Ryker would trust with their most sensitive secrets.

We were *so close* to breaking everything open. And yet we didn't get much intel tonight. What could we do except fall back to the original plan?

When we were almost back to the resort, we stopped to change out of our tactical clothes. I pulled on a pair of leggings and a patterned sweatshirt, tucking my feet into a pair of sandals. A wet wipe cleaned the greasepaint from my face. Cole put on some shorts and a linen shirt. Our dirty clothes went into a plastic bag to be discarded in an anonymous dumpster later.

We checked each other for visible bloodstains. Cole found a few flecks on my chin and wiped them clean.

Walking back into the resort, we looked like Brianna and Cameron again. Back after spending most of the night stargazing. I even had a tote with my gun and laptop stowed at the bottom, beneath a blanket and an empty champagne bottle. But we didn't see any staff on the way to our room. Certainly no guests.

Cole took out our room key, then froze. I followed the path of his eyes.

The tiny piece of paper we'd wedged above the hinge in the doorframe. It wasn't visible. Which meant somebody had opened this door while we were gone.

*Shit.*

"I guess housekeeping was here," Cole said, nodding at the missing *Do Not Disturb* hanger. But he subtly placed his hand near his waistband, where he'd concealed his gun. I reached inside my tote and closed my fingers around my weapon. My breathing slowed, blood thumping in my ears.

This hallway was lined with a dozen doors, including Westwick's and Ryker's. They could be watching us right now. Or even waiting inside our room. An ambush. Would they risk it in the middle of the resort?

Cole waved the keycard. Carefully pushed open the door.

We both drew our weapons as we stepped into the dark room.

The *Do Not Disturb* sign lay on the floor. The tiny scrap of paper lay against the wall. Through the open doorway into the bathroom, I spotted a stack of fresh towels. We'd asked for no housekeeping visits, but maybe they hadn't listened. At least someone *wanted* us to think it had been housekeeping. The bed was made, but nothing else appeared to have been disturbed.

I shut the door to the hallway with my foot. Raised my weapon. Cole signaled for me to take one side of the room, while he took the other.

The room was empty.

"Anything missing?" Cole murmured.

I glanced through my suitcase and drawers while Cole did the same. Our small stash inside the air vent was untouched. Thank goodness we had taken my laptop and the other weapons with us.

Except...

Heart leaping into my throat, I felt around in my underwear drawer, exhaling when I found my burner phone safe inside its sock.

"You good?" Cole asked behind me.

I forced myself not to flinch. Leaving the phone inside the sock, I shut the drawer and turned around. "Yep. It's all there. Jewelry and everything."

But we spent the next half hour checking every item and crevice for bugs or trackers. Once we'd finished, Cole ran his fingers through his hair and sank onto the edge of the bed. "Housekeeping doesn't show up at night. Ryker was checking up on us. But if they knew where we were tonight, they would've intercepted us on the road."

I sat beside him. "They know we were gone. When they figure out there's a guard missing from the solar plant, they could connect the two." I rubbed at my hands. I'd already washed them, but they didn't feel clean.

He reached out to put his hand over mine. "Brynn," he said softly.

How did he convey so much care and concern in one

word? I didn't think any man had ever said my name with such tenderness.

"I'm fine." I got up again, too jittery and full of adrenaline to sit still. "When we first started this, you claimed you respected my abilities. You didn't see me as weak. But all you've done since is try to protect me, and I can't—"

He caught my elbow and pulled me closer to stand between his spread knees. "You're right. I've been guilty of that. And a few hours ago, I wouldn't have apologized for it. I hate that you had to kill a man tonight. Doesn't matter that he was one of Stillwater's finest. I would much rather it was me who put him down and not you."

I tried to pull away, but he held me there, hands firm on my hips.

"But," he continued. "You saved my ass back there. You're my partner. You know what's too much for you, and nobody has a right, least of all me, to decide your limits. I respect you too much for that."

"Doesn't feel like it."

"Would you let me finish, B?" A hint of a smile ghosted Cole's lips. Then he turned serious again. "I don't want you alone with Westwick or anyone associated with him because I'm afraid of what could happen. I'm fucking afraid. I can admit that. But that fear is *my* problem, not yours. So if you're still committed to using yourself as bait to get close enough to Westwick to plant the virus, I'll...go along with it. I'll let you decide."

I stared down at him, surprised that he'd made such a concession.

It had been so important to me to prove I could handle this. But Cole had just acknowledged that his hangups were irrelevant to our mission. So I had to admit that mine were too.

I couldn't let my uncle's cruel words, all the times he'd

called me *weak* and *worthless,* dictate the choices I made now. I had to consider what was best for this mission and this partnership, setting everything else aside.

Cole and I were good together. We had chemistry, and it wasn't just sexual. In the short time we had worked with one another, we had fought side by side more than once. We had learned to read one another. There had to be a way for us to use that.

"I don't want any man touching me but you, either."

He pulled me into his lap, wrapping me in his arms. Kissed the top of my head. "Damn right," he muttered.

"But we need alternatives. We have to separate Westwick from his security team to get access to his devices. Unless we can get his phone away from him without him knowing. But Ryker will be watching our every move."

"I was coming up with contingencies on the drive home. I'm not sure you're going to like it."

"Try me."

He sighed, his breath warm against my neck. "I already told you that I never intended to let Westwick walk away unscathed."

I nodded. Cole had said as much when we were out in the desert. Could I say I was surprised? "I feel the same way. Taking out Westwick ourselves would be far more satisfying than waiting around for the legal system to do it. More efficient too. But how does that get us the rest of Stillwater?"

"You're assuming I mean to kill him." Cole huffed a laugh. "Well, I do, but not right away. I'm suggesting we kidnap Westwick. Take him to a secure location and bleed him dry of everything he knows about Stillwater."

A cold chill ran through me, but it wasn't reluctance. It was eagerness. Talk about poetic justice. Westwick had ordered Stillwater's lieutenants to kidnap my best friend torture her for information. I liked the idea of doing the same to him.

"From what you've told me about Stillwater's decentralized structure," Cole went on, "I doubt Westwick has a clear second in command. There's Ryker, but he's the muscle, not the brains."

"There are others near the top who could potentially replace Westwick and keep Stillwater going if he disappears. But if we have Westwick, we can anticipate the next moves of Stillwater's inner circle. Assuming we can make him talk. We'll also need a safe house where we can keep him. The Protectors have several."

Cole shrugged. "The Protectors also have two ex-CIA spies who can take over interrogation, should we need them. Trace and River will be more than happy to spend some quality time with Garon Westwick, given what the man has done."

We would be kidnapping a US citizen on American soil, using any means to get him to spill his secrets, all with the knowledge that he would never spend another day as a free man.

But wasn't *this* the real reason I had resigned from the FBI? It wasn't just the need for secrecy, or even Stanford's desire to give the rest of the FBI deniability if this mission went wrong. I wanted to destroy Stillwater using any means necessary. No FBI rules. No guardrails. Yet I hadn't been ready to admit that truth about myself until now.

To destroy Stillwater, Cole and I had to fight dirty. Side by side.

We had to be vigilantes.

———

We talked awhile longer about how to get Westwick away from his bodyguards. It would be tricky. Our best option was to go with a version of my original idea. Brianna would lure Westwick into meeting alone. But Cole would be waiting.

It had to happen *today*. Given Ryker's growing suspicion and that dead guard we'd left at the facility, we couldn't afford to stay here another night. It was time to make our move.

"I need to shower and get some rest," I said. The sun would be up way too soon.

"Same. I'll go after you." Cole stroked his thumb down my cheek, but his touch and his words weren't a prelude to more. It was just a small comfort. A reminder that I wasn't alone.

In the shower, I scrubbed my skin until it was red and raw. Cole trimmed his beard over the sink. I felt his eyes on me in the mirror as I cleaned up, but there was still no heat there. Just reassurance whenever our gazes met.

When I'd finished, I wrapped myself in a towel. I went to the sink to brush my teeth and try to comb out the tangles in my hair. Cole took his turn in the shower, removing his prosthesis first, then moving in that practiced way he had. Whether he was in tactical gear or naked, he was so comfortable in his skin.

Desire swirled in my lower belly, waking up from the numbness I'd been feeling earlier.

He hadn't told me much about his ex-wife. Just enough for me to know I didn't like her. What kind of fool would let a man like him go?

Trust was a battle for me, but Cole kept on working his way past my barriers. And he'd done it just by being himself. He'd told me he was no actor. Maybe he could lie when we were up against the enemy, but most of the time, Cole couldn't be anyone other than himself. That was probably the thing I liked most about him.

I had to tell him about that burner phone Stanford had given me. How I hadn't fully cut ties to the FBI like I had claimed.

"What are you thinking about?" Cole asked behind me. He was drying off with a towel.

I rinsed my mouth and set aside the toothbrush. "You." It was true.

He smiled, expression softening. "It just so happens I was thinking about you. I seem to do that a lot."

My heart squeezed.

In the bedroom, I pulled on a pair of underwear. Cole's shirt was on the floor, one he'd been wearing around the resort earlier, so I grabbed it and put it on too. I slid beneath the covers next to him.

"You're wearing my shirt."

"It was handy." But more than that, I liked having his scent on me.

Cole lifted up the blankets so I could scoot closer to him. He wore only a pair of boxer briefs. All the lights were out, curtains drawn. The blue glow of an automatic nightlight came from the bathroom.

I rested my cheek against his bare chest, my hand on his stomach, enjoying the brush of his happy trail beneath my palm.

We were supposed to be going to sleep. But my brain was wired, knowing I shouldn't let tonight end without telling Cole what I'd been hiding. How pissed off would he be? He'd kept things back from me as well.

And I had cut off all communications with Stanford yesterday. That had to count for something.

*Tell him. Just say it.*

I lifted my head. His eyes were open, watching me in the faint blue-tinged light.

"Cole—"

"We should sleep," he said huskily. "But I'd much rather kiss you. Can I?"

My confession was right there on my tongue. "I think we're past the part where you need to ask."

"Good." He shifted his body. I fell onto my back with Cole above me, propped on his elbow. His mouth sought out mine. Soft but also hungry. His free hand cupped my cheek.

"We need to talk," I said between kisses.

"We've talked for hours, B. My mind is shot. It's either sleep, or this, and I think we need this more." He pushed up the shirt to caress my stomach. "Unless you tell me no."

The last thing I wanted was to tell him no.

Desire pushed away thoughts of my confession. Of anything but how much I wanted to feel Cole, skin to skin. As if I hadn't killed a man tonight. As if we weren't in the middle of a life-or-death battle against Garon Westwick and all the ugly things Stillwater had done. As if nothing mattered but the two of us. Not even my lingering, blurry ties to the FBI.

We did need this. *I* did.

With Cole's next kiss, his tongue glided into my mouth. He tasted like minty toothpaste and kindness and comfort. Exactly what I needed in this moment. For a man roughened by his past, with so many scars, there was something sweet and open about the way he kissed. Like he was always reading my reactions, wanting to share this experience with me instead of just taking.

Cole's hands roved, exploring like this was our first time instead of the third or fourth that he'd had me spread out for him just today.

But when he touched me between the legs, finding the

dampness at the crotch of my panties, our kisses turned more intense. I felt the length of him swelling against my thigh. Growing harder and hotter by the second.

My legs wrapped around his waist. Drawing him closer. Cole pushed up the shirt until it was over my head, and I tossed it to the side, not caring where it landed. His cock nudged against my clit through the thin layers of our underwear. His beard tickled my neck, my upper chest, my breasts as he kissed and licked all over my skin.

He worked his boxer briefs down over his hips, his movements unhurried. Sensuous. "We didn't use a condom before," he said. "That still all right with you?"

"I'd speak up if it wasn't." I hooked my thumbs in my panties and shoved them down. Nowhere near as graceful as he had just been.

Maybe I should've second-guessed sharing my body with him this way, but it seemed that my instincts had been urging me to trust Cole all along, even when it took my brain slightly longer to get the message. From the first time Cole had touched me, kissed me, even when it was supposed to be fake, all I had wanted was to pull him closer.

*Closer*. That was what I needed. To get him as close as possible.

I hooked a leg over his hip and reached up to hold on to his broad shoulders. Immediately, he pressed his cock to my opening and worked his way inside with a few smooth thrusts. My head fell back against the pillow. His chest hair brushed with gentle friction against my breasts. Cole brought his nose to my temple and inhaled. As if being inside of me wasn't enough. He needed to pull my scent inside him. To lose himself in this connection and focus entirely on me.

"How do you feel this good?" he asked.

"Pretty sure it's all you."

"Not even close."

I basked in the feeling of being beneath him. His heavy weight pressing me into the mattress. Letting him control the pace.

But after a while, I nudged his shoulder. "Mind if I'm on top?"

He rolled us both and landed on his back, bouncing slightly. "I'm happy for you to be on top. I get to see you, touch you. Let you do the hard work for a while." His white teeth flashed as he smiled. "You love riding my cock, don't you?"

"I do." I spread my legs around him and lowered back down onto his hard length. Put my hands on his pecs, my long hair falling forward as I undulated my hips. Rocking our bodies against each other.

He squeezed my butt cheeks. "That's it, honey." He bucked his hips, making me gasp. "Show me how much you love it."

I shuddered with a moan. "What I *love* is finally being in charge of you."

He laughed. "For the moment, anyway."

I bent over Cole to kiss him. My smile stayed. Regardless of what we'd dealt with tonight, we'd made it through all of that as a team.

I rode him until the glow of pleasure between my legs crested, taking me over. To my surprise, Cole stayed right there beneath me instead of repositioning. A few more thrusts upward, and he grabbed my waist to hold me firmly in place as he groaned through his own release.

We ended up lying next to each other, catching our breaths. Hearts aligned as they beat quickly, but in time. I'd just joked about me being in charge, but really, we were finally in perfect sync.

And that was when I knew I couldn't tell him what I was hiding.

I'd started this op still linked to the FBI. Stanford had warned me not to let my guard down around Cole. *Even though we need the Protectors, that doesn't make you one of them,* my boss had said.

But now, it wasn't about the Protectors or the FBI anymore. This was about Cole and me. The two of us relying on each other. This had become so much more than an undercover partnership. I cared about him, and I believed that he cared about me. Our mission was stronger for it. And maybe…maybe I would be stronger for it, too.

I couldn't do anything to jeopardize that.

# CHAPTER TWENTY-FOUR

SUNLIGHT PEEKED around the curtains of our hotel room.

"Want a cigarette?" Brynn asked.

She was still lying naked beside me, legs tangled with mine beneath the covers. Her hair splayed over the pillow in a debauched mess. She looked sexy enough that I wished I was twenty years younger and could take her again right now. Maybe from behind. Get her moaning and desperate the way I liked.

But I'd had more sex in the last twenty-four hours than I'd had in a very long time. I didn't have another round in me yet.

"Excellent idea." A few minutes ago, I would've said that nothing could drag me away from this bed. But a smoke was just the thing, especially if Brynn wanted to share it with me. Not like we were getting to sleep anyway. We were due at breakfast in less than two hours.

We could sleep when this was over. In fact, I had several ideas about what we should do once this was over. More sex was high on that agenda.

Brynn and I got out of bed, threw on clothes, and went

onto the tiny patio behind our room. It was chilly, so Brynn grabbed a blanket. We sat on the small bench, her in my lap and the blanket around us both. I cast a cautious glance around, still wary after last night and the knowledge that someone had been poking around in our room. But there was no activity here except for the usual sights and sounds of the desert greeting the morning.

I lit the cigarette with my lighter, inhaling, and then held it out to her. She fit her lips around it. Took a drag while not taking her eyes off mine.

There were a few stringy clouds near the horizon, and they glowed in the sunrise. I had no doubt that workers were busy nearby, getting the resort ready for another day. But on this side, everything was quiet.

Today was going to be difficult, and there were a million ways our plans could go wrong. Yet I had never felt more alive. Because of her.

Damn. If things kept going in the same direction, I'd be falling for her before I knew it. *Might not end well,* I thought. So few things did. But I didn't want to stop.

Smoke exhaled through my nose, disappearing into the sky. "You should come see me in Mexico when this is over. I have a place in the city, but my favorite is my little house near the beach."

"Tell me about it?"

Brynn settled against me, sharing my cigarette as I told her about the small, picturesque town on the coast. The kind people I'd come to know there. The peace I felt whenever I got to hang around for a while and forget about my past sorrows, forget about work. Just be.

"We could take some time off," I said. "Do nothing but… well, each other." I squeezed her side affectionately. "What do you think?"

Brynn and I hadn't discussed much about her plans for

after this mission. Where she might go next in her career. And I had no intention of pushing. She could do her own thing. But I wanted to make sure she knew where I stood.

She smiled and tilted her chin to kiss me. "I like the sound of that." Then she blinked, uncertainty showing in the way her eyes narrowed, before it was gone. "I hope we can. We're good together."

"We are, B. We're fucking great together." The hint of emotion in my voice caught me by surprise. I'd been trying to keep things simple with her, but that just wasn't possible. I was invested.

Even when my ex-wife had left me, the blow had been worse to my ego than my heart. Shelley had accused me of never opening up. Never putting her first, never mind that I was struggling to get my life back together after losing my leg and the career I'd built in one fell swoop. But Shelley had been right that I'd refused to let my stoic exterior break.

After just a few days with Brynn, she'd already gotten beneath my skin. Those slender fingers of hers were wrapped around my heart. If we went our separate ways after this and she forgot about me, it was going to hurt like hell.

But for now, we had a mission to accomplish. We sat together and watched the sun come up. Our last day at this resort. No offense to the place, but I had no interest in ever making a return visit.

Whatever happened today, we would be leaving this place together. We'd have to figure out the rest from there.

---

While Brynn showered, I had one more quick errand to run.

When I got back, I took my turn getting cleaned up and ready. Brynn lingered in the bathroom applying makeup and styling her hair.

I stood with my hip against the counter and watched, my eyes following her every move like it was all for me. Possessive? Yeah. But that's how I was feeling.

We'd already checked the Protectors server. Nothing new from River. We had let the Protectors know about our adventure last night, and River had assured us he was keeping an eye on police activity in the area. Not that we expected Stillwater to go to the police about their missing guard.

Of course, Stillwater had recruited local officers to do their bidding before. It was just another reminder that Brynn and I were on our own out here.

Like she had said earlier this morning, we were good together. We could get this done.

Still, I couldn't keep my fingers from tapping against my side, drumming an anxious rhythm.

"Ryker will be monitoring us closely," I reminded her. The man hadn't found anything by searching our room last night, but he would still be suspicious. I expected he would assign Manning and O'Hanlon to have eyes on us.

She fluffed her hair. "Which is why we have a diversion coming. River might be obnoxious sometimes, but he always comes through. It's going to work."

"I know, but it might take me longer to shake Manning and O'Hanlon if they stick to me. If I'm not up to the roof in time, and you beat me there with Westwick—"

She arched an eyebrow at me in the mirror. "Then I'll keep him distracted. With *talking*," she added in response to my scowl. "Brianna can keep a conversation going. Westwick might have other ideas when he gets me alone, but I'll keep him talking until you arrive. And then we'll have him."

I exhaled. "We will."

She went to the main room. We had our gear laid out on the bed. Brynn lifted her dress and strapped a holster onto her thigh, sliding a small knife into the sheath. It wasn't the larger one she'd killed the guard with. That murder weapon was long gone, buried in the desert. This knife was slimmer, streamlined, but equally sharp.

If Westwick got handsy and found that knife under her dress, it would give a lot away. But if he was that close to her, then things would already have gone very wrong. I felt better knowing she'd have a weapon at the ready.

She also had the flash drive with River's virus in the lining of her purse. That wasn't our primary plan any longer, but it was a fallback. Just in case we had to scrub the kidnapping attempt.

That wouldn't happen though. We were going to pull this off.

I touched her waist. Brynn held the lapels of my shirt and pulled me into a kiss. "Come on, Cameron. We have a business seminar to attend."

Westwick had booked a special event room for a welcome breakfast. Brynn looked gorgeous in another summer dress, and heads turned as we entered the room. Most of the seminar attendees had arrived. But Westwick and his security goons weren't here yet.

Brynn put her arm through mine and whispered into my ear. "Mr. Perfect wouldn't be late to the start of his seminar. Would he?"

I knew what she was thinking, because I was wondering the same thing. Had the guards at the solar plant realized their colleague was missing? Had they sounded the alarm?

But the next moment, Westwick walked into the event room, dressed in a suit and an easy grin. I put an arm around Brynn's shoulders, feeling her exhale with relief. Ryker and Manning filed in behind Westwick, taking up a post near the exit. Ryker's eyes immediately flew to us. But I couldn't read the expression on his face.

Manning, though, lifted his chin in a friendly way when

he caught my eye. I nodded back. O'Hanlon wasn't here, and I had no idea what to make of that. But we were on track.

The other guests chatted while we grabbed breakfast. Adding bacon to my plate, I leaned into Brynn. "I guess the friend isn't coming today." I meant Eric Masterson, and her nod said she understood.

She glanced in Westwick's direction. "Solves one problem."

We hadn't known if Masterson would stick to Westwick's side today, and how much of an issue that could be. It would be easier for her to get Westwick separated without having to deal with his buddy. A stroke of luck.

As we ate and guzzled coffee, one of the hotel's staff announced the first session would begin in fifteen minutes. "Eager to get started with all of you soon," Westwick added with a grin.

I squeezed Brynn's hand, then let go. "You're on, B," I murmured. This was the first time today we would be separated, but not the last. Dropping one more kiss to her temple, I left the room, heading for the restroom.

Brynn needed a couple minutes alone to chat with Westwick, so I was giving it to her.

I used a urinal in the men's room. Then paused by the sink. I had dark circles beneath my eyes in the mirror, like a guy who hadn't slept a minute last night and was too old to get away with it anymore.

The door swung open, and Manning stepped inside. He lifted his chin at me as he passed. He went to the urinals, while I washed my hands.

I was about to leave when Manning said, "Clay. Hang on a sec."

I glanced back over my shoulder. The bodyguard strode over to the sink. Took his time rinsing his hands like I should wait all day for him to speak. And with each second that passed, the tension around my spine increased. What did he want?

Manning dried his hands on a paper towel. "Could I bum a smoke?"

Carefully sliding the pack out of my pocket, I held it out. He took it. Flipped the lid and eased a single out. "Hey, where were you and Brianna last night?" he asked conversationally. "You weren't in the lounge. Your girl was missed. She's pretty popular."

I studied him. The man seemed relaxed. But there had to be a reason Ryker trusted Manning as one of Westwick's personal guards.

I thought of the mercenary Brynn had killed last night. How he'd recited that creepy Stillwater motto right before he died.

"She wanted me to take her out stargazing."

"Romantic evening?" Manning winked. "Women eat up that shit, don't they?"

Had he been the one to search our room last night? Had he touched Brynn's things? The thought of this guy rifling through her silky underwear made me stabby.

Manning stuck the cigarette in the corner of his mouth, so it bobbed as he spoke. "I should try something like that with my girl. Hopefully soon. According to the boss man, we're going to be out of here tonight."

"That right?" So it was a good thing we planned to snatch him today. Westwick's schedule was constantly shifting. "Brianna and I will be enjoying a few more days by the pool."

Manning held out my pack of cigarettes. "With your girl providing a view like that, I can't blame you."

I snatched the pack from his fingers, hoping my grin didn't give away how much I wanted to end him.

Back in the breakfast area, I saw Brynn talking quietly

with Westwick. Then she nodded and walked away. I met up with her by the coffee jugs.

"Progress?" I asked as I poured myself another cup.

She glanced around subtly to make sure no one was in earshot. "I'm meeting with him before dinner. I mentioned you have a phone call scheduled, so I'll be free. He was very interested in a private conversation to discuss business strategy."

"I'm sure." I took a gulp of coffee. It singed my tongue.

This was good news. If Westwick hadn't wanted to meet before dinner, Brynn would have suggested later tonight. But late afternoon was ideal. Most everyone, even bodyguards, got tired around that time, looking forward to a break and a hot meal. Westwick's bodyguards wouldn't be at their sharpest. Especially if they were prepping for a departure later tonight.

Westwick probably thought he'd fit in a little fun with Brianna, have dinner, then jet off to his next locale. Instead, he'd be on his way to a safe house for interrogation.

Yet another thing going according to plan A. But if anything, the smooth runway toward our goal only wound me up.

There would be bumps in the road. It was just a matter of time.

---

One of the hardest parts of any mission was the waiting. Any soldier could tolerate boredom. That was a given. It was all about reserving your strength, relaxing your mind so that you'd be sharp when the time came to act.

But Westwick and his business seminar were really testing me.

The hours ticked by with agonizing slowness. During the

lunch break, we sat with Molly and her husband and the other attendees. Brynn, playing the ambitious young influencer, kept up the conversation, while I sat back and continued looking bored. Which was not remotely a challenge.

Luckily, Cameron wasn't supposed to be all that interested anyway.

But one thing I couldn't do was keep myself from touching her, so it was a good thing I didn't have to. Throughout the afternoon session, I played with her ponytail, massaged her shoulders. Sought out the soft places I had discovered at the side of her neck and behind her ear. Just needing to feel her there beside me, since soon she wouldn't be.

*We'll only be separated a short while,* I told myself. *No longer than necessary*. My eyes kept seeking out my watch. The minutes passed.

Just before the afternoon session was scheduled to end, I took Brynn's face in my hand. Planted my lips on her in front of everyone, including Westwick. I kissed her a few times, slow and deep, soaking in the feeling of her.

"I'll see you soon, honey," I murmured in her ear.

When I pulled back, she was smirking. "Careful," she warned. "I might get tired of you calling me that."

"You can lay down the law when it's just us."

I caught a glimpse of Brynn's determination, that strength I admired, before her sweet Brianna-smile replaced it. "Soon," she whispered back.

Westwick clapped his hands together and announced we were finished. "Thank you, everyone! I'll be happy to take all your questions this evening at dinner. It'll be in the same room where we had breakfast."

With one more kiss to Brynn's lips, I got up to head back to our room.

As I walked, I hit the timer on my watch. I had to get final word to River that we were ready for the diversion. I was on the clock now.

Brynn and I had timed things out carefully. A few attendees would linger in the seminar room, but soon, Brynn would be alone with the head of Stillwater. The very thing I'd been hoping to avoid since the start of this mission. But she was a trained soldier. Sorry, a trained *Marine*. I would see her soon. That kept repeating in my head. The very word that had been on her lips, the last thing she'd said to me. *Soon*.

As expected, O'Hanlon peeled off to follow me at a distance. I spotted the man in the reflections of artwork as I passed. If anything, his presence reassured me. I assumed Manning was prepping for tonight's late departure from the resort. Ryker would stick with Westwick, but we'd planned for that as well.

At our room, I waved my keycard and hurried inside. Set my daypack onto the bed. After the search last night, we hadn't risked keeping weapons or anything sensitive here. I'd been carrying the laptop and a gun around all day.

Taking out the computer, I booted it up and sent off a message to River. *We're a go*.

River wrote back, *Roger. Ten minutes*.

I stuffed the laptop back into my daypack. Grabbed our suitcase, which we'd packed this morning.

Then furious knocking at the door interrupted me. I went to the peephole and looked out. But it wasn't Manning or O'Hanlon here to mess up my timing.

It was Molly. The older woman from Dallas who'd taken Brianna under her wing.

"Mr. Clay, I know you're in there. I saw you go in. I want a word with you, if you please."

"Not now," I grumbled through the closed door. "I have a phone call."

"I don't want your excuses!" She started knocking again.

I almost laughed. Molly had guts. I had to give her that. She was half my size, yet acted like she towered over me. Reminded me of my foster mother. Mom had been just as fearless when she was defending her kids.

But at the moment, Molly was an obstacle between me and my timetable. Between me and getting to Brynn.

The woman was going to draw half the resort guests here to find out what was up. I had to get rid of her.

I pulled open the door, surprising her. Molly's fist was still raised to keep knocking. "Make it fast, lady," I said.

Molly puffed up, chin lifting. Then the woman actually barged past me into the room.

*Fucking hell.*

She squinted at the suitcase and my pack on the bed. Spun to face me. "I was watching you during the seminar," she said, "and I've had just about enough. You're taking advantage of that girl. Brianna deserves better than you, and it's about time that somebody stood up and said it."

Could I physically move her out of the room? Not a good idea. She might start screaming.

Hell, she deserved a medal for stepping up and doing the right thing. Too few people were willing to bother. "I'll keep that in mind. But I've got a phone call. Excuse me."

Instead of leaving, she unleashed a tirade about how I was obviously no good. A scoundrel. Not to mention too old for such a young, sweet girl. Jeez, Brynn had maybe done *too* good a job establishing her cover. What would this lady think if she knew Brianna Waverley was actually a former special agent in her thirties who'd put down a vicious mercenary just last night?

But this lady was taking up my valuable time. Minutes that Brynn and I couldn't spare.

"Save your lectures for somebody who gives a shit, lady. Get out."

Molly's face went bright red. "You should be ashamed." But my harsh words had done the trick. She took off in a huff. *Finally*.

As she left, I glanced into the hallway. O'Hanlon had disappeared, which bothered me. I'd prefer to know where he was. But I couldn't worry about that right now. I was already off our timeline, thanks to Molly's heroics. Dammit. I had to pick up the pace.

I grabbed our stuff and left through the patio door after checking the rear of the building. River had switched off any cameras that I might come across on my way. I set our bags over the metal railing. Climbed over into a flower bed. The curtains to the neighboring rooms were closed, and there was no sign of O'Hanlon or anyone else who worked for Westwick.

Still, I forced myself to walk calmly and casually around the side of the building. I was headed for the employee area. A bell hop passed me, looking curious, but he didn't try to stop me. It wasn't that kind of place. Guests had the right of way here.

I checked my watch again and saw with a surge of adrenaline that I was running out of time.

Seconds later, there were shouts from all over the resort. The fire alarm sprinkler system had just activated. Courtesy of River's hack into the hotel's systems. I didn't get exactly how he'd made that happen, but it wasn't my job to know or care.

This was the chaos we needed.

The alarm gave me an excuse to move faster, breaking into a run. When I reached the *Roof Access* door, it was still closed tight, a new padlock in place. This morning, I had borrowed the lock from the gear compartment in our vehicle and relocated it to this door while Brynn was getting ready.

She had a key to the padlock in her purse as well. But since the lock was undisturbed, that meant she wasn't here yet. Thank goodness I'd made it first, and with probably seconds to spare.

Slipping the key from my pocket, I undid the padlock and got my ass up the stairs. Brynn would be on her way. She was with Westwick right now, leading him here. I had a soul-deep need to have her beside me.

*Soon.*

That padlock had ensured that no employees would be up here. I quickly set our luggage aside and went to the hiding spot I'd made for my goody bag. The syringe to knock Westwick out and bindings to secure him. I also had one of those huge bags designed for sports equipment.

In the areas below, people shouted and ran from the buildings to escape the water. Staff called for guests to remain calm, assuring them it was a false alarm.

When the sprinklers had started, that was supposed to be Brynn's cue to draw Westwick toward the roof so they could continue their talk in peace. Even though I'd lost sight of O'Hanlon, and had no idea where Manning was, they would've been caught off guard by the fire alarm like everyone else. Same with Ryker. They were probably trying to save Westwick's belongings from damage.

Brynn would get here any minute.

Checking my weapon yet again, I took up a position so I'd be out of sight when Brynn and Westwick arrived. I waited to hear the faint creak of the hinges on the roof door, followed by their footsteps.

Thirty seconds.

Two minutes.

*Come on, honey. I need to see you and know you're okay.*

While I counted the minutes, I mentally rehearsed what would happen next. Brynn would usher Westwick onto the roof. I would strike immediately with the syringe to knock him out, and in the meantime, Brynn would head back downstairs to the parking lot. There, she would start our vehicle and pull it into the delivery bay, which wasn't far.

The hardest part would be getting Westwick's unconscious body outside. But he would be inside the equipment bag, and he wasn't more than one-sixty or so. Lean enough build. I'd carry him down, around the side of the main building, stash him in our trunk.

The whole operation shouldn't take more than five minutes. By the time the fire alarm was off and Westwick's guards tried to find him, he'd already be gone.

But a whole five minutes passed with me sitting there. Still no sign of Brynn. Sweat poured down my sides.

I knew it in my gut. Something had gone terribly wrong.

*B, where are you?*

# CHAPTER TWENTY-FIVE

## *Brynn*

COLE LEFT THE SEMINAR ROOM. I watched his back from my peripheral vision, even though I acted like I only had eyes for Garon Westwick.

*Here we go,* I thought.

I sat in my chair as a few other seminar attendees asked Westwick questions. The head of Stillwater listened and answered politely. Always the gentleman, at least when people were watching. But his gaze kept sliding to me, giving me a sly, knowing smile.

When every other straggler had vanished, Westwick sauntered across the room. "And now it's just us, Brianna. I'm glad you decided to take me up on my offer of advice."

I stood up, glancing demurely at the carpet. It had shoe prints and stray crumbs scattered over it. "Me too."

"Cameron's on a business call now, yes? He won't be looking for you?"

"He thinks I'm with Molly and her husband. I've been thinking a lot about what you said the other night. About Cameron not being the best manager?"

Westwick reached me. He put his fingers under my chin,

and it took so much willpower not to push him away. *Soon,* I repeated, just like I'd told Cole before he left.

"You deserve someone who'll be in your corner."

Movement near the doors. It was Ryker. He lifted an eyebrow at Westwick, who shook his head. Buying us some privacy, I assumed.

Ryker shut the doors to the seminar room, leaving Westwick and me alone. I smiled, my mind tracking the minutes that had passed. Cole would've made it to our room by now. Given River the all-clear for our diversion. Less than ten minutes until the fire alarm sprinklers triggered.

Somehow, ten minutes hadn't seemed like such a long time during our planning.

Chairs were set up in long rows for the seminar audience. Westwick gestured for me to take one, and he sat beside me. Draped an arm over my chair, sitting close. My small drawstring purse lay at my feet.

"Luckily, I know a lot of people in all kinds of industries. I could connect you with a top-notch talent agency." He touched my shoulder. His fingers dug in. I hid my inner cringe. "The man who had dinner with me last night, Eric Masterson, could help as well. He's actually running for the US Senate. He has even more contacts than me. In all sorts of places."

"Oh?" I hadn't expected him to bring up Masterson. "I was wondering about him after I saw him with you. Running for Senate? That's so impressive."

Westwick's grip on my shoulder got tighter. I didn't miss the fact that it was inches from the bruises Ryker had left on my skin, though the sleeve of my dress covered those. "Eric noticed you as well. So have I. You're a beautiful girl, Brianna. I'm sure you realize that. Girls like you always know their effect on men."

Ugh, what I wouldn't give to pull the knife from my

holster. Just so that I could see a flash of fear on his disgusting face instead of that leer.

I killed time by rambling about my lifestyle brand, my goals for my business. Westwick nodded along like he was listening. But with every minute that passed, he edged closer, leaning into my space as his touch grew more insistent.

Just a few minutes until the diversion. I could handle this. I was fine.

I kept talking, and he interrupted me mid-sentence. "This room isn't very cozy, is it? We should go somewhere more comfortable. We've only got a couple of hours until dinner. Might as well make the most of it."

I smiled, quick to jump up to standing. Anything to get the man's slimy touch away from me, even for a moment. I grabbed the long strap of my purse. "Sure. Let's go."

He led the way through the double doors and into the hallway. But to my shock, Donovan Ryker wasn't here. I'd assumed he was guarding the entrance to the room to give his boss privacy.

Where the heck was the bodyguard?

I dragged my feet as we walked down the hall. We were going toward the employee side of the building, which was convenient. Not far from the door leading to the roof. But aside from that, I had no idea where Westwick was taking me.

Any moment the sprinklers would go off. The passage of the seconds ticked by in my head.

A siren wailed, followed by the word *Fire*. Westwick cursed as a sprinkler suddenly rained icy water. I shrieked, even though I wanted to cheer. I grabbed his arm. "I know where we can go!" I shouted. "Come on!"

"No, this way." Westwick hustled me further down that same hallway, opposite the direction I wanted to go.

"Wait." I dug in my feet, pointing toward the exit. We had to get to the roof access. "I know the perfect spot, I promise."

When he turned to me now, water streaming down his face, the man's expression was hard. "I said *this way*, Brianna. Learn to fucking listen."

My mind worked fast. How bad of a setback was this? I could keep resisting, but then the plan would be toast. Of course, if I didn't get him to the roof, the plan was also shot.

Either way, I had to make a decision. I still had the flash drive with the virus. Should I comply? Go with him and try to upload it on his phone?

I didn't hear the door open a few feet away over the noise of the siren. But the movement on my periphery drew my focus.

Ryker stood there in the open doorway.

I went for the knife concealed under my dress. The bodyguard lunged at me. Grabbed my wrists. I kicked him hard in the knee. When his grip on my arm loosened, I aimed a punch at his throat. Ryker's eyes widened in shock.

But someone else's arms closed around me from behind. A hand covered my mouth. I bit it and screamed. The sound of the siren, and now shouts of other guests in nearby hallways, drowned me out. Large hands shoved me into the doorway Ryker had stepped out of.

I was in a laundry room. Washers and dryers, carts full of sheets and towels. Immediately I spun, my knife now in my fist. "Let me out of here!" Ryker was there in the doorway along with Manning. Westwick stood behind them in the hallway, looking on.

Manning came forward. I slashed with the knife. The knife blade opened a gash across his palm, and the man shrieked. But Ryker was quick to come at me next, attacking at high speed. I'd lost the element of surprise. He knew I was a real threat. So he didn't hold back.

Ryker slammed me against a washing machine. He twisted my wrist at an angle. Tingly numbness shot through my fingers, and my knife fell to the floor. "Enough," he said in my ear. "Or you won't like what happens."

"Try me, asshole," I taunted.

When I kicked again, he was ready with a brutal shove. My breath left me as I smacked flat on my back on the concrete. While I was still stunned, Ryker flipped me and secured my wrists with some kind of plastic cuffs. I tried to kick my legs, but he got my ankles bound. A gag went in my mouth, followed by tape to hold it in place.

"I told you, boss," Ryker said. "This one's not what she seems. The trouble's not worth it. We should get rid of her."

"*No*." Westwick's tone was sharp and ruthless. "I want her. She's mine. Go find out what the hell is happening with this sprinkler nonsense. This is screwing my entire evening."

"I will. Sir, I realize you wanted to stay through dinner, but if the fire department responds—"

"No, you're right," Westwick said. "We need to get her out of here sooner. I'll find the other seminar attendees and give them my apologies. Take care of the rest of it." The head of Stillwater stormed from the laundry room.

Ryker turned to the other guard. "Manning, make sure she's secured and then go help O'Hanlon with Clay. I'll be back here to get her."

"Yes, boss." Manning bent to drag me away from the door. Then both he and Ryker left me there. But they would return before long.

Cole was on the roof. If I could get out of here, I'd be able to warn him. But how?

The sprinklers and alarm suddenly shut off. But everything was sopping wet, which I could use to my advantage. The cuffs were tight, but there was a small amount of give. If I could get them loose enough to slide an arm free…

Then I realized I could do even better. My wrists were bound behind my back, but I could scrunch up my body into a ball and bring my arms around to my front.

It wasn't easy. My shoulders and elbows creaked from the effort. But finally I got my hands past my butt and around my legs. I brought my hands up and pulled at the tape over my mouth. Spit out the gag. Right away I used my teeth on the plastic cuffs at my wrists.

A small tear opened at the edge of the plastic. I kept working at it. *Come on, come on.* My heart was up in my throat, thumping in my ears.

Footsteps in the hall. Voices.

The door opened. *Ryker*. He cursed when he saw what I was up to. "You really are trouble." Ryker's boots met my sight-line where I lay on the ground. I screamed, but he bent to shove the gag back in my mouth and fix the tape. "Makes me wonder if you had something to do with this fire alarm glitch. But that would mean you're a very smart woman, and I don't believe that. I think you're a foolish little girl who thought she could get close to Garon. Make use of him. You did some damage with that knife you brought along. But you have no idea who you're really dealing with."

I glared up at the man, gritting my teeth around the gag. So he didn't know my real identity or my mission. If Cole could get to me...

"Nobody's coming for you," he said, as if he could see the hopeful thoughts running through my brain. "Get that through your head, Brianna. Your jealous boyfriend? O'Hanlon and Manning already tracked him down. Cameron's dead. Who knows, maybe you'll be thanking us."

*No*. He was lying.

Ryker smiled. First time I'd ever seen that expression on the man's face. "He was up on the roof, of all places. Cameron liked to play the tough guy. He even had a gun. Two of you both put up a decent fight. But in the end, Cameron went down easy."

*I'm going to watch you die,* I said through my eyes. *And I'm going to enjoy it.*

He angled his head, studying me like a bug under a microscope. But he'd forgotten about my arms. They were still bound, but in front of me. My hands shot up, claws going straight for his eyes. My nails scraped his skin before he shoved me down and pinned me, his face an ugly scowl.

"I'm not supposed to damage the merchandise, but there's plenty I can do to cause pain that won't leave a mark. Trust me, you're going to find out."

The door to the hallway opened again, and a new face looked in. It was that hotel clerk. *Lance.* I shouted around my gag. But he didn't look the least bit surprised to see me there.

Lance was sweating. Breathing hard. "The van is waiting for the dry-cleaning pickup. The driver's antsy because of the false alarm. We diverted the fire department before they got here, but the van driver says he's not going to stay much longer."

"Then get over here. Hold her."

Lance crossed the room and tried to keep my shoulders down, while Ryker pulled something from his pocket. A needle. I struggled against both of them as Ryker stuck the sharp point into my skin. But he wasn't injecting me with anything.

He was drawing my blood into a vial. What the hell?

Ryker withdrew the needle. The vial of my blood disappeared into his pocket. A bag went over my head, and everything went dark.

## CHAPTER TWENTY-SIX

THE GROUND SHOOK BENEATH ME. I blinked away the fuzzy haze in my brain. The world kept moving, jostling me back and forth. My head bumped against something. Fuck, that hurt.

I tried to remember what the hell had happened.

I recalled being up on the roof. Waiting for Brynn to show, but she never had. I'd swallowed down my panic as I packed up the syringe and tucked my gun into my waistband. My footsteps had been silent on the stairs as I'd gone to look for her…

I heard voices. Not in my memory, but in the present moment. "Holy shit," O'Hanlon said. "Look at what he had with him. What do you think is in this syringe?"

"Don't know," Manning responded. "Drugs, maybe. But Ryker had it right. The two of them were definitely hiding something."

I realized where I was now, and the irony struck me. I was tied up in the trunk of a car. The exact position that I had intended to have Westwick in by now. Instead, I was the prisoner. Shit had gone *very* wrong.

My memories cleared further, the fog lifting.

I remembered running down the stairwell to the ground floor. The fire alarm had still been going off. When I'd pushed open the door, a couple of resort employees had run past, not sparing me a glance. But as I'd taken a few more steps, Manning came around the corner.

*Ryker's got Brianna,* Manning said. *Give yourself up, and I can take you to her.*

His statement stunned me for half a second, and that was enough for O'Hanlon to sneak up behind me. I went for my weapon. Threw an elbow, catching O'Hanlon in the chest. But then Manning was on me. He put his gun to my head, forcing me to drop mine. Then O'Hanlon lifted his own weapon and brought it down on my temple.

*Ow*. That explained the throbbing I felt in my head with every heartbeat and bump in the road.

From there, my recollections got fuzzy again. They'd clearly gotten me into a vehicle. It was dark, but this was a bigger space than the trunk of the car Brynn and I had driven to the resort.

They had my bag in the front seat with them. They would have my weapons as well. The laptop. I was sure River would've encrypted it with every security feature known to man. Could be bad though. I had to assume Stillwater had its own hackers with all the dark-web stuff they were into.

Where was Brynn? What were they doing to her?

I tested my wrist restraints, my thoughts growing sharper with every moment. They hadn't bothered to bind my feet. My left leg felt oddly pinched in the socket. They'd been throwing me around. But that was the least of my worries. I had to get back to Brynn.

*Just hold on, B.*

If Westwick or Ryker hurt her, I couldn't be held accountable for what I would do to them.

But Manning and O'Hanlon were going to be first.

Eventually, the vehicle pulled off the road, bumping on uneven ground, then stopped. I heard another car behind us. It parked and switched off its engine.

Doors opened. Voices again. Manning and O'Hanlon were talking to the other driver.

Then the trunk popped open, light and fresh air rushing in. I blinked and squinted. O'Hanlon leaned over me with his hand on the lid of the trunk.

"On your knees, asswipe," he said. "Up."

"Little difficult with my wrists tied. And my prosthesis is all screwed up," I complained. This was only partly true, but anything to distract them was fine by me.

"*Up,*" O'Hanlon barked again, pointing a gun at me.

I sat up, fighting back a wave of dizziness. Quite possible I had a concussion, but there was no time for that. I quickly assessed the scene outside. The sun was setting. We were out in the desert. Possibly hours from the resort.

Manning stood behind O'Hanlon. The clerk who'd checked us into the hotel was here too. Lance. He wore his resort uniform, even the name tag. The *hell.*

"Where's Brianna?" I directed this question at Manning. He didn't respond, instead glancing over at O'Hanlon. Which made it clear who was in charge.

O'Hanlon kept his gun on me. "Get him out of there."

Manning came forward and grabbed one of my arms to help wrangle me out of the trunk. So that was why they'd left my lower half unrestrained. Didn't want to make the effort of carrying me.

I pretended to stumble, like I could barely walk. Okay, it wasn't entirely pretend. But I played it up. Pushed my weight hard against Manning, who struggled to keep me upright.

I glanced to get a better look at the other vehicle. Yep, that was the car Brynn and I had driven to Arizona. The one with the secret compartment. If I could get to it...

"Lance, move the bags to his car," O'Hanlon said. "Make sure you wipe down anything you touched in there. No evidence."

"I'm not an idiot," Lance grumbled. "What about the..."

O'Hanlon took something from his pocket and held it out.

Was that a vial of *blood*?

Pressing his lips together, Lance swiped the vial from the other man's fingers. "Do I spread this around first? Or after I put the bags in?"

"I don't care. Just get it done. Hurry."

"It would be faster if one of you helps me, you know."

"That's what Ryker is paying you for. Quit bitching."

O'Hanlon and Manning both held weapons on me as Lance transferred my suitcase and daypack to my car, pausing to spread the vial of blood around on the floor mats. Then he grabbed a cloth and wiped off the steering wheel and surfaces.

I'd figured out their plan by now. Probably would've come sooner, if not for that bump on my head still slowing down my thoughts. But the fury igniting in my veins? That wasn't slow at all. Adrenaline sharpened the world. Colors and shapes almost pulsed in my vision. My heart was beating that hard.

They'd taken Brynn's blood.

I had a pretty good idea what was going on here. And yet an ugly part of me wanted to hear them say it. Just to feed my anger.

"What did you do with Brianna?" I asked. "Where is she?"

O'Hanlon smirked. "Probably getting acquainted with Mr. Westwick. He'll have his fun with her, and then he'll pass her off to someone else."

Flames seemed to lick at the undersides of my skin.

*I am going to tear them apart.*

Manning held me while O'Hanlon stepped in front of me, enjoying the chance to rub their plan in my face. "When the police find you with a gunshot to your head, and the residue of Brianna's blood on your floor mats, they'll see a nice story tied up in a bow. Your girlfriend was flirting with other men, so you killed her in a jealous rage, and disposed of her body in the desert. But you couldn't handle the guilt afterward. Bye bye, Cameron Clay."

"Nobody's going to believe that." But I could think of one person who'd support their story. Molly would tell the police that Cameron was a possessive, toxic jerk who'd left bruises on Brianna before. Guys like that snapped all the time. Even without her body, the police would take the easy explanation.

How long had Westwick been planning this? Because there was no way they'd put this together at the spur of the moment.

Lance stepped away from my car. O'Hanlon gestured at the front seat. "Get behind the wheel, Clay," the Stillwater guard said. "Give yourself a last few moments of dignity and take this like a man." He dug into his pocket and produced the syringe I'd meant to use on Westwick. "Or I can inject you with whatever's in the needle. Who knows, maybe you really *were* planning to do your girl in." He laughed, making eye contact with Manning. "Wouldn't that be fucked up? If we interrupted his kidnapping plan with our own?"

*You have no idea,* I thought.

"I'll walk," I said. "But I wouldn't be driving my damn car with my wrists tied."

"We'll untie them later," O'Hanlon sneered.

"Then the blood flow will be all wrong." Who knew if that was true or not. I was no forensics expert. But I threw every bit of my meager acting ability into it. "And there won't be gunshot residue in the right places. Coroners look for that stuff when they do autopsies. Not to mention *my leg is twisted.* I'm supposed to walk with dignity like this?"

Cursing under his breath, O'Hanlon said, "Lance, you cut him loose. Let him fix his damn leg. I'm sick of hearing about it. Manning, keep your gun on him."

Lance and Manning approached. I heard the snick of a blade through the ties at my wrists. Felt the binding loosen.

I didn't waste a second. Turning to grab hold of Manning's arm, I twisted it in front of me. Forced his finger down on the trigger. *Bang*. The shot hit O'Hanlon in the chest. O'Hanlon had gotten off a shot of his own, but it went wide, hitting the car behind me.

Lance was shouting. I twisted Manning's finger hard, feeling the bone pop. Manning screamed. I got a better grip on the gun and yanked it, pushing Manning in front of me at the same time. He careened into O'Hanlon. The two men landed in a heap.

Lance ran off into the desert. My next bullet caught him in the calf, and he went down with a screech of pain.

Then I returned my focus to Manning and O'Hanlon. Manning pushed himself up, levering himself against his colleague. O'Hanlon was coughing up blood. Didn't look like he was going to be breathing for long. Manning reached for the other man's gun, but hesitated. His right trigger finger was bent at an angle. Broken.

"Go for it," I said. "Pick it up."

Manning reached with his left hand. But still, he hesitated.

"What's the matter, you don't want to go out in a blaze of glory?" I asked. "What kind of Stillwater guard are you? You're one of them, right?"

"You know about Stillwater?"

"I know there's no way you're as dumb as you seem. You have two choices. Either go for that gun, like you want to, and you can die right here with your friends. Or you can take me to wherever Ryker has Brianna."

"If you know about Stillwater, you know what Ryker will do to me if I mess with his plans."

"I do. It's a question of getting screwed over now, or getting screwed over later. Personally, I would always choose the second. At least then you have a chance."

Slowly, arms shaking, Manning raised his hands in the air. "Look, I don't buy into this secret-society bullshit. Ryker's wife is my cousin. She asked him to give me a job. I didn't know it was going to get this heavy."

"Sure, a real hardship taking all that money. Save me the excuses." I raised the gun.

He held out his hands, palms out. "Don't shoot! I can take you to where they've got Brianna. We were supposed to head there next! After we'd gotten rid of you."

"And what about him?" I nodded at Lance, who was moaning and crawling several yards away. "Does he work for Stillwater too?"

"Hell no, he's nobody. Ryker just paid him off. The clerk arranged a dry-cleaning pickup to smuggle your girl off-premises for Westwick. We were supposed to dispose of Lance on the way."

I scowled at the hotel clerk. He probably felt extra stupid now that he knew Stillwater had planned to kill him all along. They wouldn't want any witnesses.

And that alone made me want to spare the guy. Because I wasn't Stillwater. I saved my vengeance for those who'd truly earned it, and I wasn't going to execute some unarmed hotel clerk. Even if he'd been an accessory to kidnapping Brynn.

But I wasn't going to help him, either. I wouldn't leave him any phones or car keys. Lance could fend for himself. If he bled out, that was his problem.

Manning was still on his knees. "Get up," I said. I kept

the gun on him as he stood. He cast a single glance at O'Hanlon, who'd stopped moving.

"How long did Ryker have this planned?" I asked.

"Dude, I don't know. Since yesterday, maybe? Look, I'll drop you off where they've got Brianna, and then I want to get the hell out of here. I'm done. But are you sure your girl is worth it? Because these Stillwater people are not playing around."

"She's worth *everything*."

Whatever fierce light he saw burning in my eyes, it convinced him. Manning wiped the sweat from his face, then said, "It's about twenty miles from here. Out in the middle-of-nowhere desert."

"The solar plant," I muttered.

His brow wrinkled. "How'd you know that?"

"Don't worry about it. Now, here's what we're going to do."

# CHAPTER TWENTY-SEVEN

## Brynn

RYKER PULLED the bag away from my head. I blinked at the sudden brightness. He snapped a metal cuff onto one of my ankles before I'd even registered the movement. Then he yanked the tape away from my mouth.

"Scream all you want now. Nobody will hear you."

*Gah.* That had been…unpleasant.

I rubbed at the raw skin around my mouth. My hands were still bound with the plastic tie, but Ryker hadn't put them behind me. At least there was that.

I was sitting on a cot in a room with no windows. Cinderblock walls, low ceiling. There was a basic kitchenette across from me. A sliding door leading into a small bathroom. The place was just a step up from a prison cell. No cameras, at least none that I could see.

I bent my legs, and the metal cuff on my ankle pulled. The cuff was attached to a thin chain. The other side of the chain connected to the metal frame of the cot.

"What is this place?" I asked.

"This is the start of your new life. Time to get used to it."

I held back my sneer. *Really?* He needed to work on his

psychological tactics, because all he was doing was pissing me off.

It had been hours since we'd left the resort. Someone had bundled me with thick fabric, maybe curtains and tablecloths, then packed me up like cargo into a waiting van. We'd driven somewhere, followed by a transfer to another vehicle. I'd heard Ryker's voice through all of it. Not Westwick or the others, so I had no idea where they were.

I hadn't heard Cole's voice either. I couldn't think about him right now. Couldn't risk falling apart if he was truly gone.

I'd fought like hell earlier, and it hadn't gotten me very far. I had to come up with an actual strategy. This might be a prison cell, but it looked lived in. There had to be something here I could use.

I looked up at Ryker. He had red scratches on his face. Scratches I remembered giving him. "You have a little something here," I said, pointing at my own face like a mirror. "Looks like it hurt."

Ryker came at me, pushing me roughly by the shoulder. My back landed against the thin mattress. He towered over me. "I told you there were plenty of ways I could cause you pain without leaving a mark."

Ryker jabbed his thumb between my ribs, aiming for a pressure point. My breath stuttered, and my vision swam. The pain drove away my ability to think.

"Enough of that," Garon Westwick said.

Ryker pulled back. Westwick stood there in the open doorway. I hadn't heard him come inside. I sucked air into my lungs, shaking off the intense pain in my rib cage.

I tried to get a glimpse of what was outside the door, but all I could see was another cinderblock wall. A hallway, maybe. And the profile of a guard in black tactical clothes with a rifle across his chest.

"Keys?" Westwick held out his palm, and Ryker set a ring there, metal jangling. "Leave us," the head of Stillwater said.

"Boss, I wouldn't advise that. This one is tricky. She's already proven—"

"*Leave*. Make sure our ride is on schedule for the morning."

Ryker stalked for the exit, giving me one last glare of warning before he shut the door.

I sat up, scooting as far back as the ankle cuff allowed me. Westwick leaned against the kitchenette counter, not yet daring to come close. He watched me for a while, eyes greedy like he owned me. He clearly thought he did.

*Go ahead*, I thought. *Come over here and see what happens*.

"You're strong," he said. "That'll serve you well where we're going."

"Where's that?"

"Don't worry about those kinds of details. The only details you need to know are what your master tells you."

"My *master*?"

*Fuck that*, I almost said, but held my tongue. *Find a way out of here*. That was all that mattered.

He smiled broadly. It wasn't like his smile in that photo with his wife and daughters. The man standing in front of me wasn't wearing a mask anymore. "Ryker warned me you were spying on me. But I knew your agenda from the beginning. I've known it since the moment I met you."

I braced myself to hear my real name. To learn that he'd been playing us this entire time, and that he knew about the Protectors. About *everything*.

"What do you know?" I forced out.

"That you're attracted to power. Everyone is, but you were willing to put yourself out there to get my attention. I admire your spunk. Have to admit, you intrigue me, Brianna. You brought a knife to our private meeting. Why is that?"

I hid my exhale of relief. He didn't know a damn thing about my true mission. The guy probably believed he was infallible, too smart and too careful to ever get caught. Overconfident. And *that* was something I could use.

"I was afraid of you." The man puffed up when I said that. He liked hearing it. "As I should have been, since you kidnapped me. That's twisted. You're sick."

"I saw an opportunity and decided to take it. That's not evil, that's smart. You need to accept that you're mine now. If you keep fighting, Ryker will keep punishing you. I guarantee you don't want that. There's nowhere to go, anyway. We're in a secure location with an armed guard outside. Miles away from anyone else. To the outside world, you might as well be dead, and within a day or two, everyone will assume that's what happened to you. A victim of your possessive boyfriend."

I suddenly understood the meaning of Ryker drawing my blood. "You're framing Cameron? Like, making sure he's sent to prison for my murder? Ryker claimed he was already dead."

Westwick shrugged. "By now, Cameron will be dead. Ryker's men took care of it. He doesn't have to be convicted of killing you for the world to believe it."

Rage filled my throat. I wanted to scream. And more than anything, destroy the man sitting beside me.

Cole couldn't be dead. *Please,* my heart begged.

He reached out to stroke the back of his finger down my cheek. I managed to keep still. Not react.

"I understand your initial shock at being taken. But I don't think you're going to give me any more trouble. You're wiser than that. Especially when there's a guard with an assault rifle right outside this door. You're a practical girl. Aren't you, Brianna?"

His hand moved lower, skimming my shoulder down to my side, where I ached from Ryker's pressure-point jab.

Westwick continued along my leg, leaving goosebumps of disgust on my skin, until he reached my ankles. He produced a small folding knife and cut the plastic binding my ankles together. I imagined plunging that blade into his heart, but I didn't move. He reached for my hands and cut the plastic tying those as well. The metal cuff remained on my left ankle, securing me to the cot. But otherwise, I was free. If the word *free* had any relevance to my current situation.

Westwick folded the knife and placed it back in his pocket. The same pocket where he had the keys Ryker had handed him. "There's still plenty I can offer you. If you behave."

I lowered my eyes. "Why should I believe you?"

"Because I'm ready to give you what you wanted all along."

"Which is?" I spit out.

Westwick stood up. He fit his hands into his pockets as he walked around the small room. "Your lifestyle brand wasn't a bad idea, but it was missing the point. Real power isn't about followers on social media or selling a cheap product. It's access. You knew that, deep down. That's why you wanted to get close to me. And it's what I'm giving you. Access to rich, important men. If you're good to them, they'll be good to you."

I looked up at him, letting conflicted emotions play across my face. "Sleeping my way to the top? Are you serious?"

"Completely serious. If you're smart about it, you'll eventually be moving in the most powerful circles in the world. All from the shadows. Which is where true power always lies. But you'll actually be working for *me*. Gathering secrets and reporting back."

"I have a choice in this?"

"No, you don't. Brianna Waverley is dead. If you want to live, it'll be on my terms. But this is still an opportunity."

I pretended to consider, as if his argument made any kind of sense.

This guy truly was twisted. I had no idea if his offer was real, or if he was just playing games with his food before he sank his teeth in. But it didn't matter. For now, I would play along.

"Ryker said something about Eric Masterson. The future senator. That I'm...a *gift*."

"That's right. Masterson invested in a venture of mine, and I want to keep a close eye on him. I believe you can help me with that."

"Spy on him for you."

"Yes. But first, I have to know you'll do everything I ask. You have to impress me. Do you know what I mean?" He waited. The tension in the room crackled. Westwick thought he had me hooked. That I was some kind of trapped prey that he'd almost tamed.

But he had no *clue* what was about to happen.

I sagged against the wall behind the cot. Like all the fight had left me. "I understand," I said softly. "I'll be good."

"I know you will." Westwick came toward me. One expensive leather shoe in front of the other. He sat beside me on the thin mattress and rubbed a lock of my hair between his fingers.

Adrenaline numbed my body, my emotions, everything but the singular knowledge of what I had to do.

When he sat close enough to grip the back of my neck, I launched myself at him. My arms cinched the man's jugular in a brutal chokehold. He fell onto the mattress, kicking and grunting as he tried to get away.

I used another vicious burst of speed to twist my free leg around him, pinning him. The metal cuff on my other ankle pulled hard on the bed frame. My mouth opened in a soundless scream. Rage and fury for what Westwick had done—to my best friend, the others I'd gotten to know in Hartley, the countless victims of Stillwater. And Cole. From the beginning, Cole had wanted Westwick to suffer for his crimes. I'd tried to stay more objective. More *practical.* As Westwick had just accused me of being.

But right now, I wasn't level-headed Agent Somerton. I was just a woman who wanted vengeance against the monster who'd hurt the man she cared about.

There were a few thumps as Westwick kept struggling. Nothing loud enough to alert the guard outside. The lack of oxygen and blood flow to Westwick's brain weakened him with each second that passed.

Finally, he went limp. Unconscious. That wasn't enough for me. I wanted him dead.

Yet I had to force myself to stop.

I let go of the man, panting to catch my breath. My skin felt dirty everywhere I'd touched him.

Cole and I had agreed we would take Westwick alive so that we could deal a final blow to Stillwater. My mission wasn't finished. *Even if Cole wasn't here.* I shoved down the feelings that tried to rise up in my throat.

Finish the mission. Get out of here. Wherever *here* was. Then, I could find out what had happened to Cole. And all the while, I'd be praying that he was okay. Because if I didn't see his grumpy frown again, or hear him argue and lose his temper, or feel his warm, rough hands on my face…

*Stop.*

There would be time to wallow later. Right now, I had to move. Ryker could return any second. Especially if there were hidden cameras in here and the Stillwater guards already knew what I'd done.

# CHAPTER TWENTY-EIGHT

## *Brynn*

FISHING IN WESTWICK'S POCKET, I found the folding knife and keys. I unlocked the cuff on my ankle, then closed it on Westwick's leg instead. If the asshole somehow woke up before I was ready, he wouldn't be going anywhere.

Then, I waited for that armed guard to barge in, gun blazing. Nobody came. He hadn't realized anything was up.

*Move*, I thought.

The gag that had been in my mouth was on the floor. I shoved it past Westwick's lips, securing the gag with some duct tape that I found in a kitchen drawer. It really did seem like somebody lived here. The cabinets were full of all kinds of supplies, like dishes and non-perishable food.

A chest of drawers near the bathroom held clothing. Men's clothing.

I also found my purse lying on the ground. My phone was missing, probably cracked into pieces and scattered in the desert. But River's flash drive was still here. Somebody had found it inside the lining and probably taken a look at the drive. But they'd left it alone, likely believing it was just a tube of lipstick. Score one for the Protectors.

Unfortunately, I hadn't found a phone in Westwick's pockets, so I couldn't upload the virus just yet.

I tied up Westwick's wrists behind his back, flopping him facedown on the cot. I turned his head so that he would be able to breathe through his nose. I was merciful like that.

I had to get out of this room and figure out where exactly I was. Maybe I would find a computer or something. Means of communication, so I could send out a call to the Protectors for help.

But that meant dealing with the armed guard outside the room.

After going through the kitchen and finding only sad, dull knives, I decided to use the folding one I had taken from Westwick. I opened the blade, weighing it in my hand and getting ready.

*Breathe in. Breathe out.*

With quick, decisive moves, I yanked open the door, keeping the knife out of sight at my side. The Stillwater guard glanced at me, barely moving his head.

"It's Garon," I said. "I think he's sick. Please help!"

The guard's thick brows knit. He looked past me into the room. I brought the knife up and drove it into his jugular. He started to fall, and I eased his hand away from the trigger of his weapon.

It had taken three seconds, maybe four.

I took another breath.

The dead guard was heavy. I dragged him into the room and laid him on the floor beside the cot. After using a towel to wipe the blood the best I could, I went back inside and shut the door.

A check of the many pockets of the guard's uniform revealed a keycard and radio, which I stuck into my purse with the knife. I pulled the strap of the rifle over his head and set the weapon aside.

I needed some new clothes. My sundress was ripped, drenched in sweat, and now spattered with the guard's blood.

I put on a pair of sweats and a tee I found in the chest of drawers. Whoever normally lived in this room wasn't a big guy, since the clothes were only a little baggy on me. Sadly, his sneakers were huge. Those weren't going to work. I didn't want to wear my wedge sandals either. Why couldn't Brianna have worn flats?

No time to worry about that. I slung my purse over my arm, followed by the gun. Time to find out where exactly I was and how to get out.

Silently, I made my way down the cinderblock hallway, gun aimed ahead of me. The concrete floor was cool against my bare feet. A ventilation system whooshed, circulating air that smelled of dust and something metallic. There were no windows.

*The solar plant*. That was where they'd taken me, which made sense. This was a secure Stillwater facility. Westwick had mentioned a ride coming for us in the morning. Ryker was supposed to go check on it. He could be anywhere.

After a few yards, I passed a set of elevator doors. One button with an arrow pointing up. I considered pressing it, but what if this elevator took me straight to a bunch more Stillwater guards? I could handle one at a time, but no more than that, even with an automatic weapon in my hands.

My best hope was that they had no clue I'd gotten free.

I came to a corner. Carefully glanced around it. Sucked in a breath at what I saw.

It was a massive, open room, so large I couldn't make out the far walls to the left and right. The place looked like one of those enormous storage archives the FBI maintained for old cases. Rows and rows going almost to the ceiling. Except instead of cabinets or shelves holding boxes, it was all electronics. Stacks and stacks of black plastic and metal and blinking lights. Wires.

These were servers. It was some kind of data center.

In my direct line of sight, a glass door revealed a man at a desk with multiple computer screens. He typed away at a keyboard. Then rolled his chair to grab something, and I ducked back to hide.

If there were computers, I had to assume there would be some way to reach the outside world. I hadn't seen Ryker or any other guards yet. The guy sitting at the desk had looked more like an IT expert than a mercenary.

The man in the office swiveled away, turning his back to the glass door. I dashed forward. Hid between the rows of servers. Then made the same move again.

Once I'd made my way across, I snuck a better look at the door to the office. There was a keycard reader. Nothing else. No fancy biometrics like what Cole and I had seen on the exterior door, but that made sense. I was already inside.

I dug into my purse for the guard's keycard. When the man at the desk turned away again, I hurried forward.

He looked over as I entered. He saw my gun, and his hands shot up. "Holy shit, don't kill me!"

"Get on the other side of the room." I gestured with the rifle. "*Now.*"

He jumped up, his chair wheeling off to the side. He walked backward until he reached the wall. With a quick glance behind me, I shut the office door, still aiming the gun.

"Where is Donovan Ryker?" I asked.

"I...I don't know," he stammered. "Who are you?"

I snapped my fingers at him. "Focus. Are there cameras? Can you find out where Ryker is?"

"Uh, maybe. On the computer."

"If you raise any alarms or warn anyone I'm here, you're dead."

"Yeah," he muttered, "that's only my fiftieth death threat this week. You'd think it would've lost its effect."

"Has it?"

The guy swallowed. "Not really. No." He had shaggy brown hair, wire-rimmed glasses. Taller than me, but his build was slight. His skin had the pale look of someone who didn't get outside much.

He went back to the computer. Keeping one hand raised, he used the other to make a few quick taps on a keyboard. A window opened on the screen. It showed live feeds from several cameras. I recognized one of the views. This was the entrance to Building B of the solar plant, where Cole and I had been spying just last night. The building above me right now, I assumed.

But this time, nobody stood guard outside. No sign of Ryker either. A different camera feed showed the gatehouse. Two guards were inside, looking bored.

"Ryker was here," I said. "If he's still on the property, where could he have gone?"

"Could be upstairs. There's a break room and a bathroom. Or maybe the front office, but it's closed up since it's after hours. Aside from that, I don't know. Seriously, I stay away from Ryker. That guy is scary. Not that you aren't scary. Anybody holding a gun on me is pretty dang scary." Then he squinted at me. "Wait, are you wearing my clothes?"

I ignored that question for now. "How many other guards are on duty?"

He counted off on his fingers. "The two at the gate. One who drives the perimeter fence. And Emerson. Should be outside guarding the entrance to this building, but I don't see him there. Don't know where he is. Couple hours until the shift change, and they're not supposed to leave their post unless they're relieved. So..."

Emerson was probably the guard I'd killed. That left three

others, plus Ryker. And what about Manning and O'Hanlon? Damn, that was a lot standing in my way.

I was going to need more ammo.

The skinny guy studied me. "Who are you? For real, if it's Ryker you're after, I'm the wrong person to ask. I try to have as little to do with that guy as possible."

Whatever this man's story, he didn't seem like an immediate danger to me. That didn't mean I could underestimate him. Entirely possible he was on board with the evil Stillwater philosophy. But if I wanted answers from him, I had to get him to relax a little. He looked ready to jump out of his skin.

"To answer your original question, I *am* wearing your clothes. I'm pretty sure I just escaped from your room. Ryker and his boss kidnapped me. I'm guessing you didn't have anything to do with that?"

"Me? No! Jeez, no. I'm just an IT guy."

"What's your name?"

"Josiah."

"Josiah, I want to know about those servers. Why they're here." I kept my voice even, soothing, though it was hard to stay calm when every moment that I was stuck here meant another moment for a guard to investigate. I couldn't leave without learning more about Stillwater's activities here.

He swallowed, keeping his gaze on the gun. I pointed it at the floor instead of directly at him, and that seemed to reassure him. "The panels provide the energy to run the servers. And the routers, the ventilation, everything."

"This place is owned by Stillwater," I said in that same smooth tone. Not a question.

"Yeah. Who are you again?"

I could feel the seconds ticking by. Time I didn't have to waste. Yet I couldn't leave without knowing more.

"I'm Brianna. Ryker kidnapped me because I know about Stillwater, and that's a problem for him." That wasn't accurate, but it was close enough for my purposes. "You have to make a choice. Are you going to help me, or are you going to side with Ryker and his Stillwater bosses? You have two seconds."

I raised the gun again.

"I'll help you! I mean, I'll try. I just work here, you know? I didn't even know what I was signing up for."

How many times had I heard that excuse? "What exactly do you do here for Stillwater?"

"Keep it all running. See, Stillwater used to rely on servers overseas." He tripped over his words as he tried to answer as quickly as possible.

"I know Stillwater uses the dark web."

"Yeah, simplistically speaking, but—"

"I don't have time for an advanced degree in this," I interrupted. "Give me the fast version."

"They wanted to create their own anonymous marketplace for Stillwater members to buy and sell whatever they wanted. Here, Stillwater can host on servers that only they control. No third parties, no interference from foreign governments."

Buying and selling. That, I could understand. An exclusive online marketplace for Stillwater members to sell drugs, weapons, stolen information, even human beings. And they'd placed it here in the desert, powered by and hidden beneath a seemingly innocent solar energy plant.

I'd heard of other dark web marketplaces. Governments were constantly chasing after them, trying to shut them down. Stillwater was keeping itself several steps ahead. And doing it here in the good old US of A instead of overseas.

*Hiding in plain sight.*

"But this many servers? There must be hundreds at

least." Even with my small amount of knowledge, it seemed like overkill.

"Mr. Westwick has big plans, I guess. He doesn't share all of them with me."

But I could come up with theories myself, based on what Westwick had said to me about spying on powerful men. Maybe these servers had something to do with that. Building an empire in the shadows. "And you're their computer expert. Helping them get this all set up. You must be proud." I couldn't keep the disdain from my tone and expression.

"I swear I didn't know! They hired me to be discreet. Made me sign an NDA and all that. Which isn't so strange in this industry, because a lot of companies want to keep their IT setup secure. By the time I figured out what they were really up to, what the hell Stillwater even was, it was too late for me to get out. It was supposed to be a five-week gig, housing provided. I haven't left this place for *three months*. They monitor all my communications. I'm just trying to keep my head down until they let me go."

"Assuming they ever plan to let you leave."

He went even paler. "Shit, don't say that."

But some part of him had to know it was true. He knew far too many of Stillwater's secrets.

I dipped my fingers into my purse, pulling out the flash drive. I held it up.

"What's that?" he asked.

"Something that'll undo the damage you've helped cause."

"They'll kill me."

"Or I will. Your choice." I tossed him the drive, and he caught it.

"What do I do?"

I told him how to open it. Josiah inserted the adapter into

a port on the side of his computer. The screens flickered momentarily, then came back to life.

I kept a close eye on Josiah to make sure he didn't touch anything else. Since River had written the virus on that drive, I assumed it would quickly worm its way into Stillwater's systems.

And talk about hitting the jackpot. This wasn't just Westwick's phone or laptop. This was mainline access to all of Stillwater's servers. Its soft underbelly.

Josiah stood up, brushing off his hands. His color had returned. "What now? Because I'd really like to live through today. And if Ryker finds you here, that's not gonna happen."

I made a split-second decision. "You're coming with me. You wanted to leave. Well, here's your chance."

He nodded. "Yeah. Maybe we shouldn't take the elevator, though. If we run into Ryker on our way out? I'd prefer to avoid that."

"How else can we get out?"

"There's a fire exit through a back stairwell."

I nodded, a possible new plan taking shape in my head. "Can you shut down the front-door access to the building above us? And the elevator too?"

"That'll set off big-time alarms at the gatehouse."

"You're the computer guy. Can you bypass the alarms?"

"No. I don't have that kind of security access down here. Only the guards do." Josiah cringed. "But if we open the fire exit door, it's going to notify the gatehouse too. Either way, they'll realize something is up. They'll come running."

"You're the computer expert, I'm the gun expert. Leave that part to me."

Once we were back on the surface, I would set up an ambush for Ryker and the remaining guards. Take them out, then find a vehicle to get us the heck out of here. It was not my most detailed plan, but at least I had the head of Stillwater to use as a hostage.

"No offense, but you don't look like a gun expert."

I smirked, holding the gun against my chest and petting the top of it affectionately. "Don't let appearances fool you."

"Uh, right. Good point." He took a step back. "Are we going now? Can I grab some of my stuff?"

"Sure. I left someone back in your room. Garon Westwick."

His eyes bugged. "*The* Garon Westwick? The guy who freaking owns Stillwater?"

"At the moment, he's my hostage. I need you to help me carry him."

Josiah grabbed a wheeled cart from the corner of his office, removing some equipment. "Will this work? We can put him on top of it. And my suitcase."

"Works for me." I gestured with the gun. "Lead the way."

An alarm siren blared, and red emergency lights flashed on the wall. Josiah and I both jumped. I glanced through the glass door, but there was no sign of any guards.

"What is that?" I demanded. Had Josiah done something? Or was it the virus? Did Stillwater's system know it was under attack?

Josiah ran to his computer. "It was triggered manually at the gatehouse. Not from here."

"Check the camera."

He tapped at the keyboard. "I can't. The one at the gatehouse isn't working."

"Shit," I muttered. I had no idea what was going on. If it was good for us or bad. I just had to grab Westwick and get out of here. Maybe this alarm could work to our advantage if it distracted the guards.

Of course, our fire alarm diversion hadn't worked so well at the resort, had it?

*Don't think about that,* I told myself. *Don't think about Cole. Just get this done.*

We ran down the hall. Josiah went first, wheeling the cart, and I followed at the rear. We passed the elevator. Made it to Josiah's room. He waved his keycard and pushed open the door. Then he stopped in the doorway.

"What the ever-loving—"

Maybe I should've warned him about the dead guard. "Just grab your belongings, Josiah. We don't have much time."

Westwick was conscious and writhing on the cot, as if that could help him get free. The man grunted around his gag and glared murder at me. I used the keys to unlock the cuff at his ankle.

Josiah hadn't moved. I pushed his shoulder. "Get your stuff. We're in this now. Okay? No going back."

"Okay." Josiah threw some belongings into a small suitcase. Meanwhile, I kept the gun on Westwick as I checked the ties at his wrists and ankles.

Josiah loaded his suitcase on the bottom of the cart. We hefted Westwick onto the top, and we weren't delicate about it. He grunted his protests.

"Dude's heavy," Josiah complained. "We'll have to carry him when we get to the fire exit stairwell. That's going to suck."

"We can manage it. One thing at a time." I opened the door, checking the hallway. The alarm continued to wail, red lights flashing. I gestured for Josiah to push the cart. "Go ahead. I'll be right behind you."

Then I noticed the digital numbers above the elevator doors had changed. The elevator car was moving.

Somebody was coming down.

# CHAPTER TWENTY-NINE

## *Cole*

THE LIGHTS of the gatehouse appeared up ahead. Manning white-knuckled the steering wheel.

I kept my handgun in his peripheral vision. "Think of your girl back home. I'm sure you want to see her again."

"Fuck you, man." But Manning's fingers loosened slightly, trying to relax.

The night was pitch black aside from our headlights and the glow of the Stillwater facility. I had decided on taking Manning's SUV, which had meant leaving my vehicle behind. I'd stripped out the gear from the hidden compartment. I'd also recovered our laptop, the syringe of knock-out meds, and my gun.

It wasn't ideal to leave our car, especially considering that it was full of physical evidence. Like Brynn's blood. But the car itself was untraceable. Provided courtesy of River and the Protectors. If possible, we would go back for it. Also to bury O'Hanlon and deal with Lance the hotel clerk, should he remain alive. If highway patrol somehow stumbled upon that scene, Lance would only be able to say Cameron Clay had done it. More likely, he'd claim no knowledge. After all, he'd conspired to kidnap two hotel guests.

But those were concerns for later. I had to find my partner first. The woman who had her fingers around my heart, and if I was lucky, she'd never let me go.

If Ryker or Westwick had harmed her…

I swallowed and settled back in the passenger seat. "How many guards?" I asked for maybe the fifth time.

"I *told you*."

He rattled through the same details. One or two guards at the gatehouse. But more guards farther inside the property. Brynn would be well defended. Was he exaggerating to scare me, or underestimating to lull me? Brynn and I hadn't seen many guards when we came to the solar plant last night.

"And yet, I still don't trust you, Manning. Why on earth could that be? Oh, right. You were going to murder me."

"Asshole," he muttered. "I've done everything you asked."

"At gunpoint. Which means you're smart. Keep cooperating and you'll survive this."

"We'll have to stop at the gate. Like I told you already."

"I know. But here's how it'll go. You won't stop. You'll speed up and drive on."

Manning scowled, glancing at me. "They'll shoot at us!"

"It's possible."

I was wearing a ballistic vest from our stash of gear. Plus a hat pulled low. Last night, when I had driven past that gatehouse on the way out, the guard had barely glanced at me. He'd had no reason to scrutinize me. But this time, we were going in.

At first glance, the guard at the gate would probably take me for O'Hanlon since Manning was in the driver seat. But the masquerade wouldn't last long. Especially if Manning did something to tip them off. And I didn't have a single ounce of faith that Manning wouldn't try to screw me over at the first opportunity.

Our best shot was to just drive. The guards at the gatehouse would recognize Manning.

"They might be pissed," I said, "but they won't shoot you. I know you and Ryker were here just yesterday. Right? With Westwick and Masterson?"

"How do you know about that?"

"I'm psychic."

"They'll be suspicious. They'll try to stop the car."

"You think they won't be suspicious if they see me instead of O'Hanlon? Wave and smile. Flash your ID. I don't give a shit. Just keep driving or I'll shoot you."

We were almost there. The tall chain-link gate was open on the entrance side. By the exit, the gate was closed. I only saw one figure inside the little gatehouse building. I lowered the gun to keep it beneath the line of the windows.

Manning's fingers were back to white. Clenching and releasing.

As we neared, the guard stepped outside. Still casual. He expected this car's arrival.

"Speed up," I said.

Manning accelerated. The guard started to wave at us, like he was warning us to slow down.

But instead of just driving past, Manning suddenly veered to the right. Floored the accelerator. I realized what he was doing a second before we hit the heavy concrete post bordering that side of the fence.

The airbags exploded. I slammed into the seatbelt and the bag. The car bucked and shuddered and crunched.

Quiet descended briefly. The air smelled singed. My ears rang. I was dazed, especially because my head was still fuzzy from the hit I had taken earlier. But I snapped to awareness when I felt Manning groping for my gun.

I pointed it at him and pulled the trigger twice. The first

went through his airbag and spiderwebbed the driver's side window, what little I could see. The second hit Manning in the torso beneath his outstretched arm. He grunted. I fired again, and he slumped forward against the deflating bag and went still.

Dammit. So much for him being smart.

More pops came from outside, muffled by the deafening sounds that had already shocked my eardrums. But I knew automatic gunfire when I heard it. Had to be the guard from the gatehouse.

Bullets smacked into the SUV. More glass shattered.

I had a tactical knife in the pocket of my vest. I grabbed for it to cut the seatbelt and then the remaining airbag, shoving the puffy fabric out of the way. Pushed the door open and dove out onto the blacktop.

Getting low to the ground, I spotted the guard's boots on the far side of the SUV. He was shooting as he approached. I got into a crouch and rounded the bumper.

Took aim for a head shot. Fired. The guard and his carbine went down.

Another guard in a black tactical uniform ran into view. He ducked behind the cover of the gatehouse. I dashed across the open space. When the guard peeked out again, I fired twice. Blood spattered, but I'd only grazed him. He reached his carbine out and fired in my direction. The bullets smacked into the gatehouse, shattering the tempered glass of the windows. He shouted something too, though I couldn't begin to make out those sounds. My hearing wasn't so great at the moment.

I crouched on the other side of the gatehouse. The first guard, the one I had successfully killed, was lying a couple of feet away. I leaned out to yank his M4 carbine away from him, leaning back just as another barrage of automatic fire slammed into the concrete wall.

Distantly, I heard something that could've been a siren. Was it close? Far? I had no clue.

No sign of Donovan Ryker. No other guards came running either. It was just me and the guy I'd grazed. He was probably very pissed off about that.

I picked up a pebble from the ground, weighing it in my hand. Then I threw it as hard as I could.

It smacked into the chain-link fence. A barrage of gunfire followed.

I stood and stepped around the back side of the gatehouse. The guard was turned away from me, eyes on my distraction. One of the cheapest tricks in the books, but still a good one. Who needed fancy tech when old school still worked so well?

The next bullet from my handgun caught him in the back of the neck just as he was trying to turn.

I bent over him to take the magazine from his gun, quickly searching him for anything else of use. Keycard. Car keys. Those went in my pockets.

I went into the gatehouse. A screen flashed with the message, *Intrusion Alert*. I didn't know what impact that had, exactly, but I had to assume that any and all guards around the facility knew something was up.

I glanced around for cameras. There was one aimed at the facility entrance, but the second guard's wild gunfire had taken it out. Convenient. Thanks.

Time to find Brynn. Manning had said she'd be inside Building B at the center of the property. If so, I would go through those guards too. Anyone and everyone.

A neat row of golf carts was parked beyond the gatehouse. The most obvious strategy was to grab one of those carts and head straight up the central path. It was either that, or melt into the shadows of the solar fields in an attempt to be stealthy.

But I had left stealth behind a few minutes ago. Right around the time Manning had driven us into that concrete post in a desperate attempt to get my weapon. Nah, I was done with the undercover thing.

It was time to march up to their door and kick it right the fuck in.

Finding a cabinet of keys in the gatehouse, I grabbed one labeled #3. The cart in space three revved to life. Except for the siren, the property was eerily lifeless as I drove up the central path. Building A looked like a front office, with a sign marked *Dynamic Solar*. It was deserted. I kept a carbine aimed forward, my other hand on the steering wheel, waiting for the next attack. Yet it still didn't come.

Building B loomed in front of me. No sign of any guards out front.

But a Stillwater mercenary suddenly reared out of the shadows. Bullets pinged on the cart. I swerved to the side and returned fire. Once I'd reached the solar panels, I leaped out of the cart and disappeared in the shadows. Watching.

Movement at nine o'clock. The guard was searching for me.

I pressed the trigger gently. A barrage of gunfire burst from my weapon. The guard grunted and collapsed.

I found him on the ground bleeding from a wound to his thigh. Looked like he'd taken a hit to the artery, which meant he wouldn't last long. But he wasn't down for the count yet. He raised his gun to fire at me again, and I grabbed ahold of it, slamming it into his face. I threw his gun into the shadows beneath the solar panels and stomped on his wrist when he went for his knife.

The man cursed me as I dragged him to the entrance to Building B. I rummaged in his pockets for his keycard. Swiped it, then lifted his hand to use his fingerprints on the biometric scanner.

I let the guard fall to the ground. He didn't move again.

The lock clicked open. I kicked the door wide, raising my carbine again in case someone was waiting to take me out. I had just been standing in full view of the camera by the entrance. But aside from the ever-present sirens and flashing emergency lights, it was quiet inside.

The interior of Building B was cinderblock and concrete. On the right, a doorway led into what looked like a break room. On the left was an elevator. The button didn't respond when I pushed it. I tried waving a keycard, and the elevator came to life. The doors glided open.

I stepped in and hit the down button. It started to descend. When the doors slid open, I pressed myself against the wall, gun ready. Waiting to see who might be here to greet me.

I heard the slick sound of a gun cocking.

"I have Westwick. Drop your weapons and come out with your hands up, or his brains will be splattered against the cinderblock."

I blinked. "B? Is that you?"

The siren kept up its shrill racket, yet still, I could hear her gasp. I stepped out of the elevator, gun hanging at my side. Brynn stood there with an M4 rifle of her own.

"B," I said again, choking on emotion. Shock and relief and pure joy to have my sights on her. Exactly where she belonged. With *me*. "Hey, honey."

I held out my arm, and Brynn almost collapsed against me. I held her tight and pressed my forehead against hers.

"I am so glad to see you," she said. "Ryker said they killed you. I didn't want to believe it, but… I could've used your help a few hours ago, but better late than never."

I sputtered a laugh and pressed a quick, firm kiss to her temple. There was way too much happening inside me. A million things I wanted to say to her. All that had to wait.

Quickly, I took stock of the cart behind her with a man draped across it. It took a moment for me to register him as Garon Westwick. Duct tape covered his mouth and his blond hair was a mess.

"Figured I would swoop in after you'd already done all the work." I nodded at Westwick, who was trying to yell around his gag. "You've been busy."

"I have. And I would love to get the hell out of here."

"Me too. Who's your new friend?" I pointed at the skinny guy who was leaning against the wall like he wanted to disappear into it.

"That's Josiah." Brynn paused, considering something. "I know what Stillwater is hiding down here. They've got a bunch of servers to run a dark web marketplace for members. Josiah is the tech guy. He's been held prisoner here for a few months. He's coming with us."

"Computers," I said, and she nodded, eyes full of meaning. *The virus*, I thought.

"I have a lot more to tell you, but that'll have to wait." She tilted her head in Westwick's direction. The man was listening to everything we said.

She and I both had a lot to share, but yeah. Later. I kissed her one more time on the forehead. Just couldn't resist. She was amazing.

"Do you know how to turn off the siren, Josiah?" I asked. "It's getting on my nerves."

He shook his head. "It's controlled at the gatehouse."

"Ah. Then it's probably my fault."

Brynn smirked. "I should've guessed." She adjusted the strap of her gun. "We were just packing up, and we were going to head for the fire exit. Unless you think the elevator is safe. I wasn't sure what to expect up there."

"Seemed deserted. When I first arrived at the gate, I ran

into resistance. Three guards. They are no longer resisting. Nobody else has popped out of the woodwork."

"Manning and O'Hanlon?"

"Dead."

"Good. I haven't seen Ryker in over an hour. He's my primary concern. He was supposed to check on Westwick's ride out of here for the morning."

"Helicopter?" I wondered aloud. I'd seen Stillwater send a chopper full of mercenaries to evacuate a facility before.

"Possible."

Westwick probably knew the answer, but we'd be fools to trust anything he told us right now. "I vote we take the elevator," I said. "It'll be faster. Westwick's ride could arrive early if they got notice of the alarm going off. We need to be out of here before then. There's two of us with guns to take care of any remaining resistance. Plus Josiah." For whatever that guy was worth.

"And we have our hostage," she added darkly.

Damn. If I wasn't already crazy for this woman, that look in her eyes would've done it for me.

"Hell yeah," I said. "I'll be right beside you."

Josiah wheeled the cart inside the elevator. Westwick had stopped grunting and struggling. Wise of him. If I were in his place, I would save my strength and strategize how to get myself out of this. Of course, my job was to guarantee that didn't happen. Soon, Westwick would learn he was all out of luck and hope. Stillwater was about to come to an ugly, inglorious end.

Then I remembered the syringe in my vest pocket. I pulled it out and sank the needle into Westwick's arm. His eyes bulged in panic, and I smiled down at him for several satisfying seconds until he lost consciousness. "He'll sleep for a few hours," I told Brynn.

"Good."

I did a quick inventory of our weapons and ammo. Brynn didn't have any shoes, which was concerning. "Your clothes are different," I murmured in her ear.

Her eyes darted away. She pushed the button to start the elevator. "Don't worry about it. I can explain later."

Dread hit my gut. It took a lot of effort not to check her over for injuries. She seemed unhurt. For now, the best thing I could do for her was to get her someplace safe.

The elevator ride upstairs was agonizingly slow. I took those moments to look down at Garon Westwick. The powerful executive, bound and drugged and being wheeled around like luggage. And it was just the beginning of the humiliation and pain he had coming to him. If he had touched Brynn…

But that wasn't a road I could allow my mind to go down. Not right now. Not if I wanted to keep myself focused on our current task.

On the ground floor, the doors slid open. The red emergency lights continue to flash.

Brynn stepped out first, gun raised. She cleared the space, checked the view from the window, and led the way outside. Josiah pushed the cart, and then I brought up the rear.

Outside, the golf cart remained where I had left it. Brynn covered us while Josiah and I wheeled our prisoner over and dumped him in the passenger seat.

"You can drive. *Carefully,*" I warned. I tossed Josiah the keys, and he started the small engine. Brynn and I crouched in the cargo area at the back so we could keep our guns aimed and ready.

Once we neared the gatehouse, I told Josiah to pull the cart into the parking lot where the guards kept their personal vehicles. I had a set of keys I had taken from the second guard I had killed. The keys matched up with a Ford F150 with a crew cab and open truck bed. We dumped Westwick on the floor of the backseat, tossing a blanket over our prisoner to keep him hidden.

The plan had gotten all kinds of fucked at the resort, but here we were with Westwick, ready to get ourselves out of Arizona. Once we made contact with the Protectors, we could sort out the rest of this mess. As for Ryker, it was looking like he'd left the facility to arrange Westwick's "ride." All the more reason for us to get out before he returned with backup.

"B, you up for driving?" I held out the keys, and Brynn took them.

"You realize we haven't slept in about forty hours?" she asked.

"Well, I figured we would stop at a convenience store or something on the way. Grab an energy drink."

I loved seeing that smile break over her face. Like the sun was rising ahead of schedule.

"Where should I sit?" Josiah asked. He didn't seem thrilled at the idea of riding in the back with Westwick.

"If you're good, you can sit shotgun later." I would take the next shift driving, and that would give Brynn a chance to take a nap in the back. Assuming we switched vehicles for something with a trunk to stuff Westwick inside. That was a priority, since most people would frown on us carrying a man tied up and gagged on the floor of our backseat.

I put a hand on Josiah's shoulder before he got in. "But first, do you know how to open the exit?" The chain-link gate was still closed, and Manning's SUV blocked the entrance.

Josiah sighed. "Yeah, I can do that." He jogged over to the gatehouse.

Brynn stood by the driver's side door. I touched her cheek. Just marveling for another few seconds at how beautiful and strong she was. "We're gonna talk later," I said. "You can tell me anything."

Tension rippled over her features, and she held onto my shirt by the collar. “Cole…”

“I’m going to take care of you.”

Her dark eyes lifted. Too much uncertainty and sorrow. Yet she was willing to show it to me, when otherwise she’d been every bit the badass since I’d walked out of that elevator.

“Hey, Cameron?” Josiah called out. “It’s not working. Something is stuck.”

“On my way,” I called out. I brushed my thumb over Brynn’s cheek. “I’ll be right back. Pull the truck around? We’ll jump in once we’ve got the gate open.”

Nodding, she got into the driver’s seat and started the engine.

I crossed the blacktop. Josiah was inside the gatehouse, hand on the guards’ touchscreen. But he stood stiffly. Not pushing buttons. Not even looking at me.

Then I realized he’d called me Cameron. How did he know that name? Had Brynn called me that? Or…

I slowed my approach, lifting the carbine in my arms. At the same moment, Josiah’s head turned, panic in his eyes.

*Dammit, no.*

I pivoted and ran in a crouch as a shot rang out.

“Clay!” Ryker shouted. “Give me Westwick, or none of you leaves here alive!”

I checked the magazine on my rifle, switching it out for another. “Not happening.”

Another shot, and Ryker shoved Josiah out of the gatehouse. The IT guy sprawled on the blacktop, his head just visible from where I was crouched. *Dead.*

An engine revved. I glanced over to see Brynn driving the truck. A gun muzzle appeared through her open window. Shots slammed into the gatehouse, and glass rained onto the ground. Shit, she was trying to save me. This woman had a bad habit of doing that.

I used her cover fire to charge and collided with Ryker as he fled from the gatehouse. He was bent over at the waist, so I grabbed onto his back and brought up my right knee, smashing it into his face. His nose crunched. His arms closed around my waist, and we both went down. It was close combat now, a flurry of brutal punches and kicks, not enough space between for either of us to aim our bulky guns. Ryker tried to slam his boot heel against the socket of my prosthesis. Clenching my jaw hard, I closed my hands around his throat. Squeezed.

He managed to get hold of his tactical knife. The blade winked as he struggled to drive it into me, but I kept his arm pinned with my elbow and kept squeezing, squeezing. His other fist pummeled my side viciously, but I didn't let up.

This was for Luciana and her daughter. For Petra, the innocent nanny Westwick and Ryker had terrorized. For everyone Ryker had hurt.

For Brynn.

I bellowed out my fury. Something gave way beneath my hands. Ryker stopped fighting me.

Brynn was shouting my name. I pushed myself up, grabbed my gun, and limped to the open window of the truck. "The gate," I croaked. "We need to get it open."

Any controls inside the gatehouse were busted and covered in broken glass. But there had to be some kind of manual release. Brynn got out of the truck, leaving it idling as we went to the fence together. We managed to find the release and dragged the gate open.

Then we put Stillwater's solar plant in our rearview.

## CHAPTER THIRTY

# *Brynn*

THE NEXT FEW hours blurred together. I drove the truck until we reached a hotel parking lot in a random small town to switch vehicles and change up license plates.

Cole also took the opportunity to call River. Incredibly, Cole still had the phone he had been using as part of his cover. My Brianna Waverley phone was gone, and I assumed my FBI burner was long gone as well.

Honestly, I would've been tempted to call Michael Stanford for an FBI team to swoop in and clean up what we'd left behind. No such luck. I didn't have the energy to discuss that topic with Cole anyway. Not yet.

I was just so glad to have him here with me. Alive. We were both alive. For now, it was enough to have Cole beside me. To hold his hand or feel his fingers massaging my shoulder or my thigh. Just knowing he was close.

At a gas station, Cole bought me a pair of flip-flops so I wasn't bare-footed anymore. I dozed during the next part of the trip, while Cole drove. When I woke up, the sun had just risen, its bright rays shining through my window. I realized I didn't even know our destination. River was supposed to give us the address of a safe house to bring Westwick to.

"Where are we headed?" I asked groggily.

"River gave me an address just north of the New Mexico border. We'll be there in a couple hours or so."

I cracked a water bottle and took a long drink. "I don't even know how you got away from Ryker's men."

The corner of Cole's mouth lifted. "Manning and O'Hanlon drove me out into the desert. That hotel clerk, Lance, was helping them. They had a fancy plan for framing me for your murder, and that was their mistake."

"*Lance*. That piece of trash helped them kidnap me."

"I know. I shot him in the leg and left him. One of those loose ends." Cole reached for my hand. "If he survives, I can still track him down, if that's what you prefer. Did he do anything else?"

I settled against the head rest, looking at the sky. "Lance didn't touch me. He was just a jerk who took Stillwater's money, and it's possible Ryker didn't give him a choice." Like Josiah. He'd helped Stillwater set up their online marketplace, but more out of fear than a conscious desire to do evil. Now he was dead, and Westwick was still alive. Was that fair?

"I used the flash drive," I added.

"I figured you had. Well done, B. Thanks to you, we accomplished everything we set out to do. Including securing our prisoner." Cole's fingers smoothed through my limp, messy hair. "We're almost finished."

*What happens for us next*? I almost asked. But deeper thoughts escaped me. Despite my short nap, I was exhausted. Had I ever been this bone-tired? Maybe during boot camp. Or that really sadistic training at Quantico. Who the heck knew.

A couple hours and one pitstop for breakfast later, we pulled into the driveway of a rundown, one-story home. We had just passed the border into Colorado. The safe house had a light on the porch, a car in the driveway. But otherwise, it looked lonely. Secluded from any nosy neighbors or highway traffic, since we were down a quiet, windy road.

A thump came from the trunk of our car.

"And here I thought he was asleep," Cole said.

"Guess the drugs wore off." I rubbed my eyes, summoning my remaining energy. At least out here, nobody would care how much noise Westwick made. He was about to find out how screwed he was.

A large figure stepped out of the house onto the porch, and I barked a laugh. Westwick was not going to enjoy meeting *him*.

Trace Novo raised a hand to wave at us. I waved back. "I didn't realize T was going to be here," I said. Cole and I had already agreed to go by initials if Westwick could be listening. No need for him to know any names. He would never be a free man again, but it was still a wise precaution.

"Guess he drew the short straw," Cole said.

"Or more likely, the long one. I have to think several of our friends would be excited to meet the head of Stillwater, face to face." All of the Protectors wanted Westwick's blood.

Cole chuckled. "Yeah, now that you mention it."

*Thump, thump.*

I rolled my eyes. "Let's go say hi to our host. We can unload the prisoner later, once we find out where we're storing him."

More thumps from the trunk. Westwick must've heard. Giving me a tired smile, Cole winked and got out of the car. He stopped briefly by the trunk, opened it, and checked Westwick's restraints. The man wasn't going anywhere.

Then we met Trace by the front door, far enough from the car that we'd be out of Westwick's earshot. I was dead on my feet, but Cole's hand on my lower back steadied me.

"Good to see you both," Trace said. He clapped Cole on the shoulder, then me. "Charlotte has been messaging us constantly for updates. River was very happy to report to her that you'd called in."

His mention of my best friend set off a pang of longing in my chest. I had no idea when I would see Charlotte again, but hopefully it would be soon. "Good to see you too," I said to Trace. "I was expecting River, though. Since he was our Protectors liaison for this mission."

Trace nodded. "I was already at River's apartment when Cole called in. You uploaded the virus. Nice work. Riv woke me up the minute his computer started dinging with notifications, and I left him back in Hartley to do his hacker thing."

"That was all Brynn," Cole said. "She barely needed me there at all."

I shook my head, smirking.

"What kind of shape is our prisoner in?" Trace asked.

Cole squinted at the car. "We've treated him better than most human trafficking victims get. He's not bleeding, and he has no broken bones that I'm aware of. Aside from the fact that he's breathing, I don't have much to say about it."

"Is this a Protectors safe house?" I asked.

"Ah, no." Trace scrubbed a large palm over his beard. "It was provided by a mutual associate. Someone who's waiting anxiously inside to see you, Brynn."

"Me?" It couldn't be Charlotte. There was no way the lieutenant governor would risk coming here.

But the moment I walked in and saw his face, I realized I should've known.

"*Michael*? What are you doing here?"

Stanford stood in the entryway, arms crossed over his button-down and blazer. He frowned like I was late for a debrief. "Surprised to see me? What did you expect after cutting off all communication during a dangerous mission? You thought I would just shrug and not call the Protectors demanding to know what happened to my agent? You're lucky I didn't drive down to Arizona my damn self."

"It got complicated."

"No doubt. Now, are you just going to stand there, or are you going to give me a hug? I know it's not our style to get sappy, but I was about scared to death for you, Brynn." He opened his arms, and I let him wrap me in a hug. "I took some personal time and made a quiet vacation down here to southern Colorado," Stanford said. "Hell of a relief when I heard your partner finally called in. You're all right?"

"Good enough. I'm sorry."

Stanford patted me on the back. I pulled away just as it was starting to get awkward.

Then I realized Cole was standing behind me, still in the doorway. An unreadable expression on his handsome face. "*His* agent?" Cole asked slowly.

Shit. This was the worst possible way for Cole to find out. "It's not how it seems. I—"

Trace chose that moment to come inside, stepping between me and Cole. "When Agent Stanford offered his resources, we weren't sure at first. But last night, it became clear that your op had gotten a lot bigger than we'd expected. Stanford was already at this safe house waiting for word on your whereabouts, Brynn. It made sense."

"The minute I learned about Stillwater's solar plant in Arizona and what you found there, I assembled a strike team of agents," Stanford said. "They're already on their way to the location. On the surface, they're responding to an anonymous tip about a kidnapping. But they'll also be cleaning up the mess you left behind."

"What about the prisoner we brought with us?" I asked, an incredulous laugh bubbling from my chest. I was too tired. Too frustrated to sugarcoat anything. "Cole and I have no intention of turning Westwick over to the FBI. I told Cole this was a Protectors mission, and yes, I was supposed to send reports to you, but I'll be damned if I let the Bureau take over now and wind up setting Westwick free. Not after everything the man has done."

At that, Cole turned and walked away, heading down a hallway deeper into the house. A door closed softly. I almost followed him, but Stanford put a hand gently on my arm, making me stay.

"Trace and I already came to an agreement," Stanford said. "This is still under the purview of the FBI task force, and I have a blank check from on high to make our Stillwater problems go away. As far as I'm concerned, that includes letting the Protectors handle any prisoner who may or may not be here."

I looked to Trace for confirmation. "What about the part River is working on?" River's virus would deliver an untold amount of intel about Stillwater. The FBI would want it. *Stanford* would want it. I admired my former boss, not just as an agent, but as someone who'd treated me like family. But it wasn't like him to turn over that kind of control to a vigilante group. Stanford himself had told me not to trust the Protectors. Had so much changed?

Trace nodded. "Given last night's events, Michael and I have come to an agreement. I know how unhappy Cole is about working with a federal agency. River told me. But Riv and I were CIA. Trust me, we can handle the Bureau. Wouldn't be our first time in shark-infested waters." He smiled at my former boss. "No offense meant, special agent in charge."

"None taken whatsoever." Stanford snorted a laugh. He turned to me. "Am I to understand you bonded with your partner during the course of the mission? That's what it sounds like. Perhaps you bonded a bit too much."

I gave him a warning glare. "You're not my boss anymore. Or my father."

Trace coughed. "Brynn, you and Cole have both earned a rest before we debrief. Michael and I will escort the prisoner somewhere quiet. Someplace more conducive to…getting acquainted."

I shivered. Trace was scary when he grinned like that.

"That okay by you?" Stanford asked. "You'll be fine here with Bailey?"

"There's nowhere else I'd rather be than with Cole," I snapped. "You can save the rest of your opinions though, because I know what I'm doing."

"Did I say anything?"

"You've said plenty." I was being grumpy and petulant. Like a teenager talking to her dad. But I didn't have the patience to do otherwise.

"Just let me know if you need me." He patted my arm on his way out. Trace promised to lock up and said they'd return later on.

After the door had closed, I went looking for Cole.

In the hallway, doors led into a bathroom and several bedrooms. Cole was in the second bedroom, sitting on the made bed. I opened the door but paused there, leaning against the frame.

"Hey," I said. "Is it okay if I come in?"

He looked up. "Sure hope so."

That was a good sign. I came further into the room. "Cole, I'm sorry."

"You lied to me," he said evenly. Matter of fact. Yet his lack of anger made me feel that much worse.

I opened my mouth, ready with excuses and justifications. But he was right. "I should've told you that I was communicating with Stanford. I had a burner phone for giving him updates, and I hid it from you. I told myself I wasn't really *answering* to him, and he wasn't giving me orders, so it was okay. That burner phone was just an insurance policy, if we had no choice but to ask Stanford for help. But I should've been honest. I did cut off contact a couple days ago. Before you and I...got intimate."

"Why?"

"Because hiding it felt wrong. I wanted to trust you. Be your partner. Everything we said about the two of us, being in it together, that was real for me. Please believe that."

"C'mere," he whispered.

"What? Why?"

"Because I need to touch you, B," he said softly. "And it's killing me not to."

I swallowed around the thickness in my throat. "It's killing me too."

"Then come over here."

I crossed the room. Cole pulled me into his lap. I straddled him. He pressed kisses to my collarbone and neck, his arms going tight around my waist. Holding me close enough that I couldn't fill my lungs all the way. But I wouldn't pull away for anything.

"A week ago, I would've been furious to hear you were still updating your FBI boss," he said. "I'll give you that. I might have gotten a bit...*feisty* when I learned you were an FBI agent in the first place."

"A *bit* feisty?"

I felt the shape of his smile as he kissed my cheek. "But after all the shit we've been through in the last couple days. That *you've* been through." A shudder ran through him. "I don't care about the FBI. Just tell me what you need. Tell me what happened while we were separated."

He'd asked that same question in various ways since we'd reunited at the solar plant. Just now, he'd said it with so much care and tenderness that it made my eyes sting.

"It wasn't as bad as you're thinking."

"What *I* think isn't the issue." Cole looked at me with equal measures of protectiveness and righteous fury. "I swear, if Westwick hurt you when he had you prisoner, and you give me the go ahead, then I don't care about the Protectors or the FBI or any damn thing but *you*. I am going to make that animal suffer for it. Regardless of the consequences."

I rubbed my fingers against the short strands of his hair. He relaxed by degrees under my soothing touch. I brought my hand to Cole's face, and he turned into it, his eyes drifting closed.

"Westwick kidnapped me so I could spy on Eric Masterson for him. Other men, too. Westwick wanted me to sleep with them and pass their secrets back to him. But first, he wanted me to 'impress' him."

Cole cursed, blinking his eyes open. But I kept stroking my fingers through his hair.

"The minute Westwick came close enough to me, I got him in a submission hold. Choked him out and tied him up. Then I killed the guard outside the door. That's how I got away. I was scared. But more than anything, I was thinking of you. Ryker had told me his men killed you."

Hot tears ran down my cheeks, surprising me. Cole kissed them away. "But here I am."

"Here you are."

I rested my head on his shoulder for a while. Both our hearts were beating hard, but they eventually slowed.

I often had a feeling of emptiness after a mission, even a successful one. Today, that feeling was profound. But with every minute he held me, Cole was bringing me back to life.

After a while, Cole said, "I walked out of the room earlier so I wouldn't say something stupid in the heat of the moment. I wasn't thrilled to find your former FBI boss here, don't get me wrong, but that pales in comparison to how relieved I am that you're okay."

"Same here. I truly am sorry I kept things from you, Cole."

"We can talk about it more later. If needed. But I told you I'd take care of you. So right now, that's what I'm going to do."

# CHAPTER THIRTY-ONE

BRYNN STRIPPED down to her bra and panties. The same ones she'd been wearing when we left the resort. This bedroom had an attached bath. She went in for a few minutes of privacy while I took off my filthy shirt, discarding it in the corner.

A glance in the mirror showed a new collection of scrapes and bruises. Most were likely from my fight with Ryker. And my head still throbbed faintly. Ouch.

Then the bathroom door opened, and Brynn peeked into the room. "Coming in with me?" She sucked in a gasp, stepping out. "Jeez, Cole. You're hurt."

"Not too badly."

She gently touched my side, fingers tracing the outlines of the bruises. "Looks awful. I'd suggest going to the hospital, but there would be questions. Stanford could find a doctor to come here."

I smiled, holding her wrist and lifting her hand to kiss it. "I'm fine. I promise."

"Do you?" Brynn had dark circles beneath her eyes, and yet when she looked at me, her focus was sharp.

"Yeah. I'm going to run you a bath. Sound good?"

I went into the bathroom and knelt to turn on the water. This tub was standard, nowhere near big enough for both of us. But that was okay. Brynn was my concern right now. When the water was high enough, I coaxed her in. She was naked, but I wasn't concentrating on that. I lathered soap in my hands and smoothed them over her skin, washing away the traces of the last couple of days.

Her long hair wasn't that easy to wash without my fingers getting tangled, so she took over, but we were both laughing.

"Your turn," she said after a rinse in the shower and draining the cloudy water away.

Fresh water poured in. I pushed down my pants and boxers, my entire body conscious of her eyes on me. I sat on the edge of the tub and took off my prosthesis, which she set carefully in the bedroom.

The hot water felt like magic on my sore muscles. Though she'd barely dried off, Brynn knelt outside the tub to wash me. And now, her nakedness was a lot more…stimulating.

With heavy eyelids, she spread suds all over me. Rubbing my shoulders and arms and pecs. I couldn't help it. My cock hardened and lengthened until it was stretching out of the water. I groaned when her slick fist closed around my shaft. Stroked me.

"We should get to bed," I said hoarsely. Meaning sleep. Because I had meant to take care of her for purely benevolent, unselfish reasons.

"You're right," Brynn purred. "We should."

I groaned again. A guy was only so strong. I was so exhausted I could barely think straight. All I knew was that I had to have her.

I finished up with the bath as quickly as possible. Soon, Brynn and I were stretched out in the bed on the cool sheets, blankets pushed to our feet. Kissing with our bodies pressed together, naked skin to naked skin. I teased her nipples between my fingers while my tongue slid into her mouth.

Brynn wrapped her legs around my hips, her ankles crossed. I rocked against her, feeling how wet she was. Ready for me. Washing each other had been extended foreplay. But this was more than just a physical urge. After what we'd experienced during the mission, being close with her now meant so much. We had survived. We were here, together, and we had *won*.

But the truth was that I wanted even more.

Somehow, I gathered up my scattered thoughts. Pushed up onto my elbows to look down at her.

"What is it?" she asked. "Why aren't you kissing me?"

"The mission is pretty much over now. Stanford and Trace took it out of our hands. I want to know what you're doing next. Going back to the FBI?"

She frowned. "I thought about it. Would you blame me if I did?"

I lay on my side next to her. Rested a hand on her waist and waited for her to turn to face me. "My hang-up about the FBI was overblown. I *do* trust you now, completely, because I've seen the kind of woman you are. The kind of warrior you are."

"Thank you. I trust you too. I said that before, and I meant it."

"But you didn't really. That's the reason you didn't tell me about your reports to Stanford."

She looked guilty, and I stroked a finger beneath her chin, lifting it.

"I'm not mad," I said. "I get that trust isn't easy for you. But here's what I'm asking. Do you think, eventually, you could trust me with your heart?"

Brynn's eyes went glassy. She blinked fast.

"I know you're scared. Some asshole didn't love you the

way you deserve. And yet you've proven again and again how brave you are, no matter how scary shit gets. Give me a chance to take care of you, B. For real. Come to Mexico with me. Hang out. Give me some time so we can see where this goes."

Indecision played across her face. "That sounds amazing, just like it did when you brought it up at the resort. But I thought you meant a vacation."

"It can start as a vacation. I'm hoping it'll turn into more."

"You're serious? What you're talking about... We barely know each other beyond this mission."

"Exactly. We've seen each other's best, and some of our worst. Let's fill in the rest of the story."

"You make it sound so simple."

"Why can't it be?" We were both lonely. Both broken-hearted, in our own unique ways. But we'd found each other.

I didn't believe in happy endings. Good deeds rarely ended well, and trust ended up in betrayal. Except...my gut told me that Brynn and me could be different.

"How is it possible that you're this perfect?" she asked.

"I'm not even close to perfect. I don't have a single edge that isn't rough. But maybe I could be a perfect fit for you." I leaned forward for a slow kiss.

We made love just as soft and slow as those whispers we'd shared. Lying on our sides and facing one another, I draped her upper leg high across my hip and worked my way in. Small, rocking movements. Sweet, deep kisses. My fingers tangling in her damp hair. My cock slid in and out of her snug body. The pleasure combined with the exhaustion in my brain made me feel drunk.

I grunted against her lips. "I can't believe how good you feel around me."

"Perfect fit," she murmured. Pupils dilated, a blissed expression on her gorgeous features.

We found our release together. Mouths sealed in a kiss, arms around each other. Never letting go even as we both drifted into the oblivion of sleep.

All I wanted was a chance. I just hoped I'd convinced her to give it to me.

---

I woke a few hours later, my stomach grumbling. Brynn was passed out cold. I scooted out of the bed, careful to tuck the blankets around her. Then put on my prosthesis, got dressed, and went out to the kitchen to search for food.

Unfortunately, I found Special Agent in Charge Stanford setting down a collection of plastic grocery bags on the counter. Like he had just gotten back.

He nodded at me. "Mr. Bailey."

"Agent Stanford." My voice was rough from sleep, but that wasn't really the reason that his name had come out coated in bitterness.

"Trace is still with our guest. I expect he will be for a while. I thought I should swing by a Walmart, stock up on food and some clothes for you and Brynn. Since you didn't appear to have any luggage."

This was accurate, but for some reason, his comment made my hackles raise. "Somehow our bags got misplaced in between being kidnapped and barely escaping with our lives." Maybe his FBI strike team would recover our belongings, but I wasn't holding my breath.

He responded like he hadn't noticed my sarcasm. "Hopefully I got your sizes right. Had to call my wife, Marie, for help with Brynn's. I tried to cover the bases. Boots and coats for heading back to the mountains."

"Thanks. Appreciate it."

"Not a problem. I would do anything for Brynn."

Ah. So he was marking his territory. Stanford was way too old for her and had mentioned a wife, so I assumed this was some kind of pseudo father-daughter thing. I chose not to respond. I had nothing to prove to this guy.

Taking the bags of clothing, I quietly left them in our bedroom so Brynn would find them when she woke up.

Hopefully, she'd have answers to my questions too. The answers I wanted. But now that I'd slept and my head was clearer, I was far less confident. Would Brynn really be willing to leave Colorado and her law enforcement career to run away with me? Become a renegade bounty hunter, like I had? What kind of fantasy was I living in?

I returned to the kitchen to make myself a sandwich, thanking him again for the supplies, and carried it out to the back porch.

It was late afternoon. Open desert stretched out around us. There were no saguaro cactuses like in Arizona, but this part of Colorado was just as arid. I was alone with my anxious thoughts for a few minutes as I ate.

Until Stanford barged through the back door and took the other chair. "How's Brynn doing?" he asked. "She didn't really answer me earlier. She doesn't like appearing weak. None of us does. But I need to know."

I considered my response. "She's doing well. Resting."

"Good."

"She'd be doing even better if you can guarantee Garon Westwick will never see the light of day again. Not so much for what he did to Brynn as for all the other harm he caused."

"Gladly. On that point, I believe that we all agree."

I nodded, thinking the conversation was over. Maybe Agent Stanford wasn't such a bad guy.

But then he had to ruin the moment when he kept talking.

"Bailey, I'd like to express my gratitude to you for getting Brynn back here safe. Obviously she played a sizable role in the success of your mission as well. I'm not diminishing that. But I had serious doubts about you when this began. You managed to come through."

I felt a scowl twisting up my features. "That sounded more like an insult than a compliment."

"It was the truth. Nothing more." He brushed some invisible lint from his jeans. The denim had a crease down the legs, like he ironed them. Or his wife did. "Brynn means a great deal to me. I recruited her when she was a Marine. I've seen her growth as an agent. And also the setbacks she's experienced on a personal level. She would hate the fact that I'm saying any of this to you."

"I'm sure she would." I set my plate near my feet and stared into the distance, hoping he'd get the message.

"But as someone who cares about her like she's my family, it needs to be said. I've gotten the impression that, after the ordeal you two shared, you have come to mean a great deal to her as well."

I clenched my jaw. "I'm not taking advantage of her. If that's what you're trying to get at."

"I'm just trying to get a better sense of the kind of man you are. Do you see a future with her?"

"I do," I gritted out. "Not that it's your business."

I expected him to say more. To give me all the usual *break her heart and I'll have my agents kill you* warnings. But instead, he crossed his legs and went quiet. I thought about going back inside, but damned if I would retreat from this guy. I'd been enjoying the fresh air and the view before he barged out here.

A cigarette. That was what I needed. But when I patted around at my pockets, they were all empty.

"Ryker," I mumbled. "Asshole made me lose my smokes."

Stanford dug into the pocket of his windbreaker. And to my surprise, he pulled out a pack of Marlboros. Held them out. "Marie isn't a fan of me smoking. So when I'm out in the field, I sometimes indulge."

"I assumed you were an overgrown, uptight Boy Scout. Like most FBI agents."

He chuckled. "Then you might be surprised."

I took a cigarette, followed by his lighter when he offered it. I lit up, took a drag, and handed the lighter back. "Thank you."

"Not a problem."

Then he launched into a story.

"Marie was the girl next door when I was growing up. A few years younger than me, so our paths didn't cross all that much. But one summer, when I was home on leave, she came knocking on the door in the middle of the night. The military had turned me into a light sleeper, so I made it to the door before my family woke up. Turned out her ex-boyfriend was stalking her. He had just come by her house when her parents were out of town, tried to get inside. She didn't call the police because she had tried that before, and they hadn't done anything. Instead, she had remembered the Marine next door."

I wondered where this story was going. But somehow, I was already hooked. I wanted to know the end of it. Probably because I could imagine how I would've reacted if I had been him.

"My Marie was no damsel in distress. She wasn't looking for a rescuer. She wanted a partner in crime. By the time my leave was over about a week later, I had fallen for her hard and fast. I asked her to marry me six months later. That was forty-five years ago."

"But what about the stalker ex-boyfriend?"

A grin slowly appeared on his face. "We made sure he never bothered her again. My point is, I do understand how a stressful situation can fuse two people together. But it wouldn't have happened if we hadn't been right for each other."

I filled my lungs with smoke, frowning at the desert landscape. "Why are you telling me this, exactly?"

"Because Brynn deserves to find her partner. You know I'm not talking about a partner for one mission. I mean someone who's in it for the long-haul. If you're not him, then let her go. She can't take another heartbreak."

"If I am?"

"Then you have my enthusiastic blessing."

We said nothing else as I finished the cigarette. Just as I was stubbing it out, the back door opened, and Brynn stepped outside. She was wearing a new pair of jeans and a sweater.

Stanford and I both started to get up, since there were no free chairs, but she sidled over to me and put a hand on my shoulder. "That's okay. I'll sit here with you." Brynn settled on my lap and gave me a kiss on the forehead.

It was clear she was making a statement to her former boss and mentor. A statement I appreciated. I put my arm around her waist and smiled at her fondly.

A partner in crime. A partner in life. I did like the sound of that.

Stanford cleared his throat. "Brynn, from the moment you resigned to go undercover, I planned to ask you to return to the Bureau when it was finished. I'm beginning to suspect your answer will be no."

Brynn's eyes hadn't left mine. She returned my grin. "Sorry, sir. A very handsome bounty hunter made me a better offer. And I've decided to take him up on it."

# Epilogue

### Brynn

Cole tugged at the knot of his tie. "I hate dressing up."

"And yet you look so darn good doing it."

I fixed his collar and adjusted the knot, making sure it was just right. My guy was smoking hot in a suit, even if he did seem a bit uncomfortable. "These clothes will be even sexier when they're in a pile on the floor of this room tonight."

Cole smirked. "How am I supposed to partner with someone who sees me as a sex object?"

I patted the lapels of his jacket. "I don't know, but you seem to manage." I pulled him in for a kiss. It was a bad habit of mine. Whenever Cole was within reach, I had that undeniable urge to kiss him.

He cupped the nape of my neck, pulling back briefly to look down at me. Then he slanted his mouth over mine in earnest. Turning the kiss filthy in a matter of seconds. The silky fabric of my dress was soft on my skin as I pressed up against him.

Reluctantly, I put my palms to his chest and broke away.

"Keep going like that, and I'll have to redo my makeup. Or we'll end up undressed and back in bed. It'll be big trouble if the best man misses the ceremony."

The wicked glint in his eyes said that he was still tempted. But I also knew that Cole wouldn't miss this wedding for the world. "All right, fine," he grumbled. "Let's head downstairs. But I'm taking the tie off for the reception."

"Okay, grumpy," I teased. "I'll take it off for you."

Grabbing his hand, I dragged him out to the hallway and toward the elevator.

After the end of our mission in Arizona and the few days spent in the safe house, we'd talked about traveling to Mexico. But first, we'd taken a detour back to Hartley. With Trace and River both otherwise occupied, the Protectors had needed our help at Last Refuge.

And that visit *still* hadn't ended. We'd been here for three months so far. We had a room at the inn and a standing invite for meals at the tavern, where Aiden Shelborne cooked up excellent food and his fiancée Jessi made addictive desserts. With protectees cycling in and out of Last Refuge, Cole and I had plenty to do. *Especially* with the wedding planning going on.

Having the best man on the premises had meant Cole could listen and nod when Aiden complained about the wedding vendors or when Jessi got fed up with her fiancé. I'd gotten to know Jessi better and bonded over our pair of grumpy men. Trust that Scarlett, Trace's wife, had plenty to say on that subject too. Because as much as they got on our nerves, we wouldn't change our guys for the world.

Cole and I had also taken a few field trips for discreet missions, whatever Trace or Michael passed our way. The Protectors and the FBI had been busy dismantling Stillwater, piece by piece. But it would still be a long while before the whole job was done.

When we got downstairs, Cole kissed me on the cheek. "I'd better find the groom," he said. "I swear, Solo used to be cool under pressure."

I chuckled. "Even big, bad warriors are entitled to pre-wedding jitters."

I made my way outside to the spacious deck, where rows of chairs were set up and guests had started arriving for the ceremony. It was an ideal mountain summer day. Blue skies, high of seventy, no storm clouds or haze obscuring the view. The mountains in the distance were crisp and clear. Flower garlands were draped everywhere, and a big group of Aiden's family from California chatted nearby.

Owen was here with his girlfriend, Genevieve, plus half a dozen deputies from the Hart County Sheriff's Department. I waved at Keira, who was talking quietly to Dean. There was some kind of tension between those two lately, but Keira always brushed it off as nothing when I asked.

"Did you save me a seat?"

I turned around to find my best friend Charlotte standing there, smiling. "Hey!" I pulled her into a hug. "When did you arrive?"

"Riv and I both got back to Hartley late last night. First time I've seen my husband in a month, and I'm so glad to be home in Hart County. We're going to sneak away tomorrow for some time at the cabin."

Charlotte's career was still back in Denver, and it was strange to think how I'd used to grab lunch with her at the spur of the moment in Capitol Hill.

"Missed you," I said with feeling.

"Yeah, you too. It's hard being so far. I'm committed to finishing out my term, but sometimes..." She sighed. "It's hard. Wanted to be there for the rehearsal dinner last night, but it just didn't happen."

Charlotte's strawberry-blond hair was swept up in a twist,

and she'd worn a sheath dress. Classic and elegant, as one would expect from the lieutenant governor. I had opted for brighter colors and a shorter length then I might have dared in my FBI agent days. But Cole did have a thing for my legs, especially when I wore heels. My hair was shoulder length now, since I had cut off the dead ends from my undercover bleach job. I'd also dyed my hair back to a darker shade, and it was quickly growing out. Cole kept saying he looked forward to seeing my high ponytail again.

"What about you?" Charlotte asked. "Have you decided to give in to the pull of the mountains? Make your stay permanent? You're an official Protector now. Don't deny it."

I laughed. "I wouldn't dare deny it."

My government days were over. Cole and I were Protectors now, and I was proud to own that affiliation. I'd gotten comfortable in Trace's chair at Protectors headquarters, since I sometimes filled in as chief of operations when our leader was off-site.

Keira had made no secret of her eagerness to join our ranks. Sheriff Owen still had reservations, but I'd been giving her some one-on-one training to improve her skills. It was just a matter of time.

Heaven help me, I was really starting to fall in love with Hart County.

And maybe...fall in other ways as well.

"I can't say it's permanent, though," I hedged. "Cole and I have plans as soon as things calm down. He wants to take me to the beach. He has that place on the coast, and I can't wait to see it. We could use a vacation."

"Can't we all."

I didn't know what would happen afterwards. I had promised Cole I would give us a chance, and I'd meant it. Would we work out? Would I end up back in Hartley or someplace else? I couldn't say.

But when I closed my eyes at night and let my mind wander to the future, I always saw Cole there.

Charlotte glanced around, tugging me toward a quiet corner of the deck. "I had a meeting with the governor yesterday. The FBI will be making some big arrests early next week."

"Eric Masterson?"

She nodded. "That's one. On bribery charges related to his senate campaign. But also several members of Stillwater's ruling circle will be charged with racketeering."

I released a breath. "About dang time." Since I wasn't a government agent anymore, I was out of the loop. "And Westwick?"

"The FBI will be issuing a statement."

So far, the FBI had acknowledged that Garon Westwick disappeared from the Arizona resort where he'd been giving a seminar. But rumors had swirled about Westwick being involved in shady criminal dealings. That he'd invested in a solar plant that was really a cover for an organized crime operation, and that he'd fled the country after a gun battle with a rival organization.

But the FBI had insisted it was all an ongoing investigation, and they couldn't comment further.

Stanford had been true to his word about his strike force cleaning up the mess Cole and I had left behind. They had made sure that the scene at the solar plant looked like a battle between mafia outfits. Some competing bad guy who'd been angry at Stillwater's move to corner the dark-web black market.

The FBI had also recovered Lance, the hotel clerk who'd helped Rykker kidnap me and Cole. Lance had barely lived through his ordeal in the desert, and he had wisely chosen to claim no memory of how he had wound up there with a gunshot in his leg. With all the chaos that the fire alarm and sprinklers had caused at the resort, half the guests had left anyway. So there had been few questions about what had happened to Brianna Waverley and Cameron Clay.

But there was one guest I'd wanted to thank. Molly. Cole had explained how she'd confronted him. So I had sent her a gift with a note from Brianna, telling her I had decided to leave Cameron and quit social media. Of course, I'd made sure that no one could trace it back to me as Brynn Somerton. But I had wanted her to know that her small act of bravery mattered.

River's virus had worked exactly as it was supposed to. The Protectors and FBI hadn't just learned Stillwater's secrets and identified its entire list of members. Westwick had also amassed blackmail material on his friends and enemies. But acting on all of that information took time. Breaking down Garon Westwick himself via interrogation had taken time as well.

Next week, given what Charlotte had just shared, the FBI would finally confirm Westwick's ties to Stillwater. I could already imagine parts of the Bureau's statement. *The result of an extensive investigation based upon a trove of documentary evidence provided by anonymous sources.* There would be a lot of questions. From the media, from Congress, from legal experts and defense lawyers as the charges against Stillwater's leaders hit the justice system. I trusted Stanford to keep our cover stories solid. Nobody outside our small circle would ever know about the Protectors' involvement.

Of course, not *all* of Stillwater's secrets would result in public trials or media statements. Even more of the guilty parties would be dealt with through less official means. Like those missions Cole and I had been taking here and there. Each of the Protectors, including me, had friends we trusted from our military days, and we'd been outsourcing assignments. Our expanding network of allies was probably our greatest asset.

I was proud to be a part of it. My life looked nothing like it had six months ago, but I didn't have a single regret.

Charlotte's smile turned sly. "Apparently, Interpol is getting tips about sightings of Westwick all over Europe. Did you see the online movement to track him down and bring him to justice? There's a devoted subreddit."

"I'm sure the interest will only increase after the FBI confirms the rumors about him being a criminal kingpin."

Charlotte rolled her eyes. "If it takes attention away from where Westwick *really* is, I'm all for it. The good part is that victims are speaking out. There's going to be a joint fund to provide restitution to those Stillwater and its members have hurt. The logistics will be tough, but I plan to make sure the money gets to the people who deserve it."

I was glad for that. It paid to have some friends in high places.

"I'm sure I'll be inundated with calls for comment because Stillwater targeted me last year, and I already spoke out about them," Charlotte said. "I'm planning another interview with Genevieve. Sadly, I don't think an article in the Hartley Gazette will satisfy my media obligations."

"Thank goodness I'm staying out of that part." I grinned.

"Ha, true. But all of this *is* making a difference. Stillwater's operations have ground to a halt. Their members are being arrested or discreetly disappearing, never to be heard from again. And everyone has you and Cole to thank for it, even if most don't know it."

"River deserves the credit. I'm sure you already show your appreciation to him."

She smirked. "Any chance I get. But you're wrong. You and Cole put yourselves on the line to make this a reality. I'm grateful. You don't know how much." We hugged again, both getting choked up. "Okay, no more on that subject. Let's talk about happier things."

"Like the wedding we're here to celebrate?" I asked.

"Or maybe the fact that you and Cole are going strong. I never would've expected you to fall for your undercover partner. It's those fake relationship situations. They'll get you every time."

We both laughed.

"Cole and I are…good."

"That's all you're giving me? Really?"

"It's only been three months. I don't know yet where it's going." We hadn't exchanged I-love-yous yet, which actually reassured me. It would've killed me if he said it and then took it back.

But at the same time, I felt how much he cared for me. It was in the sweetness of his kisses and the way he always had his eyes on me, no matter what else was going on.

"But you seem really happy," Charlotte said. "Enough to make me realize you might not have been so happy before."

I nodded. "I never told you this, but I was engaged once. Before I met you. It ended badly, and I thought I could never trust a man like that again."

"Oh, B. I'm sorry."

"Don't be. I never thought I'd say this. But I think maybe it was all worth it, just so I'd recognize how perfect Cole is for me."

Charlotte squeezed my arm. "Sounds like you *do* know where this is going between you and Cole. Your heart knows. Even if your brain hasn't caught up yet."

"That's possible."

Soft music started, and I glanced over toward the wedding arch made of hundreds of flowers. Aiden had just walked up and was shifting nervously. Cole stood beside him, murmuring something, and whatever he'd said made Aiden nod.

Then Cole saw me looking and sent a smile my way. There were dozens of people around us, yet I felt that smile like a secret message meant only for me. Didn't matter where we were or what we were doing. It was the two of us, connected by an invisible, unbreakable thread. Drawing us together since the moment we'd met.

The only thing more frightening than the thought of trusting Cole with my entire heart? The thought of ever letting him go.

---

**Cole**

A hush fell over the audience as Scarlett, the maid of honor, walked up the aisle. Then the music shifted, and Jessi appeared in a floor-length, lacy dress. She walked forward on the arm of her brother Trace. Her long veil stretched out behind her. The sun was setting. A gentle breeze blew across the mountainside, shaking the wildflowers and grasses beyond the deck.

Beside me, Aiden cursed softly under his breath. Despite the crowd of people and the gorgeous surroundings of Refuge Mountain, the bride and groom didn't look away from each other as she made her way to the wedding arch. Like nothing existed except the two of them. It was a feeling I understood.

My eyes searched out my girlfriend in the third row, sitting beside Charlotte on one side and Keira on the other. Just looking at Brynn filled me up with an uncomfortable, too-big feeling. Like things shouldn't be this good, and there was no way it could keep going.

I'd been shocked when Aiden asked me to be his best

man. I mean, *me*? But I'd been honored. Even when I'd had to talk my buddy through the stress. Aiden had wanted to make every detail of today perfect for his bride, because her happiness was his happiness. Seeing them now, taking their vows? So worth it.

It had been a long time since I'd been a part of something bigger. Something important. I liked being a Protector. Especially because I had Brynn to share it with.

For so much of my life, I'd seen bad stuff happen to good people. But here we were, seeing good things unfold for some of the best people I knew. This was a new experience. I had the hunch I could get used to it.

Was I a sunny optimist now? Not even close. But my dark outlook was teetering on the edge.

When the ceremony ended, the photographer wrangled the wedding party into a slew of photos. Brynn stood off to the side and waited until I was done. The moment the photographer waved me and Scarlett away to focus on the bride and groom, Brynn came over to loosen my tie. She slid it away from my neck with a knowing grin. Then kissed my beard and my jawline as she undid the top button of my shirt.

"Better?" she whispered.

I groaned. "Way better. Will they notice if we sneak away for a few?"

"Yep, your best-man duties aren't over yet."

Damn.

Scarlett tapped me on the shoulder, holding up a phone. "Hey, can I get one of you two? You're downright adorable together."

Brynn snuggled into my side, while I put an arm around her. I wasn't a huge fan of posed photos, but I felt the grin on my face grow along with the pride of knowing the woman beside me was *mine*.

I hadn't been sure how today would go over for me and Brynn, given the rocky history we both had with the subject of marriage. But when Scarlett showed us the photo she'd taken, I saw that Brynn's smile in the image matched my own. Simple joy. So beautiful it struck me in the chest, stealing my breath for a couple of seconds.

I was probably a little obsessed with Brynn. If that was a character flaw, I had no intention of apologizing for it.

The two of us had become a fixture here at Last Refuge, which hadn't been my plan. But Colorado was easier to deal with now that the snow had melted and summer was here. My favorite time of each day was sunset, when Brynn and I could sit and watch the sun sinking behind the trees, sharing a cigarette. Marveling at how damn lucky I was. Then, after dinner, taking her back to our room and stripping off everything until we were down to bare skin. Making love slow and sensual or rough and fast, depending on the kind of day we'd had.

Sadly, our room at the inn didn't have a bathtub. There was a hot tub on site, which we had visited several times for heavy make-out sessions when nobody else was around. But not nearly as much privacy as I would've wanted.

The only thing that wasn't perfect was that I missed home. Last Refuge was a great place, but it wasn't *my* place. I was anxious to get back, whether it was my apartment in the city or my quiet spot on the beach. As long as I had Brynn beside me.

She had suggested before that she'd come with me when it was time to leave. But what if she changed her mind? Those last threads of doubt still clung to me.

After the wedding dinner and endless toasts, Brynn insisted on dancing. She tugged at my hand and pulled me to the dance floor. Then Owen and Dean started passing around whiskey shots. With that added to the obligatory champagne,

I felt pleasantly weighed down with booze and with contentment.

"Cole?" Brynn asked softly. We were swaying on the dance floor to yet another romantic song. But from the way she'd said my name, I could tell she had something important to tell me.

"Yeah, B?"

"I—"

Unfortunately, Trace decided to walk up to us that moment and rest a hand on my shoulder. "Hey, sorry to interrupt. Do you two have a minute? It's Protectors business."

Brynn lifted an eyebrow at me. "Sure," I said, reluctantly pulling away from her. But I caught hold of her hand as we walked over to the building that housed the Protectors' headquarters.

Nobody else was inside. Trace stopped in the open space in the middle, turned around, and crossed his arms. "I wouldn't have done this today, but waiting didn't feel right either. I have news that I think you'll want to hear, Cole."

Brynn's fingers tightened on mine.

Trace got straight to the point. "I spoke to Michael Stanford last night. A few weeks ago, FBI agents in the northeast busted a criminal ring who were using trafficked women as unpaid labor. They found a young woman there named Daniela Rojas. I believe you were looking for her before? On behalf of her mother, Luciana Rojas?"

"Yes." My voice was hoarse. Numbness spread through my limbs. "Where is she? Is she in custody? Or..."

"She's in protective custody at the moment. The FBI has specialists treating the victims, interviewing them, and reuniting them with their families. I understand Daniela has an aunt in Mexico, and they've already contacted her."

I cursed under my breath, rubbing my face. This was the

last thing I'd expected to hear today. But it was welcome news. I'd thought Daniela was gone forever, like her mom.

"Is there anything we can do to help?" Brynn asked.

"I wish there were. But Stanford assured me that Daniela is being well-cared for. Better that we keep you both away from the FBI operation given your undercover work." Trace nodded at me, then Brynn. "The only reason the authorities found those young women is because you succeeded in your mission. I just wanted to let you know."

We talked a few minutes longer, and then Trace excused himself to return to the reception. As soon as he was gone, Brynn slid into my embrace and tucked her head into the curve where my shoulder met my neck. I just held her, letting Trace's news sink in.

"We should head back to the party," I said.

"You sure?"

"Yeah." I smoothed my thumb over the wrinkle of tension between her eyes. "I wish I could bring Luciana back. But Daniela is free, and she'll be heading home to her family. Best news I've heard in a while."

I started to turn toward the door, but Brynn held onto me. "Wait. I'd like to finish what I was going to say before Trace interrupted."

"Is it good news? Or bad?"

"I think it's pretty good." She gazed up at me, looking more tentative than usual. "I love you. Whatever happens next, I want us to do it together."

My breath whooshed out of my chest for at least the second or third time today.

I'd known for a while that I was completely in love with her. But I hadn't wanted to scare her away by making any declarations before she was ready.

Hell, if this wasn't the moment I'd been waiting for, what was?

"B, you're the first thing I think of when I wake up. The last thing on my mind before I go to bed. It's only been a few months, but I already can't imagine my life without you."

Her eyes narrowed. "So are you saying those three words back? Or…"

My laugh was loud in the quiet space. "Yes, honey. I love you. I love you so much. So long as we can get out of Colorado before next winter." I kissed her smile, hands cupping her face. "Run away with me?" I whispered against her lips.

"Anywhere."

**There will be more books in the Last Refuge Protectors series… Coming soon!**

# A Note from Hannah

The Protectors have come a long way since Aiden and Jessi started Last Refuge in book 1, right? They now have six members, an official headquarters, and a strategic friendship in the FBI. While Brynn and Cole's story marks the end of the Stillwater arc, there will be more books with new couples to come!

But first, I have a brand new series starting in 2025, also set in Hart County. It'll have all the steam and suspense you expect, plus even more small-town heart.

I owe a big **thank you** to everyone who's supported the Last Refuge series and continued to get excited for these books, including my amazing ARC readers. Thank you all for reading!

Until next time—
Hannah

# Also by Hannah Shield

## Last Refuge Protectors

**Hard Knock Hero** (Aiden & Jessi)

**Bent Winged Angel** (Trace & Scarlett)

**Home Town Knight** (Owen & Genevieve)

**Second Chance Savior** (River & Charlotte)

**Iron Willed Warrior** (Cole & Brynn)

*- And more coming soon -*

---

## West Oaks Heroes

**The Six Night Truce** (Janie & Sean)

**The Five Minute Mistake** (Madison & Nash)

**The Four Day Fakeout** (Jake & Harper)

**The Three Week Deal** (Matteo & Angela)

**The Two Last Moments** (Danny & Lark)

**The One for Forever** (Rex & Quinn)

---

## Bennett Security

**Hands Off** (Aurora & Devon)

**Head First** (Lana & Max)

**Hard Wired** (Sylvie & Dominic)

**Hold Tight** (Faith & Tanner)

**Hung Up** (Danica & Noah)

**Have Mercy** (Ruby & Chase)

---

# About the Author

Hannah Shield writes steamy, suspenseful romance with pulse-pounding action, fun & flirty banter, and tons of heart. She lives in the Colorado mountains with her family.

Visit her website at www.hannahshield.com, where you can join her newsletter for access to bonus content, info on new releases, and more!

Made in the USA
Las Vegas, NV
05 July 2025

24471651R00194